A MURDER IN ASHWOOD

SCANDALS AND SECRETS IN THE GILDED AGE

Other Titles by
ROBERT BRIGHTON

Avenging Angel Detective Agency™ Mysteries
The Unsealing

COMING SOON...
Current of Darkness

A MURDER IN ASHWOOD

SCANDALS AND SECRETS IN THE GILDED AGE

AN AVENGING ANGEL DETECTIVE AGENCY™ MYSTERY

ROBERT BRIGHTON

ASHWOOD PRESS

A Murder in Ashwood: Scandals and Secrets in the Gilded Age

An Avenging Angel Detective Agency™ Mystery

A Novel by Robert Brighton

© 2023 Copper Nickel, LLC
All Rights Reserved

Cover and Interior Illustrations by Mark Summers

Cover and Interior Design by The Book Cover Whisperer

979-8-9876964-1-5 Paperback
979-8-9876964-0-8 Hardcover
979-8-9876964-2-2 eBook

Library of Congress Control Number: 2023931332

Find out more at
RobertBrightonAuthor.com

For Laura

CONTENTS

ILLUSTRATIONS

A WORD OF CONTEXT

IN ANY BOOK SET IN A DIFFERENT ERA, PRICES OF THINGS CAN BE particularly confusing. Today, it's tempting to marvel at luxurious houses that could be had for "only" $5,000.

This book takes place primarily in 1902, and I've chosen to present prices as they were then and let readers adjust them, should they wish to do so. Roughly speaking, $1 in 1902 would be worth about $40 today. Thus, a $50,000 insurance settlement in 1902 would probably be worth about $2 million to us.

Like the value of the American dollar, the quality of American English has also eroded dramatically in a century. While I have done my best to avoid anachronism, I freely confess to updating the conversational style of 1902 to make it slightly more familiar, and less formal or "stilted," to the modern ear. That is a concession I believe needs to be made for the changing times. Other than that, I've tried to be true to the era.

Robert Brighton
April 2023

PART ONE

A MURDER
IN ASHWOOD

ALICIA UNBOUND

Atlantic City, New Jersey
January 1, 1902

ALICIA MILLER LEARNED OF HER HUSBAND'S MURDER OVER breakfast. She had been enjoying her meal in the sunny dining room of the Traymont Hotel when a handsome young bellboy interrupted, carrying a small silver tray with a yellow envelope on it.

"Telegram for you, ma'am," he said.

She dabbed her lips with her napkin and took the envelope. The bellboy stood by expectantly.

Allie stared him down. "If you'll tell me your name, I'll make sure you receive your gratuity," she said. "Obviously, I don't have any coins with me at breakfast."

The bellboy blushed. "Oh, no, ma'am, I thought I would stand by to see if you wished to make any reply."

"That won't be necessary," she said, and the bellboy hurried away.

Allie ran her thumb under the flap of the envelope and tore it open. Inside was a single page of Western Union telegraph paper, folded once. Typewritten in the message space were the words

Edward died this morning. Come at once. Mother.

She folded the paper again and slid it back into the envelope. *So it has come to that*, she thought. With her tiny silver spoon, she excavated the last bite of her soft-boiled egg from the expertly cut shell, sitting upright in its turquoise-colored china cup. The words "Traymont Hotel, Atlantic

City" were traced in cursive gold leaf around the base of the cup. Alicia thought that she'd seen these pretty little cups offered for sale in the gift shop, and that she might take a set home with her, as a souvenir.

But first, she thought, I'll need to stop by the hotel's telegraph office. She folded her napkin and set it next to her plate, allowing herself one last look out the huge seafront windows. Such a perfect, lovely spot, she thought, drinking in the view. I'd like to remember it just like this.

At the hotel's telegraph window, she requested two sheets of message paper. One she addressed to her mother, at their Ashwood Street address. It was a little game she enjoyed, trying to write telegrams with the fewest number of characters, to save money.

Yours rec'd. Home tomorrow a.m. Allie.

The second one she directed to Arthur Pendle, Esq., at his office in the Aston Building downtown.

Returning Bflo tomorrow a.m., Express.
Meet me at Terrace Station. Allie.

Content with her brevity, she handed the messages over to the telegraph agent and went back to her room to pack her trunk in order to get to the station in time for the overnight train to Buffalo. She wished she could stay longer, to enjoy the almost empty hotel, the solitary peace of the winter ocean, her cozy top-floor room with the windows gazing over the relentless surf. It was the same room she and Arthur had always engaged, in their clandestine escapes to the shore.

The room was at the very apex of the Traymont's jutting prow, in a wing of the hotel built out perpendicular to the boardwalk, and which terminated close enough to the beach that the windows sometimes got a good dousing of spray. From her vantage point, the rest of the hotel was behind and out of view, and sometimes with the fire going and over a glass of wine, Alicia could put her book down, gaze out at the pounding Atlantic, and imagine she was a lighthouse keeper.

The salt rime would build up so quickly on the windows in this premier section of the hotel that most every day a young man would descend in a bosun's chair, holding a bucket and rags, and carefully restore the pristine, spectacular view. His schedule was unpredictable—governed by

At The Traymont

the weather, she supposed—and once, early in her stay, he had appeared as quickly and silently as a spider on silk, surprising her amidst her morning ablutions as she stood stark naked except for her gold ouroboros torc fastened around her neck, transfixed by the breakers on the beach. He'd reacted as he had to react, with ostensible and theatrical shock, but clearly not without a degree of private delight.

Allie, not wanting to give him the satisfaction of having scandalized a respectable woman of early middle age—and more than a little aroused by the young man's frank appreciation for her body, which was still taut and curvy, even at forty-two—remained stock-still and challenging, inches from the window. He'd gone about his business, wiping the dried spume from her windows, while stealing a glance between strokes at the unabashed and unflinching lady in the best suite in the house.

Since that first encounter, she'd looked forward to the young window-washer's visits, which increased in frequency. If she awoke and found the windows smeared with oily spray, she'd have a quick breakfast and hustle back to her room, where she'd disrobe, pull up a chair by the window, and wait. By the third time she and the window-washer had engaged in this little charade, the ritual was perfected. He would descend from his tether and hang, ogling her as she touched herself for him, and then on their fourth or fifth time he pulled himself out of his trousers—quite a feat in a bosun's chair six stories off the boardwalk—and despite the cold, sportingly displayed a very respectable erection. She encouraged him to go all the way, which only excited her more. They had had two more similar rendezvous afterward, each time with the same enthusiasm.

But now it was time to go. With breakfast and telegrams dispatched, she slowly packed her trunk in the nude, wistfully hoping her window-washer would appear. But he didn't. She reluctantly put her clothes on again without any release, arranged her high lace collar to cover the golden torc, and called downstairs for the bellboy. Soon she would back in Buffalo, to deal with death, and disaster, and vile humanity again. It was hard to say goodbye to this perfect, safe, solitary place, and maybe for the last time.

THE QUEEN CITY

One Year Earlier: 1901

In Buffalo—Queen of the Lakes, the Electric City—lawns were manicured, parks neatly kept, sidewalks ran impossibly straight, and order was assured.

It was assured by surging prosperity, as buildings of brick and marble elbowed aside the worn wooden façades of the old port city and new businesses popped up like mushrooms after a rain. And order was also enforced by a pitiless police force, unafraid to crack a skull or two if necessary.

Crime was thus contained mostly to The Hooks, a fifteen-block area squeezed between the Erie Canal, the Buffalo River, the New York Central tracks, and the lake. The Hooks huddled in the shadow of the great grain elevators, where the steamships disgorged numberless tons of wheat, the last link in the chain of the Great Lakes. And The Hooks supplied the staples—booze and women—that the sailors and stevedores needed to blow off steam, or simply kill time, while waiting to return to wives and sweethearts in Ohio and Michigan.

There was, of course, a price to be paid for keeping all this vice walled up inside one hellish acre, safely distant from thriving, gleaming downtown. And it was paid in bribes, to the cops for looking the other way and to many, many others, up the ladder—all the way to the mayor's office itself.

These were small problems, in the scheme of things. The city was clean and healthy, and awash in money—from business, a thousand trades, and graft. The country was replete with good cheer after a rousing little war with Spain, and there were even rumors that a pair of Ohio brothers were working on a flying machine. Dissolution, ruin, and the nagging sense that nothing can stay perfect for long were, for now—like the low life of The Hooks—comfortably distant, a generation or more away for a young, strapping city, which was, however, growing up all too fast.

Looking back, the one thing everyone could agree on was that the year 1901 had put Buffalo on the map—if not precisely according to plan.

The greatest world's fair of all time, the Pan-American Exposition, had sprouted almost overnight from the rolling green expanse of Delaware Park, only to be stunted by a sunless summer. The crowds had stayed away, and in September—when the skies finally cleared—the glow of the Electric City was snuffed out entirely by the assassination of President McKinley. McKinley had been greeting the public in the Exposition's Temple of Music when Leon Czolgosz, part-time agitator and full-time loser, drilled McKinley twice in the guts with the cheap revolver he'd purchased downtown. McKinley died a week later, still in agony, and still in Buffalo.

Meanwhile, sinister doings were brewing only two trolley stops away from the Exposition, in the upper-middle-class enclave of Ashwood. The "Ashwood Set," as the neighborhood's prosperous social clan was dubbed, were the city's widely admired nouveaux riches, the very model of modern men and women. Yet it was an open secret that the Ashwood Set could be a trifle too progressive in their attitudes—even to the occasional violation of the sanctity of marriage.

Edward Miller, his wife Alicia, and their three daughters were among the most fortunate families of Ashwood. Ed owned a thriving envelope manufacturing company and could afford private schools for the girls, fine clothing for Alicia. And she loved to dress well, in trim styles that followed the slim lines of her body—a dancer's body, people said, and rightly so.

Alicia Miller moved like a dancer too—sinuously, with a slinky rhythmic gait that men found irresistible. Even Sarah Payne's husband, Seth, who had been profoundly uninterested in sex, once in his cups had breezily observed to Sarah that Allie Miller moved like she could barely wait to get her clothes off and crawl between the sheets. At the time, his comment had surprised Sarah, but when she began observing more carefully, she had to admit that he'd gotten it right.

If Allie's body, and her sultry walk, was the thing men noticed, both sexes would avow that her eyes were her most striking feature. Alicia chose not to look directly at most people, and when she did, her eyes remained guarded by half-closed lids. Only a very few had ever looked deeply into those eyes, fully open: almond-shaped, dreamy, with jet-black pupils and irises to match, something out of an opium dream. Even Arthur Pendle himself—who should have known—said in one of his letters that looking into her eyes put him in mind of certain animals said to be able to transfix their prey with a gaze.

Arthur and his wife Cassandra lived even more fashionably than Alicia and Ed Miller did, in an opulent Columbus Avenue mansion. Arthur was a young, up-and-coming attorney and the enviably connected university schoolmate, friend, and former law partner of the Erie County district attorney Terence Penrose. In addition, Cassie was rumored to have come from money. Like the Millers, the Pendles had everything the heart could desire—except for happiness.

The Millers and the Pendles would likely have lived out their days in monotonous luxury, had not Mr. Pendle fallen in love—or a reasonable facsimile thereof—with Mrs. Miller. How it began, no one was sure. Dancing at their social club, most likely, or country drives in Arthur's expensive Babcock Electric Runabout, one of the first automobiles in the city.

For quite some time, it was unclear what exactly Arthur and Alicia were up to, what type of affair they were pursuing. Some said it was high-minded and platonic, proper in every respect, nothing more than a man and a woman showing equal regard for the other's intellect. Others were predictably less charitable. But everyone knew that *something* unusually intense was going on.

Little was known for sure until the longsuffering Mr. Miller hired a pair of private detectives to follow the pair around. In New York State, adultery was the single legally acceptable grounds for divorce, and it was difficult to prove without firsthand evidence. And despite the eye-watering sums Ed spent on surveillance, documenting Arthur and Allie's relentless goings and comings, there was nothing that could prove adultery beyond a reasonable doubt.

Until Arthur's letters to Alicia turned up.

Or, more accurately, were stolen. Allie and Arthur had engaged in a vigorous correspondence, using a shared post office box under assumed names as their pick-up point. Arthur had emphasized that the letters must not be kept, but burned upon reading, and Allie had agreed to his terms. Comfortable in that assurance, Arthur's missives became a turgid diary of passion, one which violated an important rule of his profession: never put anything in writing.

What Arthur didn't know was that Allie couldn't bring herself to destroy his love letters. Instead she kept them all, a private and explicit diary of their affair. Either she felt attached to them, in a sentimental way, or she understood that—if events turned against her—they could become evidence. Of her lover's feelings, to be sure, and those would be embarrassing and provide a certain kind of leverage. But they also present-ed evidence of something more, something far beyond his occasionally puerile endearments, more incendiary than an account of their intimacies.

What no one knew about Arthur, until his letters came to light, was that he and Terry Penrose had only briefly stopped working together. When Terry had ascended the DA's throne, their legal partnership had been dissolved. Yet Arthur had found it so difficult to forge ahead alone that Penrose soon found new work for his old friend. Highly paid, highly illegal, off-the-books work—collecting bribes, large and small, to feed the city's graft machine. In time, Arthur became a very well-compensated bagman, a fixer, shaking down illicit establishments in The Hooks and quietly settling cases for wealthy citizens who had fallen afoul of the law. Lowlifes and white-collar criminals alike knew that justice had a price tag, a price set by the only man who had that power—the district attorney.

Two-thirds of the proceeds from this graft flowed into Terry's political war chest, the police fund, and on up the line. The other third, right off the top, stayed in Arthur's pocket. It was so substantial a living that he quickly abandoned his legitimate law practice. People noticed that he was referring new cases to fellow members of the Bar Association, but if they remarked on it, it was to murmur that Arthur Pendle had either married very well indeed or was making a killing in the stock market.

All of this would have remained hidden, locked away in Allie's secret archive, except Ed Miller's fancy New York City detectives located and seized the whole trove of Arthur's *billets-doux*, despite Allie's best efforts to secure them. Dozens upon dozens of letters put Arthur's innermost thoughts on display, caught like insects in amber. And unfortunately, the letters chronicled not only his besottedness with Allie, in all its naked glory, but also his crooked exploits on behalf of the DA.

Once Ed Miller got his hands on the letters, he had more than enough proof to secure his divorce, even in a court system where Terry Penrose kept his thumb on the scale. Miller promptly, and with some righteous fanfare, filed for divorce, naming Arthur Pendle as co-respondent. And inadvertently dragging the district attorney into it.

If a divorce trial ensued, the letters would become a matter of public record—freeing Edward from his miserable marriage but also very likely sending Pendle and Penrose to prison, ending for one a lucrative lifestyle and for the other a promising political career. That meant that the former law partners now had something else in common—a reason to stop Ed Miller from ever getting into court, or at the very least with those letters in hand. For all his business savvy, in the political realm Miller was a babe in the woods, believing that justice could be done, never thinking that he was walking straight toward a tiger trap.

And on New Year's Eve 1901—as if the year hadn't already been stuffed full to bursting with misery—Edward Miller was murdered by a person or persons unknown, his skull battered to pulp in his own little den, at home on Ashwood Street. And after killing him, someone had made a thorough search of the dead man's desk and papers. Could the culprit have been looking for those incriminating letters?

What was worse, Ed had very nearly escaped his killer. Sarah Payne, by then estranged from her dissolute husband, had befriended and then fallen head-over-heels for the little envelope man. She needed a new start, and she knew Ed did too, and so on the very night of his murder she had prevailed upon him to drop his vindictive divorce suit, settle it quietly, and get on with life. But it was too little, too late. The machinery of Edward Miller's destruction had already been set irrevocably into motion.

With Miller dead, there could be no divorce trial, no public reveal of the incriminating letters. Terry Penrose, at least, had nothing more to fear. Arthur Pendle, however, was in a very different situation, in the matter of murder. The handsome seducer of Ed Miller's wife would soon become the prime suspect in the killing—but that was something that the New Year would have to confront.

And thus had 1901 staggered, gasping, to a close. In less than a year,

Buffalo had done a lot of growing up. A failed world's fair, an assassination, and a lurid case of domestic discord gone terribly, fatally wrong—these were big-city matters. Buffalo wasn't a sleepy canal town anymore but the nation's fastest-growing city, a hive of innovation in a dozen new industries. It was a place to be taken seriously. Sure, the old frame buildings of the city were being razed, replaced with brick and stone, sometimes in such a hurry that the new structures were simply built atop the collapsed rubble of the old, like Schliemann's Troy. But society was changing, too. Soon there would be votes for women who wanted more control, and Prohibition for men who needed it.

And meanwhile the good citizens of Buffalo—and especially the ones in the Ashwood neighborhood—had been busily acquiring ever more of everything modern and wondrous: electric cars, electric lighting, even an electric chair for assassins. No one could be left alone for very long nowadays without the telephone jangling and, soon, the insect hum of Marconi's wireless, which could reach where cables could not. But for all of it, no one seemed any happier. Certainly not the Millers, nor the Pendles. It was as if too many of the promises of modern Buffalo had been nothing more than the plaster-and-paint palaces of the Pan-American: enticing but ephemeral, destined to last a season only, and then only if the weather held off.

What a year it had been. And everyone in prosperous, upright, staid Buffalo was wondering what might happen next.

HOME SWEET HOME

January 2, 1902

ARTHUR WASN'T WAITING AT TERRACE STATION WHEN ALICIA stepped down from the train. It had been a long night. She usually slept very well on overnight trains, lulled by the rhythmic clicking and clacking and occasional moan of a whistle, but some woman had brought her god-damned colicky baby with her onto the Pullman car. Each time the kid would shut up for a few minutes, and Alicia would feel sleep stealing over her, the wailing would start up again, and with ever-increasing intensity. If it had been legal, she felt certain that she would have chucked the thing out the window for a little peace and quiet.

That had not been an option, and the tiny Pullman pillow was too small to pull over her head. She jammed some cotton wool into her ears, which helped a little, but somehow the specific frequency of the kid's shrieking penetrated even that dense wadding. In the morning, when the porter in his spotless uniform had come through to announce that Buffalo was an hour away, she'd discovered that the cotton was so deep in her ears that she'd come very close to asking the fellow to help her fish it out. He seemed affable enough, but it would have been unseemly to have a Pullman attendant digging around in a lady's ears. Fortunately, she'd been able to hook it out with a hairpin before having to resort to his assistance.

And now, to top it off, no Arthur. No familiar face at the busy station, only the usual throng of disheveled overnighters, piling groggily off their sleeping cars, and surly morning commuters. She asked a porter to stack her trunk and satchels next to a bench in the waiting room. Perhaps Arthur was running behind. Surely he had received her telegram—those didn't go astray, ever, and he'd received every other one she'd sent during her sojourn at the Traymont. It was puzzling, but it was fact. She waited around for about forty-five minutes, with the curious sense that utter strangers were staring at her, and then gave up on him. She hailed another porter to haul her stuff out to the cab stand for the ride back to Ashwood Street.

When her carriage approached the Millers' grand home, Alicia could see a small knot of people standing on the sidewalk in front, gawking up at the house as though they were observing a comet. Descending from the vehicle, Alicia was met immediately by the nosy old biddy from across the street, Mrs. Stoddard.

"Oh, Alicia," Mrs. Stoddard said, "Thank God you're here. I'm so sorry. It's awful."

Alicia thanked her and asked the hackman to carry her things up the stairs. "Leave them on the porch," she said. "Don't take them in."

"As you wish," he said.

Mrs. Stoddard took Alicia by the arm. "Would you want to stay in our house tonight, dear?" she asked.

Alicia looked at her, puzzled. "Why would I want . . . ?"

"I thought perhaps you and the children—and your mother—might feel safer, you know, until the police—"

"Oh," she said, understanding. "That's very kind, dear. But it's not necessary. We'll be perfectly well in our own home, I'm quite sure."

Mrs. Stoddard looked as though she didn't know quite how to fathom the notion of a wife—a widow, now—returning to a house in which, only thirty-six hours previously, someone had brutally murdered her husband. Mrs. Stoddard had seen Ed's body being removed by the coroner, yesterday about noon. The police detectives, a photographer, and the family doctor had not departed until after sundown. And then, to her bafflement, the three Miller girls and Mrs. Hall, Alicia's mother, had slept in the house last night, as if nothing out of the ordinary had happened.

Alicia smiled at Mrs. Stoddard and trudged up the porch steps, which had been scraped clean of ice and snow by the passage of what looked to be a small army of feet. Her trunk and satchels had thoughtfully been deposited directly in front of the door, making it impossible for her to open it. She huffed out steam into the cold damp and pulled the bell, hard. No answer. She banged on the door with her glove, calling for Annie, the maid. After a few long seconds, the inner front door opened a crack, and Annie's pale, nervous face peered out.

"Oh, Mrs. Miller!" the girl said.

"For God's sake, Annie," Alicia said, "will you get out here and help me move these things so I can get inside? Half the fucking world is out here, watching me." She gestured at the rubberneckers down on the sidewalk.

Annie gave the outer door a solid shove, and pushed the trunk out of the way enough so that she could slip out. Without giving the maid a second glance, Alicia dodged between her and the trunk, disappearing into the house. Annie dragged the trunk away from the door and maneuvered it into a position where she could heave it over the threshold. She waved off a couple of offers of assistance called up from men on the sidewalk. Annie was too pretty to think that they wished only to be chivalrous.

Inside the foyer, Alicia had barely time to remove her coat, hat, and gloves before her mother came bustling down the stairs.

"Oh, Allie," Mrs. Hall said, opening her arms.

Allie gave her mother a small hug and a kiss on the cheek. "What has happened, Mother?" she said.

By now, Annie had managed to hold the door open with her posterior, provoking a few hoots and whistles from the sidewalk, and was dragging in the ponderous trunk.

"Mind the floors, will you?" Alicia said. "I don't want to have to have those sanded because you can't pick up a trunk."

"No, ma'am," Annie said. "I only need to get it far enough in that I can put a little rug under it and slide it."

Alicia sighed in disgust and led her mother by the arm up the stairs. On the landing, she whispered so that the struggling maid downstairs couldn't overhear, although Annie was panting like a dog and making such a racket with the trunk that she likely couldn't hear herself think.

"So what has happened?" Allie repeated.

"Ed—" the old lady said, wide-eyed. "He was *murdered*—right in his own house!"

Alicia looked back at the rear bedroom, which was Edward's. "Where?" she said. "Where exactly?"

Mrs. Hall pointed down the stairs. "In his den," she whispered.

"Where is he now?"

"They took him away yesterday. I suppose he's in the morgue. They said they were going to do an autopsy."

"How was he killed?"

"It's dreadful," Mrs. Hall said. "Someone bashed in his skull."

"This is like pulling teeth. Will you please just tell me what happened, start to finish?"

Mrs. Hall wrung her hands. "Yesterday morning, Annie came downstairs to start breakfast, and got me out of bed. She said that the kitchen window was wide open and she was afraid someone might be in the house. We walked around and didn't see anyone, and nothing had been disturbed. The den door was closed and—Annie refused to open it. She said that maybe Ed was asleep in there. I told her to move and I opened the door, just a little—enough to see that the room had a strange appearance, things strewn all about. And then—*something* under some rugs piled up on the divan. And blood, Alicia. Blood everywhere. I called Dr. Massey, and he called the police."

"What did the police say? Did they ask you questions?"

"Yes, of course they asked me questions!"

"What did you tell them?"

"I told them I'd gone up to bed and saw Ed going into his den and that was all until the morning."

Alicia pulled her mother into the front bedroom, where Alicia slept. "Did they say how the—person—got into the house? Did they offer any theories?"

Mrs. Hall stared at her daughter. "Allie, you don't know the half of it. I did like you told me, and left the front door unlatched. And then, later, I thought better of it, and went downstairs to lock it. And at the bottom of the stairs I bumped into Arthur Pendle. Coming out of Ed's den, Alicia. He had blood—"

"That's enough," Allie said, gripping her mother's arm hard enough that the old woman winced. "Listen to me carefully, Mother," she said. "You forget about all of that. Don't you breathe a word about that door, or blood, or certainly not Arthur. You saw Ed in the evening. You retired for the night. You got up the next day, and you found what you found. That's all. Understand?"

"Yes," Mrs. Hall said feebly. "I understand. I just feel so terrible that I may have—"

"You had nothing to do with anything. There's no law against forgetting to lock the front door. We never did until all this nonsense started with Ed throwing me out and not wanting me back in the house."

Mrs. Hall said nothing. Alicia shook her. "Do you understand all that I've said? The less you say, the better. Do the girls know anything?"

"They know their father is dead. I had to tell them that. I said he'd had an accident."

"Fine. I'll tell them what they need to know. You leave that to me. They're going to be questioned too, so don't you go telling them anything else."

"I won't."

"Promise me."

"I promise."

Alicia unhanded her mother and went back downstairs, almost knocking Annie over as the maid struggled up the stairs with the first armload of Allie's belongings. The trunk was standing open in the foyer, just outside the den. Allie glanced back up the stairs, and waited until she saw Annie rounding the newel post and huffing toward the front of the house.

She put her hand on the knob of the door into the den, and listened. She heard Annie's footsteps in her room on the planking above, so she turned the knob and eased the door open.

The room was painfully bright. Normally, Ed's sanctum sanctorum was only dimly lit by a single gas chandelier—inside a perforated bronze faux-Moorish shroud—which cast barely enough light to read. Someone—the cops, presumably—had taken down the heavy brocade curtains, probably to provide sufficient light for their investigation and for crime scene photos. It was probably the first time she'd ever seen the tiny den—twelve feet square, at most—in such blinding detail. She had to squint against the glare to focus on the plush divan that stretched along most of the far wall, underneath the north windows.

Even before her eyes adjusted, she felt her nostrils close a little against the overwhelming stench of blood, like the taste of the copper penny she'd once filched from her mother's purse and smuggled in her mouth to the candy shop. Then she understood, because what she'd thought was a dark coverlet on the divan was in truth an expanse of dried brown blood, and under the divan—below where someone's head may have lain—was a big, irregular pool of the stuff, almost the size of the entire top of their kitchen stove. Stepping through the entryway, she closed the door behind her and walked carefully into the den. It was so cold in there that she thought she could see her breath. Someone had obviously closed off the heating duct to keep the smell down.

There were footprints on every square inch of floor, wood and rugs alike, except for in the pool of blood itself. The cops, coroner, undertaker, and maybe even reporters—who knows—had tracked so much snow and muck in from outside that there were areas of floor where fly ash crackled under the soles of her shoes. And more blood. Spattered on the ceiling, on the walls, on Ed's roll top desk, on the Moorish chandelier, thrown about by the rise and fall of whatever weapon had bashed in her husband's brains.

She knelt in front of the pool of blood, being careful not to drag her skirts over anything. The liquid had congealed, but there was so much of it that—despite the cold—it still looked like thin rubber spilled on the floorboards. She gingerly reached out a finger and touched the perimeter. It was tacky, resilient, and left behind a tiny fingerprint mark, which concerned her for a moment until the viscous surface swallowed the impression up again, taking it down into itself. She smelled the tip of her finger, but the whole room stank so much that she didn't scent anything. She wiped off her finger on a patch of velvet that hadn't been bloodied.

She looked at the divan blankly for a few moments, and then decided she'd best get back upstairs. On her way out of the den, she spied a framed photo atop Edward's desk, a photo of the lovely Sarah Payne. Like everything else sitting on the desk—Ed's pince-nez, some papers, pens, and pencils—the portrait of Sarah was speckled with dried blood. She curled up her lip at the notion that her husband, such as he was, had a picture of some other woman in his den, probably looking at it and playing with himself. On impulse, she grabbed the photo and put it into a pocket, and then went back to the door. She put her ear against it, listening, but there was no sound, so she slipped out of the den as quietly as she had entered, and walked slowly back upstairs.

Annie was still folding and putting away Alicia's travel wardrobe. "Where are the girls?" Alicia asked. "I ought to talk with them."

"They went out to spend the day with my sister," Annie said. "We didn't know if the police might be coming back."

"Oh, good," Allie said. "She'll take good care of them. I have a terrible headache, and I'd like to lie down for a while. You can finish this up later."

"Very well, ma'am," Annie said, and left.

Allie sat on the end of her bed, looking out the front window. She missed the Traymont, her cozy room, her enthusiastic window-washer. Here, the view was dull Ashwood Street, the coffle of the morbidly curious stamping their feet on the cold sidewalk, and nebby Mrs. Stoddard's house across the way. It wasn't even remotely inspiring, not like the great, indifferent ocean. And she knew that a storm was blowing in, and that she'd have to survive it. It won't last long, she thought. In a month, this'll all be behind me. I only have to make it until then.

🍂

RUTH MURRAY, ANNIE'S SISTER, brought the girls home a couple hours before suppertime. Allie heard the front door slam and the sound of feet on the staircase, then the quiet closing of bedroom doors. She was still lying on her bed, staring at the ceiling. She had got up only once since her return, and that was to accept a telegram from Arthur. He'd sent it directly to her house, now that there was no risk that it might be intercepted by her husband.

The Western Union messenger told her that it was "return reply requested," meaning that she should read it immediately and give him her reply so that he could take it back to the telegraph office for dispatch. She read it in the cold vestibule with a trace of irritation.

> *Allie—I was at the Falls when your wire arrived.*
> *I am shocked at this awful thing.*
> *If you wish to communicate with me say so. Arthur.*

"Your reply, madam?" the messenger asked, holding out his book of reply blanks.

"I don't have one," she said.

"Nothing?"

"No, thank you," she said, and sent him on his way. She had then gone back upstairs to lie down again. Arthur hadn't bothered to meet her at the station, so he could very well stew in his own juices a bit.

When she heard the girls return, though, she knew she had to talk with them, and soon. Who knew what questions the cops had already asked them? The damn police were no respecter of persons, and in fact Arthur had always told her that they were the worst kind of bullies, throwing their weight around with those least able to resist.

She got up, primped a little at the dressing table, and walked down the hall to the first bedroom, which belonged to their eldest daughter, Mary Anne. On her sixteenth birthday, Mary Anne had been given her own bedroom. The other two girls still shared the bedroom next door. The door was closed, and she rapped gently. "Mary Anne? May I come in?"

"Yes, Mother," said a voice, and Allie entered. Mary Anne, a pretty brunette, was sitting in her bedside chair, looking at nothing.

"Hello, dear," Allie said. "I'm back."

"Grandma told us you were on your way."

"I arrived this morning, but you were with Ruth."

Mary Anne rolled her eyes. "Yes, everyone's afraid the police would give us the third degree."

Allie smiled. "Don't worry about that. Mama's back now, and I'll tell you how to handle these people. Will you tell your sisters to come along, and we'll all talk in my bedroom?"

Mary Anne nodded.

Allie went back to her room and sat at her dressing table, looking at herself in the mirror. She felt strangely nervous. Not about seeing her children after her long exile, not even about comforting them about their dead father. She realized that it was apprehension about hearing what the police and the girls may have discussed, and how that jibed with her mother's account.

Mary Anne and the other two girls—Caroline, fourteen, and Millicent, nine—trooped into Allie's room only a minute or two later. Caroline ran to her mother and threw her arms around her, but little Millie held back. She drooped in the doorway, her eyes red and raw.

"Aren't you happy to see Mama?" Alicia said to Millie. It was hard for her to look at the little girl who was clearly suffering, but also because she was the spitting image of Edward. Everyone remarked on how extravagantly their youngest loved her father. The older sisters were more their mother's or grandmother's girls.

Millie put her head down. "Come on, Millie, Mama wishes to speak with us," Mary Anne said. The three girls sat on the bed, facing Allie.

"Mama's home now," Allie said. "For good. We're going to be a family again."

"But Papa's dead," Millie said quietly, not looking up. "We're not a family anymore."

"Yes, Papa's dead," Allie said. "He's in Heaven now, watching over us. God needed him there."

"I want him *here*," the little girl said, and started to cry. "*We* need him. God has lots and lots of other people with him."

"Now, Millie, it's not for us to question God," Allie said, feeling impatient. "We'll have to remember Papa in our prayers. Now, girls," she said, "have the police spoken with you?"

Mary Anne frowned. "There were scads of 'em here yesterday," she said. "Tromping in and out all day. They cornered me and Grandma a couple of times."

"And what did they want to know?"

"Whether we saw anyone come into the house. Where you were."

"And what did you say?"

"We didn't say anything," Caroline chimed in. "They were being very stern, and I didn't like it one bit."

"Good for you, dear," Allie said. "None of you needs to say anything today. But they will be back. They'll ask about our family."

"What about our family?" Mary Anne said. "Our family is none of their business."

"No, it's not," Alicia said. "But we'll have to put up with their impertinence. We must answer their questions patiently and never let our feelings get the better of us. We must play along, for a while. The better we play along, the sooner they'll go away and leave us alone. Do you understand? All of you?"

"Yes," the girls said, one by one.

"Good. Now tell me. What happened the night Papa was hurt? Did you see or hear anything? Did your grandmother tell you anything?"

"Millie and I went to bed at the usual time," Caroline said. "We saw Papa shining his shoes in the bathroom with that new machine he bought."

"The electrical polisher?" Allie asked.

"Yes, that one."

"Was that all you saw or heard?"

"Until the morning, when Grandmother told us that Papa was unwell and was lying down in his den. She said she had called Dr. Massey."

"Mary Anne, do you know anything else?" Allie said.

"Since my bedroom is at the top of the stairs, I thought I heard someone on the stairs sometime in the night. I thought I heard voices down in the parlor, but I fell back to sleep."

"And yesterday morning?"

"Same as Millie and Caroline. Grandma said that Father was unwell, but I didn't believe her and I took her aside to ask her what was wrong. She told me that there'd been a terrible accident and that Father was dead in his den."

"And did you tell the police all this?"

Mary Anne shook her head, sending her brown curls everywhere. "Not the part about the accident. About Father being unwell. Like Caroline said."

"You are smart girls," Allie said. "And now remember, all of you—all you do is repeat what you've already said, when they ask you again. They'll ask you the same questions, again and again, and you have to answer the same way each time."

"They did ask me and Millie about you," Caroline said. "Where you were and why you weren't at home with us."

"What did you tell them?"

"I told them that you were away because you and Papa had been arguing."

"Did you tell them what we were arguing about?"

"No," Caroline said. "I told them I didn't know."

"Why didn't you love Papa?" little Millie blurted out. "Grandmother told me that you and Papa didn't love each other anymore."

Allie looked down her nose at Millie, who was sniffling again. "Now, Millie, that's not true. Grandmother may have been exaggerating. Your father and I had had a falling-out. That happens to people. It doesn't mean they don't love each other."

"I miss Papa," the little girl said. "I want him *back*."

Mary Anne rolled her eyes again and sighed, and Caroline gave her older sister a poke in the ribs.

"We all miss your papa," Allie said. "But he's not coming back, and we have to get used to that idea. No one ever comes back from Heaven. It's going to be the four of us and your grandma now."

"I want to die and be with Papa!" the little girl shrieked.

"I'm not going to tell you again," Allie said. "You're going to get a spanking if you keep on like this. You're not going to die and be with Papa, not for a long time. Until then, you have to be grown up. Especially when you talk with these policemen and other people who will come asking questions. Mama's going to be very angry with you if you tell them that I didn't love Papa, or that you want to die and be with him. Is that clear?"

"Yes, Mama," Millie said, tears running down her cheeks.

"Good girl," Allie said. "Now girls, when anyone asks you anything, anything at all, you make sure you find me first. You are under the age of consent still, and they have no right to query you without my being present. I want you to tell me that you understand."

The girls nodded again.

"Remember, we have to play along with them. That will make them feel good, and when they feel good for a little while, they'll go away. If they feel that they can upset us, they'll only want to upset us more."

"I have one question, Mama," Caroline said.

"What's that, dear?"

"I'm worried that the girls at school will taunt us."

Allie rapped her knuckles on her dressing table. "And if they do, you ignore them. If they do it again, you tell the headmistress, and in no uncertain terms. And if they do it a third time, you tell me, and believe me they'll wish they'd never said a word to you."

"Yes, Mama," Caroline said.

"All right then, girls, remember what I've just said. It's very important. Now go get a little rest before supper.

"Millie, stay a moment," Alicia said as the girls filed out.

After the two older girls had gone, Millie remained standing by her mother's dressing table, saying nothing, looking down.

Allie put her finger under the little girl's chin and lifted it to look her full in the face. "Millie," she said, "I need you to be a very big girl for a little while."

"Yes, Mama."

"Do you know what it means to be a very big girl?"

"Don't say anything to the police. Pray for Papa's soul."

"Yes, and don't tell anyone that Mama and Papa didn't love each other. That would be lying, and lying is a sin."

"Yes, I know."

"Good. Now go and rest and try not to think about Papa."

"I'll try," the little girl said.

"Close the door when you go."

After Millie was gone and the door had clicked shut, Allie sat back in her chair. No harm done, so far, she thought. The girls will do fine. They don't know anything, anyway, and the police can't push them too hard without looking bad. It's Mother I'm worried about.

❦

"Mother?" Allie called out as she saw Mrs. Hall about to round the corner and go downstairs. "A word?"

Mrs. Hall walked into Allie's bedroom. Allie gestured for her mother to shut the door behind her.

"Mother," she said, "ought I to be worried about you?"

"Worried about me?"

"Yes, worried about you."

"I'm feeling reasonably well, all things considered. All this has been simply horrible."

"I'm not worried about your *health*," Allie said. "I'm worried that you may not understand how careful you have to be about—what happened."

Mrs. Hall looked over Allie's shoulder, out the front window, as if someone might have scaled the downspout and was spying on them.

"I know. I do understand that. I feel so—awful though. I feel terribly guilty, Alicia."

Alicia glared at her. "Don't waste another second thinking like that. The sooner you dispense with it, the better off we'll all be," she said. "If you feel guilty, you're going to *look* guilty. And if you *look* guilty, then people will think you *are* guilty. If they sense the slightest weakness, they are never going to let you—or any of us—go. This is a blood sport to these people."

"I don't know if I can bear the strain. I'm an old lady."

"You're sixty-three," Allie said. "You have plenty of spunk left in you. But I do think you're onto something. You have to play on being an old, feeble woman. They won't go after you. They'll love going after me, like the jackals they are. So you play at being feeble. Forgetful. Overpowered. And let me take them on. I'm going to give them a run for their money."

"I know you will, Alicia," her mother said. "You always were a tough one."

"I've had to be. But now that Ed's gone, we're free—both of us. No more of his whining and carrying on. You need to stop feeling guilty and start feeling liberated."

"I am so happy you're home," Mrs. Hall said. "I didn't think you'd ever come back. I didn't think he'd let you."

Allie sniffed. "You can bet your bottom dollar on that. And you can also take it on faith that as soon as he'd disposed of me permanently, you would have been out on the street. He always hated you and Father. Venomous little man."

"I suppose every dark cloud has a silver lining."

"Indeed it does."

They stood there for a moment, Mrs. Hall looking out the window again.

"What's troubling you, Mother? I know you too well, so don't deny it."

Mrs. Hall shook her head slowly. "What if Mr. Pendle is called to the inquest, and swears that he saw me—that night? When he came out of the den?"

"Do you really think Arthur Pendle is so callow as to admit to being at the scene of a murder?"

Mrs. Hall hesitated. "No, of course not. But what if he does? What would I say then?"

"You deny it. Say he made it all up. That he's delusional, or trying to implicate you for some reason you don't understand. You've told them your story, and now you mustn't change a syllable of it, no matter what. If you're consistent, then people will believe you're telling the truth. And that's all that's important."

"I understand."

"Can you do that?"

"Yes, I can."

"We have to be stronger than they are, Mother," Allie said. "And we are. They'll see, soon enough."

EDWARD'S FUNERAL

January 4, 1902
Saturday

UNDERTAKER GEORGE KOCH COLLECTED WHAT WAS LEFT OF Edward Miller as soon as the word came down from the medical examiner. Ever practical, Ed had purchased a family plot at Forest Lawn Cemetery, a rambling, leafy spot not far from fashionable Ashwood, several years before the trouble began. Yet among the changes he'd specified in his recently revised will was his express wish to be buried in his hometown of Conestoga, New York, and that Alicia should never join him there, not ever. She would be welcome to use the Forest Lawn plot, when the time came.

Only Mary Anne expressed any desire to see Edward's mangled remains, but permission was swiftly denied. Mr. Koch told Alicia that the nature and extent of the wounds, compounded by a thorough autopsy, made the body impossible to view, even to dress in respectable clothing. And the corpse, though almost entirely exsanguinated by the murder and then the autopsy, was still weeping copiously from its many wounds. Edward was accordingly wrapped in oiled silk, sewn into a plain linen shroud, laid in a suitable mahogany casket, and delivered to the New York Central station to await the family the next morning. Mr. Koch had done what he could. A memorial service in the house or at the Millers' church would be impossible amidst a throng of curious onlookers.

Conestoga lay along the Erie Canal, east of Syracuse, more than 150 miles from Buffalo. The train departed Central Station precisely at 7:00

a.m. Saturday morning, and aboard were Alicia, the children, Mrs. Hall, and Reverend Levi Duncan, the family pastor. The Miller party attracted a surprising number of gawkers, for an early Saturday morning. Mrs. Hall and the girls had the strongest reactions to them—Mrs. Hall desperately trying to hide behind her thick veil, and the girls—aside from Mary Anne—staying close by their mother. Mary Anne, on the other hand, was defiant, staring down anyone who dared to challenge her.

The train was ten minutes late in leaving, giving the onlookers on the platform additional time to catch a glimpse through the carriage windows of the mysterious Mrs. Miller. By now, the newspapers had begun to peer into the peculiar relations between Ed and Alicia—an ugly divorce in the offing, and with Arthur Pendle as co-respondent. It was only the beginning, but it was enough. Most of the faces on tiptoe as the train at last left Buffalo wore expressions of varying degrees of disapproval and disgust.

"Don't pay them any mind," Alicia reminded the girls and her mother, and possibly herself. "It's morbid curiosity, that's all it is. They'll soon grow tired of us and move on," she said, with as much conviction as she could muster. Reverend Duncan patted her hand from time to time. He was the only one in the small group who seemed sanguine about being the center of public attention. Eventually, they all fell into a stony, expressionless silence as the train chugged east.

The train—a local—stopped at most every town along the canal. Horrid little places, with discordant names like Lockport, Palmyra, Clyde, Solvay, Manlius, and a dozen more, along the tedious and plodding route east. After hours of stops and starts, their train pulled into the Conestoga station, and the group descended. Reverend Duncan informed the conductor that the casket had to be retrieved, and so the train held up there until Ed was unloaded. Allie, the girls, and Mrs. Hall all stood and watched, expressionless. News had traveled faster than their train, however, and even in the little cow town of Conestoga, there were a little gaggle of onlookers, and of course a damned reporter who was peremptorily shooed away by Reverend Duncan. The local undertaker and his horse-drawn hearse loaded up Ed's coffin, and the group followed behind in the funeral director's black carriage.

Reporters, like hydra, multiply when one is cut down, and the one pesky newsman, once back at the station, must have notified every other one within an hour's ride. By the time the funeral party arrived at Pleasant Hill Cemetery, there were—Allie counted them—seven of them loitering around the gate, waiting. Slouching, smoking, smirking away the time until the bereaved and their burden would heave into sight and give them something to talk about. Smug assholes, Allie thought. They know only what they think they know, which is limited to whatever they need to string a few sentences together and be done with it.

The cortège proceeded up a slight slope to the Miller family plot. There the black-draped horses pulled up, huffing out steam. The coffin was unloaded and carried to the open grave by a few of Ed's cousins and the undertaker's hired men. At the graveside, Allie and Mrs. Hall held hands, and the girls gathered close around, trying to keep out of sight of the reporters. The newsmen had followed them almost to the open grave, like scavengers, and stood off perhaps ten yards, at most, from the proceedings.

Reverend Duncan opened the service with a meditation and a prayer. It fell to Ed's brother-in-law to give the eulogy, which seemed to be dedicated less to the virtues of the murdered man than to the moral bankruptcy of the Ashwood Set. Poor Ed had gone to the big city to seek his fortune, and thought he had found it—only to realize too late that he was up to his neck in a cesspit of vice and self-indulgence. And eventually it had consumed him entirely. The reporters craned their necks, and the loyal brother-in-law made sure that he was heard. Allie, Mrs. Hall, and the girls stood by stone-faced, refusing to yield beneath the withering words of the eulogy and the glares of the reporters.

At last it was over, the coffin was lowered, and Allie threw the obligatory first handful of dirt into the hole. She then turned away, opening her arms so that the girls and Mrs. Hall would come with her to the carriage. She didn't say a word to the local Millers, nor they to her. Reverend Duncan thanked them for coming, for serving as pallbearers, and for the eulogy. Ed's brother-in-law shook the minister's hand, thanked him with a grave smile, and left in his palm a ten-dollar gold piece.

The group was silent all the way to the station. They stood on the platform, trying to ignore the newsmen, turning this way and that as the reporters circled around them. When the westbound train pulled into Conestoga, they all hustled aboard, and the women squeezed together into two facing seats, looking at the floor until the locomotive jerked them into motion toward home. They endured the stop-and-go cattle-car ride as best they could, knowing at least this terrible chapter was closed, and with a degree of dignity.

When they pulled into Central Station again, it was almost ten o'clock that evening. They'd been on the move, without food, with scarcely any water, and without any rest except a few stolen moments between the endless chain of stations, for fifteen hours. Even the newsboys had left the station, and without their endless crying out, it was unusually quiet. As they were passing through the hall, Allie spied a discarded copy of the *Buffalo Enquirer*—the evening edition. The reporters had been busy, and there was no way to outrun their newswires. The headline, splashed across the entire width of the front page, and in the enormous type required to sell an evening copy of the morning's news, read:

Edward Miller Buried; Wife and Daughters Show No Emotion.
Stony Silence as Murdered Businessman Laid to Rest.

Disgusted, Alicia threw the paper in the waste-box on their way out. Reverend Duncan almost fished it out when Allie's back was turned, interested in whether his role in the drama had been reviewed as well.

THE DISTRICT ATTORNEY

ALLIE DIDN'T HAVE LONG TO WAIT AFTER ED'S FUNERAL FOR HER first joust with the Buffalo justice system, at least as embodied in the person of District Attorney Terence Penrose. On Monday morning, she was finishing up a call with the family insurance agent, George McKnight, to file a claim for the death benefit on Edward's life insurance policy.

"It should be very straightforward," George had said. "Though given the circumstances, the company will want to wait to pay the claim until after the police inquest is complete."

"Whatever for?" Allie said. "He's as dead now as he will be after the inquest."

George almost chuckled but kept a cool head. "It's perhaps a little awkward, Mrs. Miller," he said, "but they will want to ensure that, um, none of Mr. Miller's beneficiaries were . . . involved in his death. In any way."

"What's that supposed to mean? I'm his sole beneficiary."

"Yes, yes, you are, Mrs. Miller. As such, the inquest will be merely a formality since you were obviously not involved in your husband's demise." He cleared his throat.

"Oh, for God's sake," Allie said. "I was in Atlantic City when he was murdered. That's in *New Jersey*, as you may know. I'd like to know how an insurance company thinks I could have bashed my husband's head in from four hundred miles away."

"Improbable, to say the least," the agent said. "You'll understand that I don't make the rules. I don't always agree with them myself."

"Fine," Allie said. "Then we'll talk after the stupid inquest."

She hung up the earpiece. She was standing in the hall, glaring at the phone with her hands on her hips, when the doorbell rang and made her jump.

"Annie!" she yelled. "If you please, answer the door before they pull the knob off the damn bell!"

"Coming, ma'am," Annie's voice said from upstairs. She jittered down the stairs as Allie disappeared into the parlor across from the den and slid the pocket doors shut.

Allie was fuming by the cold fireplace—damn girl hasn't started it again!—when Annie poked her head in. "What?" Alicia said. "What is it now?"

"There's a Mr. Terence Penrose to see you, ma'am," the maid said, holding out a calling card.

Allie snatched the card from Annie's hand. "What did you tell him? Can't you see that I'm not dressed to receive the district attorney?"

There was no time for a change of clothing. The district attorney was already in the foyer, calling card notwithstanding, whether Allie liked it or not. Annie hadn't even turned to leave the doorway when Penrose's hand appeared over her head and slid the pocket door open. Annie mumbled something about Mrs. Miller being not quite ready to see him, which Penrose ignored.

"Mrs. Miller," he said. "Terence Penrose, Erie County district attorney."

"Mr. Penrose," Alicia said, extending her hand. "It's a pleasure to meet such an illustrious figure, even if in such unfortunate circumstances."

The somewhat underweight, balding Penrose was clearly pleased to hear that he was illustrious, but demurred. "Ha ha. Hardly, Mrs. Miller. I'm simply in a notable office. I am sorry to trouble you so soon after such a tragedy—but I always prefer to discuss these matters personally, and right away."

"I understand fully. But please, do sit down," Allie said, gesturing to a velvet couch. "May I ask our girl to fetch you some coffee or tea? I can have her start the fire, too."

"With thanks, that won't be necessary. I won't stay long, and I'd like to get right to business."

"Very well," Allie said, slowly lowering herself into the chair opposite the DA.

"My condolences on your husband's death," Penrose began.

"Thank you. It's been quite a shock, as you can imagine. But I'm only a woman, and I don't have your nerve, dealing with matters of this kind almost daily."

Penrose gave an earnest frown, pursed his lips. "It's not easy, you know," he said. "Once never gets used to it."

"How interesting. I wouldn't have expected that."

He shook his head, as if to keep from getting distracted. "Mrs. Miller, I understand from your mother, Mrs. Hall, that you were in Atlantic City when your husband—died."

"Yes. Atlantic City, New Jersey. I love it there. And as I'm sure you know, Edward was considering a divorce, and we thought it best to separate for a time."

"More than considering, Mrs. Miller. He'd filed the papers. Named a co-respondent, too. It would seem he was pretty serious about it."

"Yes, but my attorney had not yet made my final response. I believe that had Edward lived to see it, he would have changed his mind. And it was terribly wrongheaded of him to name Mr. Pendle as co-respondent."

"I know Mr. Pendle well," Terry said. "We went to school together and were law partners for several years."

"Since you know him, you'll know he is not the kind of man to take liberties with another man's wife. Nor am I the kind of woman to permit it."

Terry cleared his throat. "I suppose it's a moot point now," he said. "You won't be making a response to the divorce suit. What I'd like to know is whether you have an idea of who might have wanted to harm your husband? Enemies he had?"

Allie looked up at the ceiling. "No, I don't believe I do."

"No idea whatsoever?"

Allie thought a moment. "It's perhaps wrong of me to say anything," she said.

Terry leaned forward. "You must set aside decorum, Mrs. Miller. We must get to the bottom of this."

"Could a woman have done this terrible deed?"

"Do you think a woman was the perpetrator?"

"It's not for me to accuse anyone, but as I say, there is a local woman who took a notion that she wanted to be with Ed. I would say that she was almost obsessed by it."

"*Be* with him?"

"Mr. Penrose"—Allie smiled—"we're both old enough to know what that means. She was practically *throwing* herself at him. At our local Ashwood Club dances, and elsewhere in the city. Mr. Pendle can give you all the details, because he hired detectives to follow them. And while you'll understand this is speculation only—I think that Edward had decided to take me back and drop all this divorce nonsense, and that he told this would-be homewrecker that it was over between them. Who knows what a woman is capable of, when she is scorned?"

"You are right, Mrs. Miller. It is the fundamental and almost sole reason women kill."

"Why, I should be an investigator myself," Allie said.

"You would be an admirable one, I'm sure. So you think that this woman was here, in the house, that night?"

"It's possible. Edward would never have admitted a man at the late hour that I understand he . . . was attacked. Our girls would have been asleep upstairs, and my aged mother too."

"What is the name of the woman in question?"

"Mrs. Seth Payne," Allie said. "Her given name is Sarah."

"Uh-huh," Penrose said. "Sarah Payne."

"You know Mrs. Payne?"

"Slightly," he said.

"And what do you think?"

"About what?"

"About whether she could be a suspect."

"I haven't formed any conclusions," he said. "It's early in the investigation, still."

"Yes, of course. Well, what do I know? These things are your stock-in-trade, but to me they are completely foreign."

"Yet you seem a *very* intelligent woman," Penrose said.

Allie smiled and sat quietly for a moment, hands folded in her lap. "You asked if Ed had any enemies. She's the only one I can think of. Potentially, of course. Hypothetically."

"It's plausible," Terry murmured.

"When can I clear out that horrible den?" Allie asked abruptly, pointing toward the pocket door and the hallway beyond.

"Clear it out?"

"Yes. I want to have it gutted."

"Have you been in there?"

"Heavens, no. I don't even like being here, across the hallway from it. And my girls and mother pass by that door a dozen times a day. It's very upsetting."

"It's a crime scene, Mrs. Miller. It mustn't be disturbed. We may need to examine it again."

"But my poor girls told me that the police were here most of the day, turning our home upside down. Taking awful photographs. I oughtn't to be compelled to live with the scene of my own husband's murder constantly before my eyes, wouldn't you agree?"

"Ordinarily I would, of course, but I can't authorize—"

"But you *can* authorize it, Mr. Penrose. There is *nothing* outside of your authority. Surely you can't mind if we clean it up a bit. At least get the smell out? My youngest daughter says that she can smell her papa's blood! It's giving her nightmares."

Penrose put his fingertips together between his knees and examined his shoes. "I do commiserate with you, madam. All right, you may have the room tidied."

"Thank you, sir. For being so kind."

"Of course," Terry said. "Now then—have you seen Mr. Pendle? Since your return?"

"No, I have not."

"Did you intend to meet him when you returned from Atlantic City?"

Allie's eyes narrowed. "Why, yes. I'm sure he's told you that I'd cabled him, asking him to meet me on my return. I will admit that I feared coming back to the city alone while a killer is on the loose."

"But you didn't meet with him?"

"No, he telegraphed that he'd been in Niagara Falls when my wire arrived."

"And have you spoken to him since?"

"Not a word."

"Do you find that strange?"

"Why would I?"

"He's your attorney, as I understand."

"For a divorce," she said, "that's not taking place anymore. As you said."

"True enough."

"Mr. Penrose, ought I to feel under suspicion here? It hardly need be said that I couldn't very well carry out such a crime from Atlantic City."

"No, Mrs. Miller, you're not under any suspicion. I simply want to understand the comings and goings of everyone in the family and among your close acquaintance."

"Well, neither my old mother nor my little girls would kill Edward, if that's what you're driving at."

"Oh no," he said. "Naturally not."

"Then what? You said it was plausible that a woman did this. Why don't you go and question Mrs. Payne? Don't you think I've been through enough already?"

"You have been through a great deal," he said. "Have you seen a doctor? For your nerves?"

"I haven't had time, between consoling my daughters and steadying my mother. And then just this morning I learned that I cannot obtain my husband's life insurance until after a police inquest—whatever that is. And I'm sure I don't need to tell you that without Edward, we have no income. That's why he had insurance in the first place. If something happened to him, he said, the children and I would be provided for. But now I find that we're not to be provided for until the police court has cleared me, and of what? Even though I was in New Jersey. It took me almost a full day to get back here, all by myself." She took a handkerchief from her skirt and dabbed her eyes.

"The inquest will be held starting next week, the week after at the latest," Penrose said. "Please try not to get too upset. We want to get to the bottom of this. I'm sure you want that as well as we do."

"I do, but that won't bring him back. And it won't put food on my table. I have to be the head of the household now, through no fault of my own."

"What about Mr. Pendle?"

"Why do you persist in asking me about Mr. Pendle?"

"Aren't the two of you close?"

"As you already know, he's my attorney."

"A friend, too?"

"Yes, we're friendly. He and his wife and Edward and I used to be very good friends, until Ed took his flight of fancy about me and Mr. Pendle. As you will imagine, that put a strain on things. All because I'm a woman, and Arthur—Mr. Pendle—is a man. It's so unfair. No one would bat an eyelash if I were a man, or he a woman."

"Then there's no truth to the—testimony of some—that you and Mr. Pendle are more intimately connected?"

Allie looked down, then back up at the DA. "I want to be very forthright with you, Mr. Penrose," she said. "I have had no illegal—carnal connection with Mr. Pendle, or any other man, for that matter. Mr. Pendle and I do enjoy each other's company. He and I have many things in common."

"Such as?"

"Ideas. Interests."

"Ideas."

"Yes, ideas," she said. "About society, poetry, music, that sort of thing. The things many people have in common." Allie looked at Penrose, then decided to take a chance and find out what he might know. "I'm sure you know that Mr. Pendle has written me a great number of letters."

"What was the nature of these letters?"

"His ideas about things, mostly."

Terry frowned. "What kinds of things?"

"I don't recall them all, I'm sure. Whatever came to his mind, I suppose."

"And did you reply to these letters?"

"On occasion."

"Do I understand correctly that your husband obtained these letters?"

"The detectives hired by my late husband stole them from my safety-deposit box, yes. That's what started all this divorce nonsense."

"Where are they now? The letters, that is."

"I don't know. They've gone missing."

"I see." Penrose waggled his foot. "Don't you think that Mr. Pendle might have had a reason to keep your husband from going ahead with the divorce?"

"He's my attorney. It was his job to defend me against the divorce action. To keep it from happening, if possible."

"No, I meant personally. That he might have a personal reason to want your husband out of the way."

"I don't think it's appropriate for me to discuss another person's state of mind, Mr. Penrose. Nor do I feel that I'm qualified to do so. It would be tantamount to gossip."

"You do know you'll be asked these same questions at the inquest."

"And I'll answer them then to the best of my ability."

Terry grinned. "I admire your grit, Mrs. Miller."

"I'm not always this way, Mr. District Attorney. I would have much preferred not to be forced into this situation through no fault of my own. But you'll understand that I have no choice but to adapt to circumstances, whether I like them or not."

"Well said."

"How else may I be helpful to you, between now and the inquest?"

"I'm afraid I will have to send a police detective here to take an official statement," he said. "He'll go over most of what we've talked about today."

"I understand."

"And while it may go without saying, if you come into the possession of any other information that may help me bring your husband's murderer to justice, then I would like to hear that immediately."

Alicia nodded. "I doubt very much I'll come into the possession of any such information, but I'll gladly share it with you, if I do."

"And," Penrose said, rising, "it might be a good idea not to communicate with Mr. Pendle for a while."

"I'm not permitted to consult my attorney? That seems rather strange."

"As I understood you, Mr. Pendle is your divorce counsel. I would certainly encourage you to engage counsel prior to the inquest, but I would advise you—in candor but also asking your discretion between us—to employ someone other than Mr. Pendle."

"I see. Unfortunately, I don't know a lot of lawyers."

Penrose laughed. "You're the first person who's ever used 'unfortunately' in that context, Mrs. Miller." He paused to enjoy his own joke. "I might suggest you use Bert Hartshorn. Of Hartshorn & Hartshorn—he and his brother are in practice together. You might know that he worked for your husband for some time."

Alicia scowled. "*Hartshorn*? Why, that's the very worm who prevailed upon my husband to banish me from my own home! Hartshorn was the prime mover of the scurrilous divorce suit. I wouldn't let him come within a hundred yards of me."

Terry folded his arms across his chest. "Mrs. Miller, may I offer you a word of advice? Not in any official capacity."

"Of course you may."

"Bert Hartshorn may be a worm, as you say, but that worm knows every last one of your late husband's secrets. If he had secrets, of course. Now that there's no divorce suit in the offing, hiring Bert would present no conflict of interest for him, and doing so may provide a wealth of insight for you. No other attorney could make such a claim."

Allie stewed for a few seconds. "I confess that you make an excellent point. Thank you."

"Of course. Contrary to what too many people may think, we district attorneys would generally like to see cases resolved without court battles, whenever possible. They only clog up an already overburdened system. No one wins in court."

"Precisely the point Mr. Pendle and I had tried so hard to get through my husband's thick skull," she said. "But Ed was stubborn as a mule. You had to beat it into his head to—well, that's not perhaps the most apt way of saying it."

Penrose bowed, concealing a smile. "I take your meaning as intended, Mrs. Miller. It's a very unusual set of circumstances you are facing."

"Thank you for saying so."

"Then I'll be on my way," the DA said. "You may expect a detective later today, or tomorrow at the latest. You'll receive a summons well in advance of the police inquest. In the meantime, let me suggest you consider calling Bert Hartshorn."

"I will give it my most serious consideration, Mr. Penrose," Alicia said. "Thank you for such a cordial visit, under the circumstances."

Penrose smiled and popped his hat onto his shiny head. "You're more than welcome." He put his hand on the pocket door pull. "Oh, and if you do find your letters, please ring me up immediately. They will be evidence and I'll need to have them."

"I promise I shall," Alicia said, and the DA turned to go. "Oh, one other thing, if you don't mind," Alicia said, putting her hand over Penrose's.

He turned around and looked down at his hand, where hers still rested. He didn't pull it away. "Yes?"

"Will you be conducting the police inquest? Asking the questions, that is?"

Penrose shook his head. "If we haven't made any arrests by the time of the inquest, my assistant DA, Mr. Roscoe, will handle the questions. He may one day be my successor, and I want to give him some of the limelight. If, on the other hand, we can gather sufficient evidence between now and then to secure an indictment, then I would take over at that point."

"I see. Merely curious."

"The law can be very strange terrain," Terry said. "Another reason to have a good attorney by your side, helping you navigate it. A layperson can't possibly know where the pitfalls are. If I haven't strained the metaphor past its breaking point."

"Not at all, Mr. Penrose. Thank you."

"Don't mention it. Again, my condolences. And I'm sure I'll see you again very soon."

"I'll look forward to that," Alicia said, and smiled at him like old friends as he slid open the pocket door and stepped into the foyer, next to the door of Edward's den.

"Oh my, Mr. Penrose, sir!" she said to his back as he was almost to the vestibule. "I completely forgot something."

He turned. "Yes, Mrs. Miller, what is that?"

She took from her jacket pocket an oblong piece of heavy card, wrapped in tissue paper. She unwrapped it slightly to show him. It was the blood-spattered photograph of Sarah Payne.

"This was sitting on his desk, in his den," she said. "Mrs. Payne's photograph. If I were you, I'd ask her whether a meeting with my husband went wrong and had fatal consequences."

Penrose took the photo in both hands, and slowly ran a thumb over some of the dried blood. "On his desk, you say?"

"Yes, it was right on his desk, in plain sight."

"Then did I misunderstand you, Mrs. Miller? I thought you said you hadn't gone into your husband's den."

Allie smiled. "You do pay attention, don't you? No, I didn't go in there. Dr. Massey, our family physician, retrieved this dreadful thing when he was here that morning. To spare my children from any disclosure that their father may have been behaving less than creditably with a woman not his wife."

"I see," Terry said, wrapping up the photograph again and tucking it into his coat. "That was good of him. Though he oughtn't to have removed anything from the scene."

"Of course not, and that's why I thought I should give it to you. We both know that his intentions were of the best." She shivered in the damp cold. "Well, I'm sorry to detain you, but it had slipped my mind earlier."

"I'm glad you remembered it. Good day then, Mrs. Miller," he said, and thumped down the hollow porch steps, trailing puffs of vapor from his mouth, like a little locomotive.

They're grasping at straws, Allie thought as she stepped back into the foyer. Now if Arthur can keep his mouth shut, this is going to be nothing more than a fart under my skirt.

SARAH'S RUDE AWAKENING

SARAH PAYNE HAD FINALLY SLIPPED INTO A DEEP SLEEP WHEN SHE was awakened by a loud banging at the front door. For a few minutes she lay in bed, thinking the thudding was part of a dream. But then the banging intensified. She lurched out of bed, drew her dressing gown around her, and poked her head into the bedroom next door, where Maggie, her nine-year-old, was still sound asleep.

The urgent pounding on the door was getting irritating, and halfway down the flight of stairs she wanted to scream at whoever it was to shut the hell up, she was coming as quickly as she could. She turned up the gas in the foyer fixture and jerked the door open. A wave of frigid night air cut through the tulle of her dressing gown, taking her breath away. On the front stoop were two policemen in tall helmets and a third man wearing a derby and an outsized woolen greatcoat, a shabby one and with one shoulder set at least two inches higher than the other.

"What do you mean by banging at my door, at this hour?" Sarah said, folding her arms across her chest.

"Mrs. Seth Payne?" the hunchback said.

"Yes. And you are?"

"Detective George Cusack, Buffalo Police Department."

"How can I help you?"

"I'd like to ask you a few questions."

"At this time of night?"

"Yes, apparently."

"What in heaven's name about?"

"About the death of Edward Miller."

"I don't know anything about that."

"May we come in?" Cusack said, getting impatient. "It's bitter cold out here."

"You may not," Sarah said, exasperated. She threw out her hands to push the door closed, but one of the cops stepped forward and jammed it open with his boot. He gave the door a shove that sent her reeling backward. She kept her balance, but her dressing gown came open, the thin, silk batiste camisole she'd worn to bed glowing in the gaslight, clinging to the curve of her breasts, the nipples erect in the cold draft. The cops ogled, stepped into the foyer with Cusack, and shut the door behind them.

"This is outrageous!" she protested.

"Go and have a look around, boys," Cusack said to the cops, who brushed by Sarah, one heading to the back of the house and the other up the stairs to the second floor.

She could hear the cop's heavy boots clomping around upstairs, the opening of a door, and Maggie's shriek. Sarah tried to push past Detective Cusack and run upstairs, but he grabbed her around the midsection, getting a good feel. She squirmed, trying to run to Maggie, but the struggle was futile and only gave Cusack a good excuse to prolong his groping.

The upstairs cop came heavily down the stairs, carrying Maggie in his arms. She was crying and screamed when she saw her mother pinioned in a strange man's grip. "It's all right, Maggie!" Sarah shouted. "Mama's here. Stay calm."

"Mama's here, all right," the cop said, looking at Sarah's breasts and reaching out as if he would touch one of them.

Cusack held her firmly. "If you don't settle down, lady, I'm going to throw you in the wagon and take you to the station," he said. "Open the door," he said to the cop. "Show her. In case you don't believe me."

Still holding Maggie in one huge arm, the cop opened the front door wide, bringing in another torrent of ice-cold air, and pointed to Norwood Street, where under a streetlamp a black, horse-drawn wagon was pulled up in front of Sarah's house. "You want a ride in the Black Mariah?" Cusack said. "Keep it up."

The back doors of the sinister Black Mariah—cop slang for the paddy wagon—were standing wide open, and on the driver's bench there a man was waiting, swaddled in heavy blankets. The thing looked like a hearse, except for a row of barred slits at intervals around the roofline.

"Fine, but let me go!" she said. Cusack released his grip and Sarah indignantly closed her dressing gown and smoothed her hair. "And unhand my daughter!" Cusack nodded to the cop, who let Maggie wriggle free. She ran to her mother and buried her face into Sarah's nightgown. Sarah stroked her head, trying to calm the frightened little girl.

The second cop sauntered up from the rear of the house. "Nothing back there," he said. "Kitchen, dining room, pantry. Oh, lady, you bake a delicious cake," he said, licking his fingers.

"Can we sit down?" Cusack said.

Sarah motioned for him to follow her to the kitchen. The gas was going full-bore in the lamp above the kitchen table. "You're going to burn my house down," she said to the cop who'd sampled her cake, and lowered the gas.

She sat down at the table, with Maggie on her lap. Cusack sat down opposite her, withdrew a small notebook and pencil from his coat pocket, and placed them on the table. He had terrible skin, pale but with a network of thin red and blue veins running here and there, like the tiny fibers embedded in a banknote.

"Do you know why I'm here?" he asked.

"Other than what you said after you burst through my door, no, I don't."

"I'm the lead detective investigating the death of Edward Miller."

"And I hope you find who murdered him."

"You knew Mr. Miller?"

"Yes, I did."

"You were friends?"

"Yes, we were friends."

Cusack stared over her shoulder, tapping his pencil on the table. "How friendly, would you say?"

"My husband and I have known the Millers for four or five years."

"Your husband is a dentist, I understand?"

"Yes, that's right."

"And where is he tonight?"

"He is in Batavia."

"For business?"

"No, he lives there. My husband and I live separately."

Cusack's eyes narrowed. "I might have heard something about that," he said. "You won't mind if I ask why that might be?"

"Will it matter if I do mind?"

"Mrs. Payne, the sooner we get through this, the sooner we leave."

She looked at the two giant cops leaning against her kitchen counters, dripping melting snow onto the floor. "Fine. But this is not appropriate subject matter for my little girl."

"She can go back to bed, if she likes," Cusack said.

"Thank you. Honey," she said to Maggie, sliding her off her lap, "you go back to your room. Mama must talk with these men a little bit more, but I'll be up as soon as I'm finished. Everything is going to be well."

"I don't want to go to my room, Mama."

"I know, but you have to listen to me. Now go along and get under the covers, and I'll be upstairs before you know it."

Maggie slowly left the kitchen, looking back over her shoulder at the three men surrounding her mother.

"Now then," Sarah said. "My husband and I separated because he has a drinking problem. I thought it better not to expose my child to it."

"Are you in the temperance movement?"

"No, I don't object to all drinking. In my husband's case, it has become a mania."

"I'm sorry to hear that."

Sarah nodded. "It's very distressing, of course."

"I'm sure. Will you divorce?"

"I don't know."

"Have you considered it?"

"Divorce? Yes, I have. But I have no grounds."

"Abandonment," Cusack said. "Sometimes that works."

"He hasn't abandoned us. If anything, I abandoned him."

"Do you feel badly about that?"

"How could I not?"

"Did you ever tell your friend Mr. Miller about your marital troubles?"

"Occasionally."

"And he told you about his own difficulties of a similar nature?"

"That he was seeking a divorce, yes."

"For adultery," Cusack said. "Serious business. Which brings me to something I don't understand, Mrs. Payne. Perhaps you can enlighten me."

"What is it?"

"As I understand it, Mr. Miller's complaints of his wife's infidelity are of long standing. He filed for divorce early last year, or perhaps even earlier."

"I don't remember when that was, but it was more than a year ago, yes."

"What's curious is that after he filed for divorce, he seems to have changed his mind and decided to reconcile with his wife. Do you know why that was? Things improved between them?"

Sarah looked down at the table. "No, things hadn't improved. He was deceived. By his wife, by her lover—and her lover's wife. They all told him that Mrs. Miller's affair was over, and prevailed upon Mr. Miller to take her back."

"That seems to irritate you. Am I correct?"

"He was my friend. I thought he was making a terrible mistake. He was too trusting. That's the way he was. Sometimes it was frustrating."

"And you were friendly with him then. Probably you had some hope that if he divorced—and given your husband's style of living—perhaps . . ." He drifted off, looking over her shoulder again.

"Perhaps what?"

"Perhaps you could be together, and be happy."

"What are you driving at, Mr. Cusack?"

"I'm not driving at anything," he said. "It's a feeling I have—that you were somewhat more than 'friendly' with Mr. Miller."

"If you're suggesting that I had any criminal connection with Mr. Miller, you are mistaken."

"I would never suggest that. But is it fair to say that you had hopes— that you and Mr. Miller might be together? One day?"

Sarah sat back forcefully in her chair, making it creak. "I have no idea what possible bearing this has on Mr. Miller's death," she said.

"I don't know either. But I need to know the answer."

Sarah leaned forward over the table. "Fine. Yes, I did hope for that. He did too. We *were* happy together. He was a wonderful, gentle man. And he was taken advantage of, over and over again. It hurt me to see him abused in that fashion."

"If you and he were so happy, then why would he reconcile with his wife? It seems that he was on the very precipice of divorce, had plenty of evidence, and then did an about-face."

"I told you. He was deceived. And he had an uncommon sense of duty and propriety, and like most people, he thought divorce was shameful. He thought it would reflect badly on his three daughters. So he took her back. He thought it was the honorable thing to do."

"I see." Cusack made a few scribbles in his notebook. "Mrs. Payne, after Mr. Miller reconciled with his wife, and went back to her, what happened then?"

"He very quickly learned that the affair was not over but instead had gone right ahead without interruption. That was when he made up his mind to divorce for good. He was angry, and rightly so. He'd been made a fool of."

"This affair we're talking about—do you know with whom Mrs. Miller was said to be conducting this affair?"

"I do. Arthur Pendle, a successful attorney downtown. He and his wife live on Cleveland, about five minutes from here."

"Yes, Arthur Pendle," the detective said. "Mr. Miller named him as co-respondent in the divorce case. I spoke with him, earlier tonight. What struck me as odd was—he said he didn't want the Millers to divorce."

"Didn't seem like he did, no."

"Why would that be?"

"I think you'll be better off asking Mr. Pendle that, if you haven't already."

"It's interesting, don't you think, that Mr. Pendle can now have Mrs. Miller all to himself? No cause for scandal now."

"I think that's a ghoulish thing to say."

"I'm thinking about motives," he said. "All right, then. Mr. Miller reconciles. Then you say he realizes his error, and decides to end it with his wife, once and for all. Did you again feel hopeful again about your prospects for happiness with Mr. Miller?"

"I did."

"And did he tell you he was sorry for—I don't know quite how to say it—throwing you over, the first time?" One of the cops chuckled under his breath.

"Mr. Cusack, that is highly offensive. This seems to be an investigation into my personal business instead of Mr. Miller's death."

Cusack tapped his pencil on the table. "It's my job to understand as best I can what led up to the events in question, and that means understanding Mr. Miller's personal business. In this case, his personal business was also yours."

Sarah folded her arms.

"So," Cusack said, "did Mr. Miller apologize to you for dashing your hopes with his reconciliation?"

"He did."

"And this time, he sent his wife away from their home? Banished her, good and proper."

"*Banished* is a strong word, sir. He sent her away, as any honorable man would do in such a case."

"Noted. If I may say, it was magnanimous of you to forgive Mr. Miller after what *he'd* put you through. Many women would not consider that to be terribly honorable."

"I felt he'd made a mistake. An honest one."

"Uh-huh," Cusack said. "I'm a married man myself, and I will wager that Mr. Miller knew very well that he'd better not make that particular mistake a second time."

"What does that mean?"

"Look at how resolute—angry—you said Mr. Miller became when he found that he had forgiven his wife, but that she was lying to him all along. Played him for a fool. Put yourself in his shoes, Mrs. Payne. What if, after Mr. Miller restored your hope, you found out that he was lying? And that he didn't intend to divorce at all, but was instead stringing you along?"

"Are you trying to insult me?"

"Not in the least. It's only human to become angry if one's trust is violated. Not once, but twice. I don't blame Mr. Miller for it, and I wouldn't blame you."

"Is that a question?"

He shook his head. "No. It's a fact. So now we are getting to what I'm wondering about."

"I hope we can do that quickly."

"As do I. But first, I want to ask you about this." He reached into his breast pocket and took out an oblong card. He slid it over to her. "Turn it over," he said.

She flipped it edgewise. It was a photograph of herself, one she'd given to Edward when he'd decided to take back Allie and have another try at his marriage. She had thought it would keep him from forgetting her. The image had dozens of little tear-shaped brown specks mottling the front. She pulled her hand away as if she'd received an electric shock.

"Where did you get this?" she whispered.

"That's the interesting bit," Cusack said. "It was on Mr. Miller's desk in his den. Where he was murdered." He pointed at the front. "Those little spots all over it, they're—"

"I know what they are. Blood."

"How do you know?"

"What else could it be?"

"I don't know. Did you know it was displayed in his den?"

"I did not. I gave this photograph to him, and I never saw it again. Until now."

"And yet you could sense that it had been marked with his blood. He was murdered in his den. That's where the blood was. How else would blood get on it?"

"Yes. I—" Her voice caught in her dry throat, and the cold kitchen seemed swelteringly hot now. She tried to stop her bottom lip from quivering. "I mean, I don't know. I know what blood looks like, and—it's just horrible. What I thought."

"It surely is, Mrs. Payne," Cusack said quietly. "A man lost his life, and your photo—was a kind of witness to it."

"I don't want to think about that."

"But you did, after all, give him this photograph as a keepsake, and as a proof of your affection, even after his had wavered. Isn't that right?"

"More or less."

"And then you were elated when he threw her out, and hope was restored. Right?"

"He didn't 'throw her out.'"

"Well, you know what I mean. He sent his wife away. And he had to know that he had better behave after disappointing you once."

"Behave? I hardly think a grown man has to *behave*, as a child might."

"You're still young, Mrs. Payne."

"That's an odd statement."

"No matter," Cusack said. "But I wonder—now that Mr. Miller's mind was made up, why would you wait to enjoy his companionship? He's living alone in his house. His wife is many miles away, in another state. Couldn't you visit him easily?"

"We wouldn't have done that. It would have been improper. And you know it."

"Oh, Mrs. Payne, so many things are improper, and yet they happen every day. Every day. If you only knew."

"Perhaps, but Eddie wasn't like that."

"Eddie?"

"Mr. Miller. I called him Eddie sometimes."

"It's very endearing," Cusack said, getting a low chuckle out of both cops this time. He picked up the photograph and wiggled it in the air. "Do you know what I think, Mrs. Payne?"

"I have no idea."

"I think that after Mr. Miller sent his wife away, you and he began considering a future. You are both happy and hopeful. After all you've been through! He's had to endure an unfaithful wife, you've had to suffer with an inebriate. Who wouldn't be happy? But then, his doubts set in again. Once more, he starts thinking about scandal. He thinks about his social standing. He starts thinking about the money he'll lose, maybe even his business. And then—very naturally—he starts to wonder whether he'd be happier with another woman, or happier keeping his children, and his money, and his social standing."

"That's a fable, and nothing more," Sarah said.

"But it's not impossible, is it? And if I'm right, why wouldn't he invite you over to his home on New Year's Eve? His wife is gone, your husband is in Batavia. After all you and he have been through, you can at last start a wonderful new year together. Now, at last, happiness is within your grasp."

"Quite a story, detective," Sarah managed.

"There's a little more to it, Mrs. Payne. Bear with me. You go to Mr. Miller's house on New Year's Eve. He admits you to his most private of rooms, his den. He has thoughtfully laid out food for you. You see your photograph sitting on his desk! And you are happy—happier than you've been in a very long time, perhaps happier than you have ever been. But then something happens, something which you most certainly were not expecting. Mr. Miller tells you—mournfully, I'm sure—he has developed a case of cold feet. For the *second time*. That he is going to make it up to his wife. *Again*."

"That did not happen," Sarah said, glaring.

"If you could only see it from my perspective," he said. "Look how angry you are right now. Seething—and you're in your own home, days after the terrible event. I can only imagine the *rage* you would have felt, sitting pretty as a picture, a hopeful guest in Mr. Miller's private sanctum, confronted by his second duplicity. And I wouldn't blame you at all—not one bit—if in your anger, your righteous anger, you struck him. And struck him. Again, and again, and *again*. Until you paid him back for abusing your trust."

"That's a hideous lie!" Sarah yelled. "It's a complete fabrication. It didn't happen. I wouldn't ever harm Eddie!"

Cusack smiled. "Mrs. Payne, I wish I had a dollar for every time a killer has said that very thing to me."

"I don't care about anyone else. I'm telling the truth."

"Then I have only one other question. Since you're being so truthful with me."

Sarah stared at him, then looked at the cops, who seemed to be looming toward her.

"Did you go to Mr. Miller's house on New Year's Eve?"

Sarah was trapped. She had, of course—not for any nefarious purpose, but to talk Edward out of his ill-considered vendetta against dangerous people. But given the theory that Detective Cusack had laid out . . .

"Mrs. Payne?"

"What?"

"Did you hear me? My question?"

"Yes, I heard your question."

"Then what's your answer?"

"My answer is no. No, I did not go to Mr. Miller's house on New Year's Eve."

"And if I told you that a witness or witnesses had seen you coming and going, you'd still say that?"

"I would," Sarah said, feeling a deep chill.

"You do know that lying to me is a crime?"

"Yes, I suppose I do."

"I can't help you if you don't tell me the truth. If you did go to his house that night, perhaps you did so in complete innocence. But if you're lying, well, it won't look very innocent."

"I'm not lying." She was too far in to backtrack now.

"Fine, then. That will be all for now, Mrs. Payne. I'm sorry to have disturbed you and your daughter."

"That's all? You're satisfied, then?"

He shook his head. "I don't know. I'll have to review all my interviews with my superiors, and then—we'll see. There'll be an inquest, soon, that much is certain."

Cusack got up, and the cops began shuffling toward the doorway. Sarah leaned her head back, looking up at the kitchen ceiling. I've got a real problem on my hands, she thought. I didn't see this coming. "Before you go, may I have one more minute with you, Detective?"

"Yes, of course," he replied, and sat down again, the cops huddling in the doorway.

"I want you to know that I've told you the truth about everything."

"That's good to hear, Mrs. Payne."

"Except one small thing."

"Now that's not so good to hear."

"I didn't say it only because I was afraid you'd draw the wrong conclusions."

"You'll have to leave that to me. What is it?"

Sarah paused and took a long breath. "I said I wasn't at Mr. Miller's house on New Year's Eve. But I was. Briefly. To talk him out of pursuing his divorce action." She heard the cops exhale in unison.

"You don't say."

"I wanted to persuade him to settle things quietly, and not inflame any passions—"

"No more so than he had done already," Cusack said. "So you wish to change your story, and admit that you were at his home, in his den, the night Mr. Miller was murdered?"

"I was never in his den," Sarah said. "We sat in his front parlor. I had asked him previously to settle his divorce privately, but he wouldn't listen to me. I thought it prudent to try to persuade him in person."

"I see," the detective said. "And were you able to persuade him?"

"I was. He said that the very next morning, he'd pursue a private divorce instead of a public trial."

"You must be very persuasive," Cusack said. "After all he'd been through. To sit with him in his parlor, on New Year's Eve—only briefly—and get him to change his mind about something so critical."

"That's exactly what happened. I've told you everything now."

Cusack smiled. "Everything?"

"Yes, everything."

He nodded, looking directly at her.

"What?" she said. "What is it?"

He whistled softly. "I'm not sure what to think, Mrs. Payne. If Mr. Miller had jilted you a second time, you would have had motive. But . . . no opportunity, because you told me you weren't there, in his house. You lied about that, though, and admitted you were there the very night he was killed. With motive and opportunity—all that's missing is the means. A weapon. I can't say that looks very good."

"Mr. Cusack," she said, leaning over the table.

"Detective Cusack, if you please."

"Detective Cusack. I would never have harmed a hair on Mr. Miller's head. If you must know—I *loved* him. I loved him with my entire being."

"Crimes of passion are committed every day, Mrs. Payne, by people who say they love each other. Terrible crimes, worse even than this one. Love seems to inspire people to do their very best, or their very worst. That's the great mystery about it."

Sarah looked over to see one of the cops removing his handcuffs from his belt.

"Are you going to arrest me?"

Cusack waved at the cop. "Not tonight, Mrs. Payne. And it's not my job to decide whether to arrest you. That's up to the district attorney. But I wouldn't leave the city if I were you. And you might think about getting yourself a good attorney."

Sarah swallowed hard and nodded. The cop smiled and replaced his cuffs. Cusack stood, and Sarah rose to follow the detective down the hall to the entrance foyer, cops in tow. Cusack threw open the front door and the men crunched outside onto the snowy steps. The second cop out the door made a quick grab at Sarah's ass as he went by, grinned, and then left the door standing wide open behind him, flooding the house with bitter night air.

She closed the door firmly, locked it, and leaned her back against it. Now I've gone and done it, she thought.

ARTHUR & BERT

ON A PURPLE-GREY AFTERNOON, A WEEK AFTER HER VISIT FROM the district attorney, Allie was lounging in her bedroom, trying to read a novel. The room was warm and the gloomy sky was threatening rain, and she found herself dozing. When she'd jolt awake, her first thought was always the damned inquest, which was to begin the following Monday. Getting nowhere, she slid her bookmark between the pages and looked out her window over Ashwood Street. She glanced at her little pendant watch. Only four thirty, and already getting dark.

She had almost dozed off again when she was brought to attention by a distant sound—immediate and familiar, like the sound of an old friend's voice after a long absence. It was the foot-gong of Arthur Pendle's Babcock automobile. Among the many signals that she and Arthur had arranged for their rendezvous, the gong was reserved for times when Arthur knew that Edward was not at home. The ritual began with the gong, tramped on hard precisely a block and a half south of the Miller house. Then Arthur would drive slowly past Number 101, and if the coast was clear, Allie would stand in her bedroom window and wave. Then he would continue north to Bryan Street, turn right, and pull up into a little gravel patch where the alley behind Ashwood met Bryan.

Her reaction this day was, as always, electric. At the first sound of the gong, she jumped up from her chair, stood in the window, and saw the little black—or very dark green, she never quite could tell—runabout roll slowly and silently by. Arthur was wearing a dark overcoat and a soft felt hat, which she recognized as a Christmas gift she'd purchased for him in New York, at Young's on Broadway. As he passed Number 101, he turned his face to the right and up, looking for her at the window. She waved, and he lifted his chin in acknowledgment, to keep from being too obvious. Then he motored on up Ashwood Street.

Allie, as usual, hurried out of her room and down the staircase. She took her coat and hat from the costumer in the foyer and went to the back of the house. The back door led out into the Millers' small fenced yard—not much to speak of, but a little patch of green that the children enjoyed, in the warm months. Neither she nor Edward had ever been much for gardening—so much work for so little benefit, she thought.

She crossed the yard, which despite a bit of a recent thaw was still half crusted over with wet, icy snow. Her feet were soaked and cold by the time she got to the back fence, but she was eager to see Arthur for the first time since—everything had happened. It seemed like years since he'd said goodbye to her in New York.

Allie unfastened the latch of the fence gate and stepped into the muddy, rutted alleyway that ran behind the line of houses on Ashwood Street. The alley was used by deliverymen—coal, food, ice—and for garbage pickup. Whatever dirty business was conducted by the wealthy residents of Ashwood, it was important that it be conducted out of sight, in the alley.

She'd no sooner closed the gate behind her when the DA's words began to echo in her head: Keep your distance from Arthur Pendle, for a while. She took a few steps down the alley, toward Bryan Street, and thought how silly that seemed. Why, she was free now! She could communicate with anyone she pleased, couldn't she? Yet Terry Penrose was a smart man, and cunning in the ways of the legal world that at present she had no one to help her navigate. Then the thought occurred of having arrived alone at the Terrace Station, after the long and lonely trip from Atlantic City. Where was Arthur then? He chose to visit Niagara Falls with his *wife* instead of meeting *me* at the station?

At first, meeting Arthur clandestinely had been fun, a bit of frisson, a thrill. But then it had gotten complicated—all the time running around Buffalo, playing hide-and-seek from Edward's private eyes, from familiar faces, from everyone and anyone who might recognize and report that she'd been seen in the company of a man not her husband. The thing had lost its sizzle and, in becoming commonplace, had become shameful. And it was worse for her than for him, because a woman's reputation followed her everywhere, like a shadow.

Now, walking slowly down the alley, with a cold rain beginning to fall, she remembered how shitty that had felt, and how she hadn't felt that way since Arthur had said goodbye to her in New York. She had been able to come and go as she wished, neither summoned by an impatient lover's gong nor sent packing by a jealous husband's command.

If I'm free, then I should start acting like it, she thought.

She turned around and walked back to Number 101, left her ruined boots by the back doorstep, and in her stocking feet, crept quietly back up the stairs to her bedroom.

❧

THE NEXT DAY, ALICIA was barely out of bed when Bartholomew Hartshorn III rang the bell at the Miller residence. He'd long since stopped feeling nervous about the first meeting with a new client, but *this* client was different. Very different. And given the news that morning, he'd thought it might be better to reschedule, but that had seemed craven. His heart was pumping hard by the time he pulled the front door bell.

Bert—for some long-forgotten reason he went by Bert, not Bart—was a prosperous-looking, serious man in his of perhaps 50, with a pointed nose, protruding stomach, and scrawny legs, making him look a bit like an improbable wading bird. He put on a professional smile as soon as he heard the doorknob rattle from inside. The door swung open a crack. He introduced himself to the face peeping out, and the door swung open. Annie shut the door quickly almost before Bert was fully in the foyer.

"I'll be back directly, sir," she said, and trotted up the stairs to Alicia's bedroom. "Mrs. Miller is expecting you."

Alicia's bedroom door was closed. Annie rapped lightly. "Mr. Hartshorn is here to see you, ma'am," the maid said through the varnished wood.

"Does he know what time it is?" came Alicia's muffled voice, as if she were speaking into her pillow. "Fine. Show him into the parlor. I'll be there as soon as I can."

Alicia took her time to powder her nose and preen a little at the mirror, and keep the attorney waiting a while. Then she calmly glided downstairs and into the parlor, where Hartshorn was making a show of examining some of the pottery on the mantel. He had to have heard her footsteps on the staircase, but it wasn't well to seem to be too eager. He turned around when he heard Allie enter.

"Mrs. Miller," he said somberly, holding his hat over his heart. "My deepest sympathies. You are looking very well today, considering."

"That's quite an icebreaker," Allie said. "How does that work for you?"

"What I mean to say—is that it's all been very unfortunate," Hartshorn said, shaking his head.

"That would be putting it mildly."

"Yes," he said, wringing his hands. "And I confess I don't know what to say—about *him*."

"You were his friend," she said.

"I didn't know him very well at all," Bert said.

"How well do we know anyone? But that strikes me as a rather strange comment, Mr. Hartshorn. You'd worked with him for years, and two weeks ago you were eagerly beavering away on his ridiculous divorce action against me. Which succeeded in getting me thrown out of my own house."

Bert seemed confused. "What?"

"What do you mean, *what*?" she said, putting a hand on her hip. "The divorce suit. He threw me out because of it."

"You mean Ed?"

"Who in the hell else would I be talking about? Good Lord, you're pretty thick for one of the top attorneys in the city."

Hartshorn's face went crimson. He cleared his throat with a deep, phlegmy gurgle. "Er, I take it you've not seen the newspapers this morning."

"Of course I've not seen the newspapers," Alicia said. "You started breaking down my door at the crack of dawn."

"I didn't think I'd be the one to tell you this—" he stammered.

"Tell me what?" she said. "Oh, hell with it." She turned away from Bert and strode to the telephone table in the hallway, near the foot of the stairs. Annie had placed the morning's newspapers—the *Courier* and the *Commercial*—next to the telephone, as usual. She unrolled the *Courier* and stared at the front page, disbelieving.

> *Arthur Pendle and Wife Killed By Train*
> *Miller Suspect Dashed to Death In His Auto*
> *Suicide or Blind Fate?*

Alicia wanted to drop the newspaper, fling it away from her, but instead she clutched it so tightly that she could not let it go. An odd thought flashed through her mind about an article she'd read recently, about a Niagara Falls man—a Good Samaritan, no less—who had been electrocuted by a live wire. He had tried to clear a downed line from a pedestrian walkway. At the slightest brush of his palm against the copper, his fingers had convulsed around the wire, and the thing had climbed his arm, whipping and wrapping around him like a constricting snake. No matter how his companions bleated for him to let it go, for fifteen horrible seconds he had only gripped the line ever more tightly, powerless to let it drop until it brought him death.

"Mrs. Miller?" Hartshorn said, rushing over to her and taking her by the arm. "Let's get you into a chair."

Bert led Alicia into the parlor across from Edward's den. He eased her onto the sofa and yanked the bellpull for Annie. "Some water, please," he said when the girl arrived, and Annie hurried off.

Allie was still clutching the *Courier* when Annie returned with a pitcher and glasses. The young woman poured her mistress a tumblerful and tried to hand it to her, but Alicia was staring straight ahead, unaware. Bert took the glass from Annie's hand and sat down on the sofa next to Alicia.

"Mrs. Miller," he said. "Please, have a sip of water. You've had a shock."

"I'll be fine," Alicia said, ghastly pale. She took the glass from Hartshorn and drank a little, dribbling some of it onto her high lace collar and shirtwaist.

"What—does it say?" she asked Bert, thrusting the newspaper toward him, still clenched in her fist. He gently peeled her fingers from the newsprint and waited while she relaxed a little and slumped against the back of the sofa. He set the newspaper on the floor, out of her line of sight.

"I read about it early this morning," he said softly. "Last evening, Mr. and Mrs. Pendle's automobile stalled on the New York Central tracks. Where they cross Kensington Avenue."

"What time was this?" Allie asked, her usually sleepy eyes wide.

"It was the evening Express," he said. "The accident happened about half past five."

"Half past five, you say," Alicia said to herself.

"Thereabouts. The Pendles had taken their machine out for a ride along Kensington Avenue, and on their way back the rain had started to come down in earnest."

"Yes, the rain," she whispered. "I remember."

"As the news has it, they were crossing the grade at Kensington and their electrical automobile short-circuited or something. It stalled, right atop the tracks. Mercifully, neither of them suffered. It was immediate."

"It can't be true," Allie said, putting her hand over her eyes. "It must be a mistake."

"My deepest sympathy, Mrs. Miller," Bert said. "I know that you and the Pendles were friends."

Allie snapped to attention on the sofa. "Spare me your euphemisms. If you had thought that Arthur and I were merely friends, you wouldn't have written all that rotten stuff about us in your lawsuit."

"Your husband was my client, Mrs. Miller. What else could I have done?"

"I don't want to talk about it."

"Would you prefer if I came back another time?" Hartshorn said. "Perhaps you could lie down for a while."

Allie gave him a cold, thin smile. "Unfortunately, I don't have time. This preposterous police court begins on Monday, and I'll be griddled if I don't prepare."

Bert coughed slightly into his hand. "Very well then. Let's—I'll get started preparing you and your household for the kinds of questions you'll be asked. They'll call you, your mother, your daughters, and any domestic servants who were here on the night of the event."

"They're going to call my mother and my girls? I'll give them as good as I get. But my *girls*? They oughtn't to be put through such an ordeal. It's not right."

"I'm afraid they will call them, all the same," he said.

"Can't you object?"

"In this type of proceeding, I have very limited ability to object. It's a legal proceeding, but it's not a trial. It's more a preliminary matter, to look for evidence that may lead to charges being filed. Thus, they will want to obtain a statement under oath from anyone who may have knowledge of how death came to your husband."

"For the love of God, how stupid," Allie said. "It's obvious how death came to him. Take a look in that goddamned den of his if you don't already know. It had nothing to do with me. I was out of state when it happened, and it certainly wasn't my old mother or Ed's little girls who murdered him."

"I understand that very well," Bert said. "But so far as I can tell, the police haven't any suspects worthy of the name. The police questioned a local woman last night, and word is there might be something there, but to my mind that seems like a very long putt. Women aren't savages."

"You must not know very many women," Allie said.

Bert cleared his throat again.

"Is it true that anything I say to you—anything anyone in this house says—can't go any further? Am I correct in that, Mr. Hartshorn?"

"Yes, that's true. Anything shared with me is considered what is called a privileged communication."

"Good. Then I will engage your services with that understanding. But I hope you do understand," she said, getting rather close to his face, "that I expect a very high level of service from you, if you are to win your way back into my good graces."

"I am grateful for the opportunity," Bert said.

"Then don't fuck it up," she said, stabbing her finger in his face.

The attorney looked startled. "I assure you, madam—you won't be disappointed."

She looked him full in the face, her deep, dark eyes large and distant, unfocused, the pupils black and enormous. "I certainly hope not, Mr. Hartshorn. Now let's get started. There's not a minute to waste between now and Monday."

❦

AFTER HARTSHORN LEFT THE Miller house, with a promise to return every day until the inquest to rehearse the entire family, Allie shut the door quietly behind him. She stood for a moment in the quiet foyer, between the parlor and the den, feeling strangely tempted to peek into Ed's sanctum. She wasn't quite sure why it should hold any further interest, but it did.

Instead, she walked into the parlor and retrieved the crumpled morning *Courier* from the floor. She slowly climbed the stairs to her bedroom, trying not to think about Arthur. The children wouldn't be back from school for a couple hours yet, and Ruth and Annie were busy with their chores. The hours of mock interrogation with Hartshorn had exhausted her.

In her bright room, now ablaze with the first amber rays of the afternoon sun, she kicked off her shoes and padded over to her dressing table. She flattened out the newspaper, trying not to look at the lurid headline, but it was too large and too black to ignore. The article under it was mercifully short—the evening paper would doubtless spare no detail, no matter how gruesome—but the outline of the incident was there.

The paper said that the Pendles' maid told the story thus: A reporter had called the Pendle home to arrange a meeting for five o'clock. She'd heard Arthur tell him that it had better be six thirty, instead. No sooner had the call disconnected than Arthur had put on his coat and hat, calling to his wife that he was going out for a short drive in his automobile. Cassie had tried to persuade him not to go—the sky was too low and threatening—but he hadn't replied.

The maid heard Arthur return only a half hour later. She said that he and Cassie had a quick and quiet conversation upstairs, lasting only a minute or two, and then Mr. Pendle told the maid that he and Mrs. Pendle were going out for a drive, and that they would be back before six o'clock, and long before supper. They had never returned.

Witnesses along the far, desolate reaches of Kensington Avenue had seen the two Pendles buzzing along in their little electric auto, oddly with the top down despite the cold rain that had started falling hard. At their apogee, they'd stopped for a glass of whiskey at Volkmann's Saloon—Arthur had downed his at the bar, and taken Cassie's glass out to her while she waited in the rain. Then, the pair had turned left onto Kensington, back toward the city.

At the grade crossing where Kensington Avenue went up and over the New York Central tracks, Arthur had powered his auto up the incline. Two boys playing in an abandoned shed nearby said that then—for no reason that they could make out—the car had stopped, right at the apex of the grade, straddling the tracks. The eastbound New York Central Express, which had steamed out of Exchange Street Station only minutes before, had built up a fair head of steam and there would be no stopping.

The Babcock had been hurled a good twenty yards, the bodies of Arthur and Cassie at least as far again. Bert had been wrong about one thing: Cassie had lived for as much as an hour after the impact—if life is defined as simply whatever death is not—but Arthur had indeed been killed instantly. The force of the impact had broken the Babcock's heavy storage batteries free of their moorings, tossing them skyward like a child's blocks—only for them to come down squarely on the head of Arthur Pendle. His brains had been "ejected from the skull like the pulp from a squeezed grape," the newspaper said with its usual macabre glee.

Allie put the *Courier* down again, her hand quivering. His brain, she thought. His amazing brain. Top of his class at New Haven. Greek, Latin, French, more than a little Japanese. All that education, all that experience, all of what had made him *Arthur*, lying there exposed and alone in the winter rain. What had been the point of thirty-six years of living and learning, if in a millisecond it could all be spilled and scrambled on the New York Central's filthy track ballast?

She looked out of her front window onto Ashwood Street. It was clear that he had rung the gong for her on his solitary first drive, before he'd gone back home and collected Cassie. He had come looking for her—but why? To take her in his arms and reassure her that he loved her, and now that she was a free woman, he would make her his own? To say goodbye? To ask her to join with him in the journey to whatever world he was bound? I'll never know, she thought, resting her head in her hands. She had never felt so powerless, even in the worst days of her marriage to Ed—and so utterly, inconsolably, unalterably alone. Arthur was my rock. Now that he's gone, I have nothing at all to cling to.

But then her despair was pushed aside by a sudden blast of anger. Yes, I was denied my chance to see Arthur that one last time. And no, I will never know what message he had for me before leaving me forever. And the author of all this misery—the reason I will live the rest of my life with the mystery of what was in his beautiful brain only an hour before it was spread all over the New York Central grade crossing—is Terry Penrose. It was Penrose who told me to avoid him. Penrose who said that I should find some other attorney. Penrose who had pulled Arthur's strings, for years, which had been like a living death for such a proud man.

She knotted up a fist. Enough of this useless self-pity. Arthur was my rock, but now I must be my own rock, she thought. And that is what I will do. And, she thought, with the familiar flat smile spreading across her face, I will pay Terence Penrose back a hundredfold for what he's taken away from me.

IF IT BLEEDS

"IF IT BLEEDS, IT LEADS," THE NEWSMEN LIKED TO SAY, AND ED Miller's body had scarcely left the autopsy table before the Buffalo papers began dissecting the lives and loves of Ashwood, trying to make sense of the murder. They had to, because the upstanding citizens of dull, prosperous Buffalo certainly couldn't. Murder was supposed to be a plebeian matter, confined to the brutal classes who were possessed of neither self-control nor good attorneys. That comfortable belief was now being challenged. One of the most prominent fixtures of the fashionable Ashwood Set had had his very brains knocked out, and in the sanctity of his own home.

As the scab over the Ashwood Set was slowly lifted, under it the newspapers found all manner of corruption breeding: adultery, homewrecking, ungovernable passions—creeping sin, like a colony of termites, thriving quietly and unseen among decent, upstanding folk, invading their foursquare houses like God's angel had the Egyptians.

On one level, it made for an exceptional morality play. The wages of sin had indeed been death, for Edward Miller and now—again, and so soon after!—for the enigmatic Pendles. For those who had escaped God's wrath—Alicia Miller and Sarah Payne—surely there had to be consequences. They had been up to their ears in all of it, and without a public act of contrition, nothing could ever be put quite right again.

Sarah made for excellent press. Young, achingly beautiful—many said that she was the most beautiful woman in the state—and lonely. With her wastrel of a husband a good forty miles away in Batavia, she and Edward Miller had surely been up to illicit hijinks. And from parts unknown came the persistent rumor, probably emanating from police headquarters, that if Ed Miller had jilted her, "fury and a woman scorned" was motive enough for murder. But the inside line was that Sarah was too young and too beautiful to be permanently unsympathetic, and once the assistant DA had put her in her place at the inquest, rebuked her, her sins would be expunged.

Alicia was a more complicated case. She was known to be tough, smart, no shrinking violet. The papers were openly dismayed that she had been out of the city, and out of the state, on the night her husband had met his end. With an airtight alibi for the murder, she was in the clear for the crime, but nevertheless would have to detail her adulterous affair with Arthur Pendle, which had set the whole horrible thing in motion. Would she acknowledge her shame? Would she break down in tears of remorse? It would be a luscious spectacle, that was certain, something to gorge upon.

Arthur and Cassie Pendle would, of course, miss the proceedings, but their presence would loom large nonetheless. They defied easy classification. Cassandra Pendle seemed to have known of, and mildly accepted, her husband's peccadilloes, though rumor had it that there was a limit to how far she would have allowed him to go. She might have accepted a dalliance, but she never would have agreed to a divorce. For Arthur, it was equally unclear what precisely he had wanted from Allie, or from life. He had been the envy of most every man in Buffalo, yet seemed to have been desperate to tear down, brick by brick, what had appeared to be his perfect and prosperous world.

Terry Penrose had succeeded, at first, in keeping his friend Arthur Pendle out of the eye of suspicion, but in the end it was a junior reporter from the *Courier*, Jess Murphy, who had broken the story free. Murphy's questions about Arthur's business dealings—and his dearth of paid legal work before the courts—had rattled Pendle, just as he had sensed that he was in the clear for the murder. Soon a series of articles had appeared, hinting at failed investments, graft, and large sums of investors' money unaccounted for—all of which were documented in Arthur's letters, which Ed Miller had planned to bring triumphantly before the court. As co-respondent in the divorce suit, Arthur would have had to testify, and the Potemkin village of his marriage, his work, and his life itself would have been revealed as the sham they had become.

While Edward Miller had lived, nothing had stood between Arthur and utter ruin. Hence the papers quickly pointed out cui bono, and the blame game began. Under suspicion of murder, rumored to be a swindler, and apparently abandoned by Allie, the pressure on Arthur had become intolerable. Something had had to give. And it had, on the cold, wet afternoon when Arthur had tried one final time to call Allie to him. It was Jess Murphy who had telephoned Arthur that afternoon, who had arranged for the further interview that his subject had never attended. The newspapers had done what the police had failed to do.

With the lead suspect in his grave, and anything his wife had known now unknowable, the papers were momentarily at a loss as to how to pursue the Miller case. And some did ask—Terry Penrose, chief among them—what good would an inquest do now? Why not let the Buffalo papers finish feasting on their three dead members of the Ashwood Set, and leave it at that? But that was not to be, because out-of-town report-ers—not yet so satiated as their local cousins—had begun to descend on Buffalo. Droves of them, hordes, from cities large and small across the vast continent, an ant-like caravan lured by the scent of shame. And every one of the out-of-towners had readers and district attorneys and policemen who wanted their story, their very own morality play, and there could be no story if there were no inquest. It had to happen, like it or not.

And Alicia was ready. Not because of Bert, however helpful his prepa-ration had been. Because of the crystalline hatred she felt for all of them. For the district attorney, obviously. The police, of course. Not to mention the whole clan of lawyers and judges and bailiffs, all their ilk, every single smug official anointed to cluck and smirk over her pillory. But it was all too easy to hate baleful, sanctimonious bureaucrats. Everyone hated them, at some level. The people who were more difficult to hate—which made it all the more worth the challenge—were the good, moral, upright citizens of Buffalo, and of a hundred other cities from sea to sea. Every last fucking one of them. If they were looking for a pound of Alicia's flesh, they would have to come and get it.

THE INQUEST

P OLICE J UDGE F REDERICK M ALONE SEEMED UNUSUALLY SWARTHY
for an Irishman, Allie thought, but there was something obviously wrong
with his skin. There were dozens of tiny growths, like nonpareils, on the
flesh beneath his eyes, and between two of his chins an especially large
one, about the size of a grape, which wobbled when he talked. It must
have taken five yards of black satin to cover the man's vast frame and
protruding belly, all supported by astonishingly small feet, almost like a
Chinese woman's.

Judge Malone shuffled his bulk up the two small steps and maneuvered
behind the judge's bench. Once in place, the man's enormous head slowly
settled down into his shoulders, like a roosting chicken. In addition to the
mysterious lumps, the judge's round face also sprouted a lopsided brown
mustache. It perched cockeyed on his upper lip, like a dead sparrow, broad
and bushy at one end and narrowing to a point at the other. It gave him
a permanent sneer.

The two men behind Allie were obviously having some fun at the
expense of the corpulent jurist.

"Take a gander at that mustache, will you," the one fellow said. "It
looks as though he had to shave left-handed."

"Must be hard to shave around all those *things*," the other wag said.
"One slip and his barber could send a meatball rolling out the door." Their
laughs were cut short by the firecracker sound of Malone's gavel smacking
the court into order.

"In the matter of Edward Lee Miller, deceased," the mountainous
black form intoned in a sonorous baritone, "this inquest will now come
to order."

The courtroom was packed to the gills with visitors, some of whom
had called in whatever favors owed them for a seat at the spectacle. It

was the biggest murder case in years. Sure, people were murdered all the time—but not prominent businessmen in the privacy of their own homes, and certainly not ones embroiled in titillating divorce actions. More than two weeks after the murder and without any credible suspects, almost no one expected the case to be solved. The far more interesting question was how would Mrs. Miller react to questions relating to her relationship with the other man in the love triangle, now that he, too, was dead? More than three-quarters fully expected her to disavow her former suitor entirely. That would be the most prudent tack to take.

Terry Penrose himself was in the back of the gallery, and not at the lawyer's table with Bill Roscoe. Bert Hartshorn sat in the front row, watching anxiously.

"Today we call our first witness, Dr. Michael Havilland," Judge Malone said.

A thirty-something handsome man with a full mustache and a soldier's posture was sworn in and then took his seat. Roscoe stood up slowly and approached the witness box.

"Would you state your name and title for the record?" Roscoe said.

"Dr. Michael J. Havilland, deputy Erie County medical examiner."

"Welcome, Dr. Havilland. How long have you been the county's medical examiner?"

"Since last April."

"And in that time, you've examined how many murder victims?"

"I couldn't say for sure. At least two dozen."

"My point is that you are very well versed in analyzing the remains of those who meet a violent end."

"I would say so, yes."

"Then if you would, take us through what happened on the morning that Mr. Miller's murder was reported to you."

"Certainly. I received a telephone call from Dr. Massey."

"This would be Dr. William Massey, the Miller's family physician?"

"That is correct."

"Go on, please."

"I received a call about eight o'clock in the morning from Dr. Massey, asking me to come right away to the Miller residence at 101 Ashwood Street. I went straight there and arrived about eight thirty."

"And what did you find when you arrived?"

"I was met at the door by Dr. Massey. He was conferring with Mrs. Hall, the victim's mother-in-law."

"Do you know what they were saying?"

"No, it seemed to be of a private nature."

"And then what?"

"Dr. Massey sent Mrs. Hall away and took me by the arm, directing me into Mr. Miller's private study, or 'den,' as it's called, adjacent to the front door. We went in together."

"Can you describe the scene?"

"A desk to the right, a bookcase to the left, and ahead along one of the walls was a long divan or couch, piled high with pillows and a large rug that seemed to have been taken up from the floor."

"Describe the divan."

"It was a long Oriental-style couch with no back. At least eight feet long. On it, there was a form lying, covered by the rugs and pillows. At the foot was a pair of trousers and a jacket, neatly folded. There was a large bloodstain at the left end—the head—of the divan, about twelve inches above the pile of rugs."

"Was there blood anywhere else?"

"Oh yes. It had soaked through the couch and had run down and along the floor. There was a pool of it about a foot in diameter nearby. Also, blood had been splattered here and there, on the desk and on the ceiling."

"On the ceiling? Spurting from a wound, do you think?"

"No, I believe that whatever weapon was used threw blood there as it rose and fell."

"And what happened next?"

"Dr. Massey said to me, 'It's Ed Miller under there. He's dead.'"

"Under there, meaning under the pillows and rugs?"

"Yes."

"Tell us what you did then."

"I removed my jacket and went to the divan. I removed the rug covering the body and discovered that a crazy quilt of some kind had been wrapped around the head, tightly, three times."

"Could you see that it was Mr. Miller?"

"Not at this point. The face was covered entirely by the quilt."

"But you knew he was dead?"

"Yes, there were several pieces of brain matter on the couch above the body, where the large bloodstain was. The body was cold, though rigor mortis had not yet set in."

"Did you then examine the body?"

"Yes, I did a preliminary assessment. I removed the quilt and the pillows. The body was prone, so I turned it over to see the face. It was clearly Mr. Miller."

"How was the body clothed?"

"The deceased was wearing only an undershirt, which was pulled up to just above his waist."

"No underdrawers?"

"His drawers were draped over his calves. He was not wearing them at the time of the murder, because there was a bloody thumbprint on the flesh of the outer thigh, which would have been left on the drawers, had he been wearing them."

"What would account for a thumbprint there?"

"The large pool of blood on the couch was about a foot above the head, so I believe that after the man was dead, the assailant or an accomplice pulled him down a bit on the couch, and in so doing caused his undershirt to rise up on his body."

"Was there any indication that immorality was being practiced prior to the crime?"

"None. I found no trace either of a seminal emission or of any other bodily fluids associated with immorality."

"Can you describe the nature of the body and the wounds?"

"The cranium was badly fractured—multiple fractures from multiple blows of a heavy object of some kind. There was a large fracture above the left eye, and then the rest of the wounds were to the back and upper part of the skull, which had been reduced to pulp."

"How many wounds were there?"

"It's difficult to tell. One ran into another. I would say ten or eleven, though."

"And how many would it have taken to kill Mr. Miller?"

"Any one of those wounds would kill a man dead as a doornail," the doctor said. "I suppose that he was perhaps lying face up or sitting upright when the first blow fell, and then was either turned over or did so defensively as his assailant rained down blows on his head. There was one particularly heavy blow to the base of the skull, from which about two tablespoonfuls of brain matter had oozed. That one certainly was fatal, even if the others had not been."

"Can you say what kind of person could do such a thing? A man or a woman? Such a person's state of mind?"

"It's hard to say. Most women would not be capable of the kind of strength or ferocity of the attack that killed Mr. Miller, but I can't rule it out. I would say that so many blows, most of them delivered after the man was incapacitated or dead, would indicate a furious passion. A rage."

"Were there other wounds?"

"One finger on the left hand was broken and another was badly contused—bruised and swollen. Those injuries would have likely happened prior to death."

"How would the man's fingers have been broken?"

"My estimation is that he was trying to ward off a blow and the weapon hit his hand. However, that would take a great deal of force. Perhaps more likely was that Mr. Miller fell or rolled onto his stomach and reflexively put his hands behind his head to protect himself. In such a case, if the fingers were trapped between a heavy weapon and the cranium, it would require only moderate force to break a finger. In any case, the hand injuries were perimortem. Around the time of death."

"I see. What else did you notice about the scene?"

"There was a small table near the divan with a plate on it containing a few bits of cheese, some crackers, a fruit tart of some kind, an almost empty bottle of cocktails, and a used wine glass."

"As if he had been entertaining someone?"

"Perhaps modestly, yes."

"What else?"

"There were papers on the floor, under the desk. The desk drawers were open and the papers seem to have been removed and scattered about."

"What kind of papers?"

"Some photographs. What looked to be billheads or receipts. Miscellany."

"Did you search the man's clothing?"

"Yes. There were a couple of letters in his jacket pocket, a loaded revolver, and a bill case with about a hundred dollars in notes and a few coins."

"So robbery was evidently not the motive?"

"You'd have to ask the detectives for their opinion."

"What did you do with the letters you found?"

"I gave them to the detectives when they showed up."

"And did you and Dr. Massey have any further conversation during or after your preliminary examination."

"We did."

"And what was the nature of that discussion?"

"Dr. Massey urged me to consider that this might have been a case of suicide." Dr. Havilland's mustache twitched up at the sides. "He said that the family had been through so much with a very public divorce proceeding, and that they might be spared more publicity if I judged it a suicide and not a murder."

"And what did you say to that?"

"I said it was so much bunk. I asked him whether he'd ever seen a case where a man had bashed in his own head, carefully wrapped it in a quilt, and covered himself with pillows and rugs before expiring."

The courtroom erupted in laughter, and Malone banged his gavel down. "Silence," he said.

"How did Dr. Massey respond, Dr. Havilland?" Roscoe continued.

"He said no, he'd never seen such a thing. He reiterated he was trying to spare the family further public anguish, after they had already endured so much publicity about the pending divorce."

"If you had classified it as a suicide, doctor, what would have happened?"

"There would have been no inquest. The body would have been interred straightaway."

"And the truth might never have come out?"

Dr. Havilland stared straight ahead. "I have the utmost regard for Dr. Massey," he said.

"As do we all," Roscoe replied. "Now then, doctor, after the body was removed, I presume you conducted an autopsy?"

"I did, at 10:15 on the following morning." Dr. Havilland took a paper from his breast pocket and smoothed it flat. "I can read selections from it, if you like."

"Please do."

"Male decedent, forty-two years of age. Five feet, four inches tall, one hundred and thirty pounds. Hair, black with some grey. Eyes, grey, pupils even and normal. Viscera, normal, no organic disease noted. Genitourinary organs, normal. Contusion at base and back of left thumb and second left finger. Fracture of third left finger, wound of skin of same finger. Skull, many wounds, comminuted fractures; brain membrane, lacerated. A tuft of hair not belonging to the deceased was found stuck to the pelvis with dried blood. No antemortem bruising or additional signs of a struggle."

"Thank you for that. Whose hair was stuck to the pelvis, Dr. Havilland?"

"I don't know. We compared it under the microscope and found that it is too long to be Mr. Miller's. More brown than black, too. Beyond that, we don't know."

"Any signs of alcohol or other poisons?"

"Stomach contents were unremarkable. Nothing except for the remains of a meal taken several hours before—but nothing resembling the items on the table in the den. Chemical analysis revealed no traces of alcohol or any common poison."

"So your determination of cause of death is what?"

"Edward Miller came to his death from compound, comminuted multiple fracture of the cranium."

"At what time of day?"

"I estimate between midnight and two o'clock in the morning."

"How do you know that?"

"When I arrived, as I mentioned, there was quite a large pool of blood on the floor in front of the couch. I noticed its condition and allowed no one to disturb it in the three hours or so that I was there. It had by that time almost completely clotted, so figuring back from that I estimated that he must have had this hemorrhage no earlier than midnight. And since rigor was not well advanced, I would estimate no later than two o'clock."

"And do you have an idea of what kind of weapon was used to kill Mr. Miller?"

"Something heavy and blunt, swung like a mallet to account for the spots of blood thrown onto the ceiling. Beyond that, I cannot say."

"Thank you, Dr. Havilland."

❧

THE NEXT WITNESS WAS Detective Larson Holmstrom, a tall, muscular blonde with a pronounced Scandinavian accent. After being duly sworn, Holmstrom readied himself in the witness box.

"Detective," Roscoe said, "how were you notified of the murder of Edward Miller?"

"Dr. Havilland telephoned me from the Miller house and asked me to come at once."

"And what time did you arrive?"

"About nine o'clock in the morning."

"Will you describe what you found when you got there?"

"Yes. I found Drs. Massey and Havilland, looking over the dead man's body. I let them complete that while I took statements from everyone in the house."

"And then you examined the scene?"

"Yes. I called the photographer to take pictures, and while I was waiting, I made a search of the den."

"Did the den appear as Dr. Havilland described it?"

"Yes, in general."

"What might you add or change?"

"A few things. The man's glasses were lying on the desk along the east wall, as well as a set of cuffs, a collar, and links. The gas chandelier had been turned off at the main, instead of at the fixture itself. This indicated to me that whoever turned it off was not familiar with the operation of the fixture—not turned off by Mr. Miller. Also—the dead man's slippers were next to the couch, with the heels pointing toward the couch, as though he'd stepped out of them when he sat or lay down."

"And do you think he was lying down when he was attacked?"

"That I cannot say. I believe that he may have been sitting up speaking to his assailant when the first blow was struck, but then fell over to the side."

"Was there anything else of note at the scene?"

"Dr. Havilland may have mentioned it, but the man's drawers had been laid across the backs of his legs. There was blood on the legs, but the drawers had no blood on them, so he must not have been wearing them when he was killed. My impression was that someone had laid them across the dead man's legs to provide the body a degree of modesty."

"How do you account for that?"

"I cannot."

"Were there signs of forced entry into the house or the den?"

"No. The kitchen window, in the rear of the house, was raised about three inches. The maid suspected burglary, but there was a crust of snow of a day or two's standing on the sill, which had not been disturbed. And no footprints in the snow outside the window. Mrs. Hall told me that the front door had been ajar when she came downstairs that morning. The door made a sound when it closed, so I imagine that the murderer wanted to leave without awaking anyone in the house."

"But wouldn't the door have made a sound when it was opened, if the killer entered the house that way?"

"Presumably. I suspect the door may have been open or unlatched. I tried the door myself and it was quite sticky, and on closing or opening made considerable noise."

"I see. Anything else?"

"It is puzzling who set out the tray of cheese, crackers, fruit tart, and liquor. The maid denied having done so, as did Mrs. Hall. Both also stated that Mr. Miller did not eat cheese or fruit tarts, and would not have known where those items were kept in the pantry. Yet both the crackers and the cheese had been partly eaten, and there was only about one ounce remaining in the liquor bottle."

"It appeared to you that Mr. Miller was expecting a visitor? Or that he had been entertaining a visitor?"

"Yes, I can think of no other explanation for it. Yet only someone very familiar with the layout of the house and the pantry would know where those eatables were stored."

"Did you examine the rest of the house?"

"I did."

"Did you see blood anywhere else? Anything to indicate that an assailant had searched the premises?"

"I did not. Mr. Miller's bed had not been slept in. He must have been in the den before retiring for the night, and was then murdered."

"And his clothes had been taken off and were in the den with his body?"

"Yes, but I should emphasize they were taken off before he was attacked. He was entirely unclothed, save for his undershirt. Everything else had been folded neatly and bore no trace of blood. He must have intended to sleep in his den that evening."

"I see. Dr. Havilland also mentioned that he gave a detective some letters he had found in Mr. Miller's clothing. Did he give those to you?"

"Yes, he did."

"Did you see who had sent them to Mr. Miller?"

"Yes, they were from a Dr. Warren, in Cleveland. I did not read the letters, only the envelopes, however."

"And where are those letters now?"

"I turned them in to the evidence locker," Holmstrom said.

"Yet these letters were not found among the evidence I reviewed. Did you receive a receipt for them?"

"I did not."

"Very well then. If there's nothing else to add, Detective Holmstrom, we thank you for your time."

❦

AFTER HOLMSTROM HAD STEPPED down, Judge Malone called a series of mildly entertaining witnesses, but they were not what the increasingly restive crowd had come to see. That changed when Sarah Payne was called to the stand.

Sarah looked somewhat drawn, but was still luminous. She was wearing a turban-style hat of turquoise blue velvet, and a matching velvet coat with a flaring collar and wide lapels faced with chinchilla. The coat was worn open to reveal a blue silk shirtwaist, which disappeared into a black skirt trimmed with taffeta ruffles. She was accompanied by a somewhat less prepossessing figure, her lawyer Sidney Greene.

"Mrs. Payne," Roscoe said. "I understand you were a friend of the deceased."

"That is so," Sarah replied.

"How long had you known Mr. Miller?"

"About four or five years."

"How did you become acquainted?"

"My husband and I were members of the Ashwood Social Club. A dancing club in our neighborhood. The Millers were members as well. We met them there."

"And do I understand correctly that you and Mr. Miller became good friends?"

"Yes, we were."

"Did he ever talk with you about his marital difficulties?"

"Occasionally."

"And what did he tell you?"

"That he was seeking a divorce from his wife. That they were no longer happy."

"And what did he plan to do after securing a divorce?"

"I don't know."

"You don't know?"

"No, I don't. He didn't live long enough for me to know."

"Let me try this another way, Mrs. Payne. Isn't it true that you are also seeking a divorce from your husband?"

"My husband and I are separated, but we have not filed for a divorce."

"Why are you separated?"

"Is this relevant to the inquest?" Sidney Greene chimed in.

"Mr. Greene, thank you," the judge said. "For the present, I'll direct the witness to answer the question."

"Very well," Sarah said. "My husband has health problems that made it advisable for me and my daughter to live separate from him."

Roscoe sneered. "You mean to say that he's addicted to alcohol and drugs, don't you, Mrs. Payne?"

"Really, Judge?" Greene said.

Sarah smiled sweetly at Roscoe. "It's somewhat crude, Mr. Roscoe, but if you wish to put it that way, you may."

"And isn't it true that you planned to divorce your husband, and hoped that Mr. Miller would marry you, after he divorced his wife?"

"Is that one question or two?"

"Let me break it up for you, Mrs. Payne. Did you hope that Mr. Miller would marry you after he divorced his wife?"

"Yes, I did."

"And you were prepared to divorce your husband to do so?"

"Yes," Sarah said, releasing a freshet of whispers into the courtroom. Sarah was thankful that Seth wasn't in the gallery.

"I will instruct the spectators to remain quiet," Judge Malone said sternly.

"But Mr. Miller had made promises to you on an earlier occasion, hadn't he? And then taken his wife back?" Roscoe said.

"Your Honor," Greene said, "if this is relevant to the death of Mr. Miller, that's one thing. But it's another if it's intended to embarrass my client."

"Is this relevant to a possible theory of the case, Mr. Roscoe?" Judge Malone asked.

"I believe it is, Your Honor."

"Then, Mrs. Payne, please answer the question."

"I wouldn't say he'd made me any promise, but he did reconcile with his wife."

"And you were disappointed?"

"Yes, I was. I thought he was making a poor decision."

"Were you angry?"

"Yes, I was angry with him."

"But then he took up the divorce case again, and your hopes were restored?"

"That is so, yes."

"That was very convenient, wasn't it? Did you put him up to it?"

"Are you making a joke?"

"No, I'm not."

"Then you are making a bad blunder. He took up the divorce case again because he became aware that Mrs. Miller and Mr. Pendle had resumed their affair."

This caused a general uproar in the court.

"And how do you know this?" Roscoe said, raising his voice.

"Mr. Miller told me himself. He was furious."

"And how did you feel about it?"

"I urged him to get the divorce, but to do it quietly and not with his lawsuit. But he was bent on making Arthur Pendle pay for wrecking his home."

"If Mr. Pendle was wrecking a man's home, why was it unreasonable for him to want to restore his honor?"

"Because Arthur Pendle was a very dangerous man."

"That's a serious allegation, Mrs. Payne."

In the back of the gallery, Sarah saw Terry Penrose slowly raise a hand.

"Recess for luncheon," Judge Malone said abruptly, banging his gavel. "Court will resume session in forty-five minutes."

Sarah was helped down from the witness box while the confused spectators filed out into the corridors of police headquarters to gossip or onto the cold sidewalks to smoke. Penrose slowly walked upstream against the departing crowd to the table where Roscoe was sitting, poring over his notes. Terry sat down next to him quietly.

Roscoe looked up, surprised. "Mr. Penrose," he said. "How do you think it's going?"

"What in the holy fucking name of God do you think you're doing with this line of questioning?"

"What line of questioning?"

"About Pendle. Don't bring him up. At all. If she brings him up, then you redirect her. You know as well as I do she's probably seen those letters. 'Pendle is a dangerous man'? What in fuck's name do you think comes after that? Were you going to ask her why he was a dangerous man?"

"I was trying to box her in, to suggest that Miller was going to drop her again, and that she had a motive to kill him."

"Look," Penrose whispered, "I recognize we have to make this look kosher. But you don't need to go overboard. The only verdict we want is 'murder by person or persons unknown.' That's it. We've already tried to pin it on this lady, but Pendle was still alive then and we had a chance. Now we don't. So wrap it up with her, Roscoe, and let's get on with life."

"Understood, Mr. Penrose."

"Good."

"What about Mrs. Miller? How do you want me to handle her?"

"She's the main event," Terry said. "The newspapers have had the stage set, and now it's time for the climax. Mrs. Miller is the one everyone wants to hear. They want to hear about her love affair with Pendle, her lousy marriage—the good stuff. Besides, everyone knows that she was out of town when the murder happened. She may have been mixed up in it, and so you can have a little fun with her, if you want, because there'll be no charges forthcoming. Give the people what they want, Roscoe. Something to talk about over supper."

Roscoe nodded.

❧

"We'll ask you to wait in the superintendent's office during the recess, ma'am," the bailiff said to Sarah. "I'll have something brought in for your luncheon."

"I'm not hungry," Sarah said. "A glass of water or some coffee would be very much appreciated, though."

"As you wish," he said, and led her down the corridor to the office at the end, the spacious quarters of Superintendent Ball, head of the police department. "If you'll wait here, I'll bring you some coffee. Please don't leave without calling me first."

Sarah nodded and stepped into the large waiting area of the superintendent's office and was stunned to see Alicia Miller sitting there, reading a periodical. Alicia looked up from the magazine at Sarah, expressionless.

"Mrs. Miller," Sarah said, completely at a loss.

"They must think we ought to compare notes," Alicia said.

"It does seem somewhat irregular," Sarah replied, sitting down as far from Alicia as the room would permit.

"It wouldn't be the first thing about this whole matter that is irregular," Alicia said, going back to her magazine.

Sarah didn't reply, but sat uneasily until the bailiff returned with a grubby cup of black coffee whose surface had an iridescent, oily sheen. Sarah set the cup down on a nearby table without daring to taste the fluid and looked around the room, in any direction but Alicia's.

"It's going to make for a long wait, you know, if we try to ignore each other," Allie said.

"We can try," Sarah said, still looking away.

"Oh, don't be that way, Sarah dear. We were friends for a long time before all this—circus began."

"I wonder about that. Were we really?"

"I certainly thought so. But I acknowledge I may have been wrong, since all the while you were busily at work stealing my husband."

Sarah snapped her head around and glared at Alicia. "I didn't steal anything of yours. Certainly not your husband."

"We may have to agree to disagree on that," Allie said. "But that's all water under the bridge. It's only the two of us, now. Why not let bygones be bygones?"

"You know, I think I'd prefer to wait somewhere else." Sarah got up and opened the door. A policeman was standing outside in the corridor.

"I'd like to wait in another room," Sarah said to the cop.

"There ain't another room," he said.

Exasperated, Sarah closed the door and sat back down.

"So much for that," Alicia said. "But being trapped in here with me must be preferable to being given the third degree, late at night, in your own home. As rumor has it, that is."

"It's not a rumor."

"They really did break down your door?"

"Not quite, but it was almost that bad."

"Poor dear. Poor dear."

"Please do spare me the false pity, Allie."

"See, I knew you'd warm up. At least I'm not 'Mrs. Miller' anymore. I'm back to being your old friend Allie."

"Um hmm," Sarah said.

"What did they ask you?" Alicia said. "The police."

"I don't want to talk about it."

"No, of course you don't. You deserve a rest. Take heart, though. All those people out there"—she waved the back of her hand in the general direction of the courtroom—"aren't here to eat you alive. They're here to consume *me*. They can't wait to hear all the juicy details."

"I'm sure there are plenty of those."

Alicia smiled and fanned herself with her magazine. "Dear, you don't know the half of it. It really is ironic, you know—no one would believe me, if I told the whole truth and nothing but the truth."

"Fortunately, no one expects you to."

"Touché! You look so sweet, but you can be quite salty when you want to be."

"I hope you'll pardon me if I don't sit through your testimony," Sarah said.

"Why bother? You can read it all in the newspapers tomorrow."

Allie went back to her magazine and Sarah sat in silence until the bailiff opened the door again.

❦

POLICE COURT RECONVENED PRECISELY at 12:45, on schedule, with Sarah back in the witness box.

"Mrs. Payne," Roscoe said, "when was the last time you saw Mr. Miller alive?"

"The night he was murdered."

"Where did you see him?"

"At his house."

"And did he invite you there?"

"I called him and invited myself."

"Why was that? Do you typically visit men at such hours?"

"Not typically. I wanted to talk him out of pursuing a public divorce, as I mentioned previously."

Roscoe shot a quick glance toward the back of the courtroom, where Terry Penrose was starting to scowl.

"And did Mr. Miller receive you in his den?"

"No, he did not. We spoke briefly in the front parlor."

"What time did you leave?"

"I was there about fifteen or twenty minutes. So I left around ten, or a little before."

"And where did you go then?"

"I walked home, to my house on Norwood Street."

"And did you leave again at any time later that night?"

"I did not."

"And you had nothing to do with Edward Miller's murder?"

Sarah glared. "I beg—"

"Judge," Sidney Greene chimed in, jumping up, "this has been discussed in chambers. My client has already been interrogated at length, and in her home, with her little—"

Judge Malone raised his hand. "Mr. Greene, I know the history here. But the man must ask the question for the record."

Greene sat down again.

"The witness will answer the question," Malone said.

Sarah composed herself. "I most certainly did not. And you've already done your best to suggest that I have. Let's keep going and I can tell you who I think did. I for one am in favor of finding the real culprits."

"Mrs. Payne, we're not here to make amateur speculations. We've heard from trained police detectives already. No further questions."

"You are excused, Mrs. Payne," Judge Malone said quickly.

❦

BY EARLY AFTERNOON, THE crowd was three-quarters women, most of the male visitors having reluctantly trailed away to work. As soon as someone vacated a seat, even to trot to the bathroom, two more jockeyed for her place, and all straining forward to see Alicia put on the rack.

"I call Mrs. Edward Miller," Judge Malone said.

Alicia stood and walked slowly to the front of the court, wearing a serious black crepe gown, with a heavy veil and a high collar of black lace obscuring her neck. She lifted the veil and put it back as she was sworn in, then took her seat in the witness box. She was a trifle pale, but that perhaps may have been by contrast with her deep black dress. Otherwise she seemed entirely at her ease.

As Allie took the stand, one matron leaned over to the man sitting next to her. "I simply don't understand it," she said in a stage whisper loud enough to be heard for three rows. "She's not even beautiful."

"She's something much more than beautiful," the man said. "She's *fascinating.*"

"Mrs. Miller, as I'm sure you know, I'm William Roscoe, assistant district attorney," Roscoe began. "Thank you for coming here today under such trying circumstances."

"Of course," Alicia said.

"I'd like to begin, Mrs. Miller, by asking you to describe the state of your relations with your late husband."

"In December of last year, my late husband served me with a divorce action and sent me away from our home. I went first to Niagara Falls, then to New York City, and more recently, to Atlantic City while that situation was being adjudicated."

"I see. And as I understand it, your husband had named a co-respondent in his divorce suit, isn't that correct?"

"Yes, that is correct."

"And who was the co-respondent?"

"Arthur Pendle."

"And why was Mr. Pendle named co-respondent?"

"Because my husband had the impression that Mr. Pendle was alienating my affection."

"Was he?"

"Not in the slightest. I had no affection for my husband long before Mr. Pendle came along."

Nervous laughter rippled through the courtroom.

"I see," Roscoe said. "Am I correct, though, that you and Mr. Pendle did have an intimate relation?"

"If by that you mean adulterous, nothing criminal ever happened between us. We were good friends."

"I have several letters that were found in your husband's effects," Roscoe said. "That were written to you over a period of some months by Mr. Pendle."

Alicia smiled briefly. "Very well."

"Here's one from June of last year," he said. "Mr. Pendle refers to a visit you made with him and Mrs. Pendle to New Haven College."

"Yes, they invited me to go to the commencement exercises with them."

"Mr. Miller didn't go with you?"

"No, he remained in Buffalo."

"Why was that? Was he detained by business?"

"He didn't enjoy that sort of social affair. He was content to let me go by myself."

"I see. Can you tell me what transpired between you and Mr. Pendle at that time?"

"Nothing particular. The three of us went to various parties and events. There was a football game. And a boat race."

"This letter was written to you from Shelter Island, New York, Mrs. Miller."

Alicia tilted her head.

"In it, Mr. Pendle writes, '*Yesterday, in New Haven, I was at the gate to the campus where so recently I drew you in, in the darkness. That spot is a shrine to me.*' What does that mean, Mrs. Miller?"

"I don't remember."

"You don't remember at all? That he 'drew you in, in the darkness'?"

"I do recall an incident he may be referring to. It might have meant more to him than it did to me."

"What was the incident?"

"I was to attend a ball held for guests, and Mr. Pendle was escorting me there, as a courtesy. When we passed under a great arch between two courtyards—on the campus—he took me in his arms and kissed me."

"And did you reproach him?"

"Not at the time."

"Did you ever?"

"I don't recall. Probably."

"Did you tell his wife?"

"No, of course not."

"Did you tell your husband?"

"No."

"Why not?"

"Would you? If you were a woman, that is."

"I couldn't possibly say, Mrs. Miller," Roscoe replied. "Here's another letter, from a month or so later, sent from the Waldorf, in New York. In it Mr. Pendle says, '*I will telephone you when I arrive in Buffalo so that we can meet at 1-2-3.*' What does that mean?"

"What does what mean? It seems straightforward. He planned to telephone me."

Not that part, Mrs. Miller. '1-2-3.' What was '1-2-3'?"

"I don't know what that means."

"Wasn't it a house number? A furnished rental where you and Mr. Pendle would meet?"

"I don't recall."

"It was 123 Whitney Place, wasn't it? Didn't you have to climb out a rear window when your husband's detectives discovered you and Mr. Pendle there?"

"I remember leaving a house on Whitney when I felt threatened with bodily harm by some thugs hired by my husband, but I don't know the address. And I don't remember these letters."

"You never received them?"

"Not that I recall. Where were they sent?"

"To your home. 101 Ashwood Street."

"My husband probably intercepted them."

"But you did receive letters from Mr. Pendle, didn't you?"

"Yes, I did."

"And where are those letters? The ones you say you did receive?"

"In a keepsake box in my bedroom, until my husband threatened me, after which I put them into a safety-deposit box at the bank."

"He threatened you?"

"More than that. He took me by the throat and commanded me to open the box."

"And did you?"

"No, I didn't. I'd have rather let him kill me."

"Do you think he would have killed you?"

"I don't know."

"Was your husband a violent man, Mrs. Miller?"

"He could have a temper."

"But so can you, isn't that correct?"

"I don't believe I do, no."

"Didn't things get pretty warm with your husband last year? Isn't it true that Mr. Miller had to have a doctor address a wound on his head, given to him by you?"

"We had an argument that got out of hand. I threw a paperweight at the wall, but my aim was poor, and it hit him on the forehead."

"A wound which required a dozen stitches."

"I don't remember how many. It was an accident."

"Yes, accidents do happen, don't they, Mrs. Miller? But back to the letters. Where are the letters that you put in the safety-deposit box?"

"I don't know. My husband's detectives stole them. They gained access to the box through a ruse, and took them all."

"Therefore, these letters I have are only a few of them?"

"I don't know how many you have."

"Let's say I have a dozen. I've read from two of them."

"I haven't recognized the two you've read from, so those were not among the stolen ones. I would remember those."

"How many letters were stolen?"

"I don't know."

"A hundred?"

"Perhaps. And some of my own personal papers."

"And do you know where they are? The letters?"

"I do not."

"Were you anxious to get a divorce from Mr. Miller?"

"I was."

"Why?"

Hartshorn stood up. "Your Honor—"

"Are you going to object, Mr. Hartshorn?" Malone said.

"Not specifically, Judge," Hartshorn said. "But I do not want my client held up to public ridicule. If the question will advance the cause of the inquest, then she will answer. If its purpose is merely to embarrass her or cause her to reveal matters of a personal nature irrelevant to Mr. Miller's death, then I would object."

"Understood. I think this line of questioning may be of great relevance to the matters at hand, but I instruct the assistant district attorney to refrain from questions that tend only to provoke public scorn or ridicule."

"Thank you, Your Honor," Hartshorn said, sitting.

"Go on," Malone said to Roscoe.

"What I wanted to know, Mrs. Miller, is why *exactly* did you want a divorce so eagerly? If I may say, your late husband seemed like a devoted husband, a good father to your three daughters, a sound provider."

Allie was quiet for a few long heartbeats. "Yes, he was those things, Mr. Roscoe," she said.

"Why, then, would you be so anxious to divorce him?"

"Because we had lost all love. We had drifted apart and weren't happy. And I thought I would be happier with Mr. Pendle. I loved him, and I did not love my husband any longer."

"Quiet," Judge Malone snarled at the murmuring crowd.

"Mr. Pendle is dead, Mrs. Miller," Roscoe resumed. "You needn't feel that you have to say you loved him now."

"Alive or dead, nothing's changed. I loved him. I still do."

"Even though it now appears that he may have been a swindler? And a murderer?"

"I'll caution you to speak respectfully of him in my presence, Mr. Roscoe."

"You'll *caution* me?"

"You heard me correctly."

Roscoe smiled. "I'll take your admonition under advisement, Mrs. Miller. It's not every day a witness upbraids an officer of the court. Let's talk about something that is indisputable, then."

"I am all aquiver," Alicia said dryly.

"Mr. Pendle already had a wife, did he not?"

"Whom he planned to divorce, yes."

"How would he do that?"

"He was going to take her to South Dakota, I think it was, and secure a divorce. Then we would marry."

"And you wanted a divorce from your husband?"

"Yes, very much."

"And Mr. Pendle wanted to marry you?"

"Yes."

"If that is so, Mrs. Miller, what I don't understand then is this. Why did Mr. Pendle try so strenuously—as I understand it—to convince your husband to withdraw his divorce suit and reconcile with you?"

Allie was silent.

"Mrs. Miller? Do you understand my question?"

"I do."

"Please answer the question, Mrs. Miller," Malone said. "Let's keep things moving."

"Yes, sir," Allie said. "It was Mr. Pendle who advised me to oppose my husband's suit."

"Yes, but why? You wanted a divorce, and your husband clearly did. Why not simply let it go by uncontested?"

"I don't exactly know. I followed Mr. Pendle's advice in such matters. I felt that he knew what would be best. He was my attorney."

"Yes, we know. Your *attorney*. Might it have been because Mrs. Pendle had refused to give her husband a divorce? And that Mr. Pendle knew that if you divorced your husband, you would be all alone, and Mr. Pendle might not be able to marry you? Or provide for you?"

"I don't know if that's what he thought."

"Isn't it true that Mr. Pendle wanted to keep you somewhere safe—in your own home, with your children, your mother, and a steady means of support—while he maneuvered to get out of his own marriage? And you were willing to play along—"

"Now I do object, Your Honor," Hartshorn said.

"Sustained. Rephrase that, counselor."

"Apologies, Your Honor. Mrs. Miller, were you not willing to continue in your unhappy marriage, for the sake of appearances, until such time as Mr. Pendle could free himself of his wife?"

"That was not uppermost in my mind. I was following his guidance."

"And upon your entreaties and those of others, Mr. Miller did take you back, isn't that so?"

"Yes, that is true. We decided to try again."

"You decided to try again, and that included giving up on Mr. Pendle?"

"Yes."

"And did you give up seeing him? Communicating with him?"

"For a time, yes."

"For a time. For how much time, if I may ask?"

"About a month."

"About a month. After your husband is persuaded by you and by others that you will be faithful to him if he will only stop his divorce action, and you are welcomed back home for a fresh start, in about a month you and Mr. Pendle are meeting again and have resumed—your relations?"

"That's what I am saying, yes."

"Do you think that was a fair thing to do, Mrs. Miller? To your husband?"

"My pledge to him was meant sincerely, but Mr. Pendle was a difficult man to resist. And I suppose he had an equally difficult time resisting me."

"So it would seem, Mrs. Miller. So it would seem."

The murmurs and occasional gasps in the courtroom had grown into a low and constant hubbub. "There will be silence in my courtroom," the judge said, banging down the gavel. "If I am compelled to say it again, I will clear the room and continue privately." The crowd fell utterly mute.

"And where did you and Mr. Pendle start meeting again?"

"Various places around the city."

"Such as?"

"On the streetcars, sometimes. At his office. A few times at the Genesee Hotel restaurant."

"What about rented rooms?"

"Sometimes."

"And the one on Whitney Place?"

"I don't recall if it was Whitney Place."

"The one you escaped from, through the window."

"That was rented by Mr. Pendle. The upstairs floor."

"Furnished?"

"Yes."

"With a locking door?"

"Yes."

"Was there a bed there?"

Allie could barely suppress a smile. "I should have hoped so. One does get tired sometimes."

Scattered laughs floated up from the gallery, and Judge Malone scowled. He raised his gavel and the tittering died away.

"You're saying there was a bed."

"Yes, I seem to recall a bed."

Roscoe was about to pose another question when Allie interrupted.

"You know what else I recall, Mr. Roscoe?"

"And what is that, Mrs. Miller?"

"I recall conversing quite innocently with Mr. Pendle, and then my husband's detectives breaking down the door, which frightened me so much—and gave Mr. Pendle great concern for my safety—that he felt I should flee. And I recall that those same detectives beat Arthur to within an inch of his life, for doing nothing more than lawfully renting a property in the city of Buffalo and inviting a friend over to view it. You might talk to them, Mr. Roscoe, because those men were certainly capable of deadly violence. Instead, you seem to prefer to spend time grilling me, when all I've done was to run for my life from them. And Mr. Pendle was brave enough to stay behind and defend me."

Roscoe smirked. "Thank you for that little parable, Mrs. Miller. I'm sure that others are not without blame in this for their bad actions. But for the present, we are interested in *your* actions, and those of Mr. Pendle. And we can't very well ask Mr. Pendle now."

Allie sat quietly, waiting.

"Mrs. Miller," Roscoe said, picking up a long document from his table, "why do you think that Mr. Pendle drew this up in your favor?"

"I don't recognize that document," she said.

He handed it to her. "Read over it and tell us if you remember."

Alicia looked it up and down impassively. "I don't know what this is. I've never seen it before."

"It's a bond, Mrs. Miller, made out by Mr. Pendle in your favor. In the amount of $50,000. It was found among Mr. Pendle's estate papers. It's entirely in order. It appears to have been made out early last month."

Alicia showed the first trace of surprise since the start. "I rather think you're mistaken, Mr. Roscoe. Arth—Mr. Pendle never mentioned such a thing."

"Yet here it is, fully executed," Roscoe said, waving the paper. "Why do you think a man would make out such a sum to a 'friend,' as you say? And a young man at that, not likely to die of natural causes for quite some time."

"I can't account for that. I knew nothing of it."

"Well," Roscoe said, "it seems your client is about to become a very wealthy woman. This is a pointer to help you get some more money for her."

"Thank you," Hartshorn said. Roscoe nodded and handed the paper to the clerk of court.

"Let me take you in a slightly different direction, Mrs. Miller," Roscoe said. "Where did you last see Mr. Pendle alive?"

"In New York."

"He'd been with you there?"

"Yes."

"For how long?"

"A week. Through Christmas."

"Where did you stay?"

"At the Victoria Hotel."

"And where did he stay?"

"Same place."

"With you?"

"Yes."

"In the same room?"

With a heavy sigh, Hartshorn slowly rose to his feet. "Withdrawn," Roscoe said, before Hartshorn had time to object.

Roscoe bobbed a bit, hands clasped behind his back. "Both of you at the Victoria, then. Through the holiday. And when did you see him last?"

"At the station. When he left to return to Buffalo."

"When was that?"

"It would have been December 26 or 27."

"And did you stay behind, in New York?"

"No, I left later that day."

"And did you come back to Buffalo then?"

"No, I went to Atlantic City."

"In the winter? Why?"

"I'd been thrown out of my home, Mr. Roscoe. I had to live somewhere."

"But why Atlantic City?"

"I like the shore. A lot of people do."

"Was it your idea to go to Atlantic City? From New York, that is?"

"It was Arthur's idea. Mr. Pendle's."

"Why do you think he sent you there?"

"He knew I liked the shore, I suppose. I wouldn't know."

"And he came back to Buffalo from New York?"

"Yes."

"Did you communicate with him after his return?"

"Once. No, twice. He wired me to tell me he had gotten back safely, and then I wired him when I arrived at Atlantic City."

"And that was all?"

"All what?"

"All of your communication with him?"

"Yes, until the day I was notified that my husband had died, and I wired Mr. Pendle to meet me at the station in Buffalo."

"You left Atlantic City that same evening?"

"Yes, about five o'clock, in a sleeper car."

"And you arrived the next morning—at the Terrace or Exchange station?"

"Terrace."

"And was Mr. Pendle there to meet you?"

"No. He was not."

"Why not?"

"He wired later that day that he'd been at Niagara Falls when my telegram had come in."

"This would have been the morning after your husband's body was discovered?"

"Yes."

"You know we talked to Mr. and Mrs. Pendle about that morning."

"I did not know that."

"And Mrs. Pendle said that her husband was up early and took a notion to go to see the Falls in winter. He asked her to meet him there for lunch, and to bring with her the morning papers."

Alicia blinked slowly at the assistant DA.

"Do you know why—the morning your husband's murder was discovered—Mr. Pendle would run off to Niagara Falls so early, ask his wife to meet him, and request she bring the morning Buffalo papers with her?"

"I have no idea. He did love the Falls."

"Do you think he might have known of something happening in Buffalo that would have appeared in the morning papers?"

"I couldn't possibly say."

"Doesn't it strike you as unusual, Mrs. Miller?"

"Not particularly, no."

"It doesn't seem like an indication of a guilty mind?"

"Guilt is more your area of expertise than it is mine, Mr. Roscoe."

"But you knew Mr. Pendle better than I do."

"I knew very little about many aspects of his character."

"Such as?"

Allie shrugged. "His business affairs. What he was thinking to himself. He was, in many respects, a very private man."

"How would you describe his personality, Mrs. Miller?"

"Very intelligent. Intense. Sometimes moody."

"*Intense.* That's interesting. What do you mean by that?"

"That he was a man of deep feeling. Strong emotions."

"A passionate man, then?"

"You might say that, yes." She smiled.

"Do you think that he could be a man capable of violence? Many men with strong emotions can be."

"I never saw him display any tendency toward violence."

"Did you ever hear him say anything threatening?"

"Not that I recall."

"About your husband, for example?"

"Certainly not."

Roscoe walked slowly over to his table and riffled through a stack of paper. He selected one and walked back to the witness stand.

"May I read you an excerpt from another one of Mr. Pendle's letters—to you?"

"If you wish."

Roscoe held the paper out so that Alicia could see it. "Is that Mr. Pendle's handwriting, Mrs. Miller?"

She glanced at it down her nose. "It appears to be."

"It is. This letter is dated September 18 of last year and is on the stationery of the Waldorf Hotel, New York. It says:

My dear Alicia—

I just came from telephoning you, and hearing your dear sweet voice. Am I foolish to telephone you from way down here? It was worth all it cost me. I realize more and more that you are the only woman in the world for me.

"Do you remember this letter, Mrs. Miller?"

"I do not."

"Do you remember an occasion on which Mr. Pendle telephoned you from New York City?"

"He telephoned me on many occasions, and from many places."

"Were his communications usually so mawkish?"

Allie stared him down. "Love is poetic so long as it's kept private. When it's made public, it becomes ridiculous. His letters to me were always intended to be private."

Roscoe rolled his eyes. "Very well, I'll go on.

As I looked into your beautiful eyes last night, I feared there was some trouble hidden there. If there was, dearest, I wish you would tell me, as I cannot bear the thought that you are unhappy over anything, especially when I am away from you. I thought that it might be owing to some differences with your husband. There are times when his manner toward you makes me want to kill him, but I hold my temper, knowing that any expression of my feelings would probably lead to a quick and violent quarrel, which would make matters harder for us both."

Roscoe let his hand drop to his side, still clutching the letter.

"Doesn't that sound—rather *threatening*, Mrs. Miller? Like something a man capable of violence might say?"

"I don't know about that."

Roscoe squinted at the letter again. "Do you know of any other way to interpret 'there are times when I want to kill him'?"

"A figure of speech, perhaps."

"A pretty strong figure of speech. See, Mrs. Miller, here's what I think. I think that Mr. Pendle was indeed the very kind of man capable of killing someone, and deftly, too. We know he was athletically inclined, very strong and quite competitive. You yourself have said that he was very intelligent. Passionate. Moody. And he certainly had good reason to want your husband out of the way. So that he could both marry you and also, in doing so, avoid the scandal of a very public divorce. And to top it off, we have here, in his own hand, an admission that he had—more than once—considered killing your husband. What am I missing, Mrs. Miller?"

Alicia fiddled with the fingers of her glove. "Only one thing, Mr. Roscoe."

"And that is?"

"The man himself."

"Very true," Roscoe said. "Mr. Pendle is—rather conveniently—not available. I would observe that it wouldn't be the first time in history that someone made away with himself to evade justice."

Allie gave him a thin smile.

Roscoe looked over his shoulder and saw Terry Penrose staring daggers at him again. He quickly leaned toward Alicia, his hands on the witness box. "What I wonder, Mrs. Miller, is what involvement you might have had."

"Involvement in what?"

"Involvement in your husband's murder, of course."

"Need I remind you that I was in Atlantic City when my husband was murdered, Mr. Roscoe?"

"Oh no, we all know that already. You've made that *very* clear. Also very convenient, being out of state, isn't it? And sent there at Mr. Pendle's urging, as soon he left you in New York to make his return to Buffalo."

"Is that a question?"

"No. Did you always do what Mr. Pendle told you, Mrs. Miller?"

Alicia smirked. "Most of the time."

"You didn't do much thinking for yourself, then?"

"I'm not sure I'd put it that way, Mr. Roscoe. I trusted Mr. Pendle and valued his advice, especially as concerns all of the complexities of my legal situation with my husband."

"And am I correct in the assumption that Mr. Pendle was paying for your living expenses?"

"When my husband banished me from my house, thankfully Mr. Pendle provided my support, yes. Absent his generosity, I suppose I would have been living on the street."

"Your husband had cut you off, then?"

"Entirely, yes. Without a red cent."

"And do you think that Mr. Pendle would have continued to provide for you, had he not died untimely?"

"Yes, I believe he would have."

"He was protective of you."

"Very much so."

"And did Mr. Pendle think that if he didn't provide for you, your husband might very well turn you out of the house without any means of support?"

"Of course. When Edward dismissed me from the house, he told me that very thing. That I was on my own. Arthur—Mr. Pendle—knew that."

"And what if something had happened to Mr. Pendle? As things do happen sometimes. What would have become of you?"

"I would have been destitute, of course. A woman without a husband, or a home, or income."

"And since Mr. Pendle was so protective of you, as you say, he probably thought about that?"

"I don't know." She paused. "But . . ."

"But?"

"But I do know that it was something that bothered him. He thought he had brought all this trouble down on me, and that I might be left in a very bad way as a result."

"Do you think he brought down this trouble on you?"

Alicia dabbed her temple with her lace handkerchief. "Mr. Roscoe, I wasn't kidnapped, or drugged. Nor was Mr. Pendle a Svengali. Whatever I did, I did willingly. I might even say enthusiastically. And in case you're wondering, I'd do it all again, without changing a thing. Now having said that, the risks to a woman in a situation like—his and mine— are much greater than those to a man. As such, it would be difficult for you, as a man, to put yourself in a woman's shoes. Surely you can understand that."

"I'm not sure I do. Can you elaborate?"

"A man who divorces still has his income. Except for some temporary social embarrassment, he retains his reputation. I might even say that, in certain cases, his reputation may be *enhanced* by an affair of the heart. Furthermore, it's well-known that a prosperous middle-aged man who divorces will usually attract a new wife, not infrequently one younger and more attractive than the old one. Compare all that to the situation of a middle-aged woman, sir. That woman is ruined. No independent means of support, a reputation in tatters. Faded beauty. A soiled dove. An *untouchable*. I should think you wouldn't like to be in that kind of situation, Mr. Roscoe. Does that make it sufficiently clear?"

"Yes, Mrs. Miller, it does. Do you then blame Mr. Pendle for putting you in a difficult position?"

"No. As one might say, I made my bed." More laughs from the gallery.

Roscoe smirked, but refrained from comment. "Very well. But Mr. Pendle was aware of the precariousness of your position, wasn't he?"

"I told you he was."

"Yes, Mrs. Miller, you did. And since this prospect bothered him, as you say—if he had thought something might happen to him, wouldn't you think he'd find a way to provide for you?"

"I don't know how that would be possible."

Roscoe smiled. "One way might be to settle a $50,000 bond on you, less than a month before his death."

Alicia didn't reply.

"Taking out a bond for that kind of money, only a few weeks before one's death. Doesn't that seem like very fortunate timing?"

"I didn't know about that until today."

"But it's miraculous, isn't it? Mr. Pendle dies—which ordinarily would leave you without any support—but then we learn that shortly before his death, he makes provision for you? Makes you wealthy, in fact."

"It is very much in keeping with the man. Generous and yet private about it."

"Perhaps, too, it's very much in keeping with a man who planned to do away with himself."

There was complete silence in the courtroom, not even the usual sniffling or coughing.

"I couldn't say."

Roscoe made a sweeping gesture. "Your husband is murdered. The very next morning, early, Mr. Pendle inexplicably goes to the Falls. To see the cataract—in the dead of winter. Or so he says. He tells his wife to bring the morning papers. For what reason? Could he have wanted to see about something awful that had happened, and whether the finger of suspicion pointed in his direction? If it does, self-destruction is a simple matter at the Falls. He is steps away. But in those morning papers he sees nothing to fear, not yet, so he returns to Buffalo. A week passes, and in that week the whispers begin.

"Soon it does appear that Mr. Pendle is emerging as the natural suspect. He becomes desperate, and resolves to do away with himself, and take his wife with him so that no trace will be left behind. But this suicide will not be a leap over the Falls or a bullet in the brain, which would be tantamount to a confession of guilt. No, it will be in a way that has at least the air of plausibility about it being an accident. His reputation is preserved. You are provided for."

Alicia sat quietly, observing Mr. Roscoe.

"What is your opinion of those facts, Mrs. Miller?" he said.

"I don't know that they are facts. It seems that you are asking me for my opinion of your opinion."

"My view is based on facts. A theory of the case."

"A theory, yes."

"I wonder how much you knew about all of this, Mrs. Miller? Before the fact—or after?"

"Not a thing."

"Do you have any theory on who it was that killed your husband, madam?"

"I do not."

"Do you think it could have been Arthur Pendle?"

"I do not."

"Yet someone did kill your husband."

"Yes, that is beyond dispute."

"Have you heard anything about who might have?"

"Nothing that would rise above conjecture, wonder, or mystery."

"I see. One last thing, Mrs. Pendle. Oh my, I beg your pardon—Mrs. Miller. Did you have any communication with Mr. Pendle between his return to Buffalo and his untimely death?"

"None whatsoever."

"Not a telephone call? Nor a wire or letter? No personal meeting?"

"No contact at all."

"You weren't tempted to see him? To talk with him? After all the two of you had shared?"

"I didn't say I wasn't tempted. I said I didn't have any communication with him."

"Why not?"

"I was advised not to."

"By whom?"

"That's privileged information."

"Ah, I see," Roscoe said, looking at Hartshorn. "Very well, we'll leave it at that. But will you swear that you have no knowledge of the person or persons responsible for your husband's murder, nor of any of the circumstances surrounding it, either before the fact or after the fact?"

"I do so swear."

"That's all I have, Your Honor," Roscoe said.

"The witness is excused," Judge Malone said. "You may step down, Mrs. Miller."

Alicia gathered herself up and was about to stand when she spied Terry Penrose in the gallery. She could have sworn that he gave her a little wink.

❦

By Wednesday, it was almost over. To everyone's shock—including Alicia's—Mrs. Hall kept her wits about her, and gave up nothing. More predictably, neither did the girls. A bartender and another employee from a New York hotel testified that Arthur, in his cups, had threatened to kill someone, but who, they couldn't say. It made for oceans of newspaper ink, but none of it shed any light on who had murdered Edward Miller in his den on New Year's Eve.

At last, even the diehards in the audience grew tired of the parade of late-night strollers and clueless cab drivers, all of whom claimed to have taken the murderer or murderers up, down, or across Ashwood Street that fatal night. Mrs. Stoddard had been looking forward to her moment in the limelight, when she would testify to having seen a fashionably dressed woman leave the Miller house at ten o'clock. But Sarah had already stipulated that very thing, under oath, and so Mrs. Stoddard had to step down from the witness box crestfallen.

The few personal papers that had been found in Ed's coat pocket had vanished, as had the bottle of cocktails and a golf club that had been sitting in a corner of the den. Fingerprinting was a newfangled technique, but was impossible to employ since everyone from Dr. Havilland to the detectives to the undertakers who had removed the body had pawed over everything. The police and even a few peeping neighbors had trampled the entire perimeter of the house, then tracked wet snow and ash up the porch steps, into the foyer, into the den, and up and down every hallway of the Miller house. The scene was more a public curiosity than a source of forensic evidence.

Thus when Judge Malone resettled his bulk into his chair on the morning of the fourth day, the courtroom was only half-filled, and mostly with reporters.

"In the matter of the death of Edward Lee Miller, late of this city," the judge said, "over the past three days, we have heard from a variety of experts as well as several witnesses who have given testimony relevant to the deceased man and their own relations to the deceased. For all that, much remains unknown and unknowable. The untimely death of Mr. Pendle has put beyond our reach the person who perhaps could have shed the most light on the last moments of the deceased. Further, I believe that in the testimony of Mrs. Miller there are gaps and omissions that only Mr. Pendle might have filled, but that is my estimation and not a matter of law. I wish to commend Dr. Havilland on his steadfast refusal to classify a murder as a suicide. Without his stolidity, we might not know even as much as we do about this horrible offense.

"I will close this inquest with the verdict that Edward Lee Miller came to his death by willful murder, by person or persons unknown. And I will add only that the fashionable people of the Ashwood section should reflect sincerely on what conditions—what social mores—prevail in their green and pleasant neighborhood that would create an environment in which such a sordid tale of disrespect for the marital bond, and for life itself, could be spun. This court is hereby adjourned."

❦

THE NEXT DAY, OVER lunch at The Dainty Restaurant, Bill Roscoe raised his glass to Terry Penrose. Penrose was tucking into a club sandwich, hunched over his plate as a thick piece of ham threatened to squirt out from between slices of toast sodden with mayonnaise. Roscoe had to wait an unsettling amount of time with his glass in the air, while Penrose reassembled his sandwich, wiped off his fingers, and dabbed his mouth. Only then did he pick up his own glass and touch it to Roscoe's.

"What's the occasion?" Terry said, putting down the glass, now smeared with mayonnaise.

"Closing the Miller case, but more than that, too. In less than a year, Czolgosz sent to the chair, The Hooks quieter than it's ever been, and our collections are breaking all records," Roscoe said. "May I ask what you do for an encore?"

Penrose picked at something caught in his teeth with the nib of his gold Parker fountain pen, leaving a wide ink mark bleeding across his upper lip. "Governor Odell won't be seeking another term," he said, "and his lieutenant governor is a cold fish who hasn't done anything. Career man, next in line. Or so he thinks."

"A run for governor, then?"

"Only so much I can do from this office, and I can't be DA forever."

"Well you'd be a lock. For governor."

"No one's got a lock on anything, Roscoe, but I'd have as good a chance as anyone. And it wouldn't hurt you a bit if I got out of your way and gave you a chance to sit in my chair. We could make a good team if I were in Albany and you were keeping tabs on things here in Buffalo."

Roscoe leaned forward toward Terry. "I'll do whatever I can to earn that trust, Mr. Penrose."

"The election is a year away, so let's not get ahead of ourselves. I'm sure you'll have plenty of other opportunities to earn the lead spot in the next race for district attorney. You know what they say—faith without works is dead."

"I do indeed."

"Then onward. What do they have today in the way of pie?" Penrose asked, smacking his lips. "I think pie would be nice. You're right, we ought to celebrate a little. I must say, the whole Pendle-Miller-thingummybob was heavier lifting than I ever imagined. Arthur almost made a complete hash of everything."

"Yes he did."

"He was my friend, too," Penrose said. "All the way back to college days. That made it hard, you know. But the sad fact was that he and Miller had to go. And, as they say"—he took a big swig from his greasy glass of muscatel—"you can't make an omelet unless you break some eggs."

"Very true," Roscoe replied. "But at least that's all behind us now." He watched with slight nausea as Terry stuffed the remaining quarter of his sandwich into his mouth all at once. He had to chew it down with his mouth open, but even that didn't stop him from talking.

"Not quite," he mumbled, shaking his head and at last gulping down the bolus of masticated club sandwich. "I thought for certain that Arthur would find those damn letters when he paid his little visit to Miller. But no. They're around somewhere, and until we get our hands on them, they're a liability."

"I see . . . but how do we find them."

"It's a delicate matter," the DA said. "I have an idea where they might be, but we have to step cautiously."

"Let sleeping dogs lie," Roscoe said. "As they say."

"Not if they're rabid. Those, you have to shoot, awake or—preferably—asleep."

A TRIP TO MAINE

The newspapers kept it up, for another week, and Alicia remained the talk of the town. It would blow over soon enough, but until then she kept a low profile, staying in the big house on Ashwood Street and sending Annie or her mother out whenever there was business to attend to. She was content having coffee while reading the yellow press's accounts of her and Arthur's shenanigans. They gave her a chuckle, these reporters. They always sounded so certain about everything, and yet they almost always had it almost all wrong.

It was too cold to be out and about, anyway. The Buffalo winter clung grimly on, with no signs of losing its grip. As much as she didn't mind her self-imposed exile, another part of her wanted desperately to get on with life, whatever that was going to mean. The only thing certain was that while she was stuck in her house, the rest of the world was rushing on outside. That rankled. It also rankled that her many former friends in Ashwood shunned her entirely. Not one of them dared to be seen in her company, let alone paying a visit to the Miller residence.

Bert Hartshorn was the lone visitor to the house on Ashwood Street. Almost every day, sometimes twice, he dropped by with a sheaf of papers or with news about Howie Gaines, Ed's former business partner, who had offered to purchase Edward's shares in the envelope business. Gaines's bankers were ready to write the check, but there always seemed to be some fresh detail that needed ironing out. Bert tried his best to explain the legal niceties, and Allie tried her best to feign patience.

She began to look forward to seeing the stuffy attorney, who could be officious but did seem genuinely kind. Allie came to recognize his heavy tread up the porch steps, as he hauled his paunchy frame to the door.

Sometimes she would be waiting in the adjacent parlor, but would wait to answer the door lest he surmise that she was eager to see him.

One afternoon, as they were poring over yet another set of papers, and Bert was explaining them in ever more byzantine detail, Alicia was struck by an idea. She put it to the side for the moment and tried to concentrate on what needed done with the latest set of forms and filings. Bert seemed very pleased at how attentive the usually bored Mrs. Miller was being. Legal explication gave him inordinate pleasure, and since his client seemed to be learning something, he kept at it longer than usual. Yet at last, the day's moot court neared adjournment.

"Thank you very much for your time today, Mrs. Miller," he said. "You've been most attentive."

"I find it interesting," Alicia said, "although most of it is well above my head."

"I felt the same way, the first year in law school."

She laughed. "I'm glad I'm not alone."

He consulted his watch. "I've got just enough time to get downtown and file these papers," he said. "Now that the inquest is done, and no charges have been filed, it should be clearer sailing."

"That's quite a relief," Allie said. "Thank you."

"You're more than welcome." He turned to go and stuck his hat on his head.

"Uh—Mr. Hartshorn?" She said to his back. He wheeled around, whipped his hat off again.

"Yes, Mrs. Miller?"

"I've been thinking. You've been diligently at work on my behalf now for some time, and if things are settling down—"

"Yes?"

"There is one other thing you could do for me—if you cared to."

"I'd be happy to, I'm sure. What is it?"

"I'd like to take a quick trip to Maine. With my mother. To visit Mr. and Mrs. Pendle's graves, and to pay our respects. And a change of scenery—after everything."

"The right thing to do, yes." He stood there, unsure of his role.

"And I was thinking that perhaps you could accompany us. Two ladies traveling alone all the way to Maine would benefit from a chaperone. But moreover—who knows what kind of reception I might receive from Mr. Pendle's family? I'm sure they've been reading the newspapers. They may well have formed unfavorable opinions about me."

Hartshorn shuffled his feet, cleared this throat. "Of course, Mrs. Miller. I'd be honored. You have only to tell me when you wish to go."

"Wonderful." Allie smiled, a genuine smile that bubbled up from one of her deep places. When she wore her dour face, which was much of the time, those around her wondered helplessly what might be wrong, what they perhaps had done to conjure this cloud. They'd try to humor her, ask her what might be amiss, and Allie would always say, "Nothing at all," leaving them floundering. But then when she would smile, suddenly and without apparent cause, there was release. Everyone could breathe again, stop speaking in tentative, mincing phrases, and they, too, could smile again. And like the rest of them, Mr. Hartshorn smiled back. He would go to Maine with the Miller ladies, who had apparently forgiven him for his past sins.

What he didn't know was that Alicia wasn't about to let him off the hook quite so easily.

❧

THREE DAYS LATER, ALLIE, Bert, and Mrs. Hall were rocking northward through New England. They'd broken their journey overnight in New York City, at the Victoria where Allie and Arthur had stayed during their final escape from Buffalo.

Their train chuffed past New Haven, stopped briefly in Boston, and soon after the buildings thinned out and there was nothing to see but snow and sleepy farmland. The rolling pastureland drifted on for miles until very near the southern border of Maine, where the trees sprouted up again. In Portland, they changed trains for the short final leg to Brunswick. The one small coal heater at the end of the passenger car, though blazing away like a blacksmith's forge, didn't seem to relieve the damp seeping in.

The frigid sun was still glittering like a pearl above the brick storefronts along Brunswick's wide Maine Street when they stepped onto the platform alongside the board-and-batten station.

Mrs. Hall shivered, her breath hanging in the wet air. "I do believe I took a chill on the train."

"We'll get you in your hotel room soon, Mother," Allie replied. "Get you warmed up."

"I'll be fine, dear, don't worry. Let's drop our things off and visit the cemetery first. That's why we've come all this way."

"Are you sure?"

"Oh yes," Mrs. Hall said, though without enthusiasm.

Bert hailed a carriage, and soon the three of them had deposited their luggage at The Cumberland, a sprawling barnlike monstrosity only a couple of blocks from the station, not far from the college.

True to her word, Mrs. Hall shook off her chill and in a short half hour was ready to visit the Pendles' resting place. On a summer day, it would have been an easy stroll from The Cumberland to the cemetery. But now the orange sun was struggling to stay above the trees, and the air so heavy with moisture that dew was weeping down the flanks of the carriage horse dozing under his blanket outside the hotel.

The steaming horse reluctantly hauled the three visitors around behind the campus and turned left on the main road leading to Harpswell and the coast. Only a few minutes later, they pulled up to a wide gateway with a faded wooden sign mounted to a low iron fence adjacent.

Hemlock Grove Cemetery
Established 1820

said the sign, which looked as though it hadn't been painted since that date.

"Here we are," Bert said. "Are you ready?"

"Ready as I'll ever be," Allie said.

Bert and the coachman helped Mrs. Hall and then Alicia down from the carriage. Bert told the man to come back by and pick them up in an hour, and the carriage rattled away, the grateful horse dreaming of his blanket under the *porte cochère* of The Cumberland.

Hemlock Grove Cemetery was a dead flat plot of land that would have looked like waste ground, if not for the hundred memorials of various types strewn about. Groups of cockeyed stones were enclosed in raised family plots, while single markers seemed to have sprouted wherever space would allow. Winter had not been kind to the place—carriage ruts crisscrossed the muddy ground like railroad tracks, and the three had to play hopscotch around puddles of slush that punctuated the footpaths on their way to where they hoped to find the Pendle family plot.

Twin furrows led back from the gate into the center of the cemetery, and the two ladies followed Bert as he navigated the least muddy course. A hundred yards in, past a whole townful of Reids, Hutchinsons, and Orrs, they stopped at a kind of crossroads, where various paths led off into different corners of the burying ground.

"Good heavens, which way now?" Mrs. Hall said, her skirts spattered with the glutinous graveyard mud. She was plainly not enjoying herself.

"Look for a recent burial," Bert said. "There can't be too many of them."

The three scanned around them. Allie spotted it first, and pointed. "Over there," she said. Twenty yards south of the crossroads was one of the elevated family plots, surmounted by a tall obelisk. Near the base of the obelisk were two fresh-looking hummocks of earth, stretched out neatly side by side, slowly collapsing in on themselves under the weight of the Maine climate.

"Wait here," Alicia said.

The ground sloped away in that direction, and a large pool of dark water lay between her and the likely graves. She had to take the long way around, deeper into the cemetery, before she could stand in front of the raised plot and its obelisk. Sure enough, the stone plinth read "Pendle."

At the foot of the twin mounds of earth were two polished granite markers, one freshly engraved with "Arthur" and the other with "Cassandra," and their dates. As Alicia confronted the graves, a pattering rain started up again, and she hid underneath the crepe of her umbrella to study the rivulets of mud creeping down the turned earth. It was hard to fathom that *he* was in there, down in that hole. That in the darkness of a seeping wooden box were the remains of the man she'd known so well, whom she had testified in open court to having loved, who had set her free. It was strange to think of him reduced to—this. He's down there, in this ground, forever.

She had thought she would feel something beyond curiosity. She had wondered, all the way on the train, not whether she would cry, but whether she could bear to cry in front of Hartshorn and her mother. Now she knew with confidence that there was no risk of such an embarrassment. Not only did she not feel like weeping, she didn't feel anything at all, other than a bitter, morbid fantasy about what Arthur's battered body might look like now, moldering away in the muck.

Bert and Mrs. Hall, standing off to the side, seemed profoundly uninterested in the gravesite. Their eyes were on Allie, instead—Bert to gauge how best to respond to any torrent of emotion, and Mrs. Hall to sense how soon they could dispense with this lugubrious duty and warm up back at the hotel. Neither would have long to wait. There had been no wave of grief—not so much as a sniffle—nor did she inclined to stand for long in the damp chill. She looked absently for another minute or so, trying to recall the sound of Arthur's voice, and then turned to take the long way around the Pendle plot and back to where the others were standing. Mrs. Hall was huddling sourly under Hartshorn's umbrella.

"How do you feel?" Bert asked gently, when she returned.

"About as you might imagine," she said. Bert was unsure how to respond to this with sufficient chivalry, so he extended his umbrella and his arm to escort Alicia back to the main road. Mrs. Hall, now exposed to the rain and irritated at playing second fiddle, trailed along behind the other two. Clearly Mr. Hartshorn knows where his bread is buttered, Mrs. Hall thought. Allie glanced back and handed her unused umbrella to her mother.

At the crossroads, Allie stopped and pulled away from Bert. "Is everything all right?" he asked.

"Yes," she said. "I almost forgot something." She dug into her handbag and fumbled for a moment, then took out a little folded piece of paper. She opened it carefully. Inside was a tiny maple key, deep crimson in color.

"Arthur loved anything Japanese," she said to her puzzled companions. "I brought along a Japanese maple seed to plant at his grave." She looked over at the viscous pool of mud between them and the Pendle plot. "I forgot to plant it there, but I suppose this will do." She walked over to the edge of the rutted path and bent down, taking off her glove. She drilled a little hole in the sodden ground with her forefinger, and put the seed into it. Then she tamped the ground around it with her heel.

Bert handed her his handkerchief, and she wiped off the mud. "Thank you, Bert," she said. "You are a gentleman."

He bowed slightly. "Not at all."

"I rather doubt that will germinate," Mrs. Hall said. "Probably drown down there in this soup. What passes for soil in these parts."

The failing sun was now barely scraping above the treetops, and they were getting soaked by the drifting mist that swirled and condensed on the smooth granite markers. Allie thought again about Arthur's coffin, and quickly banished the image.

"Maybe so," she said to her mother. "But it seemed like the right thing to do."

"You would know, I suppose," Mrs. Hall said, now sporting a full-blown scowl. There was something about her expression that stirred up Allie's rage. She pointed at her mother.

"You know, you can wipe that smirk off your face anytime you like," she hissed. "I know very well you never liked Arthur. And you never liked Ed, either. Now you're standing there, looking like you've eaten an unripe persimmon. At the very least, you could pretend to show a little respect."

Mrs. Hall's sour look intensified. "Respect, you say?" she said quietly. "That man"—she hooked her thumb in the direction of the Pendle graves— "caused this family untold heartache. And I'm supposed to respect him?"

"I meant for *me*," Allie said. "Anything else you want to think, think away. But so long as you enjoy staying dry under my roof, you'd best watch how you handle me."

"And you had better keep a civil tongue in your head when you—"

Bert cleared his throat, and stepped between them like a boxing referee. "It's been a long day, ladies. It's probably best if we get you both out of this damp."

Allie's dark hair had come undone and was hanging over her eyes like a forelock. She brushed it away. "You go with her, Mr. Hartshorn. I'm walking back."

"You can't very well walk back, Mrs. Miller," he said.

"I can, and I will. You can take my mother back. I refuse to ride with her."

"Oh, but please, be reasonable—"

Allie speared him with a look that made his legs feel unsteady.

"I'll walk back with you, then," he said. "I will not allow a lady to walk in the dark in an unfamiliar town."

"Then let's get her back in the coach and send her on her way," Alicia said.

At the main road, they stood by the iron gate and waited for their coach to return. Ten long, silent minutes later, the old Cumberland rig and unenthusiastic horse reined in. The driver and Bert helped Mrs. Hall into the coach, and then the coachman moved toward Alicia, who shook her head.

"We're walking back," she said.

The driver looked mystified. "There's plenty of room, ma'am," he said.

Bert tried to look less morose than he felt at the prospect of a twenty-minute walk in the misty winter twilight. "That's all right," he said. "We'd prefer to walk."

"Suit yourself," the puzzled coachman said, and remounted. The pair watched the artless black conveyance pull away into the gloom, Bert thinking wistfully about the fire in The Cumberland's hearth.

They crossed the main road and got away from the traffic rattling by, Allie's little boots squeaking after getting soaked in the boggy cemetery. A block away from Hemlock Grove, they ducked under the skeletal trees of the college, half hoping that they'd provide some shelter from the drizzle. They didn't, but the footing was better. On the paved pathway, the squeaking of Allie's shoes became comically loud. Bert didn't dare say anything, though it would have been difficult to think of what to say without acknowledging the rhythmic squeaking.

"I sound like the bedsprings in a cheap hotel," Allie muttered.

Bert glanced over at her, and saw that she had developed a wry smile. "That's very droll, Mrs. Miller," he said, feeling safe.

"It was worth ruining a pair of shoes to tell Mother to go pound sand," she said. "Sometimes that woman drives me out of my mind."

"She loves you very much, I'm sure."

Allie gave a little snort. "She loves herself."

They walked along in silence, punctuated by the creaking soles of Allie's shoes.

"Those shoes really are a distraction," Bert offered.

"Would you rather talk about something else?" she said. "Do you wish to have supper when we get to the hotel?"

"Well, yes, I suppose I would. There wasn't any food worthy of the name on the train, that's for sure."

"Good. I'm positively starving. How would it be tonight if I bought you a nice steak?"

He wasn't sure if she was putting him on. "Anything would be quite welcome."

"No, I mean a *steak*. A proper dinner. You've been a prince this whole time, putting up with me and my mother, and this damn weather, all so that I could pay my respects."

"It's the least I could do, Mrs. Miller," he said. "I think it was a very proper thing for you to want to do."

"I'd be content with a nice cup of coffee," she said. "I'm chilled to the bone."

"We'll get you one as soon as we get back. May I offer you my coat?"

"No," she said. "You'll catch your death out here." She paused for a second and then gave a little chuckle. "One dead lawyer is enough for one day."

Bert tried to read her face in the deepening twilight, but failed. "Er, yes, true enough," he managed.

"You know," Allie said, as the trees thinned, "I met him a year ago today. On Valentine's Day."

"Oh, I am sorry," Bert said.

"It seems like forever ago. I wanted to move here, with Arthur. To Maine."

"You did?"

"Yes, I did. It was my idea, in fact."

"Why didn't you?"

Allie raised her eyebrows. "He said he wasn't ready to ask his wife for a divorce."

"It would be a hard thing to do," Bert said.

"It oughtn't to have been as hard as he made it. But now I know that wasn't the real reason he didn't leave her. I learned that at the inquest."

"You mean all the debt he'd racked up?"

"Presumably. Hundreds of thousands in bad investments. He couldn't afford a divorce after that. That was news to me, at any rate."

"He hadn't told you about the losses?"

"No. That wasn't his nature. He would have tried to find a way out of it on his own."

"I suppose in the end, he did."

"Are you trying to be funny?"

"No, no," he said. "I mean to say that he was in a desperate situation. And sometimes people do desperate things when—"

"I take your meaning."

"Now that you've seen it, is it what you expected? Brunswick, that is."

She pondered this for a few squeaks. "More or less."

"Would you mind if I asked what you mean by that?"

"It's a bigger place than I thought. The streets are wider than in Buffalo. Yet for all that the town seems somehow claustrophobic, as if one might never escape once one wanders in."

"We're accustomed to the city, I suppose."

"And it feels as though everyone here is watching us. It reminds me of Ed's detectives all over again. Did you notice the people passing by the cemetery when we were there?"

Bert laughed. "I did. They were staring at us like we'd dropped in from the moon. I saw the same couple stroll by three times. In the rain."

Allie playfully squeezed Bert's arm with her glove. "You do have a sense of humor after all, Mr. Hartshorn."

"I'm human," he said. "I like to laugh. In different circumstances, you would see that."

"You might see me differently, too," she said.

That was a remark best left unaddressed, so Bert contented himself with the feeling of Allie's hand gently resting on his forearm. It was quite dark when the hulk of The Cumberland hove out of the mist, a line of gas lamps flickering along the broad front porch. Allie's shoes squeaked up the boards to the front door.

"After you've had a chance to thaw out," Bert said to her, opening the door, "ring my room and the three of us can have supper."

Allie rolled her eyes. "God, and here I was hoping I wouldn't have to see my mother again tonight."

Bert smiled. "I'm sure my own children have said the same about me and my wife, and more than once."

"Touché. I'll ring you in an hour or so."

❧

MUCH TO BERT'S SURPRISE, dinner was altogether pleasant. Neither Allie nor Mrs. Hall seemed to have an appetite for pursuing their quarrel, if equally little for The Cumberland's rather limited bill of fare—lobster soup and buttered bread.

"I'm sorry I couldn't get you that steak," Allie said, looking downcast. "I never thought for an instant they wouldn't have a piece of beef in Maine."

"When in Rome," Bert replied, shrugging. "The lobster soup was excellent. I can always have steak, but one can't find lobster in Buffalo."

"And if you could, you wouldn't trust it," Alicia said. "Imagine what a lobster would look like, dredged up from the Buffalo River."

"Disgusting," Mrs. Hall said. "Every year they say they'll do something about that river, and then nothing happens. It's little better than an open sewer."

"Prosperity has its price," Hartshorn said.

"I suppose so," Mrs. Hall said, putting her napkin on her plate. "But that's a problem for another day. For the present, I should get these brittle bones of mine into a soft bed," she said, standing. "Thank you both for the company."

"She's not quite sixty-three years old," Alicia said under her breath as her mother hobbled off. "You'd think she was ninety."

Allie and Bert left the table shortly afterward, and Allie suggested a stroll to the lounge for a cup of strong Irish coffee. They talked for a little while about nothing in particular, sipped their coffee, ordered another. It felt good to be warm and sleepy. They dragged it out as much as possible, but by about nine o'clock there was nothing left to say and Hartshorn was looking a bit weary.

"Well, Mrs. Miller," he said, eyeing the clock above the fireplace, "I think it's time for me to turn in. We'll have a long ride tomorrow back to Buffalo."

"Yes, I'm tired too. Would you mind escorting me to my room, Mr. Hartshorn?"

"Aren't you on the ladies' floor? With your mother?" he said, puzzled.

"No. They wanted to put me there, but I told them nothing doing. I'm too old to be bunking in a girls' dormitory."

Hartshorn chuckled. "Well then, it'd be my pleasure."

The pair went to the elevator. "We're on the fourth floor," she told the operator. He glanced at their hands, out of long habit, and looked away when he saw that both wore wedding rings.

On the fourth floor, Hartshorn gave Alicia his arm and walked her to the door of her room.

"Come in and sit with me for a little bit," Allie said. "I do have one further question about the settlement of Ed's estate, and it wasn't something I wanted to discuss in public."

Bert looked up and down the hallway. "Mrs. Miller," he said quietly, "I'm not sure that it would be appropriate—"

"Don't be a ninny," she said. "I'm not dangerous."

She handed him her key and he worked the lock. Once inside, he turned up the gas to reveal a spacious two-room suite, with an adjoining bath. In the front room was a davenport, presumably for people with children so that they could have a second bedroom. Allie stepped spritely over to the davenport and sat down on the far end. "Sit down, will you? You look like you've seen a ghost," she said.

"I really had best be going to my room," Hartshorn said, looked around. His eyes glued to the door behind and to the left of the sofa, the portal to the main bedroom.

"You have quite a case of the heebie-jeebies, don't you?" Allie said. "I only want to ask you a couple of questions. Then you can go off to your room and be all by yourself."

He sat down on the near end of the davenport, putting as much fabric between him and Alicia as possible. "So, then," he said, clearing his throat, "how may I help? With the estate?"

"I'm concerned about how long all of this will take," she said. "Edward's business and everything else. How long before I get my share and the children get theirs?"

Hartshorn immediately felt less ill at ease. He loved questions like this. They gave him an opportunity to show off his many years of experience.

"Hard to say precisely," he intoned, "but I'd estimate another several months. Things go faster after the preliminaries are done, and the inquest. Those are both things that must be settled on before any monies can change hands."

"I only hope that Howie Gaines doesn't renege on his agreement to purchase Ed's share of Miller Envelope," she said.

Bert shook his head. "I don't see him as the type to back out on a deal. He cared a great deal about Edward. And also, I'm sorry to say, Edward's demise presents Mr. Gaines with the opportunity of a lifetime. He can be majority owner of his own business now. That would not have been possible if Edward were still alive. I hope that's not being too blunt."

Allie nodded and rubbed her face gently. "No. Blunt is good. No pussyfooting necessary with me, Mr. Hartshorn."

"I do hope you'll call me Bert," he said, gratified.

"Bert." She smiled, trying out the name. "Bert. Very well. Thank you, that's what has been preying on my mind these past weeks. Until you came into the picture, frankly I didn't have anyone else to ask. Whom I could trust."

"I'm happy to hear that I can be of service."

"Well you have been, and thank you," she said brightly, shifting to sit on the front edge of the davenport and turning to face Bert. "Now, then, don't let me keep you. I know you have to be going."

"Yes, I ought to," Bert said, shifting his weight toward the front of the davenport, though Allie was half-blocking him. He felt a curious mix of relief and dismay. He hadn't known what to expect in this woman's room, though in truth he had been flattered to be invited in, and had almost hoped that someone might see him with a much younger woman. No one knew him here, so it would be a bit of a thrill. But, on the other hand, it was better it had been all business. Now he could go to his own room, unfasten his pants, and have a glass of whiskey before falling asleep.

She caught his arm before he could stand. Her eyes had gone black, all pupil in the dim gaslight. "In the spirit of bluntness—there is one other thing I wish to say before you go."

"Yes?"

"I've been thinking that I owe you an apology."

Bert's eyes widened. Alicia Miller didn't seem the type to offer apologies.

"Why would you say that?" he blurted.

"Because I misjudged you, Bert. I concluded when you joined forces with my late husband—against me—"

"That was a different set of—"

She held up a finger. "Let me finish. I thought that you were—not to put too fine a point on it—a scoundrel. A nasty opportunist. Isn't that simply terrible?"

"I suppose I can—"

"But on this trip, I've changed my mind entirely. You've been a prince. Simply a *prince*. So I wanted to apologize for getting it so wrong. No, I *need* to apologize."

Hartshorn was momentarily taken aback, but not for long. Winning over the redoubtable Mrs. Miller would mean a very, very good fee, and for a couple years.

"I owe you my sincere thanks," Allie went on.

"Oh, not at all, Mrs. Miller," Bert said. "I do very much appreciate the sentiments, and realize it can't have been easy to offer them. I am very sensible of that."

Allie scooted closer to him on the davenport, close enough that Hartshorn started to feel slightly uncomfortable. "No, Bert, I do. I do owe you something."

She put her hand on his trouser front and pressed down on the fabric.

"Mrs. Miller!" Hartshorn said, stunned and a little embarrassed by her discovery of his partial arousal. "I hardly think—"

"Then don't think so much. You lawyers all think so much. And," she said, putting her lips next to his ear and purring in her husky contralto, "do call me Alicia."

Hartshorn's round face had flushed beet red. Allie didn't wait for him to calculate his next move. She had him on his back foot now, and wasn't about to let him regain his balance. She slid off the davenport like a raindrop and kneeled next to his legs, which were a little skinny compared to his rotund torso, and then forced herself between them. She worked on the buttons of his trouser fly. Her fingers remembered the trick, having done it so many times with Arthur.

"Oh, my," she said softly. "What have we here? We'd better hurry, or it's going to be too big to get out." She fixed him with her dark, dreamy eyes. Bert sat there frozen.

Sure enough, he'd responded quickly, a promising sign in a middle-aged man. She tugged him out of his pants, none too gently, and took a good look at her prize. Bert had an older man's cock, worked up into a purplish-grey, almost the color of eggplant, against the bland white of the rest of his skin. Best not to look too closely, she thought, and took it into her mouth. Hartshorn uttered a low moan, and some syllables she couldn't make out, possibly Alicia's name. She expected that he might try to escape—being the nervous type and all—but after a few seconds, he laced his fingers through her hair, behind her head. He wasn't going anywhere.

It didn't take long after that. After she'd finished him, she patted his rapidly deflating tool. "I'll bet you weren't expecting *that* tonight," she said, slipping back up onto the davenport next to him.

"I don't know what to say—Alicia," he mumbled, trying to catch his breath. "I—you know I'm married—"

She laughed. "Oh, I know that very well. I don't mind. Isn't it nice to—you know—and then go home to your wife? I don't want a husband. What I do need is a good lawyer and someone with whom I can blow off a little steam. Discreetly. The best of both worlds."

"Uh—"

"And if you don't mind my saying, my dear Bert, you blew off quite a *lot* of steam just now. You poor dear. I wonder how long has it been—since—?"

"I don't know—a month or two?" he stammered. "I don't really keep track—"

"It was a rhetorical question," she shot back. "I don't need to know the actual details."

"Oh, sorry," he said, sheepishly. He sorted himself out and buttoned up his fly. Should he go now? Stay?

Alicia saved him the trouble. "Now that we've cleared the air, I'll let you be on your way. I certainly feel worlds better for getting a load off. Of my chest." She smiled the flat, little smile that was her sign when she had thought of something that amused her. "I hope you feel better, too."

"Well, indeed I do. Very much so."

"Good. It's been an awfully long day," she said, "so I won't ask you to return the favor tonight, if you take my meaning. But next time—"

"Oh—of course," he said. "Yes, I will be h—"

"Shhh," she said, putting her finger on his lips. "Let's not talk any more about it. Now before you go, let me make sure there are no spies in our hallway," Allie said. She got up, smoothed her skirt, and peered out the door. She turned and gestured to him. "The coast is clear."

He walked up behind her and was going to inch by and out the door, but then he couldn't resist an urge to place his hand in the small of her back and trace downward along the curve of her buttocks, giving them a little squeeze.

Allie didn't give anything away, merely smiled at him. One little lark and he thinks he's in charge, she thought. Good, let him.

"Sweet dreams," she whispered as he left.

❧

"Sleep well?" Allie asked as Bert joined her and her mother at breakfast.

"Like a baby," he said with what might have been an awkward wink, which made Alicia want to throw her scalding coffee in his face.

"The rain seems to have stopped," she said instead. "We'll have time for a little ride around the area before the afternoon train. I'd like to see Harpswell and a few other places that Arthur spoke about. After you've had your breakfast, naturally."

"Very good," Bert said. He motioned the waiter over and ordered fried eggs and toast. "I'll be finished before you know it."

"Never a truer word spoken," Allie said.

Mrs. Hall looked mystified by this, and Bert carefully arranged his napkin on his lap.

"Lovely pancakes here," Mrs. Hall said.

"They are," Alicia agreed. "We should ask Annie to make these when we get home."

"The most important element is the maple syrup," Hartshorn said. "We can take some back to Buffalo, if you like."

"Bert, why don't you enjoy your breakfast and call us when you're ready to go?" Alicia said, getting up. Bert stood too, dropping his napkin on the floor.

"I'm sorry I'm holding you up," he said. "Why don't I just cancel my order?" He patted his stomach. "It wouldn't hurt me to miss a meal every now and then, you know."

Allie made a wry face. "One meal isn't going to make a difference, Bert. Enjoy your breakfast, and let us know when you're ready to go to Harpswell."

❧

HARPSWELL LOUNGED ALONG A narrow promontory, bordered by lapping grey-green water tugging at the stony foreshore. The thin beaches, mostly pebbles, nestled under rock outcroppings, on which a few houses balanced, facing the sea. Not far off the beach—probably reachable by a strong swimmer—lay a few tiny islands, each bristling with a few dozen pine trees defiantly standing sentinel against the relentless tides and currents.

There seemed to be nowhere on the promontory where the water could not reach. If the waves couldn't soak it, the whirling haze of spray would finish the job. Turn one direction, and the wind would shift perversely in the other. Turn away, and as if by magic, the reward was a face full of cold mist.

Bert had engaged the hotel carriage to take them to see the sights. It seemed like a cozy way to view the wild scenery. But with three people sealed in the little closed compartment, the cozy coach quickly became stifling and humid, the windows opaque with the fog of breath. The driver would have to call down when they were approaching something of note, and then Bert would use his soggy handkerchief to clear the windows enough to peer out. Finally, even that stopped working.

Soon, the only creatures in Harpswell sullener than The Cumberland's hired horse were the three humans trapped inside the hired carriage. Allie begged Bert to have the driver stop a couple of times, braving the drizzle for a breath of air. One promising stop was at what had to be the narrowest part of the promontory, where there was a view in both directions—landward and out across the endless ocean. There was even a little wide spot where carriages seemed to park to take in the view. When the three of them tumbled out of the coach, though, squinting against the wind, they had no sooner gotten to the stony beach when Mrs. Hall cried out sharply.

"Oh my good Lord!"

"What is it, Mother?" Allie said, holding down her hat to keep it from blowing into the briny.

"For heaven's sake. Look, will you? What is the world coming to?"

Allie and Bert hurried across the pebbles to where Mrs. Hall was standing, transfixed. She was pointing at the beach near her feet, where a used condom had been discarded.

"God in heaven," Bert breathed. "Ladies, please, I suggest we go back to the carriage."

"Imagine, right on the beach," Allie said. "There's a story here."

"Don't be horrid, Alicia," Mrs. Hall said.

"I'm merely saying, Mother—imagine it—on these hard, wet pebbles?"

"Surely this was tossed from some carriage—oh, why on earth are we discussing this?" The old lady turned on her heel and strode back to the waiting carriage. "May we leave, please?" she shouted back down to Bert and Allie, trying to raise her voice above the whistle of the wind.

Allie nudged the condom with the toe of her boot. "Bert, I tell you, it's a sign," she said, and laughed.

Bert's round face went crimson. "We'd better get back to the coach," he said. "What say we go back to town and have a coffee?"

"There's one more place I want to visit first," she said. "I want to see where the Pendles built their ships. Arthur's father was a shipmaster, and Arthur grew up on shipboard. He told me so many stories of the days of sail. Then I'll be done."

"Yes, naturally," Bert said, offering her his arm.

The three bumped back up to town from Harpswell, not caring enough for the view to wipe off the streaming windows. From Brunswick, it was a short ride to the defunct shipyard that Arthur's father and brothers had owned.

There wasn't much left. A few old barns and the rotting ways running down and out into deep water, waiting for a new keel that would never be laid. These ways—long, sloped wooden tracks used to ease a new ship from land to water—had launched the last great Pendle Brothers ship back in 1874. Arthur's father had died aboard it four years later, and with him had died four hundred years of history: four centuries in which the Pendles' tall ships had nosed into every ocean, bay, and estuary. Then, in only four decades, they had been vanquished entirely by steam.

An old fellow was taking advantage of a break in the drizzle and was sitting on one of the old pilings, smoking a cigar and looking out over the quiet water. Bert approached him.

"Is this all of what remains of the Pendle Brothers operation?"

"Yup," the man said. "This all there is now." *Now* sounded like it had at least three syllables.

"Must have been a busy place years ago."

The old man leaned to one side and spat. "You wouldn't recognize it. When I was a young feller, this place had hundreds of men crawlin' all over. The whole town would come out to see 'em launch the newest one."

"Seems a shame," Bert said.

"Progress, is all, they say," the old man replied. "Times change."

"What became of all the workers?"

"Oh, most of them boys went to work in the mill. The weavin' factory."

"The big one in town?"

"Yup, that's the one."

"That's a rather sharp change for a shipwright."

"Yup. Too big for most of 'em," he said. "Lots of 'em just turned into drunks. But—that's the only work 'round here these days, except fishing, and once you've built boats, I expect you don't care to be out in 'em." The old man spat again, to the other side of the piling, and resumed smoking in silence.

"Well, thank you for your time," Bert said.

"Yup," the man replied, without turning his head away from the water.

Bert hustled back up the sloping bank to where the ladies were standing. "This is—or was it," he said.

"Thank you," Allie said. "Let me stand here for a minute, and then we can go back to town."

"I'll wait in the coach, if you don't mind," Mrs. Hall said. Bert escorted the old lady back to the carriage and, after she'd gotten settled, stood there discreetly while Allie had a moment to herself.

She gingerly stepped down the bank along an abandoned cartway, whose cobblestones were slick with a layer of mud. She avoided the old man and walked upwind from the smoke of his cheap cigar. Arthur had liked cigars, which she'd found slightly less deplorable only because his were always of excellent quality, not the ones that—she smiled as she recalled his scornful description—smelled like smoldering socks soaked in piss.

Near the water's edge, where the ways disappeared into the black depths, she thought back to what she recalled about Arthur's boyhood, spent with his mother and younger brother John aboard his father's ships. He'd been born on shipboard, somewhere in the trackless Southern Ocean, and on a dozen or more voyages had been from Japan to Peru, around raging Cape Horn and all the way to Liverpool, and along the coasts of Africa. Travel had given Arthur a worldly quality—and a somewhat standoffish, supercilious manner when talking to local Buffalo people—which Allie had found quite intoxicating.

But if Arthur loved travel, he hadn't loved the sea. Not the way his father had, whose love for the ocean and the creak and strain of wood and hemp was a passion matched only by his love for Arthur's mother. Arthur had never aspired to be the next, and certainly not the last, in the long line of Pendle captains. Even though his body was lean and hard—another thing that Allie had found intoxicating about the man—and he had inherited the large and powerful Pendle hands, Arthur was too bookish and intellectual for command. His mind was too open to possibility to plot a single, direct course without becoming ensnared by other equally attractive alternatives. A sea captain had to be both an autocrat and a diplomat, someone who could command sailors before the mast and then play at equals with the rich businessmen who owned and underwrote the ships. That was certainly not Arthur, and his cool, nuanced reserve would never have inspired men in the way it had inspired women.

She looked down at the pebbly strand, shook her head. How different life would be right now, if Arthur had lived. But no, he'd been too complex a creature to survive long in such a simple, brutal world, in which reward and punishment were doled out arbitrarily, heedless of intellect or sophistication. It had turned out he could no more live on land than he could aboard ship, for in both realms the laurel always went to the glad-handers, the fakers, and the hard cases—to men like his father, men who could be whatever other men needed them to be.

Since the inquest, most everyone had concluded that Arthur Pendle had possessed most everything in life, except integrity. He'd stolen another man's wife, abandoned his own, and very likely swindled his own relatives out of their substance to fund his ignoble, personal pleasures. And yet, as Allie stood there looking out over the wreckage of the Pendle dynasty, she felt something that she hadn't felt since the inquest, and not even when standing in front of the hole in which Arthur's body had been laid to rest. She felt pity for this man she had not known until just now, a man who could be neither a captain of industry nor a captain of a ship. Like the half-built vessels that once stood at the top of the ways, he had been equally ill at ease on land and water. But one had to acknowledge that he had remained true to himself, whatever that was, until the end. And with that rising feeling, Allie again felt an equal and counterbalancing need to get even. She would strike back at the people who had disgraced and hounded to death the only man she had ever loved, until the only place left for Arthur was neither water nor earth, but the sorry mud of the little town he'd been desperate to leave behind.

She reached down, picked up a pebble off the beach, and walked back up the slope. The rain was coming down hard again by the time they got back to Maine Street and the shelter of The Cumberland.

❧

MRS. HALL AVAILED HERSELF of a few hours' repose in her room, while Bert and Allie had an early lunch in the restaurant of The Cumberland. They would soon be southbound and west again, and were due to arrive in Buffalo the next morning.

They were seated at a small table at a window with a view over the broad backyard of the hotel, and the black trees defining it like a giant's picket fence. Allie peeled off her gloves and sank back into her chair. They discussed the menu, and quickly agreed to split a ham steak. Then they lapsed into an awkward silence, looking out the window at the dripping trees. Alicia was hungry and not in any mood for chitchat. Like any good attorney, in such a situation Bert knew enough to be quiet. Each was feeling that something had changed irretrievably.

"What's next, Bert?" Alicia said after their food had been served.

"How do you mean?"

"Take it any way you want to."

"Oughtn't we talk about"—he leaned forward—"last evening?"

"What about it?"

Bert sat back and swallowed his mouthful of ham, dabbed his lips.

"Well, it seems to me that—I don't quite know—"

"Best not to dwell on it too much," she said. "Things happen. They're not always as significant as we may think."

He looked down. "I suppose I thought that—I know I've said it before, but I very much regret that you and I had such a difficult stretch, Alicia. Maybe last night was a new beginning. That's what I've been thinking."

"It is certainly long past time to move on," she said. "We've got a lot to do. Finish settling Ed's estate and then get Arthur's bequest paid. That money belongs to me. It's what Arthur wanted."

Bert looked up and pursed his mouth. "Yes, I'm sure it is what he wanted. But it might not be that easy, in practice."

"How hard can it be? It's right there, in black and white. In the man's will, with his signature affixed. What else could be required, pray tell?"

"The facts are in our favor. But I wouldn't be surprised if the family contests that provision in the will. His brother John has already tested the patience of the executor more than once. Courts have wide latitude to adjust bequests based on circumstances."

Allie sat back forcefully in her chair, almost knocking herself over backwards. "For heaven's sake," she said. "Arthur's executor is the district attorney himself. As if that inquest wasn't enough ordeal to put me through. Now this—you tell me we have to convince Terence Penrose to do his job." Allie sniffed and looked out the window.

"It's the way the system works. You should listen to your attorney, you know," he said.

"And you should listen to your client. I'm not happy about this."

"I'm sorry. I'll do the best I can to make you happy."

"Fine, fine," she said, stabbing at the ham steak with her fork. She looked up at him, her eyes all black. "One hand washes the other, Bert. You have a lot to do for me. And I have plenty I plan to do for you, if you follow me. How does that sound?"

Bert stopped mid-swallow. "It sounds—wonderful," he said, lowering his voice. "But I can't help worrying a little—about my wife."

"Bert," she said quietly, putting her fingertips on the table, "It's you I'm going to be fucking, not your wife. Two's company, three's a crowd. And moreover, I've seen your wife."

"For goodness' sake," Bert said, staring.

Allie laughed so hard that the waiter looked over to see what was so funny.

❧

FOR THE FIRST FEW weeks after their return from Maine, Bert felt like a young buck all over again. At forty-two, Alicia was more than a decade his junior, and he'd thought that after a certain point in life—children grown and gone, he and his wife settled into a comfortable routine—that the urges he had had as a young man were only that, the urges of a young man, a thing to be remembered fondly but indistinctly, like the smell of burning leaves.

Allie had rekindled all of that. Now, being with her—plunging into her warm and willing body—was nearly all he could think about. He didn't even listen to most of what she had to say anymore, sometimes even if listening would have been advisable as regarded his legal and fiduciary duty. Her voice would fade into a kind of background drone, and the rush of his fantasies about her lithe, sinuous body as he watched her chest rise and fall with her complaints about the delays in getting her payouts or the goddamned district attorney or whatever would give him a lump in his trousers that became the central fact of his being, impossible to ignore. This turgid upwelling of desire—of lust, he exulted privately—drove him nearly to distraction.

She knew it, of course. It was fine with her, too, most of the time. They would sometimes be sitting in the parlor, talking idly about something, anything, and she'd see him shift, cross his legs, display the little tells that his mind had gone somewhere else—namely, upstairs to her bedroom. And she would stand, give him a look that almost made him think he might release in his trousers, take his hand, and lead him upstairs. He was self-conscious, at first, about his protruding belly, his hairless legs, the one bad tooth he had, his stale breath. But she didn't seem to care about any of it. All he had to do was stay up long enough for Allie's lips to part, just slightly, enough for her to let out a long, low, hissing moan. That was her tell. Whatever Bert got along the way was fine with her, and kept him around.

It kept him around so much, though, that one day he told his wife that Mrs. Miller was having a difficult day—grief, worry, stress—and that he would stay at the Miller residence that night. It was unprecedented, but Mrs. Hartshorn would never suspect that Alicia Miller would have the slightest interest in her husband. One sleepover became two and then three and ten, though, and as the sun declined each day, the rituals of closing up the Miller house for the night developed into a kind of fetish. The simple act of locking the front door at twilight could give him a hard-on. He knew it was stupid, but he also knew that he felt more alive now than he had in years.

He'd even started trying to lose weight. He took off twenty pounds, fast, which to his delight prompted Allie to observe appreciatively that his cock was looking positively enormous these days. Bert and his wife had been married for more than twenty-five years, had raised two children, and yet he felt sure that the missus would not have been able to identify his penis in a lineup. And here was this beguiling, vital, younger woman, *admiring* it. He'd won Bar Association awards, bested some top-notch attorneys at trial, raised two fine children, and yet he could recall no greater honor than Allie's hungry compliment about his pecker.

She didn't tell him she loved him, and he hadn't the courage to ask. That would have been treading on thin ice, and especially since in intimate settings, Allie maintained a grim, directed silence. And Bert wasn't sure what this rush of youthful feelings meant, not in any sense larger than the thrill of the moment. For the present, he was having fun, and getting paid for it. One of those things would change, soon enough.

IN LIKE A LION

ALMOST A FULL MONTH HAD PASSED SINCE THEIR RETURN FROM Maine, and Buffalo was slogging through another long, cold March. Alicia was beginning to get a touch of cabin fever. She loved golf, bicycling, outings to the picnic grounds downriver on Grand Island. Yet all those outdoor things were still another month and a half away, and that was with luck. Maine may have been gloomy, but at least it had given her a chance to get out of the house.

Along with winter, the process of settling Ed Miller's estate dragged interminably on. Allie was seething over Ed's will, which he had rewritten only a few weeks before his death. In it, he had cut Allie off entirely, "for reasons which will be obvious to her." Instead, he'd left the entirety of his estate in trust for their three daughters. To add insult to injury, he had also named Howie Gaines as the children's guardian until they each became of legal age, effectively firing Allie as their mother.

Edward's state of mind when he had filed for final divorce was now abundantly clear: not only to disinherit Allie but also to ensure that she never set foot in their house again, or saw their children without his permission. However harsh, his wishes were explicit enough, and the Gaines camp asserted that they must be carried out to the letter, as was only right and proper. Yet if they prevailed, Allie and her children would be entirely at the mercy of her late husband's best friend and business partner—and soon to be new majority owner of Miller Envelope Company.

Whatever her initial doubts, it quickly became clear that Terry Penrose had done Allie an enormous favor by prodding her toward Bert Hartshorn. Bert was an artist before the judges, who, like every other soul in the city, had heard Allie's testimony at the inquest and were predisposed to agree with Ed Miller's uncharitable opinion of his wife. Hartshorn deflated all that, deftly pointing out that under New York law, death changes everything, even the wishes of a dead man—if the dead man's wishes assumed that he would be unmarried when he died.

Had Edward lived long enough to secure his divorce, then cutting Allie off would have been simple. But by pure mischance, death before divorce meant that Allie, as his lawful wife at the time of his death, could not be disinherited entirely. Whether Edward willed it or not, his wife was automatically entitled to one-third of the estate—the so-called widow's dower. Nor was Edward's wish for someone other than his still-lawful living wife to care for their children going to pass legal muster. Bert put on a strong legal case, and in short order the judges had little choice but to grant Allie her one-third of everything, and uphold her as the children's legal guardian. Gaines was out as guardian, and frankly probably relieved to be. He wasn't married and didn't even like children. Most likely he had never expected his friend to die.

And yet facts were facts. And after the guardianship matter was settled, Howie lived up to his word and honored his fair—even generous—offer to buy the children's two-thirds of the envelope business. With no charges filed, and Ed's life insurance soon paid, after Howie's check cleared the Miller bank account was looking very healthy indeed. Once she could secure Arthur's unexpected $50,000 bequest, Allie would be a very prosperous woman.

❦

EVEN IN BUFFALO, WINTER can't hold on forever, and a blustery March eventually blew itself out. As the month wore down, and the first daffodils peeked out of the fresh earth piled atop the dead, the newspapers lost interest in the Millers and the Pendles, and gradually the tired grey snow melted away. Life began to resume something of the usual course it had followed prior to the disaster that had been 1901.

When the inquest had concluded, Sarah turned her attention back to Maggie—and to Seth, who had spent the winter drinking himself into insensibility. Yet alcohol had become a disappointment. He couldn't drink enough these days to feel free, and to his cocktails he was adding laudanum, ether, and chloral hydrate, all legal and all from his medical kit.

Under the weight of all the intoxicants, Seth's flailing dental practice had finally capitulated, and when Sarah visited him one weekend late in the month, their little house in Batavia smelled like urine, and Seth smelled worse. She helped him out of his clothes and into the bath, shocked at how thin and brittle he had become in the two months of her absence. Before dental school, he'd been a gravedigger—hard and strong—but now, as she gently soaped his wasting limbs, he looked like a shade of the man he'd been only a decade earlier. True, he was eating very little, but she feared something else was going wrong on the inside, that his body had begun to consume itself.

At the end of March, Sarah closed up the house on Norwood Street and moved herself and Maggie to Batavia. She took two rooms in a row-house a couple of blocks from Seth, not wanting Maggie to see her father's dissolution day by day. When Seth was lucid, and Sarah had freshened the house, then she would bring the little girl down for a visit. Maggie was always delighted to see her father, and Seth to see his little one—but then again, he always seemed on the verge of weeping. He knew that after a couple hours he would get the itch again, that Sarah would try to stop him, fail, and then whisk Maggie away to safety lest the girl see her father's slow suicide.

Sarah might as well have been dead herself, going through the motions of caring for her ailing husband and her daughter, taking secretarial courses at the Bryant & Stratton Business Institute so that she could support all of them, and every morning, tamping down "for some other time" her own grief. Often, she thought she'd been judged for trying to escape her marriage, that she was being rightly cudgeled for desertion. Maybe it served her right, but she had to keep those thoughts to herself.

She tried to pray—for the first time in years—but it only made her feel lonely. No one seemed to be listening. The only person she wanted to talk with, Eddie, had been stolen from her, by person or persons unknown, and all the king's horses hadn't been able to shed any light on who or why. It made her angry, knowing that someone—maybe even a handful of people—knew what had happened in Ed Miller's den on New Year's Eve 1901, and that no one seemed to care. Not the police, not the newspapers, not even the good people of Buffalo.

❧

ON APRIL 1, ALICIA was going through the morning mail. In the stack was an envelope from Hartshorn & Hartshorn, Attorneys at Law. What's this? she thought, sliding a finger under the flap and opening it.

It was a bill. An invoice for $450 for legal services over the preceding month, including travel to Maine, hotel, and meals. That fat old shit, she thought. We'll see about this.

Later, when Bert dropped by the house to check on her—she was, after all, very fragile just now, as he continued to tell his wife—Alicia sat him down in the rear parlor, the private one, and stood in front of him, tapping her foot. He knew the look by now, and hoped he could settle her down quickly. He was feeling more than a little randy.

"Is something wrong, Alicia?"

"Look what arrived today," she said, pulling the bill from her jacket pocket. She unfolded it and looked daggers at it, then dangled it in front of his nose. "A four hundred fifty dollar invoice from—can you guess?—Hartshorn & Hartshorn."

"Yes, I reviewed that myself," he said. "It's all in order. That was for all the hours for the trip to Maine and quite a bit of work on Ed's estate. You'll see all of the details right there."

She glared at him, which made him wilt. "Oh, I see all the details."

"Then you know it's all in order."

"So you actually expect me to pay *you*? Four hundred fifty dollars?"

"Um, yes, that's customary."

"Don't be a smart-ass. You know what I mean. If anything, you should be paying *me*."

"Alicia, my bill is for legal services. Whatever else we—it's a completely different—nonlegal matter . . ." He trailed off.

"Your wife puts your invoices together, doesn't she?"

"Yes, she does."

"Mattie, I believe?"

"Yes, Mattie."

"Good. Does Mattie know about any of the 'nonlegal matters' we get up to?"

"Of course not."

"And I suppose you'd like to keep it that way?"

"What—"

"What I'm saying, Bert, is that if you are going to have Mattie bill me for services, I am going to start billing her for *mine*. And mine will be every bit as detailed as hers are."

"That's not necessary, Alicia," Bert said, looking desperate.

"Well then, so long as I don't send bills, you don't either. I know this will sting, Bert, but here goes nothing—" She tore up the bill in front of him, letting the pieces of paper flutter to the floor at her feet.

"How am I supposed to tell her—my wife—not to invoice you like every other client?" He was getting red in the face.

"Are you really that thick? Tell her you're working on contingency. You'll get paid if you get my money. I know a thing or two about how lawyers operate, you know."

Bert cleared his throat. "I could tell her that, I suppose."

"Yes, you can, and no one will be the wiser. We have a good arrangement, Bert. Don't fuck it up."

He shook his head.

Alicia exhaled. "I'm *so* glad we got that settled," she said. "I confess I was feeling rather frazzled until just now."

"I'm glad, too," Bert said with something in his voice that wasn't enthusiasm.

"Now then. We do have some actual legal things to discuss—a few papers that I want to ask you about," she said. "But before we get to that, maybe you'd like to sanctify our new arrangement with some nonlegal activity?" She lifted her skirt a little up her leg, and smiled.

Bert could feel himself growing despite himself, though simultaneously wanting to punch Alicia. There was no point in fighting it. He needed what she had, what she offered up, and he would take it on any terms she set. He knew there wasn't a damn thing he could do about it, or wanted to do about it. And as angry as he was with himself sometimes, he didn't care.

❦

SETH PAYNE DIED IN early May, peacefully, as the lilacs were starting to bloom. Although at some point Sarah had accepted that the end was inevitable and that neither she nor God could divert Seth from his quest for self-destruction, his passing hit her hard. She tried to console Maggie, but her words seemed hollow and meaningless, like the trite blandishments she'd heard her minister father offer a thousand times to a thousand grieving families.

Sarah knew that a full year—sometimes two—was the obligatory period for a widow to enter deep mourning. She was to wear deep black from head to toe, eschew jewelry and other ornamentation, and conduct herself with conspicuous probity. For two months, she endured the process as best she could, receiving near strangers at her home with an appropriately grave countenance. But the visitors—and the clothing—only irritated her, and suppressed her mood further.

I gave ten years already to Seth, she thought each evening as she kicked her shoes across the bedroom and peeled off the layers of crepe and black lace. And now I'm supposed to give two more? I could pretend, I suppose, that I'm wearing mourning for Eddie, but that's nothing short of cowardice. Wanting other people to think that I'm someone I'm not, and never was. I'm stalling, that's all it is.

On the Fourth of July, she and Maggie lined up right in front of the Genesee County Courthouse, the best spot from which to watch the parade. It was a tiny little celebration, mostly made up of aging veterans of the Civil War and the local fire brigade. The entire parade lineup took all of five minutes to pass by the courthouse in one direction and then, presumably to extend the festivities, turned right around and came back by again. On the second pass, the participants stopped in front of the limestone building, beneath the huge American flag, to recite the Pledge of Allegiance, introduced not ten years before and still a novelty.

I pledge allegiance to my Flag and the Republic for which it stands: one Nation indivisible, with Liberty and Justice for all.

Justice, she thought wryly. Whatever that is. Justice had not been done in Buffalo, and the longer she buried herself in Batavia, the less likely it would ever be done. The person or persons unknown who had stolen her future had got away scot-free, and she could not let that stand. And by the time the Pledge had concluded, when the cheers had died away, and the hats tossed aloft had returned to earth, Sarah knew what she was going to do next. She was going back to Buffalo, to get justice for Eddie.

PART TWO

THE AVENGING ANGEL
DETECTIVE AGENCY

DOG DAYS

July 12, 1902
Saturday

SARAH'S TRAIN WAS FULL OF EXCURSIONISTS, ESCAPING HOT AND muggy Batavia for a weekend in hot and muggy Buffalo, or perhaps hoping to catch the steam ferry to the cooler summer resorts of Grand Island. While Maggie was staying with a friend in Batavia, Sarah had two days, three at most, to reopen the house on Norwood Street and see a few office properties.

The first office she saw captivated her, and she didn't need to waste precious time shopping around. She signed, on the spot, for a furnished spot on the fifth floor of the Hudson Building, directly across from the Erie County Courthouse. There were two rooms, only: a small inner office that would be hers, and a larger outer space spacious enough for two or three other detectives. When the company grew, of course.

The best part of it, to her mind, was that her private office window overlooked Delaware Avenue and lined up with the four large windows of the office of the district attorney.

As far back she could remember, Sarah had wanted to be a detective. Why, exactly, she didn't know. Something about mysteries and disguises, or the inscrutable art of deduction she'd read about in *A Study in Scarlet* when she was a teenager. She had told Eddie once or twice, when he'd engaged his New York City sleuths for surveillance on Allie and Arthur, that she even knew the name of the agency she dreamed of opening, one day: The Avenging Angel Detective Agency. And if in time Maggie joined the practice, she'd merely make it "Angels," and that would be that.

As soon as she was given the keys, she arranged to have the name of the new agency painted on the glass of the front office door, with her name under it as principal. She walked down to the busy Bell Telephone office and registered for a telephone, and from the printer in the ground floor of her building, ordered a hundred engraved calling cards—all of which any detective worthy of the name would need from the start. At the Bell office, she was careful to insist that her name be shown as "S. Payne, Principal," to not reveal that she was a woman. In the long run, she thought, *my being a woman may be a benefit. But at first, best to play it safe.*

With a proper name on the door, a nice new telephone (and free city directory for opening an account), and her little stack of business cards, Sarah sat proudly behind the old but serviceable partners desk that had been supplied with the office. A partners desk looked a bit strange for a one-person operation, but soon enough she'd have an associate in the outer office, and she could call him in to work on a case right there at the huge desk. That would be handy.

She took the streetcar over to Norwood Street. Everything at the house seemed in good order. Thankfully, given all the other new bills she'd have to pay, the house was paid off. Seth had made a good living, until the drink and drugs began eroding it, and soon she would sell the Batavia place lock, stock, and barrel. That would leave her with enough money for five months of office rent, food, and necessities. By then, she expected that the agency would be producing a steady income. Yet that, too, was a problem. She would have to serve as a consulting detective to bring in funds, but she knew as little about how to chase down clients as she did about chasing down the culprits behind Eddie's murder.

On Sunday, she aired out and tidied the house, and took a little walk around Ashwood to see if anyone would say hello. No one did. Whether it was her bright pink parasol that put them off, or that so many of them thought of her as a homewrecker, the neighborhood seemed strangely deserted. It made her more than a little sad, walking down Cleveland and Ashwood and all the familiar streets, passing all the familiar houses, Eddie's and the Pendles.' Their once-grand homes now seemed worse than abandoned.

The Pendle house was, in fact, vacant. An extravagant crop of dandelions had colonized the front yard, and the windows were streaked and opaque, the eyes of a blind man. She understood that Arthur's younger brother owned it now, having prevailed upon the executor—none other than the district attorney himself—to square a few accounts on the cheap, and to allow enough room on the ledger to ensure that he got something out of his wealthy brother's demise.

The wealth—more than $200,000 of insurance, from a variety of policies taken out over several years—had gone mainly to creditors. Arthur and Cassie had apparently lost, or spent, whatever money their relatives had invested with them. Their untimely but perhaps fortuitous deaths had saved them from scrutiny and disgrace.

Without anyone to talk with in Ashwood, Sarah returned to her new office. She sat there for a good half hour, not knowing where to begin on the trail of finding justice for Eddie. Her mind kept snapping back to practicalities, top among which was to find someone to look after Maggie. With school out for the summer, Maggie could come to the office with her and play, but in September she'd be enrolled again.

With five months' funding in hand, though—six, if she economized—she had time. I need to be patient with myself, she thought. I have a lot to learn, and five months will go by all too quickly.

❦

"GODDAMN IT, ANNIE! THE door!" Alicia shouted over the upper staircase railing. The sound of feet clattered up from the basement.

"Yes, Mrs. Miller?" Annie said, breathlessly, looking up at the face leaning over the stairwell.

"Are you deaf?"

"I'm sorry, I was in the basement with the furnace man."

"The furnace man? It's July."

"He was doing the maintenance, before winter," Annie said.

The doorbell rang again, this time insistently.

"Will you answer the door? Someone's been pulling the bell so hard it's going to come out of the wall. It's probably another of those damn salesmen."

"Yes, ma'am, right away."

Allie went back into her bedroom and flopped down on the bed. I am so tired of that tedious girl, she thought.

Annie Murray was a family friend of Ed Miller's family, from Conestoga. As a girl, she'd known Ed before he went off to Buffalo to seek his fortune. By the time she'd come of age, Ed was starting a business and a family, and needed a girl-of-all-work who could do the marketing, cook, and clean, while Allie tended to their expanding set of social obligations. Annie was a natural choice, and her parents were delighted that their daughter could step into a position in the big city, but safely and without having to make her way among strangers.

After four years in service to the Miller family, Annie had developed into a rather pretty young woman in her early twenties, but as yet hadn't shown any particular interest in marriage and a family of her own, mainly because working for Mr. Miller was a source of genuine happiness. Ed Miller was kind to her, more like an uncle than an employer, and he and Annie had something else in common: a love of hobbies.

Ed Miller was an inveterate hobbyist, and he had the money to pursue as many of them as he liked. Annie shared his love of every new craze, but her own resources would have been far too scanty to indulge in very many of them. Ed, on the other hand, jumped feetfirst into golf, cycling, photography, astronomy, electrical gadgets, and a dozen other things. He was endlessly interested in new things.

But he was a dilettante, a dabbler, and never had enough time to become an expert in anything before his interest shifted. But he inoculated Annie with his enthusiasm, teaching her the intricacies of every one of his new interests and then giving her free rein to play with his toys whenever she had time to herself. And she was different from Ed in that she went deep into each, to the point where what were pastimes for Ed became raging passions in Annie. And in the process of learning about each one, she developed a love for science and engineering, and dreamed that one day she might become an inventor herself, another Edison.

It would have been perfect, had Mrs. Miller not been in the mix. Working for Ed Miller was a joy. Working for Allie was a very different story. Allie felt that hired help should know their place, and resented that Edward treated Annie as an equal, or worse, a kind of friend. Allie tried to get Annie fired at least four times a year, but each time Ed put a stop to the plot before it could be consummated.

Then Ed Miller was slain, in his den, while Annie slept soundly upstairs in her third-floor bedroom. If Annie had known that her Uncle Ed was being attacked two flights down, she would have willingly died trying to protect him. But she hadn't known. She'd been in what she came to see as a deep and guilty sleep while poor Ed's brains were being strewn about like so much garbage on his own divan.

No living soul in the Miller household gave a damn about what Annie—nothing more than the house girl—felt about the death of her old friend. Not Mrs. Hall, not the children, and certainly not Alicia. Of course, each of them had her own feelings to wrestle with, but at the same time, Annie had never felt so alone. She considered returning home, to Conestoga, but there was nothing for her there. Buffalo was her home now, and yet with Ed gone, working in the Miller household was like living behind enemy lines. She would have to wait for some other situation, yet she had to be careful. Alicia Miller was too well placed, and soon to be too wealthy, to double-cross.

Annie had managed to survive six months of Alicia, Mrs. Hall, and the girls. But as she hurried to the door to stop the bell from ringing so, she wished for about the millionth time that her Uncle Ed might still be sitting in his den, next to the front door, smiling at her as she bustled around, or calling her in to show her a catalogue of wonders that he'd received that day in the mail.

"Good afternoon," she said, opening the front door.

"Good afternoon," said a tall lady dressed in a heavy winter suit, oddly out of season. "Mrs. Warren to see Mrs. Miller."

Lord, no, Annie thought. Helen Warren, the wife of a prominent Ashwood surgeon, had telephoned the day before. She and her husband had unaccountably moved to Cleveland, of all places, almost three years before, but now had moved back to Buffalo. She'd called to set an appointment to pay her return respects to Allie, as she was expected to do with all the prominent women of the Ashwood Set. And Annie had completely forgotten to mention it to Allie. My goose is cooked but good, she thought.

"Won't you come in, Mrs. Warren?" she said in a quavering voice. "Allow me to seat you in the parlor while I fetch Mrs. Miller."

After getting Mrs. Warren situated, Annie climbed the stairs with a sinking stomach. This is going to be very, very bad.

At the top of the stairs, she turned right and went twenty feet to the door of Allie's bedroom. She rapped on the door.

"Mrs. Miller?" she said.

"What is it?" Alicia's voice replied.

"Mrs. Warren is here to see you," Annie said.

"Mrs. Warren? Helen Warren?"

"Yes, ma'am."

"I'm not expecting her," Allie said.

"I know, ma'am." Annie gulped. "She telephoned yesterday, but I neglected to make a note of it."

"She thinks I am expecting her?"

"Yes, ma'am. I'm terribly sorry."

The door flew open, and there stood Allie, still in her dressing gown, although it was already midmorning.

"Do I look like I am in any condition to receive visitors?" she hissed, her gown gaping open from neck to knees. Annie quickly looked down at her feet.

"No, ma'am," she said. "I mean to say, you look lovely as always, but no, not quite ready—"

"Not quite ready."

"No, ma'am."

"Look at me."

Annie lifted her eyes from the floor, scanning upward. Her body really is perfect, Annie thought, firm and curvy, the morning sun coming through the little tuft of hair between her legs, the breasts, half shadowed by the dressing gown, and then that strange golden snake *thing* around her throat. There was something about the woman's directness that made her wish Alicia would drop the dressing gown entirely, and something about Allie's challenging stance suggested that she would, if asked.

"What do you think?" Alicia said. "Is this what 'not quite ready' looks like to you?"

"No, ma'am."

"Thank you. And now I've got to think of something," Allie said. "I can't very well send her away." She thought a moment. "Go downstairs and tell her that I spilled something on my dress just before she arrived, and that I have to change clothes. I need ten minutes. Get her a drink or something to eat. You idiot!"

"I truly am sorry," Annie said, looking down again.

"We'll talk about this later," Allie said. "For now, buy me some time."

Annie went back downstairs and made the excuse seem quite credible. In ten minutes, Allie glided down the stairs, looking not only presentable but positively fetching, a slim jacket atop a high-collared shirtwaist and a form-fitting skirt. Annie hid out in the kitchen, at the rear of the house, pushing away the image of her mistress's body.

After Mrs. Warren had gone, Annie asked whether Mrs. Miller might like something for luncheon.

"I've lost my appetite, running around like a chicken with its head cut off, trying to get ready for a guest I didn't know was expected," she said.

Annie didn't think another apology would help. She stood there, downcast.

"To answer your question, no, I don't want any luncheon. And moreover, I've had it up to here with your lack of attentiveness. You've been like this from the start, but my husband always stuck up for you. Always excused your demeanor. That's over now. I will expect that you will pack your things and leave by the end of the month. I'll pay you two weeks' severance in addition to your regular wage, but we have no further need of your services here."

"But, ma'am," Annie began, wondering why she was trying to keep a job that she'd come to hate, "it won't happen again. I must have been distracted."

"No, it won't happen again, because—you are *fired*. End of the month, I want you gone."

"Yes ma'am," Annie said. "End of the month."

"Good. I'll have your last pay envelope ready for you then."

"May I also expect a letter of introduction—a good reference from you, ma'am?"

"I'll have to think about that," Allie said. "I'm certainly not going to guarantee it now, because then you'll lay about all month and do nothing. We'll see how things finish up, and then I'll decide."

"Very well, I understand."

"It'll be so good not to see your little face around here anymore," Allie said, angry that Annie didn't seem more disconsolate.

"I'm sorry you feel that way, ma'am," Annie said, touched by an odd mix of sadness and the unaccountable feeling of having been jilted.

THE WANT AD

NOW THAT SARAH HAD AN OFFICE, WITH NOT ONE BUT TWO VACANT desks, she needed to find some other detectives to help her launch a proper agency. Where to find them was a new problem. She couldn't very well ask the ladies of Ashwood for suggestions—the private sleuth business was a man's world, and most of the hired detectives in Buffalo and elsewhere were men hired by other men to keep tabs on their women. Ed Miller himself had hired detectives to do the self-same thing, and Arthur Pendle had countered by hiring a competing team to dig up dirt on Edward.

It was hot as blazes in the office, but the windows were open, and at her altitude a light breeze was lofting down Delaware Avenue, hinting that autumn couldn't be far away. But soon enough would come the killing winter, and the snow, and the squalls off the lake. Her finances would last only so long without paying work, and in a Buffalo winter, even straying wives had to hunker down by the fire with their dull husbands. If she didn't get things going now, the money might run out before she had another chance.

Putting a want ad in the newspaper seemed a likely step, so she flipped open her stenographer's pad and scribbled away for a little while, frowning and scratching out. After a few sheets of paper had been wadded up and thrown into the wastebasket, she looked at her handiwork with an air of satisfaction.

Man wanted. New detective agency seeks energetic investigator. Full- or part-time a possibility. Reply with résumé via this paper to AA Detective Agency.

I don't think I can improve on that, Sarah thought. Short and sweet. And the "AA Detective Agency" doesn't give anything away that the business is owned by a woman. That might turn away some men before I've been able to set the hook.

Sarah folded up the page of steno paper, put it in her bag, and went downtown to place the ad in the *Courier* and the *Commercial*, the two more serious newspapers in town. The ad duly placed, she had only to be patient and let the applications roll in.

NICE WORK,
IF YOU CAN GET IT

"Mr. Murphy is here to see you," Terry Penrose's secretary said, as the clock chimed half past five. A young man squeezed past her into the office, slightly out of breath.

Terry rocked forward in his chair and half-stood. "Jess," the DA said, shaking the young man's hand. "Good to see you again. It's been a while. How long, I wonder?"

"Six months?" Jess said.

"Could very well be. Time does fly. How have you been keeping? What are you doing these days?"

"Working in a hat store. That's why I'm so late—I had to work all day."

Terry smiled. "A good business. Everybody needs a lid. Twice a year, too."

"Maybe, but I never imagined I'd come all the way from Rhode Island to sell them. But I had to do something with myself, after you cut me loose."

"Your assignment had concluded," Penrose said. "And you had done a fine job."

"If by 'fine' you mean driving a man to suicide."

"You're being unkind to yourself. It was Arthur Pendle's decision to take his life—if that's what he did, and we'll never know. In any case, neither of us is responsible for another man's mad act."

Jess cleared his throat. "You're right. We'll never know for sure. Now why did you ask me here today, Mr. Penrose?"

"Because your father asked me to check on you. And I have something that may interest you."

"He did, did he? How much trouble does the honorable Judge Murphy think I could cause, selling hats?"

"He worries about you. You can't blame a father for that."

"He worries about how I might reflect on him. He's too great a man to have the likes of me dangling around his neck."

"Perhaps you've forgotten just how difficult things became back in Newport."

Jess shrugged. "If I do, there's always someone ready to remind me."

Terry took off his glasses and began to shine them with his handkerchief. "Your father's intentions are of the best, young man."

"I'm thirty," Jess said. "If my math is correct, only seven years younger than yourself."

"You look younger," Penrose said. "But at your age, I was already preparing myself to sit in this chair." Penrose pointed at his lap. "Your father wants the same for you."

"I'm sure," Jess said. "Everyone tires of being disappointed."

"Well. I didn't bring you here to spar with me. Your father asked me to look in on you, and as I said, I might have another little assignment for you."

Jess watched Terry's small hands fluttering in the air, like a pair of pale butterflies. "Anything that gets me out of the damn hat store," he said.

"Good, good. Then have a look at this." Terry picked up a folded newspaper from a stack of papers on his desk and spun it around so that Jess could read it. He pointed out a few small lines of type.

Man wanted. New detective agency seeks energetic investigator.
Full- or part-time a possibility. Reply with résumé via this paper
to AA Detective Agency.

"The AA Detective Agency," Jess said. "Never heard of them."

"You wouldn't have. It's as bright and shiny as a new-minted penny. But it's my business to keep an eye on people who keep their eyes on other people. And this one"—he tapped the page with his forefinger—"this one is potentially trouble. Does the name Sarah Payne ring a bell?"

Jess thought for a moment. "It's not an unusual name."

Terry smiled. "It's not. But in this case, it belongs to a very unusual woman."

"Do you want me to interview her? I don't work for the *Courier* anymore, obviously."

"No, I don't want you to interview her. Not exactly. I want you to apply for this position."

"Whatever for?"

"So that you can keep an eye on her."

Jess sat up straight. "I know you like keeping me guessing, but you're going to have to tell me more about this woman—and why you want someone watching her."

Terry chuckled. "I'm sorry, old prosecutor's habit. I do like to draw out a story. I'll come to the point. Mrs. Seth—Sarah—Payne was in love with Edward Miller, and he with her. You may recall that I brought her in for questioning soon after his murder. On a tip I received."

Jess nodded slowly. "I remember. You wanted me to do an article about her, fingering her for the crime."

"I never asked you to finger her, but I wouldn't have blamed you if you had." He laughed.

"Very funny."

"I thought so. Be that as it may. I told you at the time that she was a suspect and that you should have a look at her. But then you picked up on Arthur Pendle's scent, and we were overtaken by events."

"What interest do you have in Mrs. Payne? Miller's dead. The Pendles are dead. Seems like everything's gone by the board. And nothing is terribly unusual about opening a detective agency these days, with all the divorces going on."

"My instinct tells me that she'll resurrect the Miller case."

"I wonder how. She can't very well resurrect the man."

"No," Terry said, drawing out the word. "But there is an element to that whole mess that I didn't share with you last year. But as you were at the inquest, you heard a little—hopefully precious little—about it there. And I think Mrs. Payne knows about it."

"That sounds intriguing."

"Oh, it most certainly is. When Arthur was, oh, I don't know what to call it, *courting* Mrs. Miller, the two of them exchanged scores of letters. Some of them rather explicit. Arthur did the gentlemanly thing and burned the ones that Mrs. Miller sent to him, but Mrs. Miller couldn't bring herself to destroy the ones from him. Instead she squirreled them all away in a safety-deposit box."

"These were the ones purloined by Miller's detectives?"

"You have an excellent memory. Yes. They gained access to the box, and took away with them all the letters. Miller was going to use them as evidence against Pendle in his divorce suit."

"But that's all moot now. No Miller, no Pendle, no divorce case."

"That's the problem. I'm sure the letters still exist, somewhere," Terry said. "And I have a feeling that Miller told Mrs. Payne about them. And I'm concerned that she's smart enough to find them. Or knows where they are."

"So what?" Jess said. "They're of no use to anyone without a divorce action."

Terry picked up a pencil and tapped on his blotter. "If only it were so simple. I learned about these letters early—before Miller died—because his detectives visited me and read excerpts from a few of them. They wanted me to keep my beak out of it, and not intervene to save Pendle."

"Why would a bunch of someone else's love letters keep you from meddling?" Jess said, puzzled. "I'm lost, Mr. Penrose."

"Because Arthur was, shall we say, rather indiscreet in these letters. And not just about his cavortings with Mrs. Miller. They were also a kind of diary in which he recorded things he was doing—*professionally*, one might say." Terry paused. "With me. For me."

Jess tilted his head back. "*Now* I understand. You can't have these letters seeing the light of day."

Terry rapped on the desk with his knuckles. "If they still exist, they need to be located and disposed of before I start my run for governor. And that's why I want you to use your boyish charm to land that position at the AA Detective Agency. Keep an eye on Mrs. Payne, which if you remember her so well, will not be hard duty—in a manner of speaking. If she doesn't find those letters, no harm done. If she does, though, you'll need to get your hands on them before she attempts to use them for her own ends."

"Understood," Jess said. "And what do I get out of it?"

"You get out of the hat business, for one."

"You know what I mean."

"You'll be well compensated for your time, as previously. And if you locate and secure these missing letters, there'll be a substantial additional reward."

"How substantial?"

Terry stared at Jess. "Jess, I'm doing you a favor," he said. "Beyond that, you'll have to trust me. Your father and I go back all the way to our college days. I'm not going to cheat you."

"I don't think you will."

"Then what do you say?"

"Why not? What have I got to lose?"

"Good. Now before you meet with Mrs. Payne, you and I should go over a few things. Get our story straight, as it were."

"You let me know when you want me to come by. In the meantime, I'll reply to the ad."

"Very good. And when you speak with your father, please tell him I send my best regards."

Jess smiled flatly. "I think you'll probably speak with him before I do."

"Have a good evening, all the same," Penrose said.

AVENGING ANGELS

The two newspapers ran Sarah's ad several times, and in the morning mail the following week there arrived a little stack of replies, neatly wrapped in paper and twine. Sarah was delighted. *Somewhere in there may be the man I'm looking for.*

She cut the twine away, removed the paper wrapping, and spilled the contents across her big desk. Inside were a good dozen envelopes, of various types and sizes. Some were neatly addressed, and others were almost illegible scribbles of ink. A few looked as though someone had reused an old envelope. *Haven't people heard about first impressions?* she thought, wrinkling her nose. She held up one particularly rumpled envelope that looked as though it had been splattered with little dots of oil. She sniffed it. Bacon. She put the ones that were neat and tidy into a pile. About a dozen remained.

She slit the first envelope open, and a little snippet of newsprint fell out when she unfolded the letter inside.

Dear Sir:

Pursuant to your item in this paper (enclosed), I wish to apply for the position of Investigator. I have extensive experience and indeed am a world-renowned detective. Address 221B Baker Street, London.

Sincerely, S. Holmes

Very funny, she thought. *Why would someone waste a stamp on a practical joke?* She threw Sherlock's letter in the wastebasket. *Maybe the next one will be better.*

It wasn't, or not by much. One by one, she tossed out eleven letters without the requested résumés, résumés without relevant experience, and a few more that were simply bizarre. When there were only two left, she was almost afraid to open the first. Here goes nothing, she thought, and slit it open.

This one was neatly written in a schooled hand, and on a sheet of decent paper, too. It was from a Mr. Jesse Murphy, who announced that he was a former reporter for the *Courier*, looking for a change of career. In the envelope was a neatly typed résumé. Now this one looks promising, she thought, setting it aside. I'll call him and set up a conference.

She turned to the other remaining envelope. It, too, was very neatly addressed, but in a woman's hand. Odd. A man with a secretary wouldn't likely be looking to hire on with a private detective agency, she thought. She slit the envelope open.

Inside was a typed résumé and a handwritten cover letter, both on very nice ladies' stationery, smelling faintly of clover. This is strange, she thought. I'd obviously advertised for a man. She smoothed the letter out on her desk.

Buffalo, NY
August 10, 1902

Dear AA Detective Agency,

First, please understand that I recognize that your advertisement clearly stated a preference for male candidates for your Investigator position. I can't apologize for being a woman, naturally, but I would nevertheless like to request your consideration.

Sarah chuckled. Sounds like a plucky lady.

Recently I lost a long-term position as a domestic, in which capacity I managed a complex household and not infrequently had to solve difficult problems and act with considerable discretion. In addition, for many years I have dreamed of becoming a professional woman, preferably a detective, as I have great interest and some skill in inventing new mechanical and electrical devices that could benefit a modern investigative agency.

I do hope you will give my enclosed résumé your earnest consideration, in which spirit it is offered. I can be contacted at my

*current position until the end of this month. Your favorable
interest may be directed to me c/o Mrs. Edward Miller, 101
Ashwood Street.*

*Yours very sincerely,
Annie Murray.*

Sarah almost dropped the letter. Annie Murray? Care of the Millers?
Why, this must be Annie, their maid. Sarah had met Annie many times,
back when she and Seth were frequent guests at the Millers' home. This is a
coincidence too rare to let pass by, she thought. And after all, my girlhood
dream was to be a detective, too. I ought to at least give her a fair hearing.

She pulled out two pieces of her new agency stationery and began to
write to Mr. Jesse Murphy and Miss Annie Murray. Murphy and Murray,
she thought. We'd certainly have some fun on St. Patrick's Day here in
the office with a couple of Irish around.

16

JESS MURPHY

Two days later, precisely on time—3:30 in the afternoon—there was a rap at the outer office door. Sarah got up, smoothed her hair and dress, and opened it. On the threshold was a good-looking young man, late twenties or early thirties perhaps, of middle height and build, with abundant sandy hair that had been creased down in a ring by his derby, which he was holding in his left hand. He wore rimless gold spectacles, which made him look a little older and more studious than he might have otherwise.

"Mr. Jesse Murphy?" she said.

"Yes," he said. "Well, Jess Murphy. I'm here for my conference with the AA Detective Agency." It sounded a bit like a question, his voice rising at the end of the sentence.

"I'm Miss Payne, head of the agency."

"Yes, Miss Payne," he said, showing no surprise at all that the head of the agency was a woman, and a stunning one at that.

This was not what Sarah had expected. She'd assumed he'd think she was the office girl. "Do we know each other?"

Murphy looked somewhat taken aback. "Oh, no. I meant, very pleased to meet you, Miss Payne."

The two sat down in the outer office. Sarah picked up his neatly prepared résumé. "It's not Jesse, then?" she said. "It says here 'Jesse J. Murphy.'"

"Only my parents call me Jesse," Jess said, smiling crookedly. "My full name is Jesse James Murphy, after *the* Jesse James. My father loves those outlaw stories from the West."

"But you're from Rhode Island."

"True enough, but if Mother hadn't had family in Newport, I'm sure Father would have pulled up stakes for the Arizona Territory."

"Newport is quite an impressive place," Sarah said.

"I can assure you that I'm not from *that* Newport. My father is a lawyer, and my mother is a schoolteacher."

"Both very creditable occupations," Sarah said. "You know, when we received your résumé, I felt sure I recognized your name, perhaps from your time at the *Courier*."

"Yes, I wrote for them for about a year."

"Not now, though? Are you with a different paper? Your résumé didn't specify where you are currently employed."

"No," Jess said, smiling a slightly crooked smile. "I couldn't get a job selling newspapers in this city, let alone writing for them."

"Why would that be?"

"I rubbed someone the wrong way, I guess. They let me go in February."

Sarah didn't quite know how to respond.

"I shouldn't have said it that way," he said, shifting in his chair. "Suffice it to say that sometimes a reporter can be *too* good at finding things out," he continued. "And that's why I think I'd be very well suited to detective work."

"But you haven't had any detective experience."

Jess looked at her. "I don't mean this to sound tart, but I wonder how much detective experience this place has now?" He looked around the vacant office.

"That sounds pretty tart to me."

"I'm sorry, I didn't mean—"

"It's fine. You're not wrong," Sarah said. "I *won't* say it doesn't sting a little to hear it, but it's true all the same. We don't have much experience. We're new."

Jess leaned forward. "That was really the point I was trying—poorly, it would seem—to make. As a reporter, I have written about many, many things I knew very little about before I began digging into them. But I know how to ask questions, I know how to learn, and I can tell when I'm being hoodwinked."

"Fine qualities."

"And I do have an excellent memory for names and faces. For example, the moment you opened the door I knew exactly who you were."

"And who exactly am I?" Sarah couldn't tell if she liked the young man for his candor, or was beginning to find him irritating.

"I covered the Edward Miller case for the *Courier*. I sat through the entire inquest."

"I see," Sarah said. "Yes, I suppose then I'd be familiar."

"Oh, very," he said, with that same crooked smile. Something about the way he drew out the syllables of "very" made the hair on Sarah's neck stand out.

"You know the whole sordid tale, I take it?" she said.

"More than I ever wrote about, that's for sure."

"Now that's intriguing. What do you know that hasn't come out?"

He fidgeted with the hat on his lap. "As one example—long before the inquest, I knew you were in Mr. Miller's house the night of his death. This was when the cops were trying to pin the thing on you. And," he added hastily, "I knew very well you weren't complicit in his death. So I kept that detail to myself, even when I could have written the kinds of article that the *Courier* was desperate for me to write."

"Ought I to be thanking you, Mr. Murphy?"

"No, no, not at all. I wanted to show you that I knew how to do my job—and do it ethically, which isn't something reporters normally care much about."

"That took courage."

"Courageous or unwise, I'm not sure which," Jess said. "That's why I was sacked."

"Do tell."

"I'll be happy to. I started snooping around in the affairs of Mr. Arthur Pendle. You see, directly after the murder, I made him out to be the number one suspect. He had motive, means, and opportunity. And I knew from some of my police contacts that he was involved in some pretty rough stuff. I started talking with people. Here, and in Connecticut, and in Maine—where he was from. And then I went and talked with him, too. Face to face, twice. The last time I saw him, he more or less threw me out of his house, because he knew I'd uncovered things that no one else had dared to try to uncover. He was untouchable, that's what everyone told me. But I wasn't about to let it go."

Jess sighed deeply and went on. "And that's what got me fired. Someone political—high up, too, I'm sure—made a call to the *Courier*'s editor-in-chief about me. My editor pulled me aside and said that if I didn't stop nosing around in Arthur Pendle's business, I would be gone. You can imagine how I took that. I was fired the same day."

"That's unfortunate," Sarah said. "And that's why you say other newspapers won't hire you?"

"Precisely. My reputation now is a fellow who won't take a direct order. Newsrooms are like the Army. You follow orders, or you get court-martialed."

"I see."

"Now, if I may," Jess said, "what do you know about *me*?"

"That you wrote for the *Courier*," Sarah said. "You're from Rhode Island. And the other things that are on your résumé."

"I could easily have falsified all of that."

Sarah was nonplussed. "Did you?"

"Not a word of it. But you don't know anything that I haven't told you. Which could all be lies."

"That's a very strange thing to say, Mr. Murphy."

"It oughtn't to be—not in a detective agency. I'm not trying to be critical. I am trying to demonstrate that I can bring a useful frame of mind to your agency. A frame of mind that accepts *nothing*, and questions *everything*. The frame of mind that a good reporter has. Or should have."

"You do have a sharp tongue, but I am beginning to like you, Mr. Murphy, all the same," Sarah said. "You have an edge."

"Thank you. Now tell me," he said, "don't you think I could help you here? Detective experience or no? What I have—what I *am*—is something you can harness. I loathe that certain people get away with things because they *can*, and that no one's willing to stop them."

Sarah stared down at her hands, clasped before her, and realized for the first time that her knuckles had gone white from clenching them together so tightly.

"I'll need to think about it a bit. Besides, I don't know yet whether we can afford you."

"I made fifty dollars a week at the *Courier*," he said. "But I'm not making nearly that now. I'm working at Adair's, the men's hat store over on Main. I'm lucky to make twenty dollars now."

"That must be difficult to get by."

"You were kind enough not to judge me by the condition of my only decent suit," he said. "I brushed it so much this morning that when I was done, I thought I could see daylight through it."

Sarah laughed.

"How about this," he said. "Pay me what you can. I'll keep working at the hat shop part-time. I live with two other fellows now, near Michigan and Vine, so I live cheaply. You probably wouldn't believe how cheaply. When the agency is on its feet, you can pay me more. I've put up with the hat shop for six months, so I can put up with it for a little longer. Especially if I have something interesting to sink my teeth into."

Sarah slid her chair back. She stood and stuck out her hand. "I know I ought to think about this more, but I haven't time to waste," she said. "I'd like to offer you the position."

Jess rose and took her hand, didn't so much as shake it as hold it lightly in his.

"You won't regret your decision," he said.

"I can't imagine I will," Sarah said, thrown off-balance a little by this somewhat peculiar fellow.

"I can start when you like," he said. "I have to work at the shop all day tomorrow, but I'm off on Friday."

"Then let's try Friday. Perhaps come by a little before lunchtime, if that would suit you, and we'll get started discussing the future. Then we'll have something to eat to celebrate."

"Capital," he said. "I'll be here then."

Sarah smiled. Jess gave her his little twisted grin, and left. Well, that was easier than I'd imagined, she thought. But I still should meet Annie Murray this afternoon, if only to let her down somehow.

ANNIE MURRAY

ANNIE MUST HAVE BEEN WATCHING FOR HER, BECAUSE THE DOOR-bell rang only a few minutes after Sarah got home from the office, after having retrieved Maggie from Mrs. McKelvey next door. The neighbor had been kind enough to volunteer to look after the little one until Sarah found someone she could trust.

Maggie was chattering away while Sarah made her a snack in the kitchen, which was a happy place again, now that the midnight interrogation was long past. It was a spacious, cheerful room, with a table large enough for six, wide countertops, and a white and black tile floor. The kitchen faced west, so in the afternoon the setting sun turned the room and everything in it shades of red and orange, which for some reason Maggie found unspeakably funny.

"Eat your snack, honey," Sarah said, wiping her hands on a towel. "I'll see who's at the door. We'll have supper a little later tonight."

The little girl nodded and tucked into her cucumber and mayonnaise sandwich. The bell summoned Sarah a second time, and she trotted to the front of the house, forgetting to leave the towel behind. She opened the front door with the towel waving in one hand. Standing on the porch was a pretty, young lady in a pale blue summer dress, with a crocus flower pinned to the front, and wearing what looked like a man's slouch hat, but also in pale blue, atop a mess of light brown curls.

"Annie!" Sarah said. "Surprise!"

"Mrs. Payne? What are you doing here?"

"I live here. Come in!"

Annie looked confused and remained frozen on the doorstep. "But I'm supposed to—"

"I know. You're here for the AA Detective Agency. That's me."

"It is?"

"Yes, it is. Come in, come in."

"Well, thank you," Annie said.

"You're right on time," Sarah said, showing her into the parlor. "You always did seem like the punctual type."

"I think it's important. But I arrived well before you got home. I stood at the corner of Utica and Norwood for an hour." She laughed. "I'm surprised someone didn't call the police, but no one seemed to notice me."

"Compliments for being so inconspicuous. I had no idea you were watching. Too much in my own world."

"How have you been, Mrs. Payne? My deepest condolences. I understand your husband passed away recently."

"I'm doing well enough. And thank you. It was only in May that Seth died, but as you can see I've dispensed with the widow's weeds already. Didn't feel like me. I came back to Buffalo to start over."

"That's wonderful," Annie said. "About starting over, I mean."

"And condolences are due to you, as well. On Mr. Miller's passing."

"He was a very special man. I'd known him my entire life."

"I had the pleasure of knowing him only for a little while, but I agree with you—he certainly was special."

"To you, as well, to us both—if—" Annie stumbled, not knowing quite what to say.

"In different ways. I understand. You read the newspapers. And I'm sure we both miss him every day, each of us in her own fashion."

Annie nodded, blinking back a tear. "I'm sorry to be so morose," she said.

Sarah waved her hand. "Not a word of it. I can tell you that if I let myself, I can become very blue over it. It was starting to bring me down so, that it goaded me to do something about it instead of mope my life away."

"May I ask what you're going to do? I could perhaps take away a lesson."

"Of course. I decided that justice was not done for Eddie— Mr. Miller—"

"It most certainly was not."

"—and that it would make me feel somewhat better if I could get justice for him, however much after-the-fact. So I determined to open my own detective agency."

"When I saw the advertisement in the paper, I had no idea that you were the owner."

"I'll tell you all about it," Sarah said. "I happen to love your outfit, by the way. Wherever did you find a crocus this time of year?"

Annie smiled and looked down, fiddling with the little flower. "It's silk," she said. "But it does look real, doesn't it?"

"It does. And it means you're cheerful, as I'm sure you know."

"It means I'm cheerful?"

"Oh yes, the language of flowers. Every one of them has a different meaning. I've been reading about it lately. Crocuses are the symbol of cheerfulness."

"I suppose I'm normally a cheerful person," Annie said, smiling. "Though lately things have been a little discouraging."

"I'm terribly sorry about that," Sarah said. "Mrs. Miller let you go, I take it?"

Annie tried not to roll her eyes, and failed. "I knew the handwriting was on the wall from the time Mr. Miller passed. But it's been a difficult adjustment. She—Mrs. Miller, I mean—fired my sister, too."

"Ruth, is it? I didn't know she was working at the Millers."

"You have a good memory, Miss. Yes, Ruth, my younger sister. She started at the Millers about a year ago, looking after the youngest girl, Millie. She loves children."

"Who is the pretty lady, Mama?" said a little voice from the doorway. Maggie had finished her cucumber sandwich and come to investigate. Annie smiled broadly.

"You must be Maggie," Annie said.

"I am. Who are you?"

"Margaret," Sarah said sternly, "that's very rude. You know that's not how you talk to adults. Apologize to Miss Murray."

"It's quite all right," Annie said.

"No, it's not. Maggie?"

"I'm sorry, Miss Murray. I ought to have said, 'I'm delighted to make your acquaintance, madam.'"

"Well, I'm delighted to make your acquaintance too, Miss Maggie. You're even prettier than I heard."

"You're *very* pretty too," the little girl said. "I love your little flower."

Annie unpinned the silk crocus from her dress and held it out to Maggie. "Then I want you to have it," she said.

"May I, Mama? May I keep it?"

"Annie, you really oughtn't to," Sarah said.

"I'd love for her to have it."

"Then you may keep it, Maggie. Now thank Miss Murray properly and go upstairs and play a little before supper."

The little girl thanked Annie, and the young woman held out her hand. Instead of shaking it, Maggie threw her arms around Annie.

Sarah and Annie laughed. "Now go along, Maggie," Sarah said.

Maggie disappeared up the stairs, clutching her silk crocus to her chest.

"She's adorable," Annie said.

"Thank you. I love her to pieces, naturally. And she seems to love you, too. Now, then. Where were we? Both you and your sister are looking for a new situation, I take it?"

"Yes, and when I saw your advertisement, I thought there was no harm in trying. I've wanted to be a detective for as long as I can remember."

"As have I," Sarah said.

"Such a series of coincidences," Annie said. "Can you tell me a little about the AA Detective Agency?"

"We're downtown in the Hudson Building, across from the courthouse. The double *A* stands for Avenging Angel."

"Ohhh . . . I do love the name!" Annie said. "How exciting! And to think you could bring the men behind Mr. Miller's death to justice."

"Men?" Sarah said.

"I certainly never thought a woman did it. And the more I think about it—and think about the things I saw in the house as the trouble got worse—yes, I do think that there had to have been more than one person in on it."

Sarah leaned forward. "Why do you think that?"

"Mrs. Miller was mixed up with Arthur Pendle, as you know. And Mr. and Mrs. Pendle were at the house a lot, for years, before the troubles began. I observed Mr. Pendle very carefully—he was a very *interesting* man."

"He was that."

"First off, regardless of what anyone said in that inquest, I think Mr. Pendle was perfectly capable of killing someone. Not even speaking specifically of Mr. Miller. I mean to say, if I'd heard that Arthur Pendle had murdered someone, I wouldn't have batted an eye. He could be very high-strung, but at the same time he could be extraordinarily cold and rational. I almost felt sometimes as though his occasional outbursts, or flares of temper, even, were calculated. For effect."

"How fascinating. Go on. I'm very interested in your observations."

Annie smiled nervously. "You are?"

"Very much. Please, go on."

Annie settled in her chair. "All right. That's Mr. Pendle. But then there were a group of people that he—Pendle—was associated with. Sometimes he'd come to the house with one or two of them. They never said much, but they'd sit with Mr. Miller in the den. I got a very bad feeling from them."

"Do you know who they were?"

"I don't, but they were rough types. One thing that fascinated me about Mr. Pendle—he knew how to behave, how to fit in, with anyone. From the upper crust to these rough types he'd bring by. Mrs. Miller is the same. I think that's part of what they saw in each other."

"Perhaps because Mrs. Miller is equally abrasive with everyone," Sarah said.

"She can be difficult to like," Annie said. "But I will tell you this—the people who do like her, *love* her. Mr. Pendle would have done anything— and I mean *anything*—for her. And frankly, Mr. Miller hung onto her a lot longer than most men would have. She has a certain something."

"She has charisma."

"Charisma?"

"It's a mysterious quality that some people have. One which draws other people to them."

"Perfect," Annie said. "What an interesting world you're in."

"And one that I know far too little about. I don't know if I'm a natural detective, or if I merely want to be one."

"I'm sure you'll be very successful."

"I hope so, but there are days when I have my doubts. For example—"
She paused.

"Yes?" Annie asked.

"For example. How long have you been here now?"

"I don't know. Ten minutes?"

"Let's say ten minutes. Fifteen, at most."

"All right."

"You were waiting for me on the corner of Utica, you said."

"Yes."

"For how long, do you think?"

"Almost exactly one hour."

"And in that time, no one called the police? No one seemed in the least suspicious of you?"

"Not so far as I could tell."

"I didn't notice you either, although I must have walked right past you on my way from the trolley."

Annie smiled. "That you did."

"All right then. You came here, and in ten minutes you have demonstrated how carefully you observed Arthur Pendle, Mrs. Miller, and Pendle's cronies. You observed, too, your own visceral reaction to them."

Annie nodded, but looked confused.

"My point is this," Sarah said. "I have a hunch you may be a better natural detective than I am. Oh, I like to read and I have a good mind. But you are more observant than I am. I breezed right past you, in my own world."

"You weren't looking for me."

"And neither is the subject of any investigation. But you managed to be inconspicuous. I always stick out like a sore thumb."

"That's because—look at you," Annie said. "You're stunning. I'm run-of-the-mill."

"You are anything but run-of-the-mill. My daughter thinks you're lovely, and she's always right about these things. And frightfully blunt about them too. You simply have a way of blending in, when you want to, or need to. That's a gift."

"Well, thank you."

"And you study people—don't deny it."

"That I can't deny, Miss. I find people fascinating."

"Right. I oughtn't to be going on like this, but I do want you to know you're an excellent candidate."

Annie brightened. "Thank you for saying that, Miss!"

"There's only one little problem."

"Yes?"

"I've already hired someone for the position, just today."

Annie looked crestfallen. "Probably best I gave that crocus away," she said. "But I understand. I'm sure there are many better candidates with more experience."

"Please don't be discouraged, Annie. I'm very, very impressed—"

"You know, I'm a good cook," Annie blurted. "I keep a clean house. If you don't already have a domestic, I know I would simply adore little Maggie, and my sister, Ruth, could help. You could pay me and Ruth whatever you can, and we would split it up. As long as we have a roof over our heads, we don't need much money. I'd simply love to work for you, Miss, and I could always observe what a detective does, at least."

"No," Sarah said. "That's not what I was thinking at all. I don't want you to keep house."

"Oh, darn. I'm sorry to hear that," Annie said.

"No, what I'd like you to do is to join my new agency. As a detective. If Ruth is interested, I do very much need someone to look after Maggie and keep house. But she would be paid for her work, and you would be paid for yours."

"But you have already hired someone at the agency," Annie said. "And I can't be nearly so well qualified as he is. I assume it's a man."

"He is, but he's new to this too. So now I've found two members of the team in one day, and that must be fate, so I'm not ignoring it. As I said, you have qualities and abilities that I don't. Oh, and—I neglected to mention the best part—you know the Miller household as well as anyone can. If we're investigating Mr. Miller's death, you could be very, very useful."

Annie sat back in her chair, stunned. "I don't know what to say."

"How about yes? You and Ruth will live here, with me and Maggie. I have three empty rooms upstairs, gathering dust. You and I will go to the office in the day, and Ruth can handle everything here. See Maggie to school when it starts, do the marketing. I assume she can cook."

"Oh, she's a much better cook than I am," Annie said. "This sounds so wonderful—I could never have imagined such a thing could happen to me."

"So it's a yes?"

"Yes, most certainly it's a yes!"

"Wonderful. You two move in as soon as you are able, and we'll get started."

"I should probably ask my sister to make me an outfit like yours," Annie said. "I have working clothes for housework, and a couple of dresses, like this one, but I haven't needed anything like what you are wearing, until now."

"No need," Sarah said. "I'm going to take you shopping downtown. We'll get you fitted up right away."

And with that, the Avenging Angel Detective Agency had filled up its new office.

THE OUROBOROS

The lamps were off, the girls and Mrs. Hall were finally in bed, and Hartshorn tiptoed down the corridor to Allie's room. It wouldn't do—who knew whether Mrs. Hall could keep a secret?—to be *too* obvious. It had been a long day, and he was looking forward to snuggling up against Alicia's curves.

Her room was dark and quiet, the only sound the jingling of occasional harness bells along Ashwood. He slid into bed beside her, and she turned on her side, toward him. He curled his arm around her and pulled her close. She seemed to be dozing, or pretending to.

"Alicia?" Hartshorn said, after a few quiet minutes had passed. He looked down into her rich, dark hair, spilling over his shoulder. He could feel her gold torc pressing into his skin.

"Yes?" she murmured.

"May I ask you a question?"

"You just did."

"I mean another one."

"I was kidding. Go on," she said.

"I've been wondering," he said. "You always wear this—*thing* around your neck." He tugged gently at the collar.

"True. What of it?"

"What is it?"

"It's an ouroboros."

"I know that. But you never take it off. Have you always had it?"

"Not always, no."

"Where did you get it?"

"I thought you were going to ask me one question," she said, propping herself up on an elbow.

"It's unusual, that's all. I've often wondered about it."

"Arthur gave it to me," she said, touching the metal collar gently. "It symbolizes eternity. Rebirth. The snake eating its own tail. He gave it to me because we used to say it was hard to tell sometimes where he stopped and I began."

"And you never take it off?"

"I can't."

"Why not?"

Alicia slowly closed her eyes, remembering. "Because when Arthur gave it to me, he took me to the old man who made it—at Benedict Brothers, in the jewelry district in New York. And he put it around my neck, and had the hinge sealed shut. Soldered. And I can tell you, it burned the hell out of my skin when the jeweler did it. So now it can't be removed unless it's cut off."

"You let him do that to you?"

"Why not? It made me—oh, never mind."

She flopped onto her back, staring at the ceiling. "Now is that all?"

"Did you love Arthur? Really *love* him?"

She let out an exaggerated sigh. "What kind of a question is that?"

"I want to know you better," he said. "Here we are, in bed together, and yet I feel I don't know much about you."

Oh God, not this, Alicia thought.

"You know me well enough, Bert. Better than most anyone."

"But I want to know more."

"Yes, you want to know more. Not about me, though. About Arthur."

"Yes. Arthur. Did you love him?"

Alicia lay there for a moment, considering. "He was my golden boy," she said. It was honest, and in an eyeblink, she longed to take it back. It was only opening a door that she ought to have slammed in Bert's face. I'll never learn, she thought.

"Golden boy?"

"I don't know why I called him that. He was young, handsome, fearless. He showed me the way out of a life I hated. He was like Alexander the Great. The perfect man."

"I say," Bert sniffed, "that's awfully strong language."

Allie looked daggers at him in the moonlight. "You jealous, Bert? What's the problem? You're the one fucking me now."

"Alicia, sometimes you can be simply crude."

"And sometimes you're an old stick-in-the-mud who stirs up trouble where there needn't be any. Why do you care about Arthur—or anything—before this moment? Here's an idea," she said, warming to her topic. "What say we play a game. It's called 'The Past is Dead.' We pretend that every single new moment is the beginning of our lives, and we never talk about anything that may have happened before that."

"I'm sorry I asked," Bert said.

"So am I. Bert, sometimes you are such a hemorrhoid. You really are."

"Don't say things like that, Alicia."

"Oh, fine then. What else do you want to know about Arthur? A list of things we did together? How about that?"

"No, I don't want to hear anything like that," he said.

She smiled a terrible smile. "Well, guess what, Bert? I'm not going to tell you anything that he and I got up to. Some of it would be very strong medicine for your delicate constitution. But you know what I am going to do?"

Bert sighed, wishing he could be catapulted out of bed, nude if necessary, and land someplace else. Anywhere else.

"What are you going to do?"

"I'm going to *show* you. And when I do, you'll be able to imagine how things *were*. And the best part of it is that we won't be talking about the past—we'll be living it, in the present. I don't mind taking a trip down memory lane, either."

Bert hadn't time to respond before Allie had cupped the lawyer's balls in her hand, working him up with the other. He lay back, vanquished. She straddled him and impaled herself with a low moan, rocking back and forth, and he was beginning to fall into his usual trance when Alicia unceremoniously slipped her thumb up his ass. Hartshorn gave a little grunt of surprise, or something. Hard to tell.

"You like that?" she said, looking down at his red face. He craned his neck and looked down at her arm disappearing between his legs.

"Uh, it's—different. Peculiar."

"I want you to like it."

"Well, I suppose I do. I like whatever you do."

"Maybe we need to up the ante a little," she said, and then without waiting for his reaction, worked two and then three of her fingers in. This made the attorney yelp.

"What in the devil! That hurts—"

"Give it a second—you'll see," she said, leaning back and pushing her fingers deeper, until they were swallowed whole. Hartshorn moaned, as much in resignation as in pleasure, and gave himself up to her. It hurt like hell, but as she had promised, there was something compelling about it, like salt on sweet. When he unloaded, Allie smiled down at him indulgently.

"Now see?" she said. She took her fingers out of him and lay down by his side as he wheezingly caught his breath. "Told you you'd like that. And now you know something—that you didn't."

Hartshorn didn't say anything, lying there with his belly heaving. She put her head on his shoulder and rested with him for five minutes or so, and then reached down and felt his balls again. She rolled them around in her palm, squeezing each one carefully, assessing them like a person at the market inspecting produce.

"I suspect there's still something left in there," she whispered, "And besides, it's my turn. I'm going to wash up, and when I come out here, we're going to have some more fun."

Allie slid out of bed and tiptoed into the bathroom, closing the door behind her. She washed Bert off her hands, feeling a trifle disgusted when she thought about the body lying on the bed. Old, still portly, fish-belly white. *He wants to know what Arthur was like, does he? I wouldn't have the heart to tell him that he's not at all like Arthur, my golden boy, only thirty-six, and a champion college athlete at that. And creative! No one could imagine some of those things . . . oh well.* She wasn't looking forward to getting fucked tonight by her lawyer, but that's what things had come to these days, and it would have to do.

She urinated and then walked back into the bedroom, where Hartshorn was still lying on top of the sheets, shriveled. He was snoring.

He's asleep? Allie thought, wanting to punch him in his flaccid sack. *God, nothing like Arthur, who would have popped right back up again by now, ready to go. I'll be damned.* She jumped into bed, which bounced like a trampoline, creaking like old machinery. Hartshorn woke up. "Oh, Allie," he said, "I must've dozed off."

"You hear that sound?" she said as the squeaking bed slowly settled down on its springs.

"Yes," Bert said. "I think we may have broke the thing. I'll get us a new one downtown." He attempted a winsome smile. "Just now, I'm tired, thanks to you, dear Alicia."

"Well, guess what, dear Bert? You're not going to sleep yet. You're going to do whatever you've got to do to get that thing"—she flicked his limp organ with a finger—"up again and inside me, and make this bed creak like a ship in a storm."

"Allie, I don't think I—"

"Run along," she said, "behind the dressing screen, and play with yourself. I don't care what you have to do, so long as you come back out here and show me what you're made of."

Bert dutifully climbed out of bed and padded over behind the dressing screen. He was there quite a while, but when he finally did reappear, he was at half-mast. Allie leaned up on one elbow.

"I suppose we'll have to work with what we've got," she sighed. "Now hurry up, before you lose it."

Bert was tired and confused, and once again the errant thought crossed his mind that he wasn't charging this woman a cent for any of the hours he was spending. But he kept at it stolidly, until he forgot everything except the sight of her golden torc as she arched her head backward into the pillow.

THREE'S A CROWD

WHEN JESS ARRIVED ON FRIDAY FOR HIS FIRST DAY OF WORK, SARAH and Annie were both in the office to greet him.

"Very pleased to meet you, Mr. Murphy," Annie said.

He looked at her with an eyebrow cocked. "Are you our office girl?"

After a short but uncomfortable silence, Sarah said, "Oh no. Annie is another Avenging Angel. She's a detective."

"Well, knock me over with a feather," Jess said.

"Why?" Annie said, not terribly amused.

"No reason," he said. "I didn't know we'd be a threesome so quickly."

"I predict we will all get along famously," Sarah said.

"I have no doubt of it," Jess said.

"We have two main challenges off the bat," Sarah went on. "One is to start looking at what might have been missed in the investigation of the Miller case. The other is to find other cases that will pay the bills."

"I might suggest I take the lead on the Miller case," Jess said. "As I mentioned to you, Miss Payne, I followed that story quite closely," he said. "I'm sure I know it better than Miss Murray. I was at the inquest, and met all of the personages."

"Um, I worked for the Millers in their home for *four years*," Annie said. "I think I know the family particularly well."

"You worked for them? In what capacity?"

"I was in domestic service."

"I see," he said.

Annie was taking a distinct dislike to Jess, but wrestled it down. Not on my first day, for God's sake, she thought. "Miss Sarah, perhaps Mr. Murphy and I can work on it together? You are probably best suited to finding new clients, since you are the head of the agency."

"That makes sense to me," Sarah said, "and it'll give the two of you a chance to get to know each other."

"I thought I was coming to work for you," Jess said.

"And you are. We'll all be working together."

"I see," he said, seeming somewhat disappointed.

"In any case," Annie said a trifle brusquely, "I know one thing we could look at that was never presented at the inquest. Something that even you, Mr. Murphy, couldn't have seen."

"What's that, Annie?" Sarah said, before Jess could respond.

"I was at the house—that morning, and I know for a fact that there was a photographer who took pictures of everything in the den. And of Mr. Miller, I'm sorry to say."

"I *knew* I recognized you," he said to Annie. "I saw you at their house— after the murder. I was with the *Courier* then."

"That was a dreadful day," Annie said. "I remember only bits and pieces of it."

"It's true they never brought those photographs out at the inquest," Sarah said. "I wonder why not?"

"They may show something they didn't want to be seen," Jess said. "That's the way these people work. At a simple inquest, they can suppress anything they want. Then, if it never comes to an actual trial, it's suppressed forever."

"I know I don't want to, but if we could see those photos, we might obtain some clues," Sarah said. "But we probably can't get at them."

"But we can," Jess replied. "A fellow I know from my *Courier* days is buddies with the cop who handles the weekend shift at the evidence locker. If we borrow them on a Saturday, and get them back on Sunday before anyone is the wiser, I'm sure I can get them. They'll be glass negatives, though. Not prints."

"Not a lot of time to make photographic prints," Sarah said. "And we can't very well take them to a local camera shop."

"I know how we can copy them," Annie said.

"Don't keep us in suspense," Jess said.

Annie ignored him. "Mr. Miller was a camera enthusiast. He set up a little darkroom in the basement of the house. He liked to go down there when Mrs. Miller was in one of her moods."

"I remember him telling me something about that," Sarah said.

"So, a couple of times when Mrs. Miller was away from the city, Mr. Miller showed me how to use the equipment."

"And you remember how to do it?" Sarah asked.

"It's easy. And I was so amazed by the whole thing—it's like magic, watching an image develop in a little tray of chemicals."

"The *Courier* has a darkroom, of course," Jess said. "Quite an extensive one, as you would imagine. But how would we smuggle you in, I wonder?"

"We wouldn't need to go that far," Annie said. "I can develop them in a closet or even put up some curtains in a basement. Anyplace dark. That's what Mr. Miller had done. What we need is an enlarger—it looks like a large camera on a stand—to magnify the negatives. Then we'll need some chemicals and paper, but we can buy those at any number of places here in the city without arousing the least suspicion."

"Is there a way to borrow an enlarger?" Sarah asked.

Jess smiled. "Sure there is. The *Courier*. They have any number of them, and I have plenty of friends still who'd let me abscond with one for a couple days."

"Perfect," Sarah said. "We can do it in the basement of my house. Jess, when do you think you can get the negatives and the enlarger? And Annie, the rest of the material?"

"Next Saturday morning?" Jess said. "I may not be able to get the enlarger until then, and the negatives. Depends when the coast is clear."

"Sounds fine to me," Annie said. "I'll get the chemicals and paper in plenty of time."

"Agreed then," Sarah said. "We've planned our first investigation already. Now, how about we have that luncheon I promised you, Jess?"

❦

"TELL US A LITTLE more about yourself," Sarah said to Jess over lunch at the Three Pyramids Luncheonette, a place near the office curiously done up inside in faux Egyptian décor. The menu was standard fare, nothing more pharaonic than egg salad. "About your family, hobbies. Anything you like."

"There's not that much to tell," he said.

"Everyone has a story," Annie said.

"I don't." He took a gulp of his coffee. "You're new here too. Why don't you tell us yours instead?"

"She will," Sarah said. "You first, though. You were officially my first hire."

"If you insist," he said slowly. "You know I'm from Newport. My father is an attorney, and my mother is a schoolteacher."

"Brothers and sisters?"

"No. Just the three of us."

"Your parents must miss you terribly," Annie said. "Ruth and I have two brothers, still in Conestoga. I don't think for an instant that my parents would have allowed us girls to leave if they were left all alone."

"Well, I guess mine aren't like yours," Jess said.

Annie set her teacup down gently. "I'm sorry, I meant no offense. I was—"

"No offense taken," he said, with his odd smile. "I was kidding around."

"What interested you in coming all this way, to Buffalo?" Sarah asked.

"I needed my luck to change," he said. "I thought this might be the place."

"You've been unlucky?" Sarah asked.

Jess stared into his coffee cup for a long moment. "You might say that. I was engaged to a girl, back in Newport. We were very much in love," he said softly. "But she—her family—didn't think it an advantageous match for their daughter, so they forced her to break it off."

"Oh, I'm terribly sorry, Jess," Sarah said, and Annie nodded.

"It's all right. But that's why I came here. I couldn't stay in Newport."

"That would be difficult, after you and—I'm sorry, I don't know her name . . ."

"Cynthia. She's the most beautiful girl in Newport. Everyone says so. You know," he said to Sarah, "she looks a lot like you."

Sarah blushed. "What a coincidence," she said. "Well, then, I do regret we pushed you onto a painful topic. Perhaps you can tell us more about your time at the *Courier*."

"Her family is very prominent, so they're always in the newspaper," Jess went on. "And you know, it took them about a week, after I was disposed of, to find her an upper-crust Newport fellow to replace me. I sent her letters, telegrams—even walked past her house a dozen times and put things directly into the mail slot. But I never heard a word, until I saw her engagement announcement in the newspapers. I guess her parents were intercepting our letters."

Sarah sighed. "Families can be so nearsighted. I'm sure you would have been a fine husband to her, and a credit to them. If they'd given you a chance."

Jess looked at Sarah for a moment and then looked quickly down again. "Thank you for saying that," he murmured. "But I got a little bit even, at least."

Neither Annie nor Sarah knew how to follow that, so they quietly chewed their egg salad.

"I'm pretty good with my fists, you know," he said, balling them up and adopting a mock boxing stance at the table. "The manly art, you know. I saw the new fellow on the street soon after and I called him out."

"You didn't!" Sarah said.

"I did indeed, and I sure taught him a lesson!"

"You oughtn't to have done that," Annie said, frowning.

"He stole my girl," Jess said. "Any self-respecting man would've done the same."

"She wasn't *your* girl," Annie said. "She was *a* girl, and if things didn't work out, that's a shame and all that, but one doesn't go around beating the daylights out of people because they didn't. I'm sure Cynthia didn't approve of your behavior."

"How would I know?" he said, testily. "Her parents were intercepting my letters."

"Um hmm," Annie murmured.

"Is there a problem?" Jess asked her.

"No, there's no problem. I simply think that men are too apt to try to solve things with violence."

"See?" Jess said, turning toward Sarah. "You see why I don't like telling my so-called story. Because people pick it apart."

"I'm terribly sorry, Jess," Sarah said. "We're not judging you. And I'm sure Annie means only that violence sometimes creates more problems than it solves."

"See, I knew it," he said, tapping the table. "See, I knew *you'd* understand. You're just that way. You *listen*."

Annie sat back in her chair exasperated.

"In any event, Jess," Sarah said, "I hope this new situation will bring the kind of luck you want. Everyone deserves a fresh start. Now, Annie, why don't you share your story?"

"All right. I'm from Conestoga, and I have two older brothers and a younger sister. Mr. Miller brought me here to work for him, and then later, my sister. That was four years ago. After the crime—I stayed on another six months, until I answered a little want ad. And that's what brings me here. I like tinkering with mechanical things and reading about the science of crime. Fingerprinting, Bertillon anthropometry, that sort of thing. And photography, as you know."

"I can't tell you how happy I am that you both are here," Sarah said, raising her glass for a toast.

"Now, Miss Payne," Jess said, touching her glass, "are we going to hear your story?"

"If you like," Sarah said. "I'm from a little north of Buffalo, but have lived here most of my life. My father is a Presbyterian minister—well, he's retired now—and my mother is at home. I have a little nine-year-old girl named Margaret, but we call her Maggie. My husband was a dentist—he passed away in May. And, like Annie, I've wanted to be a detective since I was a little girl. Hobbies . . . I suppose I'd have to say shopping, when I have some money." She laughed.

"I'm not surprised," Jess said. "Your clothing is astonishing."

"Why, thank you," Sarah said. "I'm fortunate that I have a few dress-makers and milliners who are friends, and make clothing for me in styles they'd like to advertise around town. You might say I'm a kind of walking billboard."

"A very beautiful one, if you'll permit me to say," Jess said.

Sarah looked down at her plate. "I'll make sure I pay that compliment to the people who deserve it—the ladies who make these things. They'll be delighted to hear that you like them."

❧

PENROSE WAS ROCKED BACK in his desk chair, looking out his enormous window at the clouds scudding by, slowly streaming smoke toward the ceiling. He sprang forward so fast when Jess came in that he jettisoned sparks from his cigar all over the front of his waistcoat. He jumped up, brushing embers onto the floor.

"Jess! How goes it?"

"As well as can be expected," Jess said.

"You got the job, I take it?"

"I did."

"I never had any doubt," he said. "Who wouldn't want to hire you?"

"Other than my father?"

"Jess," the DA said, "be kind. You have a minute? Sit down. Cigar?" Penrose showed Jess the well-masticated stub of his stogie.

"Don't smoke, but thanks."

"More for me then. Now, tell me, what's the situation at the AA Detective Agency? Mrs. Payne? What are they working on?"

"The 'AA' stands for Avenging Angel."

Terry laughed. "Didn't I tell you? She's out to settle a score. What else?"

"It's Miss Payne and one other person, a girl who used to be the maid for Edward Miller."

"Not sure I like the sound of that," the DA said, squinting as a string of smoke drifted into his eyes.

"She's one I'll have to watch. Miss Payne is awfully sweet, but the other one—Annie Murray—is a real shrew. And I don't think she likes me."

"You'll have to kill her with kindness," Penrose said. "Win her over. Whatever it takes."

"Hmm. We'll see about that. Their offices are in the Hudson Building, right across the street. Fifth floor."

Penrose nodded. "And do they have any cases yet?"

"Nothing paying."

Penrose chortled out a great gust of smoke. "God, women. It's bad enough they're—well, women. But now they're playing at being detectives. What's next—doctors? Lawyers? Keep an eye on them and let me know personally what they find, if anything. And don't get on the bad side of the Miller maid girl. That's not the way you want this to go."

"I'll do what I can," Jess said. "Anything else?"

"I've already mentioned those letters. Those would earn you the blue ribbon, and a lot more. Other than that, you're an intelligent fellow. If you hear or see anything that you think I'd like to know, you know how to find me. I don't like these detective-ladies meddling around. Amateurs can get lucky, when you least expect it. Even a blind squirrel finds an acorn every once in a while."

"I'll keep an eye on them, don't worry. I'll keep you informed."

"Look sharp. Women can be a lot smarter than they appear."

20

IN THE DARKROOM

Jess arrived at Sarah's house early the following Saturday, lugging a large wooden crate about half his size. He also had a messenger bag slung across his body.

"Don't tell me you walked all this way from downtown," Sarah said, opening the door for him.

"No, I hailed a hack at the *Courier* building. But just hauling this thing up to the porch was plenty. Why is it still so hot?" He put the crate down gingerly. "It's heavy *and* delicate, both," he said, exhaling. "I hope it's all in one piece."

"Well, come on in and have something to eat. Ruth just made some brunch."

He took off his hat and wiped his forehead with his handkerchief. "Sounds wonderful." He took the messenger bag off his shoulder and removed a large, heavy envelope from it. "The negatives," he said, handing it to her gently.

She cradled the envelope with both hands. "Thank you for doing this, Jess. I'll put them in my room and meet you in the kitchen. It's in the back."

In the kitchen, Jess introduced himself to Ruth—who resembled her sister, if a few years younger and well beyond merely pretty—and sat down to wait for Sarah to return. She was gone for a good five minutes when the doorbell rang.

"I'll get it," Jess said to Ruth. "It's probably your sister."

Sure enough, Annie was standing on the threshold, holding a folio of paper and some metal trays. When the door opened, she motioned to the driver who'd brought her, and he lugged into the foyer a wooden crate of brown glass bottles. He made a second trip to return with a second crate with a large piece of equipment in it. She tipped him, and she and

Jess stood in the foyer, looking at the crate with the enlarger and all the chemicals and equipment.

"Glad you know what to do with this stuff," he said.

"Well," she said, "I hope Miss Sarah won't mind, but I also purchased a book from the camera dealer. In case I forget anything. Which is very possible. I've done this only a few times."

"There's some brunch coming," he said, gesturing toward the kitchen. "Miss Payne went upstairs with the negatives."

"She's going to have a very difficult time with this. I feel terribly sorry for her."

"I do too," he said, as they walked back to the kitchen. Ruth hugged her sister.

"While we're waiting for Miss Sarah," Annie said, "why don't you and I move the chemicals and other things from the foyer to the basement?"

"You wait here for Miss Payne," Jess said. "I'll do it. It won't take me long."

Annie gratefully sat down at the kitchen table while Jess made a few trips between the kitchen and the foyer. An armload at a time, he lugged everything down the narrow stairs into the dark, musty basement.

As hot as it was upstairs, down here it didn't seem much cooler, only more humid. Under the low ceiling, a rusty boiler and a huge furnace squatted in the corner, near the coal chute. The furnace was covered with age and dust, and had multiple ducts running from it and disappearing between the beams of the ceiling, heading off to parts unknown. The contraption looked like a giant spider, and for some reason gave Jess the willies. He put the gear down on a rickety wooden table that sat forgotten in the corner farthest from the machinery. It would be easy to tack up some partitions to the wooden ceiling beams, and then he wouldn't have to see the weird machinery.

He was a little relieved when he heard Annie call for him down the basement stairs. He ran up to rejoin the ladies, brushing cobwebs off his shirtsleeves. He almost barreled into Sarah, who had just returned to the kitchen, carrying the envelope of negatives and wearing a very strange look on her face. Her normal rosy color seemed to have fled.

She sat down quietly with a thin smile. "I'm sorry to keep you waiting," she said. "You really didn't have to. Let's have some of this delicious food Ruth prepared."

Annie and Ruth did most of the talking over brunch. Sarah didn't eat much—she never did, but today she ate even less—and Jess chewed his food slowly, looking sidelong at Sarah. When they had all finished, they sat there in silence.

"I suppose we should get started," Sarah said. "We don't have a lot of time."

"Everything's downstairs," Jess said. "We'll need some blankets or something that I can tack up to keep out the light."

"I got down some old curtains from the attic," Ruth said. "They're in the pantry."

"Sounds good," Jess said. "Annie, do you want to come down with me and set up your chemicals and the enlarger? When we have everything ready, Miss Payne, we can call for you."

Sarah looked him with her deep blue eyes, almost violet. "That would be wonderful," she said. "Thank you."

"Ruth," Jess said, "would you mind helping your sister with those curtains? I'll be down in two shakes."

Annie and Ruth went into the pantry and then disappeared down the basement stairs with what looked more like the black sails of a pirate ship than a set of old curtains.

"Miss Payne," Jess said softly, "are you unwell?"

"Only a little."

"Did you look at the negatives when you were upstairs?"

"I looked at a few of them with a magnifying glass I use for sewing," she said. She looked up at him. "I probably oughtn't to have. They're horrible. No—horrible doesn't begin to describe it."

"I'm terribly sorry."

"I know you are, Jess. I've got to get through today somehow, that's all."

A tear rolled down Sarah's smooth cheek, and it was all Jess could do not to wipe it away, not to lean over the two feet between them and kiss it as it passed her lips. He caught himself with a jolt.

She brushed the tear away with the back of her hand. "I oughtn't to be feeling so sorry for myself," she said. "I'll be fine." She paused. "I imagine you've seen a lot of photos like these. How did you cope?"

He looked at the ceiling, then back to her. "I have seen quite a few. I think it's different, though, because I never knew any of the people in them. That made it easier. They were strangers."

She pursed her lips. "Yes, naturally. I suppose I can try to pretend that it's not—Eddie. That it's someone else."

"If it's any help at all," Jess said, "when those photographs were taken, the Edward Miller you knew had already gone."

Sarah blinked a few times, looking down at the table again. "Yes, yes. That is very wise. That will help."

She put her palms on the table. "Time to snap out of it," she said. "Thank you for your advice. It's very much appreciated." She put her hand on his forearm and patted it. "You're a good man, Mr. Murphy."

"My mother would be pleased to hear it."

"*And* the first reporter I've ever met who was a decent human being."

"I won't disagree with you there."

"I thought not." Sarah stood. "Time to get this show on the road."

She picked up the envelope with the negatives, and the two of them walked to the basement stairs.

☙

IN THE BASEMENT, ANNIE and Ruth had tacked up the old curtains to make a tall, narrow enclosure that looked something like a shower bath. Jess and Sarah picked across the rubble floor of the basement and peered into the makeshift darkroom.

Inside, Annie had a little kerosene lamp going, and by its light had set up the enlarger and four shallow trays on the old table, with the folio of paper nearby. Ruth had gotten a basket of clothespins, and she'd strung a length of clothesline from one corner of the darkroom to the other, presumably to hang the prints up to dry. In the dim light, it looked rather impressive, a setup any hobbyist would have been proud of. Annie looked over her shoulder at them and smiled.

"Not too bad, eh?" she said. "This enlarger has an electric bulb in it. Fortunately, it's powered by a battery, but I don't know if it'll last long enough. We'll have to hope."

"So that's why it was so blame heavy," Jess said. "But it'll be worth a slipped disc if that battery holds out."

Sarah and Jess ducked under the clothesline and stood next to Annie. "Are you ready to begin?" Sarah said.

"As ready as I'm going to be."

Sarah put her arm around the young woman's shoulders. "I know. Jess told me to try to think that it's not Eddie—Mr. Miller. That the person in the photos wasn't him anymore."

"I'll try," Annie said.

"Then let's go," Sarah said, pulling on some cotton gloves. She handed Annie the first negative. It was a shiny black square, made of thin glass, about four inches on a side. Annie carefully sandwiched it in a little metal frame, and slid the frame into the enlarger.

"We don't have enough battery or paper to do test prints, so we'll have to adjust as we go," she said. "Some of the prints may be a little too light or too dark. If we have enough material at the end, and the battery holds up, we can always go back and redo any we don't like."

"Makes sense," Sarah said. "It's so wonderful you know how to do this."

"Thanks to Mr. Miller. I am going to think that he's here with us, helping us solve his murder."

Annie then lowered a tin cage with panels of red glass over the kerosene lantern, turning the whole darkroom and their four apprehensive faces blood-red.

"It's called a safelight," she said. "The red light won't expose the photographs. But first, I need to get this thing focused."

Annie flipped a little switch on the base of the enlarger, and an electric bulb glowed to life, shining down through the negative and casting a shadowy image on the white base of the device. Annie turned a knob on the side of the enlarger and the image crisped up, came into focus. When it did, all of them gasped and had to look away.

"I'll be upstairs," Ruth said, and ducked out of the little darkroom.

Annie clicked off the enlarger. "It's focused," she said. They stood there catching their breath. Sarah put a hand on the table to steady herself, and then Jess reached out and took her elbow, gently. "I'm in your way, Annie," Sarah said, taking her hand off the table and leaning on Jess's forearm.

"This negative has a smudge on it," Annie said, removing the glass square and holding it up. "I should clean it or we won't get a good image. The smudge is on the glass side, fortunately."

"What do you clean it with?" Jess asked.

"Benzene would be best," she said. "I don't suppose we have any of that?"

"No," Sarah said. "Anything else?"

"Any kind of light solvent. I can try with water if I have to, but this looks oily."

"Wait a minute," Sarah said. "I may have just the thing." She ran up the basement steps and they heard her run across their heads and then up the main staircase. When she returned, she was holding a small apothecary bottle with a cork stopper.

"I'll bet this will work," she said. "I brought a little piece of cotton wool, too." She unstoppered the bottle and tilted it, soaking the ball of cotton. Immediately the little darkroom was filled with fumes, sweet and cloying.

"Whoa," Jess said. "That's strong stuff. It's making me dizzy."

"Oh shit—douse that, quick," Sarah said, stoppering up the bottle again and pointing toward the kerosene safelight.

"Why?" Annie asked.

"Just do it!"

Annie hurriedly turned down the wick and flicked on the electric bulb of the enlarger so that they could see.

"Thanks," Sarah said. "I'm awfully sorry. The fumes from this are highly flammable. That was very stupid of me."

"Well, give me the cotton wool," Annie said, trying to hold her breath. Sarah handed the cotton to her, and she and Jess hurried out of the darkroom to catch their breath. Annie followed a few seconds later, looking terribly faint.

"What is heaven's name is that stuff?" she gasped, putting her hands on her knees.

"It smells like burned cotton candy," Jess said. "Reminds me of the Pan-American."

"It's ether," Sarah said. "I took it away from Seth because he was sniffing it."

"No wonder I feel sleepy," Jess said.

"I didn't realize it was so potent," Sarah said. "I'm terribly sorry. It will dissipate quickly, though. But for God's sake, don't ever get it near a flame."

The three waited a few minutes, and then Annie poked her head into the darkroom and gave them the thumbs-up. "It's fine now," she said, and they gathered around the enlarger again. She relit the safelight.

"All right then, let's make a picture," Annie said. She took out a sheet of photo paper from the envelope and placed it under the enlarger. "Jess, does your watch have a seconds dial?"

"It does."

"Then you tell me when I should start. You then start timing and tell me when half a minute's gone by."

Jess nodded, bathed in the red light. He took his watch from his vest pocket without letting go of Sarah. "I'll tell you when to start. Ready—go."

Annie flipped the switch again.

Sarah and Jess paid attention to Jess's watch and didn't look at the image. Annie looked away, too, keeping her hand on the switch.

"Twenty-five, six, seven," Jess counted. "Thirty."

Annie switched off the enlarger. She carefully removed the paper.

"It didn't work," Sarah said. "There's no image."

"Not yet," Annie said. "That comes next. Jess, give me sixty seconds when I put this in the first tray." She slid the blank paper into the first tray, gently rocking it to slosh the fluid over the paper. Jess and Sarah peered over her shoulder.

And sure enough, faint as a will-o'-the-wisp at first, an image began to develop on the paper. It darkened as Jess counted down the time. When he called time, Annie pulled what was now a photo from the first tray and slid it into the second one. She counted down from ten, and then shifted the photograph to the third tray.

"Thirty seconds, Jess."

When thirty seconds had elapsed, she put the photo into a fourth tray of clean water, and swished it around for a few moments. Then she took the photo out and hung it on the clothesline.

Annie removed the red-glass cage from the kerosene lantern so that they could see the finished photograph, hanging limp and dripping in their little darkroom.

"Oh my God," Sarah said, squeezing Jess's arm involuntarily.

The image was of Edward's den, his private sanctuary in his otherwise very unhappy home. The photo showed the Moorish gas fixture hanging from a coffered ceiling, a rolltop desk with a photo sitting on it, and a small table with a bottle and a plate of food of some kind. Against the far wall, facing the photographer, was a long Turkish divan. And on the divan was the nearly nude body of a man, the underwear pulled down around the ankles, the upper torso and head buried under a small heap of pillows and rugs.

The divan, the rugs, the bottom of the man's undershirt—all were soaked in disturbing quantities of blood, which looked inky black in the photograph. More blood was spattered on the wall near the desk, on the ceiling above the divan, and a great deal of it seemed to have seeped from the man's head through the divan to pool on the wooden floor beneath.

"My poor Eddie," Sarah breathed. "You poor, poor man." She let go of Jess's arm and sat down suddenly on the rubble floor of the darkroom, shaking her head.

"Sarah?" Jess whispered. "Do you need some air? I can carry you upstairs, and we'll finish down here."

"No," she said, struggling to her feet. "I'll be fine now. It was a shock, that's all." Once standing, she turned to Annie. "How are you?"

"Not terribly well, Miss. But I'll manage. I have to keep my mind on the developing."

"Then let's keep going," Sarah said. "No more stopping. I'm sorry."

"Don't be sorry," Jess said.

One by one, they printed the negatives. After about a dozen, the electric bulb seemed to be growing fainter, and Annie had to leave the light on longer to get the right exposure. The clothesline became so filled with photos that Jess had to string up another one outside the darkroom. Once the photos were fixed—in the third little chemical bath—there was nothing more to fear from the light. By the time they were done, about twenty photographs hung drying from the lines.

"Good, our little storage battery held out for us," Sarah said. "Well done, Annie, and Jess. You make a good team."

"Thank you, Miss," Annie said.

"Now may I borrow your little lantern?" Sarah said. "I need to study each of these with my magnifying glass and then—if we can coax a little more energy out of our battery—I may ask you to print enlarged portions of some of the images. Jess, would you mind holding the lantern behind me so that I can focus the light with my glass?"

Sarah went down the line, one at a time, examining the photos with her magnifier. About half were of the murder scene, taken from different vantage points in the den. The last half were photos of Edward's body taken, it would seem, at the morgue. Those were beyond belief in the degree of savagery—of overkill—visited upon the man's trim, compact body. The forehead and the top and back of the skull had been turned to pulp, the brain tissue hanging out in stringy clumps. The eyes, mercifully, were closed, but the whole upper part of the face was a mass of cuts and contusions.

Sarah was all business now, though. Something seemed to have come over her, a change of weather, and without hesitation she showed Annie places in a half-dozen photos that, if possible, she wanted her to enlarge.

"I'll do it, Miss," Annie said. "It's rather close in here, though, with all the chemicals and so on. Why don't you and Jess go upstairs and get some air? I'll be up as soon as I'm done. We'll let these dry down here overnight."

"I think that's a good idea," Jess said. "Let's wait upstairs. Annie can handle it from here."

Sarah nodded and they walked up the stairs. In the kitchen, they sat down heavily at the kitchen table. Sarah glanced at the clock on the wall—nearing seven. They had started in earnest no later than noon.

"How do you feel?" Jess asked.

"Like I've survived Pickett's Charge," she said. "You?"

"Pretty bad. Worse because I have some idea of how hard this is on you."

They sat limply at the table for another half hour, and then Annie reappeared from the depths. She looked exhausted. They were all covered with dust and grime from the cellar.

"Look at you," Sarah said. "Look at all of us. And I thought that detective work would be glamorous."

Sarah took the pins out of her hair, shook it, and let it fall in waves around her shoulders and face. She looks even more beautiful with her hair down, Jess thought, if that's possible. And she also looked sultry, more a real woman than a fashion plate.

"I'm beat," Sarah said.

"Me too," said Annie.

Sarah gestured feebly toward the front of the house. "Jess, there's a davenport in the parlor. Pull that out and stay here tonight. It's too late to go anywhere."

"Are you sure?" he said. "Mightn't your neighbors think ill of you?"

"So far this year, my neighbors have seen the police almost break down my door, put in a witness box, and then vanish to Batavia and return. Nothing's going to surprise them. And at this hour, anything naughty you might've come here to do to us would have been long done by now, and everyone would be fast asleep."

He laughed. "Fine, then. I appreciate that."

"Thank you again, Annie," Sarah said as the three wearily got up from the table. "Fine work today."

"We'll get to the bottom of this, Miss. I know it."

"Yes, that part starts tomorrow. All of us—we'll have to study those photographs for clues. But first we all sleep late."

❦

RUTH'S BREAKFAST CHEERED THEM somewhat. After the dishes had been cleared away, Sarah asked Ruth to look after Maggie, who, like her mother, could sleep the morning away. "I'll go up and kiss her awake, and tell her that Mama's busy for a while," she said. "Best not to have the little thing coming down here while we have those photos spread out."

While Sarah was upstairs waking Maggie, Annie retrieved last night's prints from the clotheslines in the basement and brought them up in a slightly curled sheaf.

"How do you want to do this, Miss?" Annie asked Sarah on her return, touching the stack of photos.

"Let's lay them out on the table—grouped by the part of the den they show."

"All right," Annie said. The three of them arranged them in four vertical lines, like a Solitaire hand, each showing a different view of the room. The first column showed the north wall of the room—with the divan and the body—and then the columns moved clockwise around the points of the compass to the desk, to the doorway back into the corridor, and finally, to the bookcase and windows facing west, onto Ashwood Street.

They hovered over the photos for a half hour, passing Sarah's magnifying glass back and forth among them.

"Annie," Sarah said, "were you nearby when the photographer was in the house that morning?"

"Off and on, yes. I was continually running back and forth to the front door, so I had to pass by the den dozens of times."

"And do you remember how long the photographer was there?"

"I'd guess about two hours. He arrived with a couple of police detectives, set up his equipment, and took some photographs. Then the head medical examiner arrived—I answered the door for him—and everyone left the den to give him room to move. After the medical examiner was done, the photographer and the detectives went back into the den, took some more photographs, and left a little before noon."

"That's very interesting," Sarah said.

"What about it?" Jess asked.

"If I understand correctly, there were two sessions of photography," she said, "with an interval between, when the photographer wasn't in the den."

"Yes, that's right," Annie said.

"Now take a look at these photos," Sarah said. "They're all of the same view of the room, which would be the east wall, with the rolltop desk. There are five of them, and I've arranged them in a particular order, which you'll understand when you study them."

Jess and Annie bent over the column of photographs. "They look the same to me," Jess said. "Slightly different angles, of course, but the same desk. Drawers are hanging open, papers on the floor—"

"Wait . . ." Annie breathed. "It's so obvious I can't believe I didn't see it right away."

Jess looked puzzled. "What?"

"Look at this photo of the desk," Sarah said, selecting an image. "What's on the desktop? Everything you see."

"A couple of ledgers," Jess said. "Some papers. Pen and ink. A pair of nose glasses. A photograph of—"

"Of me," Sarah said. "I gave that to Eddie."

"All right," he said. "That's all that's on the desktop. Have I missed anything?"

"No," Sarah said, switching the photograph for another one that looked identical. "But look at this one. Anything different?"

Jess adjusted the magnifying glass. "Looks the same to me—whoo!" he said. "Of course. What is that thing?"

"Look in the corner, near the right side. Partially shadowed by the side of the rolltop."

"The black thing?"

"Right," Sarah said. "Now look at this other view." She brought back the first photograph and set it next to the other.

"It's not in this one," he said.

"That's right. That item was on the desk in one photograph, and was removed before the second one was taken. Probably when the medical examiner arrived."

"Very sharp work, Miss!" Annie said.

"Why thank you, Annie. But this image is too small for me to tell what the thing is. Do you think your enlarger battery has enough life in it to magnify this area of the photograph?"

"I'll soon find out," Annie said. "Let me take this photo downstairs. I'll find the corresponding negative and give it a try. Jess, may I borrow your watch?"

"Sure," he said, unfastening the chain from his vest.

Annie took the watch, picked up the photo with the black shape, and trotted down the basement steps.

Jess and Sarah sat quietly at the table, Jess stealing a glance over at his new boss when she seemed to be lost in her own thoughts.

"Do I have something in my teeth?" Sarah said at last.

"Pardon?"

"You keep looking over at me."

"I'm sorry," he said. "I didn't think I was doing that. Only sitting here waiting to see whether Annie can pull one more rabbit out of her hat."

"If anyone can, she can."

Jess looked in any other direction but Sarah's for the next half hour— at the various cans and boxes of food on the kitchen shelves, even at the patterned ceiling—to the point where he almost tipped his chair over backward. As he was running out of things to examine, and beginning to develop a crick in his neck, Annie's footsteps echoed up the wooden stairs. She popped into the kitchen and brushed back a wisp of hair.

"It worked," she said. "It's drying now."

"That's wonderful," Sarah said. "How long should we leave it before we have a look?"

"A few hours, at least."

"Then if we have some time," Jess said, standing and rubbing the back of his neck, "unless you think we'll still need the negatives and the enlarger, it's probably a good idea for me to hoof them back to their rightful owners. I'll come back afterward, and by then the photograph should be ready."

❦

WHEN JESS RETURNED TO Norwood Street, it was lunchtime and the ladies were sitting on the front porch, having a glass of lemonade. Sarah was fanning herself with a folded newspaper.

"It was too hot inside," she said.

"Yeah, it's awfully muggy today. But I got the stuff back into the right hands before I got heatstroke," he said.

"I hope you don't expect a raise just yet," Sarah said. "Annie, do you think the photograph is dry enough?"

"Dry enough to have a look, I'm sure. I'll get it off the line."

The three went back to the kitchen, and Annie clumped downstairs to retrieve the enlargement.

"It's still a little tacky," she said when she returned, the shiny photograph dangling between her thumb and forefinger. "So long as we don't touch the surface, we can look, though." She laid it out on the table and let the curled paper relax.

"You first," Jess said to Sarah, handing her the magnifying glass.

Under the glass, the enlargement showed tiny details unseen in the smaller original. The grain of the wooden desktop, even some words on the papers strewn about—and dozens upon dozens of tiny, black specks.

"Was there dirt on the negative?" Sarah asked.

"No," Annie said. "You mean all those spots?"

"Yes."

"Miss—um, I believe that's blood."

Sarah closed her eyes for a moment. Then she bent back over the print and moved the magnifying glass over to the corner of the desktop.

"You did a magnificent job on this, Annie," she said. "I can make the object out quite clearly now."

"What is it?" Jess asked. "The black thing."

"It's a tool of some sort," she said. "Have a look."

Jess leaned into the print and squinted through the glass. "It's a wrench," he said.

Annie took the magnifying glass from Jess and peered at the photograph. "It's a wrench, no doubt about it. It looks like something my father used to use on our farm. One end is a crescent to fit over a big nut, and the other end tapers to a chisel point. Looks to be a good eight or nine inches long, and heavy."

"Anything else?" Sarah asked.

Annie bit her lip. "I'm sorry to say—it's got blood all over it. And—on the crescent end—what looks like hair."

"That's the murder weapon," Jess said.

Sarah nodded. "At the inquest, the medical examiner testified that the weapon must have been something quite heavy, and blunt. But everyone testified that nothing in the den—golf clubs and whatnot—could have been the right size and weight."

"Only one explanation," Annie said.

"Yes," Sarah said. "The murder weapon was in the den, until someone took it away before the second set of photographs was taken. And whoever took it lied about it."

"Someone official, too," Jess said. "One of the detectives, the cops, or the doctor."

"I wonder what's become of the thing?" Annie said.

"At the bottom of the canal, most likely," Jess said. "Maybe from the photograph, though, someone can tell us what kind of wrench it is."

Sarah nodded. "I have a hunch about someone who can tell us definitively."

"Who?" Annie asked.

"Tomorrow morning, you can come and see for yourselves, if you'd like."

"I have to work at the damn hat shop," Jess said.

"Annie and I will handle this one," Sarah said. "By the time you're done with work, I predict we'll have an answer."

❧

THERE WASN'T A BREATH of air stirring, even on the second floor. Jess shuffled up the staircase to his apartment as slowly as he could, trying not to work up more of a sweat than he had done already in his walk from the streetcar.

He was panting by the time he got to the apartment, where he found his roommates, George and Philip, lounging and fanning themselves with newspapers, but looking none the cooler for the effort.

"Try not to breathe so heavy, will you?" George said to Jess. "You're heating up the place even more."

"Go soak your head," Jess said. "I've had a hard day." He flopped down on a worn throw rug on the floor, with the back of his head against the dirty plaster wall.

"What's wrong?" George asked.

"I'm officially in trouble, boys."

"What'd you do this time?" Phil said.

"I've gone and fallen in love with my boss."

"Well," George said, savoring the moment, "who could blame you? Mr. Adair is a very captivating gentleman."

"Not the hat store, idiot," Jess said. "The detective agency."

"That didn't take you long," Phil said.

"It wouldn't take you long, either," Jess replied. "If you saw her. Or heard her. Or watched her move."

"Down, boy," George said. "You'll get even more overheated than you are."

"I don't expect you two to understand, but it's a *problem*," Jess said. "I try to look at her when she's not noticing, but sometimes I think she knows I am."

"Ladies don't like to be ogled, pal," Phil said.

"You wouldn't say that if you could see that body—that face. Her eyes! And when we were in the darkroom, she was leaning on me, and I could smell her powder. Like clover or carnation or something. It was intoxicating. I thought I'd die."

"Better watch yourself, old man," George said. "You remember how it ended in Newport."

"That was completely different," Jess said.

"I don't know," Phil said. "What if some handsome swain comes along and sweeps Miss Sarah off her feet? Then what will you do?"

"That's not going to happen. Her husband died three or four months ago. She's not going to have anyone else for quite some time. I've got time."

"I wouldn't get your hopes up," Phil said.

PART THREE

PURSUIT

21

JOHN PENDLE

"Do we really have to meet with him?" Alicia asked.

"The insurance company told me that he's the one protesting your bequest, so yes."

"Arthur told me all about that weedy little whelp brother of his," Allie said. "A little mama's boy. I don't care to see him."

"I can meet with him myself, but since you are the beneficiary, I think it's wise to have you there."

Alicia squinted. "I'm not so sure. John Pendle has a phobia about women. I'm sure that's part of the reason he's being such an asshole about my bequest. In addition to being a greedy little bloodsucker, that is."

"Even if he had his way, that money wouldn't go to him," Bert said. "The coroner saw to that. Cassie was still alive—unconscious, but alive—when the doctors reached them after the wreck. Arthur was long gone. Which means that Cassie was Arthur's sole beneficiary, except for named bequests."

"You're smarter than you let on, Bert," she said. "That's interesting. So anything that's not distributed according to Arthur's will goes right to Cassie's family, the Lanes. And if there's one thing the Lanes don't need, it's more money."

"Now, even if he can't get the money himself, he can stall this thing indefinitely. And normally you'd be bleeding legal expenses with all the motions and countermotions. But I'm sure I don't need to remind you that you're not paying me."

"You want to open that can of worms again, Bert?"

"No, I'm simply making a point. That his strategy is probably to waste your time and money, until you either give up or settle with him and the insurance company for a fraction of the $50,000."

"He hates me. That's the simple answer."

"But why? What does he have against you? You've never met."

"I am everything that man despises, in the flesh."

"Surely not simply because you're a woman?"

"Because I'm a certain *kind* of woman."

Bert felt a pit in the bottom of his stomach. He cleared his throat and hoped Allie would volunteer more information. When she didn't, but instead continued to glare at him, he mustered up his courage.

"What kind would that be?"

"I'm sure he'd have a Roget's Thesaurus of words for my kind," she said. "*Strumpet* comes to mind. But in my own defense, I'd say 'direct' or 'forthright' instead. He doesn't like women who speak their minds."

"That's not unique to John Pendle," Bert said. "Not every man is as broad-minded as I am."

"Well played, Bertie boy. Don't throw your shoulder out patting yourself on the back, though. I will say, however, that you're made of strong stuff. Don't make me say it twice."

"I won't. Now then, why does Pendle have this woman phobia?" Bert was genuinely curious now.

"Arthur told me the story of little Johnnie's problem," she said. "His father died on board ship when the family were with him on a long voyage. Little Johnnie was only eight or nine, and when they came back to dry land, the boy—who'd apparently been quite gregarious beforehand—became quite withdrawn."

"Lots of little boys are shy. My son was."

"Of course, and most of them grow out of it. But remember—Arthur's family were all seafaring types. Shipbuilders, sea captains. Not a namby-pamby in the lot of them, and no sissies need apply, either. After Johnnie's father died, a couple of his uncles—Arthur's father had seven brothers—took Johnnie in hand and decided to raise him up to be a proper man. They had him scrubbing spittoons, whatever they could think of, to toughen him up. Nothing worked. He was still a little dandy. Then, when shy little Johnnie turned thirteen, one of the uncles—imagine this!—hired a prostitute to visit the boy in his room. Turn him into a man.

"The way Arthur told the story, the hired girl showed up after supper, when everyone had retired for the night. She raps on Johnnie's door, and he opens it, not knowing who this lady is from a hole in the ground. She invites herself in and shuts the door behind her. Then, you know, she goes to work on the kid."

"Good Lord," Bert said.

"It's not the worst thing in the world, a young fellow having the chance to learn from an expert. It's a hell of a sight better than fumbling around in the dark, wondering how all the pieces fit together, for the next ten years. But it didn't work that way for Johnnie. Apparently, the boy was terrified. No matter what this poor girl did to get him going, he was having none of it. She kept at it for a while, but finally, Johnnie fled the scene. He went to Arthur's room and woke him up and begged him to save him from the succubus. 'Artie, Artie! There's a horrible woman in my room, trying to play with my pecker!' On and on, like a maniac."

"What did Arthur do?"

"Knowing Arthur, he probably strolled calmly down the hallway and got his uncle's money's worth." She laughed. "I don't know, but he told me that after the girl went away, the poor boy refused to return to his room for a while, as though it were haunted. He insisted on sleeping with Arthur, too."

"The uncles ought to be ashamed of themselves."

Allie rolled her eyes. "God, you really do surprise me sometimes, Bert. Well, have it your way. All I'm trying to say is that John . . . has a phobia about women. He sees us all as dangerous. See if I'm not right about this when we meet him. I'll bet he goes weak as water at the sight of me."

"We'll soon find out. And when we do, try to keep your mind clear of whatever you may think about him. It won't be helpful when we are trying to be diplomatic."

"I'll do my best. When someone has his hands around my throat, I know enough not to make him angry."

A VISIT TO
BABCOCK ELECTRIC

AT THE FRONT—A THREADBARE OLD PARK ALONG THE BUFFALO waterfront, where Lake Erie gushed into the Niagara River—Sarah and Annie climbed aboard the Belt Line train north. For a nickel, the Belt Line took passengers in a twenty-mile-long loop around the city. The Buffalo Electric Carriage factory stood a hundred yards from the Military Road Station, about a third of the way along the loop.

At the station, the two hopped down from the coach, crunching cinders under their shoes, and walked up the long asphalt path to the brick automobile factory.

"Sarah Payne," Sarah said to the girl at the front desk. "And Miss Murray. We're here to see Mr. Babcock. I telephoned him earlier to arrange a visit."

The receptionist pressed an intercom button on her desk and leaned toward a mouthpiece mounted on a flexible gooseneck. "A Miss Payne and a Miss Murray are here to see Mr. Babcock." She released the button.

"Mr. Babcock's secretary will be out presently," she said.

In a few moments, a neat young lady appeared. She scanned Sarah quickly, from the extravagant hat atop her strawberry-blonde hair down to the ribbons of her shoes. "I'm Miss O'Connor, Mr. Babcock's secretary," she said. "Would you follow me, please? I'll take you to his office."

A few doors down the corridor was an office door much like Sarah's, oak with a large pebbled glass window that read:

Frank J. Babcock
President

They went into a small outer office where Miss O'Connor's desk sat.

There was another door behind her desk, off to the left. Miss O'Connor rapped on it and opened it a crack. "Mr. Babcock?" she said. "Misses Payne and Murray are here to see you."

"Send them in," a man's deep voice responded, and Miss O'Connor opened the door.

The two eased into Mr. Babcock's large paneled office. Behind his desk were huge bookshelves, though without any books. Instead, they were chock-full of scale models of his automobiles, motors—various bits and pieces he presumably used as props when talking with potential purchasers.

Babcock looked up from his desk and didn't even try to conceal his shock at Sarah's perfect light pink dress, which followed her shape from the ruffled neck to a fringed hem that just brushed against the lavender ribbons holding her shoes on. He was used to seeing rich, dour old ladies who wanted an electric car that they could show off at picnics. He got up and hustled around the desk, with surprising agility for a middle-aged man with a bit of a belly.

"Well, hello there, Mrs. Payne."

"It's Miss Payne," Sarah said.

"Is that so?" Babcock said, smoothing back his salt-and-pepper hair. "Charmed."

"I'm Annie Murray," Annie chimed in, poking her head around Sarah's huge hat.

"Yes, you are," Babcock said. "Nice to meet you. Why don't you make yourselves at home?" He gestured to a round table in a corner of his office.

"Thank you for seeing us today," Sarah said.

"No need to thank me," he smiled. "It's my job. Can we offer you anything to eat or drink?"

"Ice cream is the only thing I eat at this hour," Sarah said.

He looked disappointed. "I'm terribly sorry, Miss Payne, but I don't believe we have any ice cream on hand. Why don't I send Miss O'Connor—"

She laughed. "I'm joking," she said.

"Ah ha!" he said, wagging a finger. "You caught me out with that one! You have quite a sense of humor."

He stared into Sarah's violet eyes for a long few seconds, seeming to forget why precisely he was there.

"Now how may I be of service today, Miss Payne?" he stammered. "And Miss . . ."

"Murray," Annie said.

"Miss Murphy, yes. Are you two shopping for a nice little runabout that you could take on shopping excursions, perhaps?"

"That sounds magical," Sarah said. "But we're not here to purchase an automobile. Not yet, anyway. I've only recently started my own business."

"You have? How interesting! Let me guess. You're a milliner? Your habiliments, if you don't mind my saying, are magnificent."

"No, I can barely sew on a button. Miss Murray and I run a detective agency."

"A detective agency?"

Sarah removed a card from her little handbag and slid it across the table. He studied it.

"'Avenging Angel Detective Agency,'" he read aloud. "Well, you don't say. A lady detective agency."

"It's not a 'lady detective agency,' exactly," Sarah said. "It's a detective agency that happens to be run by ladies."

"A very useful distinction."

"Now, Mr. Babcock, I recognize your time is valuable. And while one day I'd love to purchase one of your automobiles, I wonder if today you might tell us a little about one that belonged to someone else."

"Whose?" he said.

"Arthur Pendle's."

"*Finally*," he said. "Did the police send you?"

"No. I don't work for the police."

"Well, I'll be. You see, I called the police about our break-in, but they never sent anyone. Not so much as a patrolman, let alone a detective. That was Friday, and still I've heard nothing. I thought perhaps they'd sent you to follow up."

"Break-in?" Annie said.

"When you said you were interested in Arthur Pendle's automobile, I assumed you were here about the break-in."

"I must confess I've lost the thread," Sarah said.

"Well," he said, rubbing his face, "it's a bit of a mystery."

"A mystery?"

"Yes," he said. "It'll be easier to explain if I take you down to the factory floor. A picture is worth a thousand words."

On the way out of the office, Babcock looked back over his shoulder at Miss O'Connor. "No interruptions, please," he said. "I want to show Miss Payne the factory. And Miss Murphy, too, of course."

"Murray," Annie said to the back of Babcock's head as he followed Sarah out into the corridor.

Miss O'Connor nodded with her thin smile and then, as soon as Babcock turned his back, rolled her eyes and went back to slitting open a pile of mail.

The factory was attached to the offices, and soon Sarah, Annie, and Frank Babcock were on a wide expanse of smooth floor, brightly lit by sunlight streaming in from floor-to-ceiling windows. Automobiles in various stages of production were being worked over by teams of craftsmen. The place smelled of wood and varnish. It was remarkably quiet.

"I had expected noisy machinery and smoke," Annie said.

"We do have a machine shop, in the back, where you can have your fill of noise and sparks," Babcock said. "This is where the cars are finished, and it's more like a coachbuilding shop than an automobile factory. When I conceived the whole idea of the Buffalo Electric Automobile, it was quite simple, really. I took the designs of the most popular horse-drawn carriages and put electric running gear in them. Simply eliminated the horse."

"How clever," Sarah said. "I've seen your machines around the city, and they are lovely."

"Would you like me to take you on a little test drive, Miss Payne?" he asked. "I've got plenty of time. Miss Murphy, I can arrange a tour of the machine shop, if that would interest you."

"We would love to do that some other time, if you'll invite us back," Sarah said quickly. "Today Miss *Murray* and I are somewhat pressed for time."

"Of course, yes," he said.

She smiled brightly. "Wonderful. Now tell us a little about this break-in. What were they trying to steal?"

"That's the curious part. Follow me."

They strolled over to a newly completed automobile, gleaming under many coats of varnish. The graceful black fenders were outlined in gold pinstripes and accented with little bunches of painted flowers. The seat—a leather-covered bench wide enough for two—was beautifully upholstered in rich leather.

"Our nicest runabout," Babcock said with evident pride. "The Stanhope model. It'll make fifteen miles per hour, right off the floor, and go fifty miles on a single charge. Then it takes only forty-five minutes to recharge the storage batteries."

"It truly is a thing of beauty," Sarah said.

"Gorgeous," Annie added.

"Each one is hand built and customized according to the owner's desires. Type of leather, various appointments, even monogramming on the front and rear."

"Was this one here when the break-in occurred?"

"Yes, indeed it was, and that's the strange thing. When my security man was alerted by the alarm bell, the burglars weren't anywhere near this beauty, nor any of the others in the various stages of build. They didn't take any tools, either. None of the things you might expect a thief to steal."

"Where were they, then?"

Babcock crooked his finger. "Right over here."

The three walked over to a far corner of the vast floor, where they came to a pile of something, covered over with a large canvas tarpaulin, and some wooden crates scattered about, some with their tops pried open.

"This is why when you mentioned Pendle, I thought for sure you must be working with the police. The scoundrels came in at the front of the shop. They came all the way back here, where my security man found them snooping around this." He pulled off the tarp with a flourish.

Beneath the canvas was what was recognizable—if barely—as having once been a perfect example of the new Stanhope they'd seen a few minutes before. But this one looked as though it had been crushed by a steamroller. The wooden frame was broken like so many shattered bones, the running gear twisted and bent. The leather bench was soaked in what looked to be dried blood.

"My God," Sarah said. "What in the world?"

"This was Arthur Pendle's automobile," Babcock said.

"Stalled on the New York Central tracks," Annie interjected.

Babcock's face flushed with indignation. "My automobiles do not *stall* on train tracks, Miss Murphy," he said.

"We don't mean anything by it, sir," Sarah said. "It's what we read in the newspapers. You know how they are."

"I do, and you have no idea how many wanton lies those blasted reporters wrote about my machines. It almost did my business in. But my customers, God bless them, stood by me."

"I understand, and I do sympathize. But tell me more about these burglars. They were looking at this wreck?"

"Yes. They'd removed the canvas and were nosing around inside it. Two of them. Then there was another fellow who was prying open these crates and digging around in them."

"Whatever for?"

"That's the mystery," Babcock said, shaking his head. "This machine has been here ever since the accident, and not a soul has shown the slightest interest in her. Mr. Pendle's brother came once, right afterward, and told me to sell it for whatever I could get. But then the very next day he telephoned and said he'd changed his mind and wanted at least a thousand dollars, which is preposterous. That's why it's still here, after all this time.

"Anyway, I have no idea why three burglars—and to judge from the slick way they entered the factory, they were professionals—would spend ten seconds on this. Why, they might better have blown the safe in my office."

"That is very strange," Sarah said.

"You know, I remember the day Mr. Pendle ordered it," Babcock said. "Top of the line. Every possible option."

"I'm sure it was lovely, once. Did you get to know Mr. Pendle very well?"

"Well enough. He took meticulous care of his machine. He had us handle all the maintenance to keep it in top condition. And again, another reason why she"—he jerked his thumb at the heap—"didn't *stall*."

"And the police never asked you about any of this? Never came to look this over?"

"Only the reporters. Not a single cop. Ever."

"What was Mr. Pendle like?" Sarah asked.

"Nice enough. Very polite. Seemed well-educated. Soft-spoken. Quite serious, though, as if he always had a lot on his mind. He never really talked with me about anything, other than his automobile. He loved it. I think it was his prized possession."

"I'd imagine so. But nothing of a more personal nature?"

"Not a thing. I knew he was married because he'd say that he and his wife had taken the machine here or there. And he was clearly a very successful young man, or else he wouldn't have been able to afford a machine like this. But more than that? No. I would offer to buy him lunch or take him for a drink, as I would with any customer, but he always politely declined."

They looked at the wreck for a moment. "If the automobile didn't fail, Mr. Babcock," Sarah said, "is there any way to determine why it stopped on the train tracks?"

"We can ask Louie. He's my best engineer." Babcock walked over to a rangy man who was bent over some drawings at an adjacent assembly point.

"Good day," the man said, walking back with Babcock. "Pleased to meet you ladies. I'm Louie Sueur."

"Louie *Sewer*?" Annie said.

"It's S-U-E-U-R," he said, with some irritation. "It's a French name, originally."

"Mr. Sueur," Sarah said, "it's our pleasure. My partner Miss Murray and I are detectives—"

"No kidding?"

"Not at all. We're detectives, and we're interested in this automobile."

"Seems like everyone is these days."

"So we hear," Sarah said.

"I know this poor girl very well," he said, nodding in the direction of the remains. "I've passed her every day since the accident. A very sad ending."

"Two people killed," Annie said.

Sueur blinked. "Oh, right. Yes. This machine was special. You know she has an extra forward gear so she could make twenty miles per hour? And I know for a fact she'd exceeded that easily. I test-drove her myself after I modified the gearbox." He shook his head slowly. "Now look at you," he said quietly to the wreckage.

Sueur gathered himself and turned back to Sarah and Annie. "What is it you want to know?"

"They read in the papers that she *stalled* on the railroad tracks," Babcock sneered.

The engineer scowled. "Those reporters don't know their ass from a hole—oh, I am sorry, ladies. I mean, newsmen don't understand automobiles. I went over this machine myself not a week before the crash, and she was in better-than-new condition. Top to bottom. When this automobile stopped on those tracks, she was stopped on purpose or through some error on the operator's part."

"What do you think happened?" Annie said carefully. "Is there any way to find out?"

Louie stroked his chin with a hand. "I do have an idea," he said. "But since no one until now was interested, I haven't verified it."

He trotted over to one of the mechanics' stations and came back with a jack. He placed it under a solid piece of the mangled frame of the vehicle and began to lift it, each click of the jack ratcheting the hulk a little higher. When the underside of the automobile was well off the ground, he removed the rear wheel. Once the wheel was off, he began fiddling with the central hub, carefully disassembling it.

He held out in both hands a donut-shaped metal ring. "This is the brake drum from this wheel," he said, gesturing with his head. "When you activate the brake, there's a leather pad—it has tiny bits of metal in it too, like hobnails—that comes down and contacts this ring. The friction slows down the automobile.

"And over time, you can see that the action of the brake shoe—as we call it—makes all these little scratches—grooves—in the metal drum. These scratches run along the drum, circumferentially. Lengthwise, that is," he said, tracing the wear with his finger. "But look at this." He held out the part. "Perfectly normal wear, as I would expect. Except here." He rotated the ring in his hand until he came to a spot on the other side. "Now this isn't normal. *At all*."

He pointed out a patch of about three or four inches where there were deep, emphatic scratches running perpendicular to the normal pattern he had shown them.

"Brakes don't wear this way," he said. "They can't. It's impossible."

"What does that imply?" Sarah asked.

"Well—and I believe we'll find the same thing on the other wheel, as soon as I take it off—what happened here was that the brake pad was pressed down hard against the drum and then, when the crash happened, it was torn away, violently enough to scratch the drum—against the grain."

"So that would mean . . ." Annie said.

"It means that when this machine was hit by that train, the brakes were set and locked. Locked down tight—as tight as it's humanly possible to set them."

"I could kiss you," Sarah said. "You're a marvel."

The engineer blushed and looked down at the brake drum. "My," he said gruffly, "it's nothing but physics."

It took only a few minutes for Louie to set the car down, jack up the other side, remove the brake drum, and hand it out to Babcock. To no one's surprise, that drum showed the same across-the-grain scratching pattern.

"I'd say that's the solution to your mystery," Sueur said, unfolding his long frame from under the automobile. He let the wreck down off the jack tenderly, giving it a little pat on a crumpled fender.

"I can't thank you and Mr. Babcock enough," Sarah said. "There is one other question I have, if you both don't mind." She reached into her bag for a large envelope.

"This is a photograph of a tool," she said, "that I hope you gentlemen will be able to identify." She took out the close-up of Ed Miller's desktop. Babcock and Sueur huddled over it.

"Armature wrench," they said nearly in unison.

"One of ours, too," Louie said. "No doubt about it."

"What's an armature wrench for?" Annie asked.

"We supply one in each of the tool kits that go with our automobiles," Babcock said. "It's a large wrench—about yea long." He gestured with his hands. "One end has a crescent for fitting over the armature nut, and the other end is a tire iron. Which is used for prying off damaged tires and replacing them."

Louie walked over to the car that was nearing completion and rummaged around in a steel box under its seat. He came back with a large wrench exactly like the one in the photograph.

"This is what's in that picture," he said.

Sarah hefted it in her hand. It was a good three pounds of forged steel, the tapering end providing a natural grip. She passed it over to Annie, who held it in one hand and the photograph in the other.

"Where did you get that photo?" Babcock asked.

"It's from a case we're working on," Sarah replied. "You say there's one of these in every one of your automobiles?"

"Standard equipment," Babcock said. "Each one has a fully stocked toolbox."

"Would you still have the toolbox for the Pendles' vehicle?" Sarah nodded toward the wreck.

"I have it," Louie said. "I put it in my office, though, because tools tend to walk away."

"Would you mind getting it?" Sarah asked.

"Not a bit," Sueur said, and loped off again on his long legs. He was back in a minute or two, during which interval Babcock found enough time to ask Sarah at least four questions about her new agency, whether she liked golf, and so on.

"Here you go," Sueur said, setting down a badly scuffed metal box on one of the crates containing the remains of the Pendle automobile. "You can see how tough these kits are." He rapped on the lid. "Solid as a rock—the lid hasn't even popped open, that's how strong the closure is."

"Yet another reason to be proud of your products, Mr. Babcock," Sarah said.

"Oh, that is *so* kind," Babcock said. "I really could see you in one of my machines, Miss Payne. You're our kind of customer."

"I can see myself in one, too," she said. "Now, Mr. Sueur, would you mind showing us the contents of the tool kit?"

Sueur worked at the hasp that secured the lid. He flipped it open, unrolled a little leather mat tucked inside, and one by one laid out the tools.

"One adjustable pipe wrench. Three screwdrivers. Four serpentine spanners. Electrical pliers and wire cutters, one of each. Wheel knockoff tool. Hammer. Three drifts, one brass and the others steel. Chamois. Flat pliers."

"Quite a complete set," Annie said.

"Not quite," Sueur said, peering into the empty toolbox.

"What do you mean?" Sarah asked.

"The armature wrench is missing."

THE INVESTIGATION
TAKES A TURN

AFTER THEY'D THANKED LOUIE SUEUR, ANNIE AND SARAH WALKED with Babcock toward the door, Babcock chattering away and clearly not relishing their departure.

"You've been so generous with us today, Mr. Babcock," Sarah said.

"It's nothing at all, Miss Payne," he said with an attempt at a little wink, but which came across like a kind of nervous tic. "It was such a pleasure to meet you. And Miss Murphy, of course. Perhaps you'd come back again, and I could have Miss O'Connor cater a little luncheon for the two of us? I have a private dining room upstairs that I use with customers."

"That might be fun. Let me—" She reached out and put her hand on his sleeve. "You know, I have another idea."

He didn't move a muscle, for fear this heavenly creature would remove her hand. "You do?" Babcock fidgeted a little, inadvertently causing Sarah's hand to slip off his forearm.

"I do. Come to our offices downtown sometime, and give Annie and me that spin in one of your fine machines."

It wasn't perfect, but it was good enough. "I'd like nothing better," he said. "I'll have Miss O'Connor telephone your girl."

Sarah smiled and almost laughed out loud. She found that she genuinely liked Babcock. "I'm my own *girl*," she said. "So you may telephone me directly. And you know what? I'll make sure I have a dish of ice cream waiting for you that day."

He clapped his hands like a gleeful little boy. "That sounds grand, Miss Payne. I will be in touch very soon."

Back on the Belt Line train, Annie and Sarah settled into their seats.

"Should I start calling you Annie *Murphy*?" Sarah said, giving her a nudge. "I kept thinking that you and Jess might have eloped."

"I recognize that you're ravishing, but is it asking too much to remember my name?" Annie said. "And of all people I might elope with, I hardly think it would be Jess."

❦

THAT EVENING, JESS CAME over to the house and sat down with Annie, Sarah, Ruth, and Maggie to a delicious dinner Ruth had made of cod and fried potatoes. The conversation about the visit to Babcock was in full swing when Maggie asked to be excused so that she could go upstairs and play with her dolls.

"Of course, dear," Sarah said. "Help Ruth wash your plate and silverware first. Then you can go."

After Maggie had gone, Sarah put her hands on the table. "All right, now that my little one is safely upstairs—I know it's only Monday . . ."

"I'd love one," Annie said.

"One what?" said Jess.

"Rye whiskey," Sarah said. "The official cocktail of the Avenging Angel Detective Agency. Well, as of now. Join us?"

"Of course."

They sipped their whiskey and finished the tale of the Pendle automobile, and the tool kit.

"The armature wrench was missing?" Jess said.

Sarah and Annie nodded.

"I suppose it could have been anyone's armature wrench," Jess said.

"Oh yes," Annie said, "there are dozens of them wandering around Buffalo on any given day. Showing up at murder scenes, and then disappearing again."

"Sarcasm not required," Jess said into his glass.

"I think the odds are greatly in favor of the wrench in the photo being the one missing from Pendle's toolbox," Sarah said, throwing the rest of her whiskey back. Jess looked sidelong at Sarah's neck, watching her swallow. "Which can only mean that it was Arthur Pendle—or someone with him—who murdered Eddie Miller."

"Is that it, then?" Annie said. "We've solved the case?"

"Part of it, I think," Sarah replied. "But was there anyone else there that night?"

"The biggest question of all," Jess said, "is whether he was acting on his own, or whether he was ordered to kill Mr. Miller."

"Do you think that's possible?" Annie said. "He certainly had plenty of motive to do it."

"That he did," Jess said, pouring Sarah and himself another glass, "but he wasn't the one who removed the murder weapon from the crime scene. The only reason someone other than the murderer would do that—"

"—is to cover up for one," Sarah said.

"Exactly. And since the only people in that den that morning were detectives and policemen, it suggests that it was someone above them who ordered them to clean up the scene, so that nothing could be traced back to Pendle."

"In case he might talk," Annie said.

"And a week later, both Pendles die under mysterious circumstances," Sarah said. "And are silenced forever."

Jess took a big gulp of whiskey. "Exactly. And don't forget, if that wrench in the den was Pendle's—and I do agree that it probably was— whoever took it out of that den did so while Arthur Pendle was still alive. And I'll bet that whoever did told Pendle about it, and used it as leverage."

Sarah shivered. "He may have had no choice but suicide, if that's true," she said.

"Then we need to find out who might have been pulling Arthur Pendle's strings," Annie said.

Sarah took a swig and put the glass down with a smack. "I may have something that will help," she said. "Be right back."

Jess and Annie sat at the kitchen table as Sarah disappeared upstairs. "I wonder what she's got up her sleeve?" Annie said.

Jess turned to look at Annie, but he didn't seem to be listening— rather, he was looking through her as if she were transparent. "Did you say something?" he said.

"I said, I wonder what she's got up her sleeve."

"No idea."

Sarah was gone a few minutes when Jess said, "Do you think I should go up and see if she's all right?"

"You can't very well go upstairs to her private quarters."

"Perhaps she's unwell," Jess said, pushing back his chair and standing. "I think I ought to check on her."

"Sit down, Mr. Murphy. You can't go up there, and you know it."

Jess's eyes went cold and distant. "Did it ever cross your mind that she might want me to check on her? Did it?"

"Never crossed my mind, no," Annie said. "And I'm pretty sure she doesn't."

"You might know less than you think," he said quietly.

"What is *wrong* with you?" she said.

"I could ask you the same question," he said, sitting down slowly. "But in your case, I think I know the answer."

Annie glared at him, still standing with her hand on the back of her chair. "In my case? What does that mean?"

"Yes," he said. "I think you like having your Miss Sarah all to yourself. But I was here first, so you'd better get used to it."

"What has gotten into you?" Annie said.

"I know what you're thinking, that's all."

"I'll wager you don't know what I'm thinking *now*," she said, sitting down again because her legs suddenly felt weak.

They heard Sarah's feet on the upper landing. "And don't be a tattletale, either," Jess said, not looking at her. "Because I'll know if you say anything."

Annie was about to open her mouth when Sarah walked into the kitchen, carrying a large pasteboard box. Sarah immediately sensed that something was amiss.

"Is everything all right?"

"Oh yes," Jess said. "Annie and I were talking politics, and you know how that can be."

"Politics and religion are best avoided, even amongst friends," Sarah said. "And you two must be friends. Our agency depends on our all getting along, you know."

Annie said nothing, but tapped her little finger hard on the table.

"Sorry that took so long," Sarah said, "but I'd forgotten how much stuff I had moved around when we came back from Batavia. It turns out it was a good thing, though, because I wouldn't have wanted the police to find *this*."

She set the box down on the table and pulled up a chair. She took off the lid and laid it aside. The box was chock-full of envelopes—letters, dozens upon dozens, all of which seemed to be addressed in a single male hand. Annie knew what they were immediately, having heard Mrs. Miller's frequent and bitter complaints about her husband's theft of her letters.

"Oh, Miss, you know, it's getting a little bit late, don't you think?" Annie said. "To get started on something? Why don't we wait until tomorrow, when we're all more rested?"

"I feel energetic," Sarah said. "We seem to be getting somewhere, and that's exciting."

"I've got all sorts of energy," Jess said.

Annie wanted to scream, but couldn't make a sound.

"Any guesses at what these are?" Sarah said.

"Miss—"

"They're Arthur Pendle's letters, aren't they?" Jess said. "The ones that went missing before Mr. Miller's death."

"That's right," Sarah said. "How did you know about them?"

"From the inquest. Mrs. Miller said that his letters had been stolen from her safety-deposit box, and that their whereabouts were unknown. It caused quite a stir in the courtroom."

"I see. I didn't sit to hear Mrs. Miller's testimony, though in retrospect I ought to have. In any case, I've had them all along. Eddie gave them to me for safekeeping, because he thought someone might break into his office and steal them."

"I know the DA was in quite a flutter about them," Jess said.

"How would you know that?" Annie said.

"I—I interviewed him. Before the inquest. He mentioned them."

"But how would he know about Pendle's letters, at all?" Sarah said.

"Oh, as I recall, there was something about their being evidence in the Miller divorce trial. Pendle probably told him."

"So?" Annie said. "What would the Erie County district attorney care about some unfortunate family's divorce proceeding? Surely he had bigger fish to fry."

"I suppose I don't know," Jess said.

"Well, that's a first," Annie said under her breath.

"I heard that," Jess shot back.

"Come on now, you two," Sarah said.

"Let's read them," Jess said.

"I don't think we should," Annie said. "It's not right. They're someone else's private correspondence."

"You make a good point," Sarah said. "Though Eddie did entrust them to me, and asked me to read them."

"With all due respect to Mr. Miller," Annie said, "perhaps he oughtn't to have done that. I wouldn't want someone reading my letters, under any circumstances."

"What do you think, Jess?" Sarah asked. "Annie makes a very fair point."

"We're investigating a *murder*," Jess replied. "And the person who wrote these letters is the leading suspect. I don't think the usual rules of etiquette quite apply."

"I tend to agree with Jess, Annie," Sarah said.

"Then I can only protest," Annie said. "Strongly. I don't think it's right. At the very least, Miss, you might read them privately before sharing them with us. After all, Mr. Miller entrusted them to *you*, not the—whole world."

"We two are hardly the *whole world*," Jess said. "And Mr. Miller didn't know he was going to be killed—and possibly because of these letters. Nor did he know that Miss Payne would start a detective agency to bring his killer or killers to justice."

"I think we can find a compromise," Sarah said. "I'll read a few of them aloud, to get your perspective. Then we can decide if we need to read further."

"It seems rather contrived to me, but if that's the only way we can satisfy Miss Murray," Jess said, "I suppose we'll have to indulge her."

"Annie?" Sarah said.

"I'm not in favor," Annie said. "But it seems I've been outvoted."

"Only a few, then," Sarah said. "When I read these last year, I put them in chronological order. Let's pick an early one, then one in the middle, then one of a more recent date."

"Let's go," Jess said.

"Fine," Annie said.

"All right. Here's one of the earliest ones. Postmarked New York City, March 1901:

My Darling—

I feel we've passed a kind of test by securing our new post office box, where we can now correspond without your husband's interference. Tonight and tomorrow I'm in New York, stopping at the Hoffman House for a Bar Association meet. It is all I can do to listen to the droning on about statutes and precedents, with your dear face—and more—before my mind. Then I go back to my room and I look at myself in the mirror and think of how you might look at me, and I begin to . . ."

Sarah's voice died away. "I don't think I need to read the rest of this one," she said, looking a bit pale.

"What does it say?" Jess said.

"It's, um, rather personal."

"Oh for God's sake, this is simply untoward," Annie said. "We don't need to hear that sort of thing."

"No," Sarah said, swallowing hard and refolding the letter. She slid it back into the envelope and tucked it back at the bottom of the box.

"I'm sorry to say it," Annie said, "but it was unworthy of Mr. Miller to have these letters stolen. From a safety-deposit box, no less."

"He had every right," Jess said. "They were his wife's, and everything of hers belongs by right to him. She used his money to set up post office boxes and safety-deposit accounts, merely to carry on an illicit affair with another man. Using cute pseudonyms, no less. She had no right to conceal any of that."

"She wasn't *property*," Annie said, flushing. "A woman has a right to her privacy."

"Not once she is married, she doesn't."

"What century are you living in?" Annie said to him. "Can we *please* quit now, while we're ahead?"

Jess ignored her and turned to Sarah. "Two more," he said. "We've already agreed to that."

Sarah fished out another envelope from the middle of the box and slid out the contents. An unused train ticket to Atlantic City was folded inside the letter.

My Dear One,

If you can get away from him for the weekend, I have enclosed a ticket to meet me at the shore. We can take our usual suite at the Traymont. Send me a wire at the Waldorf, one word, simply yes or no. And remember—burn my letters. All of them. Destroying yours is like cutting my own flesh, but I do it because we can never risk these missives coming under anyone's gaze but our own.

Your Arthur.

"See what I'm saying?" Annie said. "They didn't want anyone seeing these. They're *personal*."

Jess laughed. "You're unbelievable."

"Last one, then," Sarah said. "This one's not a letter either, so it won't have anything personal in it. I remember it well. It struck me as very peculiar." She unfolded a sheaf of four sheets of legal-size yellow paper. On each was a series of rows and columns.

"It's all in Arthur Pendle's hand. As you'll see, the first column is the date," she said, spreading the papers out on the table and smoothing them with her hands. "Starting in 1899. The first three sheets are similar, and they come up almost to the end of 1901."

"What's marked in the second column?" Annie said, despite herself.

"Some lines are blank. Some have initials. Either WR, HP, or TP. Some others have 'Wkly,' which I imagine is an abbreviation for 'weekly.' Then the next column is either blank or a name. This one, for example, says 'Barker.' Next to the name, in the next column, is a number with a dollar sign. For 'Barker,' it's $750. Then in the last column there is generally some kind of notation in shorthand. But it's not Gregg or Pitman—I know both of those systems—so it seems to be some more personal code that Arthur was using."

Jess studied the pages. "Doesn't look familiar to me, either."

"Since this isn't a letter," Annie said, "why would it be in this box?"

"As I understood it from Eddie, everything here was in Allie's safe-ty-deposit box. It must be a document she obtained, somehow."

"These dollars are large," Jess said, adjusting his glasses on his nose. "Payments or receivables, I'd think."

"What about the initials?" Annie said. "WR, TP, HP? Who are they?"

"I thought perhaps TP was Terence Penrose, the DA, since he and Arthur were partners once," Sarah said. "But they weren't partners after 1898, so why would that be him?"

"William Roscoe," Jess blurted out. "If TP is Terry Penrose, WR must mean William Roscoe, the assistant district attorney. HP, I don't know."

"Do you recognize any of the other names?" Annie asked.

"I'll bet if I had a list of the dates and names," Jess said, "I could go to the *Courier* archive and find what was happening in Buffalo on those dates and with those people. Or near them in time. But if I guess right—and I'll be surprised if I'm off base—I think these are lists of monies collected for favors. Political favors. Graft."

Annie and Sarah sat back in their chairs at the same time. "That's right," Jess said. "If these are what I think they are, these four sheets of paper alone are something quite a few people would have killed for. To keep them from seeing the light of day."

Sarah exhaled and set the first three sheets aside. "Let's take a quick look at this last page," she said.

It was also a chart or ledger of sorts, but this one had a list of names—a lot of Pendle and Lane surnames—dollar amounts again, and then addresses, mostly in Tonawanda or the new outer suburbs of Buffalo.

"I know for a matter of fact what this one is," Jess said with a degree of smugness that made Annie want to knock him over the head. "I have no doubt that this is a schedule of the investments that Pendle made on behalf of his relatives. This is precisely what I was asking him about in the week prior to his death, and in fact what I was going to talk with him about the night he died." Jess studied the paper. "I called him about this before he had his fatal accident."

"Called him about what?" Sarah said.

"I had heard rumors that the Pendles had been making investments—real estate investments—on behalf of several family members. Collecting money from them to buy properties that would pay rents, and become more valuable as the city expanded. But then I caught wind that a couple of the family members hadn't seen any money back at all, and were getting nervous. I tracked them down and the story was always the same.

"Arthur and Cassie had told them that the investments had been made, had given them the addresses of the properties and copies of the deeds, but that it was taking longer than expected to pay out. I went to the addresses in question—and none of them had been built yet. All vacant lots in godforsaken places like Kenmore, and certainly not owned by the Pendles. Whatever deeds they had sent were fakes. That money had been used for something other than real estate investments.

"When I confronted Mr. Pendle, of course he denied it all, but he was squirrelly about it. Something was off. The more I pressed him, the weirder he became. And then"—he snapped his fingers—"next thing you know, he and his wife are *gone*."

"But why would someone bilk his own family?" Annie said.

"People do strange things," Jess said.

"You can say that again," Annie said.

Jess put his head into his hands and rubbed his eyes. "Who knows what the motive was? Maybe he was gambling with the money, or investing it in something else, or spending it on Mrs. Miller. He may have been hoping to kick the can down the road until he could clean up the mess he'd made."

Sarah folded the four sheets back together, put them back into the box, and closed the lid again.

"I'm sorry, Annie, but I think I'll need to read all these again. What's in here may be the key to the whole matter."

"I would say only this," Jess said. "No one—but no one—can know you have these. The best thing to do, probably, would be to burn them all, as was Pendle's intention. So long as they exist, you—all of us—could be in danger."

"I think you may be right," Sarah said. "I've always felt that I've been sleeping above a bomb."

"Sleeping?"

"I've had this box under my bed this whole time. But I'm going to hide them better now."

"If you like, I'll take the whole box away tonight and destroy it," Jess said.

"You won't do anything of the sort," Annie said. "I mean, I think that's Miss Sarah's decision to make, and not on the spot, either."

"Annie, you are a sweetheart," Sarah said. "Jess is only trying to be helpful." She turned to Jess. "Annie's very protective of me."

"As well she should be," Jess said. "This world is full of odd types. Some odder than they appear."

Annie looked sullenly down at the tabletop. "Can we call it a night?" she said. "I'm exhausted."

"Yes, let's do," Sarah said. "Thanks to both of you for giving up your evenings for this."

After Jess had left, Annie said a quick goodnight and made for the stairs. She was almost to the upper landing when Sarah's voice stopped her.

"Annie? Do you have a moment?"

Annie turned on the step and looked down at Sarah's upturned face, which looked worried.

"Yes, Miss?"

Sarah came up the stairs. "Let's chat in your bedroom, if you don't mind," she said.

The two sat on the edge of Annie's bed in her cozy room, appointed with photos of her family and a few Currier & Ives lithographs she'd saved up to buy while at the Miller house.

Sarah reached out and took Annie's hand. "I'm sorry about being such a pill," she said. "You know I value your opinions. And it would always be more pleasant to agree. But I don't want to overlook anything, either."

"Of course not," Annie said. "Nor do I."

"Is there any reason—other than the ones you mentioned, and very effectively, I might add—that you didn't want me to read those letters tonight?"

Annie looked down at Sarah's hand and patted it with hers. "No, not especially."

"Annie," Sarah said, putting her finger gently under the younger woman's chin and lifting her eyes to meet hers, "now I need you to tell me the truth. If there's something you feel I did that was improper, I want to hear it."

"It wasn't anything you did, Miss."

"Then what was it?"

"It's Jess," Annie said. "I'm beginning to think there's something not quite right about him."

"Why would you say that? It does seem you two seem to rub each other the wrong way, but—"

"Because—when you were upstairs, getting the box of letters, I nearly had to stop him bodily from going upstairs to you."

"Surely you mistook him."

"I didn't. He told me that you might want him to go up to you. That you might want him to check on you. If I hadn't jumped up and stopped him, I'm sure he would have."

"You're sure about this?"

"I would never make such a thing up. And he was rather curt with me when I stopped him, too. He seemed like a different person altogether. You ought to have seen his eyes. It still gives me gooseflesh to think of it."

"Perhaps he merely wanted to ensure everything was well with me?"

"That's what he claimed. But you know as well as I it's simply not done. If he had a concern, Ruth or I could have investigated. Every man knows that he doesn't march up the stairs to a lady's boudoir."

"True," Sarah said. "I don't know how to account for it."

"I don't either. That's not the only thing, though. It's only a feeling— but I think there's something very queer about him. I don't feel I can trust him. I want to, but I don't."

"Perhaps I've been too trusting," Sarah said. "I suppose I've felt we ought to be 'all for one and one for all.'"

"And that's a beautiful sentiment. But Mr. Miller may have died because of those letters, and I don't want anyone handling them we can't completely trust. They're like nitroglycerine."

ROOM TWO

John Pendle had maintained his brother's former office space as his headquarters as coexecutor of Arthur's large and complicated estate. Room Two, Aston Building, was more a partitioned-off section of another tenant's larger space than an office in its own right.

The best feature of Room Two was a row of tall windows that looked out onto bustling Franklin Street, though the ground floor location made it seem like living inside an aquarium. Arthur had therefore kept the blinds drawn most of the time, even on fine days. Alicia had been inside Room Two only once before, and that had been in the dead of winter, when Arthur had been at his most abject—raging, pleading with Ed to take his wife back, if only to buy them time. Ed had stood where Alicia was now standing, just inside the office door, pressed against the wall, listening gravely, refusing to look at Arthur, keeping his eyes on the worn floorboards. That was what she remembered most—that and the scent of Jockey Club eau de toilette, Arthur's favorite, filling the small, humid space, its windows sealed shut long ago by decades of paint.

Alicia had no sooner stepped into Room Two when she was dragged bodily back into the past by a faint trace of Jockey Club, even months after his death: lingering, as though it had seeped into the pores of the wainscot. She closed her eyes for a moment, and in a rush recalled the feel of his skin, the smell of his chest when she would lay her head on it.

She was rudely jostled out of her reminiscence by the horrifying awareness that the scent was emanating from John Pendle, who was sitting in Arthur's chair, at Arthur's rolltop desk, staring down at some papers, feigning ignorance of their arrival. He didn't stand. He didn't turn his head toward the door. He studiously ignored them until Bert cleared his throat.

"Mr. Pendle?" he said.

The younger Pendle swiveled Arthur's chair toward them with a long squeak, still neither standing nor welcoming them into Room Two. Instead, he looked past them coldly, as though they were as much strangers to him as the beggar on the streetcorner. Bert removed his hat and stepped into the room uninvited. He stuck out his hand.

John Pendle stood, slowly and deliberately, and tentatively took Bert's hand in his, giving it a weak shake with a small white hand traced with deep blue veins. He may have smelled like Arthur, but that was where the resemblance ended. John was shorter than his brother and more slightly built, if equally well-dressed, to the point of dandiness. His eyes were soft and brown to Arthur's penetrating blue, his hair sandy compared to his brother's deep chestnut. Arthur had often said that he took after his father's side of the family, and his brother resembled his mother's.

Ten to one, Alicia thought with a flash of pique, it's Arthur's bottle of cologne he's splashing on. Little shit.

"Mr. Hartshorn," Pendle said, continuing to ignore Alicia. "I'm sorry that my brother's office is so Spartan. But feel free to have a seat." Calling Room Two "Spartan" was being generous—in addition to the rolltop desk and chair, there was a single guest chair, a telephone table, and that was all. Nothing on the walls, nothing that would indicate anything about the man who occupied it for half a dozen years. "Please," Pendle said, waving his hand at the vacant chair.

"I trust you remember Mrs. Miller," Bert said, stepping aside to give John Pendle a full-frontal view of her. The little man did not extend his hand, only glanced at Alicia with a slight smirk under his neat mustache.

"How could I forget?" he said, and sat down emphatically into his office chair, which creaked like a ship's hawser.

Bert moved the empty chair over toward Alicia and motioned for her to sit. "Thank you, Mr. Hartshorn," she said. "You're a gentleman."

John Pendle looked up at Bert, steadfastly avoiding Allie's eyes. "Mr. Hartshorn, you requested a conference," he said, "but didn't specify the reason for your request."

"The telephone is too indiscreet, I tend to think, for sensitive matters," Bert said. "Although I suspect you can guess at the topic."

"I wouldn't presume to *guess*," Pendle said, smiling, "at the nature of any matter too sensitive for the telephone. It would be overweening on my part, as I'm sure you would agree."

"I can't imagine someone finding you overweening," Alicia interjected.

Hartshorn squeezed Allie's shoulder gently. "Mrs. Miller and I are here today, sir, to ask you if there is anything we can do to answer any remaining objections you may have to Mrs. Miller's receiving your brother's bequest."

"I see," he said. "No, there isn't anything you can do."

"Then you have no opposition to the bequest?"

Pendle shook his head. "I didn't say *that*."

"Pardon me?"

"What I said was that there is nothing you can do to answer my objections."

"And do you still have objections?" Bert said.

"Yes, I do."

"Would you be so good as to outline them? So that we may perhaps address them to your satisfaction?"

Pendle tapped a long index finger on the desk blotter. "I think that would be a better topic handled man-to-man, Mr. Hartshorn. It would be most awkward with the subject of the discussion present."

Alicia threw her head back and looked up at Hartshorn. He looked back and shook his head. "Mrs. Miller is my client," he said slowly. "There aren't any secrets between us."

Pendle smiled again, his little mustache creasing. "I find that difficult to believe, but I'll take you at your word. I remember not long ago she was also my brother's *client*"—he drew the word out—"so that must be what Mrs. Miller calls the peculiar fondness she seems to have for her legal counsel."

Bert cleared his throat. "May I once again request, respectfully, that you share with us the reason or reasons for your opposition to the settlement of my client's claim on your brother's estate?"

"Simply put, I see your client's claim as lacking a moral basis, and that, in effect, she inveigled the bequest out of my brother. She played upon the guilty conscience of a man of honor who was desperately trying to put things right—and repair the havoc your client had wrought on his otherwise spotless character. My brother took Mrs. Miller on as a client, and she promptly compromised his good name and reputation by intimating that there was more than a professional liaison between them."

Alicia wanted to spring out of the chair and throttle the little man, whose smugness infuriatingly reminded her of Edward. She felt the growing pressure of Bert's hand on her shoulder.

"Mr. Pendle," Bert said, "you are entitled to your opinion. Yet one must not confuse 'opinion' with 'fact.' The *fact* is that your brother loved Mrs. Miller and was afraid that, in the event of a divorce from her husband, his repeatedly avowed feelings for her might leave her vulnerable to retribution, and penniless. It was clearly his intention to provide for Mrs. Miller's security."

"I would suppose that's what courts are for, Mr. Hartshorn," Pendle said. "You have your facts, and I have mine. Unfortunately, you don't have any proof backing yours up, other than your client's claim. Anyone can make such a claim without documentation. It's my understanding that certain correspondence between your client and my brother has gone missing—if, that is, it existed in the first place."

"I don't need any *proof*," Alicia said, unable to keep quiet. "Arthur made dozens of bequests, and they've all been satisfied. Except for mine. It's not necessary for you or anyone to know *why* Arthur made *any* of them. It was his wish, not mine. I didn't even know he'd made it until the inquest."

Pendle still didn't look at Alicia, and instead responded to Bert. "In this case, unlike every other bequest, the basis of this bequest was illegitimate. To fulfill such a wish would be repugnant and beneath the dignity of the law. Almost every dollar of Arthur's estate went to settle his debts, as I'm sure you know, and if this sum is paid out, there will be nothing at all left to distribute to his lawful family."

"Oh, I see what it is," Alicia said. "You want the money."

"Al—Mrs. Miller, please," Bert said. "Mr. Pendle, my client is correct. There is no—to use your word—*moral* requirement for a bequest. If the bequest is made according to the law, it must be honored. Surely you know that."

"As I am not an attorney," Pendle said, "you might want to take that up with Mr. Penrose. As you already know, he has volunteered to assist me in my duties as my brother's executor. And he believes we are on firm ground in opposing this supposed bequest."

"*Supposed*?" Alicia said. "It's written in black and white, you—"

This time, Bert squeezed her shoulder so hard that she winced. "I have spoken to Mr. Penrose, and he has told me that if you withdraw your opposition, he has no remaining objection."

"That's not as I understand him. If only he were here, we could ask him. But he's not."

"It would seem we are at loggerheads," Bert said.

"It would indeed. Now if there's nothing else I can do for you today, I ought to get back to my work. I'll have to return to New York soon."

"You do recognize that this bequest is to be paid by one of Mr. Pendle's insurance policies," Bert said. "If the bequest isn't paid, it's only the insurance company that is enriched."

"Not so," Pendle replied. "Each policy has one or more contingent beneficiaries. Should a primary beneficiary be judged to be ineligible, benefits are paid to the next in line. In the case of the policy in question, Arthur's mother and I are the contingent beneficiaries. And your client is ineligible."

Alicia stood up so forcefully that she knocked the chair over backwards. "You little shit," she said, jabbing her finger in his direction. "Everything your brother said about you was true. No wonder he thought you were nothing but a mama's boy."

If her comment wounded John Pendle, it didn't show. "I presume that means 'good day,' Mr. Hartshorn, in your client's parlance."

Bert was holding onto Allie's arm and began edging toward the door. "Don't get up, sir," he said. "Thank you for your time today."

"Oh, Mrs. Miller?" Pendle called as Bert half-dragged Alicia toward the door. She tore free of Bert's hand and wheeled around.

"What?"

"I do want to thank you for something. I found it very touching, how you defended my brother at the inquest."

Alicia didn't know how to respond. "What is that supposed to mean?"

"My, you still don't know," John Pendle said, shaking his head sadly and placing his hand over his mouth. It wasn't a question. "I'm sorry. I oughtn't to have brought it up."

"What do you mean?" Alicia said, her voice rising. "What don't I know?"

"Mr. Pendle," Bert said, "what say we conclude this conference?"

"Oh, no you don't," Alicia said sidelong. "Out with it, Pendle. Be a man for a change and tell me what you mean."

Pendle leaned back in the office chair and laced his fingers behind his head. "If you insist, Mrs. Miller. What I mean to say is that I found it very affecting that you stood up so for Arthur—and your love for him. You could have easily scuttled his reputation, and you didn't. I'm grateful to you for that. Though I realize now that you did so unaware of the full scope of the situation. I'm sorry I mentioned it."

Bert stepped toward the little man. "All right, now, Mr. Pendle, if you are going to bring things up that my client should know or should have known, I would urge you to lay them out for us."

"Fine, fine, then," Pendle said. "If you insist. Mrs. Miller, you said that Arthur thought I was nothing but a mama's boy."

"I did. And he did."

Pendle shrugged. "And possibly he did think that. Well, probably he did. I suppose I was always the steadier of the two of us boys."

"What does that have to do with anything?" Alicia said, glaring.

"What I mean is—Arthur told you something about me. And I believe you. It has the ring of truth. But he also told me a lot about you."

"Well, I don't believe *you*. He wasn't that kind of man."

He laughed. "My brother was the kind of man he needed to be, whenever and wherever he needed to be. How else do you think he could graduate magna cum laude from New Haven College, and then make his living roughing up crooks in the slums of Buffalo? No need to answer: I'll tell you. He was an *actor*, Mrs. Miller. And a very good one. He could take on whatever role was required, and do it well. And with you, my dear—"

"I am most assuredly not your dear!"

"Excuse me. That was impertinent. With you, Mrs. Miller, he was playing the swain, the suave man-of-the-world, who could so easily charm a country girl like yourself off her feet."

"This has become insulting, sir," Bert said. "I think it's best we leave. Alicia?"

"No, I want to hear what this little turd has to say to me," Alicia shot back. "Go on, Johnnie."

"What I find ironic is that while you were committing suttee on my brother's pyre—at the inquest, you know—you had no idea of what he thought of you."

"I know very well indeed. I had dozens—a hundred—letters from him. I spent many nights with him. Arthur loved me, and I loved him. Whether you like it or not. You're just jealous, because he didn't love you."

"You know, I think you're right about that, too," Pendle said, leaning forward and putting his fingers together between his knees. "I do. I don't think that Arthur loved me. And I also think you're right because Arthur never loved *anyone*. Not even himself. Do you happen to know why my brother—while so in love with you—would beseech your husband—beg him!—to take you back to his home and hearth? And why he pleaded with you to help him in that goal?"

"Yes, I do. He said that Cassie was not yet prepared to grant him a divorce, and that I needed to wait for him in a safe place until he could prevail upon her. Otherwise, he feared I'd be turned out by my husband and left without resources."

Pendle shook his head slowly. "Poor Mrs. Miller," he said. "No, I'm afraid that's not the reason. I mean, that may well have happened to you, but that's not why my brother moved heaven and earth to convince your husband to take you back. The reason is that my brother enjoyed your company—a certain type of company—but he had no more desire to marry you than he did to marry Mr. Hartshorn here. Arthur was his usual seductive self with you, and you fell into it entirely. To such a degree that you wanted him to divorce his wife and make you his forever.

"But you see, Arthur wasn't that man. It was a *role* he was playing. Cassandra Lane was the only daughter of one of the wealthiest families in Connecticut. Not only would she never have consented to a divorce, for her family's name's sake, but Arthur would have been giving up a king's ransom. And for what? For a frowsy middle-aged Buffalo lady without means and past her prime? All those things that people said about you after the inquest, Mrs. Miller—your catalogue of sins— no one ever put their finger on your most fatal flaw. And that is *credulity*. You believed Arthur because what he told you matched up with what you thought of yourself. And the reason for that is—he could sense that that was what you needed, and he gave it to you to get what he needed in return.

"Now, now, let me finish," he said, holding up a finger. "I'm almost done. You wanted to know what my brother told me about you—himself. And this is it. He said that he'd had his fun with you. Lots and lots of fun, and there was more of it to be had, but things had gone too far. You had to be put back into your box, because what had been a little harmless lark had become deadly serious. Your husband had filed for divorce and couldn't be talked out of it a second time. And it looked as though he had enough evidence to secure one, at that.

"And then what? After a trial and all the attendant public scandal, you're divorced, and yes, you would be flat broke. Cassie might then have divorced him, if only to save face. And then my brother—champion athlete, magna cum laude legal scholar—would have to marry *you*, to salvage what little would remain of his reputation! And live the rest of his life like a plebeian. That's not nearly so much fun as—and I shall quote him verbatim, so please do pardon my French—'fucking that amazing body of hers in a rented room now and again.'"

"That will be quite enough!" Bert shouted. "I insist that we leave, Alicia." He gripped her arm, and she didn't resist but turned wordlessly toward the door. Bert guided her to the corridor and in the doorway turned back to John Pendle, sitting placidly in his brother's office chair. Bert stabbed his finger at him. "You are a cruel, heartless man," he said. "And no gentleman."

"You may be right," Pendle said impassively. "But I'm the only one in this room whose word can be utterly depended upon. Now if you wouldn't mind, please close the door behind you when you leave."

Bert closed the door quietly and hurried Allie down the corridor and out onto Franklin Street. "I'll hail a coach," he said. "I don't want to take the trolley."

In the coach, Allie looked away from Bert, out the window. He placed his hand over hers, but she pulled it away. When he looked over, he saw her dab a tear with her glove.

"I'm truly sorry, Alicia," he said softly, holding out his handkerchief. She pushed it aside. "That man ill-treated you. I've half a mind to go back and teach him a lesson, man to man."

Alicia turned toward him, and he could see her eyes were red and watery beneath her veil. "Don't you dare," she said.

"Why not? That little bastard gave you a terrible shock."

"You've got it all wrong, as usual," she said. "He gave me a priceless gift."

"Excuse me? Then why are you weeping, my dear?"

"I'm weeping because he's the first person in my life who cared about me enough to tell me the truth," she said, and turned back toward the window.

The pair rode in silence back to 101 Ashwood Street, and when they arrived home, Alicia quietly hung up her coat and hat and started up the stairs.

"Alicia," Bert said to her back. "Can I be of any assistance?"

She stopped on the stairs and turned around, a flat smile on her face. "No, Bert. What's wrong with me, you can't fix. But thank you."

❦

JESS HAD LET MORE than a week pass since the crime scene photographs were returned to the evidence locker, without reporting on any of it to Penrose. Each time he resolved to visit the DA, he remembered how Sarah's graceful hand had felt gripping his forearm. And he had been stalwart—not the Jess Murphy that everyone expected, but upright and noble, a pillar of strength in Sarah's worst moment. He had felt it, too: a flooding, electric paroxysm of grief shivering through her body. And in his imagination, he extended the scene, bit by bit: holding her close, whispering comfort, drawing her to him.

To sit down with hawk-faced Terry Penrose and share what had passed between the two of them in that makeshift darkroom seemed nothing short of profane, something that would turn a towering moment, a triumph, into something tawdry and common. And then there was the delicate matter of the letters . . . the thing Penrose wanted most.

It took another week before Penrose finally forced the issue.

Jess returned to his lodgings one evening, after a long shift at Adair's Hat Emporium. He opened the door and, to his delight, found no one waiting for him. His conversations with Phil and George could be helpful, but these days he felt a growing suspicion that they disapproved of his growing feelings for Sarah. Accordingly, he was trying to keep more and more to himself, and they tried that much harder to pry their way in.

On the board floor of the apartment, just inside the door, was an envelope. He rarely got mail—he had never told his parents his actual address—so seeing the envelope surprised him a little. He picked it up and saw that the return address was from the Office of the Erie County

District Attorney. Inside was one of Terry Penrose's calling cards, and on its back was written, in a neat cursive:

See me immediately.—THP

There could be no more stalling.

☙

"You've been quiet as a church mouse," Penrose said when Jess walked into his office. "Should I be concerned?"

"Not a whole lot is happening. And I've been busy at Adair's."

"Now, now. Jess. It's been weeks. Surely there's been something going on at Miss Payne's little detective operation."

"Well," Jess said, "she and Annie Murray saw the Pendle automobile."

"Were you with them?"

"No, like I said, I've been stuck at the hat store."

"What did they say? About the machine?"

"Only that it was a complete wreck."

Penrose put his elbows on his desk and leaned toward Jess. "Why do I feel that you're not telling me everything?" he said, looking at him squarely.

Jess tried, but couldn't meet the man's eyes. "I don't know why you'd think that. I am telling you everything."

"How are things with the Murray girl? Getting along better?"

"Yes, somewhat. She irritates me though. She's so—protective of Miss Payne, as though she's her mother or something."

"Women look out for other women," Penrose said. "They see men as threats."

"That's silly."

"You aren't having any—I don't know—warmer feelings for Miss Payne, are you?" Terry asked. "You seem a little bit protective of her, yourself."

"Only to the extent that I am sympathetic to what she wants to do," Jess said. "She feels that the legal system failed in the Miller case. She's trying to right a wrong. It's hard not to think she's doing the right thing."

"Just remember, Jess, you're speaking to the 'legal system' right now," Terry said, making quotation marks in the air. "And you're working for it, so please try to remember whose side you're on. Keep a cool head. Is that clear?"

"Yes, it's clear, but—"

"But?"

"But if anyone has warm feelings—it's Miss Payne."

"You lost me."

"I think she's a little bit smitten with me, if you want to know." Jess removed his spectacles, breathed on them, and wiped them clean with his handkerchief.

"You think so?" Penrose said. "What gives you that idea?"

"Sometimes you can just tell."

"Yes, a man does sometimes know such things. If she is, though, that could be useful to us. The warmer she feels about you, the more open she will be with what she's thinking."

"I'm confident she thinks Arthur Pendle did the deed."

"As do ninety-five percent of the people in Buffalo," Terry said. "That's hardly a revelation, but all the same it's nothing more than supposition. There's no evidence of his culpability—no weapon, nothing traceable to Mr. Pendle. And he can't very well be questioned now."

"True, I suppose it's a hypothesis."

"Good word! I swear, I've got to get you back on a newspaper sometime. Now then," Terry said, standing, "anything else for today?"

"No, that's it." Jess stood and shook the man's hand. "Don't tell my father, will you? About Miss Payne's feelings."

"I wouldn't dream of it," Terry said. "Your father would not find it comforting if he learned you'd become involved in another affair of the heart."

"He won't be satisfied until I join a monastery."

"I don't think that's it at all, but after the last—issue—he'd rather not take any chances."

"Lightning doesn't strike twice in the same spot, Mr. Penrose."

"It does if you're a lightning rod."

"Very funny. Well, sir, I'll leave you to your other work." Jess began edging toward the door.

"Thank you, Jess," Penrose said. "Let me leave you with one small request, if you don't mind."

"Of course. What's that?"

"Do not—*ever*—make me send you a card again requesting a conference. It's beneath my dignity. Once was more than enough. A second time will not endear you to me."

"I promise I'll be more regular in my reports."

"Thank you for understanding. I would like to think that you think about me more than I think about you."

FERE LIBENTER HOMINES

For a full week after the meeting with John Pendle, Alicia kept mostly to herself in her bedroom. Melissa, the new domestic, brought up her meals, though she didn't eat much. The children would pop in for a kiss now and again. Bert contented himself with asking after her through her door, and told the girls that Mama was unwell, nothing serious, no cause for concern—but best left alone while she got better.

She passed the time jotting in her diary, which she'd resumed keeping after the inquest. She'd kept a diary for years, before the trouble began, but then it became more a thing potentially incriminating than beneficial. And she'd found that while she was with Arthur, her thoughts were mainly trained on him: when she'd see him again, what they'd say, what they'd do—and then, when his next letter was going to arrive. There was no room at all for any other thought.

Not that her diary entries were especially profound. She held her deeper thoughts close—and the liveliest ones of all seemed to lose their breath as soon as the ink had dried on the page. There wasn't any way to capture—not really—what she felt about John Pendle's revelation, which from the moment he'd uttered it could not be dismissed. His words had had the cold, crystalline ring of a tuning fork, indisputably on key, the one sound she'd never been willing to admit. And now it could not be unheard. She had lived a long and intense period of her life in error, she now knew, and undoing that was impossible. But what to change? She had always prided herself on her perspicacity, and yet with Edward and Arthur both, she seemed to have chosen unwisely. *Credulity*, she thought. What other blind spots might she have?

She also engaged in another favorite activity—one that hadn't ever altered—and that was staring at herself in the mirror, sometimes clothed, though more often not. Her favorite times to be naked were first thing in the morning, and in the lamplight before retiring. She would wear one of her shining satin dressing gowns, and would glide in front of the full-length cheval mirror, letting the smooth silk slide away from her shoulders and puddle on the floor at her feet. Then she would examine herself, posing this way and that, running her hands over her skin.

She liked her touch. She liked it better than she had liked Edward's, or Arthur's, or Bert's. There was something about the caress of her own hands that felt safe, never ticklish and not always arousing, merely a familiar warmth. Not that she couldn't become aroused, when she wanted to, but that was her choice, not linked to a lover's urgency. And she could touch herself precisely the way she wanted to be touched, at that moment—an impossible requirement to place in another person's hand. Often her palms would glide over her thighs, her belly, her breasts, mimicking the liquid feel of the dressing gown. And sometimes she might be far tougher on herself, rubbing, pinching—sometimes hard—and knowing all the while she would have slapped any other person had they taken such liberties. When she did it to herself, it hurt—sometimes a lot—but in a good way, like biting down hard on a toothache.

Sometimes she traced with her fingers the torc, the golden snake, around her throat. For the first time since it had been burned on, the warm gold seemed alien, a thing perhaps affixed for reasons different from those she'd imagined, or had been given. I wonder what John Pendle would say about it? she thought, if he knew. Then again, maybe he did.

As the days went by, and the lines in her diary dried as fast as the ink could flow, the most difficult thing of all was the thought that Arthur Pendle had done away with himself—and his wife—because of her. Had death seemed preferable to a life with her? Had things gone so far that he knew that they would have to marry, like it or not? She had never thought to ask him anything of the kind when he was alive, and however frustrating it might be, she could never know now. And would she believe it, if she could?

She picked up her pen again, stabbed it into the inkwell, and wrote the single Latin maxim that had stuck with her since high school.

Fere libenter homines id quod volunt credunt.

People believe what they want to believe.

26

THE MORGUE

WHEN ANNIE WALKED IN THE FRONT DOOR AROUND SUNDOWN, Sarah was standing in the hallway, looking through the mail. She glanced up and smiled. Annie's hair was disheveled and her whole face was smeared with what looked like soot.

"Have you been auditioning for a minstrel troupe?" Sarah said.

"Very funny. I told you I was going to see if I could turn up more information on our friend. I've been at the *Courier*. In the morgue, which is apparently what newsmen call the storage area. I never thought detective work would be so filthy," she said, looking down at her clothing.

"What were you doing over there?"

"Research. Looking for things relating to articles written by you-know-who. He's not here, is he?"

"No, of course not. What did you find?"

"Let me wash up and change out of these clothes, and I'll tell you."

A half hour later, Annie joined Sarah in the kitchen, carrying a stenographer's pad. "You look like a new woman," Sarah said.

"I'll sleep well tonight, at least. It was exhausting, lugging all those stacks of newsprint around."

"Did you learn anything?"

"I learned that I wish you'd teach me stenography, because I had to copy articles out longhand, but yes, I found some very interesting things." She opened the steno pad. "Seems like Jess had bylined articles starting in late 1901, local things mostly. Nothing crime-related." Her finger traced down the page in her notebook. "Demolition of the Pan-American buildings. Closing of the canal for the year. Then a couple of things that may have been crime-related—a fire of mysterious origin in December."

"Nothing much there," Sarah said.

"No, and the writing is straightforward. Not crude, but not Julian

Hawthorne either. But then on January 2, directly after the murder, he seems to have been put on the crime beat, or at least assigned to the Miller case.

"He was telling us the truth when he said he was pressing pretty hard on Arthur Pendle. He clearly thought he was guilty from the first word. You can tell from the tone of the articles. I almost feel sorry for Pendle—Jess makes him out to be terribly smarmy."

"Smarmy?"

Annie laughed. "That's a word I read in one of the newspapers today. It's a new term that means sleazy or dishonest."

"That's a good one! I'll have to remember it. What happened next?"

"There are no more bylined articles by Jess until just before the inquest gets going."

"What then?"

She flipped to the next page of her notebook, which was covered with pencil scrawling. "That's when it gets interesting. The first mention of you—specifically—was when you were interviewed by the police."

"He covered that?"

"Because he seems to have been convinced that Pendle was guilty, yes, he spends a lot of time on your interrogation. He writes that—well, here, I'll find it." She pored over her notes. "Yes. He says that the police '*burst into the home of a local woman suspected of having had illicit relations with Miller on the night of his murder, but have failed to bring charges to bear.*'"

"For heaven's sake. I know people thought that, but it's hard to hear it."

"There's more. A lot more. The day after the police showed up, he must have spied on you, because he writes, '*The woman interrogated by police, Mrs. Seth Payne, though undeniably beautiful, has about her the slightly disingenuous air of someone who knows more than she reveals.*' And then in another article the very next day, he says, '*This reporter has learned that the radiant Mrs. Payne, presumed to have reunited with her husband after her ordeal with the police, is in fact living independently on Norwood Street, while her lonely husband carries on his dental practice in Batavia.*'"

"Nice of him to find me beautiful—even radiant!—but it makes me sound rather . . . *smarmy*, you might say."

"You might say that," Annie said. "Now listen to this. The Pendles die, and Jess begins covering the inquest. He writes something every day, but the most interesting is his coverage of your testimony."

"I'm on tenterhooks," Sarah said.

"Here goes, then. *'Today, the lovely Mrs. Seth Payne took the stand. She maintained her composure throughout a withering examination by the Assistant District Attorney, her dainty booted foot tapping occasionally in impatience with Mr. Roscoe's probing, her violet eyes flashing with disdain when asked a pointed question. After it was done, the proceeding succeeded only in confirming the opinion of many that Mrs. Payne is culpable of nothing beyond being a pretty simpleton, a charming country girl ensnared in, but also enshrined by, the Ashwood Set's wicked web. If she was ashamed of her relations with Edward Miller, she bore that shame with aplomb, even with a kind of willful pride. When Mrs. Payne at last stepped down from the witness box, one could feel that the star actress of this morality play had left the stage, and possibly forever.'"*

"Well, how about that?" Sarah said. "Demoted from 'beautiful' to 'pretty' this time, and made into a simpleton. A wicked one at that."

"His descriptions of other persons involved in the matter are nowhere near as, um, colorful."

"This is good work, Annie. You are a natural detective. I wonder where this leaves us, though?"

"I'm not sure. But the—intensity—of his writing about you concerns me. I'm beginning to wonder if this is a case of obsession."

"He's certainly a bit overwrought, but I don't know if I'm willing to go that far."

"Let's say I'm wrong," Annie said. "What harm is done? If we conduct ourselves with additional care? None."

"The harm is that we don't give Jess the benefit of the doubt. That wouldn't be treating him fairly."

"An ounce of prevention," Annie said.

DROIT DU SEIGNEUR

ANNIE WAS ALREADY IN THE OFFICE WHEN JESS ARRIVED THE next morning. At first, she barely looked up from her work to say good morning, but then immediately chided herself. She snapped out of it and managed a reasonably cheerful hello. It was doubly difficult after having read the man's articles.

Jess hung up his hat and turned to look at her with a steady, somewhat challenging gaze.

"I thought so," he said.

"You thought so what?"

"I knew you'd tell her. About our little disagreement."

"I don't know what you're talking about."

"And I know you do." He sat down at his desk and leaned back in his office chair, looking at the ceiling. "I talked with my roommates last evening about you. And they agreed with me."

"Whatever are you talking about? You talked about *me*?"

"Yes, and they think I'm on the mark about you. I know your type. I knew people like you at the *Courier*, and in Newport too."

"People like *me*? Tell me, if you would—just what kind of person am I?"

"A jealous one."

"Jealous? Of what?"

"You're jealous that Sarah likes me. You want to keep her all for yourself."

"It's 'Miss Payne' to you," Annie said. "And I don't want to keep anyone to myself, whatever that means. And I'd like to know how do your roommates know anything about me?"

"They don't know you. I said they know your type."

"What are their names?"

"Why do you want to know?"

"I'm curious. Maybe I do know them."

"You don't."

"But perhaps I'll meet them someday. What are their names?"

"Why should I tell you?"

"Why wouldn't you?"

"Phil Henry and George Barfield," Jess said, looking away. "And you won't meet them. They're professional men. They wouldn't be rubbing elbows with—what did you call it again?—a *domestic*."

"It's very fortunate for you that they don't mind rubbing elbows with a hat salesman."

"Hmm," he said. "Sarah needs me, and she's not going to like you trying to drive a wedge between us. I mean it."

"You're crazy," Annie said. "I mean it."

❦

IT WAS ALMOST NOON on Monday when Sarah got to the office. The autumn air was light, the sky a deep blue, with a few high clouds. The crisp, fall weather had put her in good spirits, and she greeted Annie and Jess with a broad smile.

"Guess where I was this Saturday?" she said.

"Where?" Annie said.

"On Friday I received a call from Mr. Charles Kendall, requesting a conference with me on Saturday. We may have a new case!"

"Charles Kendall?" Jess said.

Annie squeezed her eyes shut. "That name rings a bell, but I can't place it."

"How about Kendall Electrolytic Abrasives?" Sarah said.

Jess seemed to recognize the name. "In Niagara Falls?"

"Oh, I know," Annie said. "He's a multimillionaire. A big businessman. His house was featured in the rotogravure section of the paper some months ago. It's amazing—like a castle."

"Right. That's where he wanted to meet with me. It's called Kendall House, and it's perched along the gorge, not far from Lewiston, looking out toward Canada. It's magnificent."

"Why did he want to meet you at his home?" Jess said. "And on a Saturday?"

"The matter in question relates to what he called 'industrial espionage,' and so he couldn't very well meet me at his factory. The factory is on the High Bank in Niagara Falls proper. Ten miles from Kendall House."

"That is wonderful news," Annie said. "I can't imagine how beautiful his home must be."

"It's stunning," Sarah said. "But mainly, he would be an excellent client, and the case seems very intriguing."

Jess tilted back in his desk chair and whistled at the ceiling. "Well, so long as we're careful," he said.

"Careful?" Sarah said.

Jess rocked back into an upright position. "I'm remembering the great Charles Kendall now," he said. "Handsome, tall and straight, a captain of industry. He has fifty million."

"My kind of gentleman, if you want to know," Annie said.

"I'm sure he is. But he wouldn't be interested in you," Jess replied. "But oh, now, Miss Sarah," he said in a voice thick with sarcasm, "now *that's* a different story."

"I have no interest in his appearance," Sarah said. "But a man like that as a potential client is like a dream come true."

"Imagine, fifty *million*," Jess said with a snort. "What does any person need with fifty million dollars? While people are starving on the street."

"I don't know how much money he has," Sarah said. "I understand he's a self-made man."

Jess snapped up in his chair. "A self-made man! How delightful. But I wonder whether he would have invited *me*—as a representative of the firm—to discuss a case with him?"

"What are you suggesting?" Sarah said.

"I'm a man. You're a woman. And a certain *kind* of woman."

Sarah was going red in the face. "What in the *hell* is that supposed to mean? Just what *kind* of woman do you think I am?"

"Calm down, it's a compliment," Jess said. "You're beautiful, Sarah, and you know it. Mr. Moneybags knows it, too."

Annie stared at them, unsure of whether to intervene, and shocked that Jess had used Sarah's Christian name.

"We'd never met before today. He wrote us a letter. He's heard good things about our agency. For God's sake."

"Oh, but I'm sure he's seen you. Probably in the photographs published in the articles I wrote for the *Courier*. I probably am the one to thank for introducing the two of you."

"The two of us?"

"Well, if he offers you the case, just make sure he doesn't think the agency fee also entitles him to droit du seigneur."

Sarah looked incredulously at Jess.

"Did I hear you correctly?" Sarah said quietly, in the most threatening tone Annie had ever heard come out of her mouth.

"Hear what?"

"You know what you said. Did I hear it correctly? *Droit du seigneur?*"

"It's a metaphor."

"A metaphor for a belief on your part that my person is for sale to the highest bidder."

Jess looked away. "I didn't mean it that way."

Sarah was simmering. "Is there another meaning to that very specific phrase? I don't think so."

"Sorry I said anything," he mumbled.

"As am I." Sarah turned on her heel and went into her office, slamming the door, hard, behind her.

"What the hell was *that* about?" Annie said. "What does that gibberish mean, anyway? *Dwah duh* what?"

"It doesn't mean anything."

"It means something, or it wouldn't have set her off like it did."

"Look it up, if you care so much."

"Then I will," Annie said, reaching for her desk dictionary. "How do you spell it?"

"Are you completely illiterate? D-R-O-I-T-D-U-S-E-I-G-N-E-U-R."

Annie found the term and then looked up, her eyes wide. "What in the what? She should have slapped you into next week."

"Men with money think they can have anything they want. And generally they can. That's all I'm saying."

"That doesn't include her. You owe her an apology."

"For looking out for her?"

"For being an asshole. And for calling her Sarah."

Jess stood up and grabbed his bag. "I'm leaving," he said. "I'm not going to take abuse from the likes of you."

"Fuck off," Annie said.

Jess strode out and slammed the outer door as he went. Annie waited a few moments for her heart to stop thumping, then got up and rapped gently on Sarah's door.

"I'm busy," said her voice, muffled through the door.

"He's gone," Annie said.

"Come in."

Annie opened the door enough to sidle in, and gently closed it again. Sarah was at her desk, the mail strewn about haphazardly, the prized letter from Charles Kendall thrown onto the floor. She was staring down at the desktop. When she looked up, her face powder under her eyes was streaked.

"Miss," Annie said. "I'm so sorry about what he said."

Sarah smiled feebly. "To imagine that someone, anyone—and in my own employ, no less—would suggest that I'm little more than a common whore."

"I don't know what to say. It's repellent."

"Maybe he thinks I don't know what droit du seigneur means?"

"I certainly didn't, and I wish I still didn't."

"Do you think that's what people think of me?"

"Oh, Miss," Annie said, reaching across the desk and squeezing Sarah's hand. "You are a princess. You *are* beautiful, and a hideous creature like Jess is jealous. He wants you to like him."

"Surely not!"

"I'm not wrong about this," Annie said. "He's got you on the brain. Has from the first time I set eyes on him. That's why he doesn't like me. He thinks he has to share you with me."

"What nonsense." She looked down again. "I wish I didn't have to admit this, but he really wounded me."

"Who wouldn't be? But consider the source. He's an oaf. We're going to have to do something about him, Miss."

"I'm so sorry I got us into this, Annie," Sarah said, putting her head in her hands. "I hired him right away, and now I'm living to regret it. I've made a mess of everything."

"You've done nothing of the sort. He's the one to blame, not you. Don't let him give you his shame. And he's going to be sorry, I promise you. I'll make him howl, by the time I'm through with him. I lived with Alicia Miller for *four years*. I can handle his kind with one hand behind my back."

"What would I do without you, Annie?" Sarah said, blinking back tears.

"You're never going to find out, so long as you'll have me."

❦

THE NEXT DAY, JESS showed up in the office early, hoping to catch Sarah alone. He was in luck—Annie had awakened with a throbbing headache and was off to a slow start that morning.

Sarah heard him sit down at his desk, but she didn't call out a hello as usual. She went on typing a letter to Charles Kendall, thinking carefully about how to put her best foot forward.

After a few minutes, Jess appeared in her office doorway. "May I have a word?" he said.

Sarah stopped typing and looked up. "What about?"

"Could we sit in the outer office?"

"Yes, I suppose," she said. She got up and followed him out to his desk and sat in the adjacent guest chair.

"What's on your mind?" she said.

"I think you know," he said. "I felt terrible about yesterday, and I wanted to clear the air. I want to apologize."

"Thank you, Jess. I forgive you. But I will say it will be a hard thing to forget. I do feel that it's driven a wedge between us, and certainly between you and Annie. That's a problem for our agency, as I'm sure you can understand."

"It was a stupid thing to say. I didn't intend to say it. I hate myself for it."

"You couldn't have come up with something like that without some thought. Is that what you think of me? Really?" She studied his face.

Jess looked back into Sarah's violet eyes and then did something that took her quite by surprise. He half-stood out of his desk chair and bent toward her, and kissed her impulsively on the lips. The kiss was brief, a second at most, but for another such second with her soft, warm mouth against his, Jess probably would have been willing to throw his entire life away.

Sarah jumped up, knocking the chair over backwards. "What in the *world*?"

Jess looked straight at her. "Now *that*, I intended."

"What the devil? Have you lost your mind?"

"I can't help it. I'm in love with you, Sarah."

"I won't tell you again, but it's 'Miss Payne,' and you don't know me well enough to be in love with me. Not to mention the fact that we are colleagues, not sweethearts."

"I had a long conversation with my roommates about this," he said, closing his eyes slowly and leaning back in his chair. "They understood."

"Understood what?"

"I said to them—'I'm officially in trouble, boys. I've gone and fallen in love with my boss.' They thought I meant Mr. Adair, the owner of the hat shop. Isn't that funny?"

"I'm not laughing, Jess. It's not amusing in the slightest."

"Oh, come on, it's funny. Anyway, I told them that I've been working with you only for, what is it, a few months, and I've gone positively batty over you."

"Why am I listening to this drivel?" Sarah said, almost to herself.

"Phil—my one roommate—said to me, 'Can't say as you had much choice in the matter. Who wouldn't fall in love with that goddess?' I'd shown him your photograph. And I said, 'Oh, that's not the half of it. She's gorgeous, and I've seen her with her hair down—'"

"Jess, please stop yourself. You've said quite enough!"

Jess shook his head. "No, there was more. I stuck up for you. I said, 'She's so much more than merely beautiful. She's sharp as a tack, completely fearless, loves her daughter . . . who's a little doll, by the way . . .' Then George, my other roommate, says, 'Well what in the hell would a woman like that want with someone like you?' And I know I have nothing to offer you, Sarah—"

"I can't hear any more of this," Sarah said, heading for the door.

"Please, don't leave," he said, getting up. "Phil said to me, 'You never know, old man! She may be in love with you, too, and is afraid to admit it.' And George said, 'Why not roll the dice! Kiss her, and tell her you love her. What have you got to lose?'"

"Your job, for one," Sarah said, trying to put an arm through her coat and missing the arm hole over and over. She flung the thing over her arm.

"You can't fire me for being human," he said. "Simply for having emotions. For being in love with you!"

"I *can* fire you, if I so choose. And not for *having* emotions, but for *acting* on them."

"It was one little kiss!" he said. "It was heaven, too. You must have felt it. I'd die for you, Sarah. Don't you want someone like that looking out for you?"

"I think you should think about finding other employment, Jess," she said, trying to steady her voice. "I would never let someone go now, before Thanksgiving and the holidays, but after the New Year, you'll have two weeks to find another situation. I can't have this. I *won't* have this."

"Please, please," he said, clasping his hands. "Don't send me away. It just—started. At the inquest. And I couldn't stop it. It's who you are—you are intelligent, and kind, and beautiful—but there's also something more, some deep pain that I want to take away. Perhaps I oughtn't to have kissed you like that. But please, Sarah, don't dismiss me. I can keep a check on myself. This agency is all I have."

"For the last time, stop calling me Sarah. It's most unwelcome. And this agency is all I have, too—besides Maggie. But I insist on having a *real* detective agency, and *real* detectives don't go around kissing each other. You think that Pinkerton men are smooching on the job?"

He wanted to laugh. She's thawing out, he thought. "No, I expect they're not. Look, we'll laugh about this one day. Let's put it behind us."

Sarah glared at him from the door.

"Please—just think about it. If January comes and you still want me gone, I'll go."

"I won't be changing my mind."

"Please, let's leave it for now. But I wonder—if we didn't work together, do you think you could have feelings for me?"

"No," she said, raising her voice. "I don't have romantic feelings for you, and I don't expect them to develop. I was enthusiastic about hiring you—learning from you—but that's as far as it goes."

Jess rubbed his eyes. "You haven't seen me at my best," he said. "You've seen a desperate man. A man tormented—consumed by feelings for someone he can never have. No, I'm not well-dressed, or rich, and I live in a lousy place in Chinatown and not in some grand mansion like Charles Kendall"—he waved his arms—"but damn it, I can *love*! I could love you more than anyone!"

"That'll be more than enough. Right now, I don't want to hear you, I don't want to see you, and no later than the middle of January I want you gone. I'm tempted to say I'm sorry, but I'd be lying. I'm going out now for a while. If you want to make yourself useful, please get to work filing all those"—she pointed in fury—"horrid piles of paper keeling over on top of your desk. It looks like a pigsty in here."

She didn't wait to hear his reply, and all he could hear were her footsteps growing more distant and the voices of his roommates, who he knew would tell him, as soon as he got home, how terribly he'd overplayed his hand.

❧

AFTER THE DOOR CLOSED behind Sarah, Jess sat down heavily for a few seconds, breathing hard. How did that go so badly? he thought. I apologized, for God's sake. And for what? Only to be abused and rejected. Who the hell does she think she is?

I'll give her pigsty, he thought.

He stood and, with both arms, swept everything off his desk—papers, ink, books—onto the floor, then kicked the mass of it all over the office. He pounded on the desktop with his fists, feeling a rage he hadn't felt since—well, since back in Newport. Tilting his head back, he roared at the top of his lungs, a kind of wounded animal howl, until he had no breath left. He sat down weakly in his chair and put his head on the desk, and then lifted it and brought it down, hard, three or four times, until he saw stars.

The door rattled and Annie rushed in. "What is going on in here?" she said. "I heard screaming!" Then she saw the mess, and her eyes went wide.

Jess lifted his head off the desk. His forehead was bleeding, and blood was running down along the bridge of his nose and over his lips.

"What in the—"

"It's nothing!" he said. "Mind your own goddamned business for a change, will you?"

She kept the door partly open behind her in case she needed to escape.

"It is my *goddamned* business when our office looks like it was hit by a tornado, and you're bleeding all over the place. What gives?"

"Yeah, well, fuck you," he said, getting up. "That's what gives." He barreled toward her and grabbed his coat, knocking her into the wall. "And get the hell out of my way." He yanked the door open so quickly that Annie's foot got wedged underneath it, stopping it, which made him angrier. He tugged on the knob, hard, wedging her instep under the door. Annie howled. "Fuck's sake! My foot's caught!" she yelled. "Let up!"

He glared at her. "I'd cut it off, if I could," he said coldly, and tugged again on the door, enough so that he could fit through the opening and catapult himself out of the office.

Annie tried to wriggle her foot out from under the door, without success. She had to bend over awkwardly and untie her boot so that she could extricate her throbbing foot. It was already beginning to swell. She yanked the boot free from under the door and then stood on one leg, rubbing her injured foot and looking ruefully at the ruined leather of her best pair of boots.

"That son of a bitch!" she muttered. "I'll be damned if I let him get away with this." Ignoring the pain, she pulled her damaged boot back on, resolved to chase him down. She grabbed a leather-wrapped lead blackjack that Sarah kept hanging by its wrist strap on the costumer and dropped it into her coat pocket. I'm going to knock him into next week, she thought, and hobbled quickly down the corridor.

Jess was long gone, down the hall and down the steps, but she made the best time she could, limping but on fire inside and muttering every curse she'd ever heard Alicia Miller say. Annie popped out onto the cold sidewalk and looked both directions. No Jess. She walked toward city hall, where the streets got wider and she thought she might have a longer view.

Then, almost at city hall, she spotted him. Gritting her teeth and tightening her grip on the cosh in her pocket, she crossed the street and did pretty well closing the distance. He lived over off Michigan, she knew, so he'd be going past city hall, heading east. I'll catch up to him in a block or two, she thought. Won't he be surprised when I brain him. Not putting up with—

But then, instead of going past city hall, Jess turned at the plaza in front of the great stone building and walked straight up the steps and into the grand front entrance. She hobbled after him and, at the end of the vast marble lobby, saw him hop onto an elevator car, going up.

Now what have we here, she thought, feeling the stabbing pain in her foot for the first time and almost buckling under.

WHAT THOU DOEST

"I'm here to see Mr. Penrose," Jess said. His face was red, but his freckles had gotten even redder, making it appear as though he might have measles.

"Do you have an appointment?" the lady behind the desk said, with the practiced calm that came from dealing with angry strangers most of every day.

"I do not. Where is Mrs. Harrison? She knows me."

"Mrs. Harrison is not here today, sir. Are you aware that you are bleeding?"

Jess whipped out his handkerchief and mopped his forehead. "Sorry. I tripped and fell on the stairs in my haste to see Mr. Penrose."

"Well, then, perhaps you can leave a card, and I'll tell him you called."

"I need to see him now."

"He's in court," the lady said. "You can't see him now, and in any case, you'd need an appointment."

"Tell him it's Jess Murphy about—something he'll want to hear. He knows me. He's friends with my father. I'm from Newport."

"A lovely spot," the lady said with a bland smile. "My husband and I went there on our honeymoon."

"Yes, yes, it's a very nice place," Jess said. "But I need to see Mr. Penrose."

"Now, Mr.—Murphy, was it? I have already told you quite clearly that the district attorney is very busy, in court at present, and if you'll only leave your card, I promise you I will present it to him with all of the others left with me."

"I'm not leaving until I see him," Jess said. "I can wait." The lady at the desk nodded over Jess's shoulder, and an enormous pile of a policeman sauntered up from his post next to the door. "What seems to be the problem?" he said.

The lady smiled. "Mr. Murphy here wants to see the district attorney. I have told him, twice, that Mr. Penrose is not available, but he's become rather insistent."

"All right, buddy, let's go," the cop said, grabbing Jess by the upper arm so hard his hand went numb. "Let's not bother the nice lady anymore, what do you say?"

Jess craned his neck and shouted into the offices. "I am Jess Murphy, and I'm here with information for Mr. Penrose!"

The cop growled and started dragging Jess toward the door, looking forward to teaching him a lesson in the alley behind city hall.

"Hold on there," said a voice from behind the lady's desk. "I'll speak with him."

"Mr. Roscoe," the lady said, "this man is being rather obstreperous. Are you sure?"

"Yes, it's fine. I'll speak with him. He does know Mr. Penrose."

The cop reluctantly loosened his grip on Jess's arm and shoved him toward the desk. "Your lucky day, pal," he said.

"Come on back," Roscoe said to Jess, and opened the wicket between the lobby and the office area. Jess followed him to his office and took the seat offered at a small conference table.

"Now what, pray tell, are you yelling about, Mr. Murphy?" Roscoe said. "Consider yourself fortunate that I rescued you from a nasty fall on the ice behind the building."

"Thank you, sir," Jess said. "I had assumed Mr. Penrose would make my name known to the desk staff. I'm working on a very important assignment for him. It's very irregular to come here and be treated like a common criminal."

"Yes, I'm sure it is. I know about your assignment. Why don't you tell me why you're here? I'm having lunch with Mr. Penrose today, and I'll be happy to pass along anything you wish. If he wants to see you personally, he'll be in touch directly."

"I don't know you," Jess said.

"We haven't been formally introduced, but I'm William Roscoe, assistant district attorney." Roscoe reached into his vest pocket and took out a card, which he advanced across the table to Jess. "Now, will that do?"

Jess examined the card, flipped it over. "Yes, I've heard of you. I used to be with the *Courier.*"

"Indeed you did. Now then, as you'll imagine, I'm rather busy myself. Would you be so good as to get to the point of the matter?"

"You know that Mr. Penrose has me working for Miss Payne—at the detective agency."

"Yes, the 'Avenging Angels,' or some such. Yes."

"I have something very interesting to report."

"Yes?"

"First, they've deduced that Arthur Pendle was the probable killer of Edward Miller, and that Pendle then committed suicide."

Roscoe made a wry face. "Quite a few people—perhaps a majority—in Buffalo hold those beliefs, Mr. Murphy. I don't find that such remarkable detecting."

"That's only the start. They think that the district attorney was somehow involved in Miller's murder."

"Now that's a strong statement. I doubt very seriously that they have anything to back it up."

Jess smiled and rapped his knuckles on the table. "And that's where you'd be wrong," he said.

Roscoe leaned back in his chair, looking skeptically at Jess. "I don't have all day, sir," he said.

"Miss Payne has the *letters.* The Arthur Pendle letters. A whole box of them. She's had them all along."

"And you know this how?"

"I saw them. She read a couple of them to me."

"And when was this?"

"Couple months ago, I guess."

"Interesting that you're only now coming forward with this. That seems—peculiar."

"I've been busy," Jess said.

"Oh yes, and you were blinded by the full moon. You know I'm in the business of falsehood, Mr. Murphy—discovering it. And you're not telling me the whole truth. Why did you wait so long to tell us something this important?"

"I wanted to gain her trust," he said.

"She's a very attractive woman, isn't she?" Roscoe said.

"She is. What does that have to do with it?"

"I think it's difficult, sometimes, for a man to—give over a woman like that to the hands of the law."

Jess looked away briefly, then snapped back to Roscoe. "I made a pledge to Mr. Penrose," he said. "It is difficult. And Miss Payne has—well, she's become my lover. I've taken her as my lover."

"Now that is unexpected, sir. Is she still your lover?"

"Yes, but at last I had to make a choice between doing my duty and pursuing an affair of the heart. I chose duty."

"How remarkable. In all candor, truly noble," Roscoe said. "Do you know how rare that is? I don't know one man in a thousand who would take such a stance. And not one in ten thousand—a hundred thousand—who would take it if Miss Payne were his lover. Such a man would sooner cut his own balls off with a letter opener, Mr. Murphy, than bear witness against such a woman. Unless—of course—he'd been *jilted*."

"I've not been jilted. If anything, I may well jilt her."

"I would imagine that if she learns that you've been here, and revealed her little secret, that'll put a swift end to your affair of the heart." Roscoe chuckled.

"As difficult as it is, it's what I vowed to do."

"Very well. Tell me, then: Where exactly are these letters?"

"In her house. I don't know specifically. But in her house. That's where I saw the box."

"A big box? Small box? How big, would you say?"

"I'd say a good-sized box. About the size of, um, a typewriter."

"And how many letters are in this box?"

"I don't know. I'd say at least a hundred."

"And can you get them for me?"

"No . . ." Jess said, drawing out the word. "I think they're upstairs, where she and her daughter have their bedrooms. I can't go up there."

Roscoe leaned forward over the table. "I don't quite follow you," he said. "She's your lover. Aren't you visiting in her bedroom from time to time?"

"Well—I meant, I can't go up there unaccompanied . . . to mount a search."

"Delicately put, sir. You needn't trouble yourself about it further." Roscoe drummed his fingers on the table. "This is very useful information, Mr. Murphy," he said. "I'll see to it that Mr. Penrose knows. And I'll see to it that he understands the sacrifice you're making for the cause of justice."

"He said I'd be rewarded," Jess said. "Will you ask him about that, too?"

"Of course," Roscoe said, smiling broadly. "We *never* forget a friend. And you're most certainly one of those."

"Thank you," Jess said. "I'm feeling much relieved now that I have this off my chest."

"It always feels good to do the right thing," Roscoe said. "Now you leave the rest to us. Keep going into work, same as usual. If you see or hear anything else, let us know right away."

"I will. And you won't tell Miss Payne anything, will you? About our talk?"

Roscoe made a motion of locking his lips and tossing the key over his shoulder. "We are nothing if not discreet, Mr. Murphy. Discretion is our stock-in-trade."

"Thank you," Jess said. "Thank you for seeing me today."

"I'm very glad I did. You're a most unusual man, Mr. Murphy, and it's been my pleasure to meet you."

Jess wasn't sure about being unusual, but he smiled and extended his hand. "Then I'll wait to hear from Mr. Penrose? About the reward?"

"Either Mr. Penrose or myself, yes. We'll make sure you're well repaid."

❧

ANNIE WAITED FOR A solid hour in the shadow of one of the stone lions flanking city hall. She was beginning to take a chill, and wondering whether Jess might have exited from some other door, when he breezed by her, so close she could have seized his lapel. He didn't notice her, though, and turned left at the corner of the city hall grounds, walking east at a furious pace.

She felt the weight of the cosh in her coat pocket, and was tempted to run after him and give him a good knock, but her blood had cooled. I should tell Miss Sarah first, she thought. I can follow him any day I want.

She limped back to the Avenging Angel office, her foot throbbing and now so swollen that it kept popping out of her shoe. If it had been summer, she would have made the rest of the distance in her stocking feet, but it was too cold and too wet for that. She finally peeled the shoe off when she entered their office building, and climbed the stairs with one shoe on and one shoe off.

Sarah had returned and was sitting in her office poring over a thick book. She looked up when she heard Annie in the outer room. Annie looked in at Sarah and saw that she was wearing a little pair of silver wire-rim spectacles, which she quickly took off when she caught sight of Annie.

"My eyesight has been tricky lately," she said. "How embarrassing."

"I think they look cute," Annie said. "Very fetching."

Sarah shoved the glasses away and covered them with some paperwork. "When I purchased them, I was terrified that someone would walk into the shop and recognize me."

"I wouldn't worry about it. Do you have a minute, by the way? There's something I need to tell you about."

"I was about to say the very same thing to you. Of course. Should we talk here, or go out?"

Annie held up her one shoe. "I don't think I can do much more walking for a little while," she said.

"Sit down, for heaven's sake. Whatever happened? It looks like a tornado went through this place."

"That's what I want to tell you about. When I arrived today, Jess was raging about something, throwing things around, and he—I got my foot caught under the door, and he yanked it something fierce onto it. My foot is the size of a watermelon."

"He didn't!"

"Oh, but he did," Annie said slowly. "And then I made matters worse by running after him." She pulled the cosh out of her coat. "I was determined to brain him."

"You didn't, I hope," Sarah said. "That's only going to get you into hot water."

"No, I couldn't catch him. But I did find out something very peculiar from following him. I thought he was going to his apartment—but instead he stopped and went into city hall. He was in there for almost an hour."

"City hall?"

"That's right."

"What business does he have there, I wonder?"

"I don't know, but I'd like to find out," Annie said. "I'm going to follow him around a little more. After I put ice on my foot, that is."

"That's simply awful. You say he did it on purpose?"

"Without a doubt. He was cursing at me, yelling at the top of his lungs. He was terribly angry about something."

Sarah tapped her desk with a pencil. "I know what about," she said. "That's what I was going to tell you. This morning, when I got here, he was waiting. He sat me down and apologized for what he said to me."

"About time."

"Yes, and I would have left it at that. Had he not then leaned over and kissed me."

"*Kissed you?*"

"Kissed me. Right on the lips."

Annie looked horrified. "I hope you knocked him for a loop, the masher."

"I didn't. I was too stunned."

"You let him get away with it?"

"Not quite. I told him he was dismissed. I told him he could finish out the holidays and a couple weeks in January, to give him time to find a new position. Then he has to go."

"That's mighty generous, considering," Annie said. "You'd have been within your rights to call the cops on him."

"I don't need to make an example of him. I felt sorry for him—afterward. Now that I know he hurt you, I don't feel that way. But I did at the time. Perhaps I ought better to let him go immediately, given these new circumstances."

"No—don't," Annie said. "Don't. I want to find out what he's up to."

"What does it matter? He'll be gone soon."

"Maybe, but I want to make sure he stays gone. Someone like that isn't likely to go quietly. I think it's better if we learn more about what makes him tick."

"How do we do that?"

"I'd suggest we try to be as normal as we can be with him. I would like to see if he goes back to city hall, and I want to see if I can talk to his roommates. They don't know me from Adam."

"Do you know where he lives?" Sarah asked.

"I know he lives above a store on Michigan Street, between Clinton and Vine," Annie said. "I know he's over near where there is that little cluster of Chinese laundries."

"Do you know the number?"

She shook her head. "No."

"And since he's a boarder," Sarah said, "he's not in the city directory. We can't get the number that way."

Annie thought for a moment. "That's not a problem. I'll follow him home," she said.

"What if he sees you? Jess is rather observant, you know."

"I think I can be discreet. I know that area over there well, so I can stay out of the line of sight. I used to drop off and pick up the Millers' laundry in that part of the city."

"Would anyone else recognize you, do you think?"

"If someone did, it would be a Chinaman, and they aren't going to say anything. They keep to themselves."

Sarah mused on this. "If you think it'd be safe," she said.

"After work, it'll be light enough that I'll be in no danger. And I'll wear my clothes from my employment with the Millers, so I'll look like every other domestic girl carrying laundry."

Sarah nodded. "Good idea. It may not turn up anything, but you never can tell. For now, I'm paying for you to take a carriage home and put that foot on ice."

❧

"ALICIA," BERT SAID WHEN Allie came downstairs for breakfast. "We need to discuss what next to do—about the John Pendle chat."

"Oh joy," Alicia said.

"We still haven't talked, you and I, about our conference with him."

"There hasn't been anything to say."

"I've wondered if you've thought any more about it."

"I've thought about it a great deal."

"Is there anything you'd like to share?"

"I don't like Pendle. Not even a little. But I don't blame him. Arthur was his brother, and he needs to find someone to blame his brother's sins on. Imagine, his brother a swindler, a murderer, and then a suicide? And possibly taking his wife along with him? John Pendle can't have that. The only thing left to do is to smear me."

"You seem to have adopted a rather philosophical view," Bert said.

"If I think about it too much, philosophy goes out the window."

"We need to, though. If I don't get this unstuck, I'm afraid as long as John Pendle stays on his high horse, the insurance company will delay and delay and delay."

"He's not budging, I can tell you that," she said. "And where else do we appeal? And as foul luck would have it, the district attorney happens to be the executor of the estate."

"That's what I wanted to talk about. I'd like to appeal to Terry Penrose directly."

"How will you manage that?"

"He and I are both members of the Buffalo Club, and I know him well enough to talk with. The club's having its annual ball on Saturday, and I'm sure he'll be there."

"With his wife? Do I have to go?"

"This is a stag affair."

"Oh," Allie said, rolling her eyes. "One of those. So much the better, because I don't want to see him. Just don't come home stinking of some dancing girl's pussy."

"I'm not that sort of man," Bert said.

"No, you're not. It's a pleasant change, actually."

29

THE CONTRACT

"You'll never guess who came to see me today," Roscoe said later that day, over lunch.

"Probably not," Penrose said, chewing his steak vigorously and lubricating it with some wine.

"Jess Murphy."

"You don't say," Penrose said. "It's been quite a while, again. It's really starting to bother me. Had he any report on that little pest, Sarah Payne?"

"Yes, that's what brought him in."

Terry swallowed hard, with a look of momentary alarm as a bolus of steak lodged in his throat.

"Are you all right?"

"Yes, yes, I'm fine," the DA said, coughing into his napkin. "These people here have got to get some better beef, though. They're going to kill me one day with this horseflesh."

"That's why I have the fish."

"At least my beef came from some nice pasture in East Aurora," Penrose said. "You have no idea where they got that fish. Buffalo River, maybe."

Roscoe put his fork down. The Buffalo River was more like an open sewer than a river.

"So what about it?" Penrose said.

"The fish? Nothing. I'm certainly not going to eat it now."

"Not the fish. The Sarah Payne thing. You look like the cat that ate the canary."

"Yes, of course. Listen to this. He claims he's taken her as his lover."

"Woman, the eternal mystery," Penrose said, waving his fork like a wand. "But of course she's his lover. What a headful of glue that boy has. You've seen Mrs. Payne?"

"Of course. At the inquest, remember?"

"I know, I know, merely a figure of speech. And you've seen Jess Murphy. So you know that he doesn't stand a Chinaman's chance of taking her as a lover. It's in his head. The poor man's delusional."

"It would seem so."

"You don't know the half of it. If it weren't for me and his father—who calls the shots in Newport—the lad would have been in prison long ago."

"Is that right?"

"His father sent him to Buffalo for me to keep an eye on, because Newport got very hot for his dear Jesse."

"May I ask why?"

Penrose took another bite of steak and nodded. "Why not? About a year ago, Murphy junior dreamed that some fellow had stolen his girlfriend. A girlfriend he'd dreamed up, by the way. I mean, it was a real girl, but she didn't even know him. Our Jess followed the unfortunate real boyfriend home and spent a good three-quarters of an hour cutting the poor fellow up with a rather fearsome knife."

"Did he kill him?"

"No, he did worse than kill him. Severed the man's nerves, tendons, whatever it is makes the limbs work as they do. One by one, took his time about it. Left him a near cripple, numb everywhere. Very bad. Murphy senior pulled the strings that only he could pull, and called me. Sent him here. I put him to work at the *Courier*, a little bit before the Miller thing. He was very useful there, but he began acting so strangely after the inquest that the editor told me he had to go."

"Is that someone that we want roaming around our city?"

"Judge Murphy owes us in a big way, Roscoe. So yes."

"Understood."

"Anyhow. Go on. What did nutty Jess Murphy have to say for himself?"

"He said he's been sitting on some information for a couple months. Because she's his lover, agonizing over his duty. My guess is that his feelings for her aren't mutual, and he wants to get even with her."

"The green-eyed monster's got him good. Wish I'd seen that myself. Did he tell you anything interesting, or just piss and moan about unrequited love?"

"Oh yes," Roscoe said, drawing it out. "He told me something very interesting."

"What do you think I have to do to get you to tell me?" Penrose asked, stopping midchew, his fork and knife in midair.

"I was getting to that. Murphy told me that Sarah Payne has the letters. The Pendle letters."

The DA finished his mouthful of steak and thought about this for a moment, Roscoe watching the DA's straining mandible.

"How does he know that?"

"Because—she read them to him. Out loud. She had a whole boxful."

Penrose put down his knife and fork. "Do you believe him?"

"It certainly had the ring of truth."

"Well, how about that? Miller must have given them to her before he met his maker. He was even smarter than I gave him credit for."

"Seems that way."

"I hardly need to say that Murphy needs to get them for us."

"He says he can't. She has them in her bedroom. I asked him, 'Aren't you her lover?' And he said he was too busy when he's up there to look around. Ha ha."

Penrose laughed. "God, I wish I'd been a fly on the wall. That must have been rich. In any case, he doesn't want to do the wet work, that's all. He's happy to stab her in the back. Fine. Doesn't matter to me. Come to think about it, it's better if he doesn't take them—no trail leading back to us."

"He says you promised him a reward," Roscoe said.

"I'm sure I did. Give him a hundred bucks. If he's lying, we'll get it back, and if he's not, it's the deal of a lifetime. That's easy. Let's focus on getting those letters."

"We could hire someone to toss the place when she's at work," Roscoe mused.

"In the daytime? Don't think so. Too risky. She lives in Ashwood, not Chinatown."

"Do you have a better idea?"

Penrose glared at him. "What the hell did you say?"

Roscoe cleared his throat. "I'm sorry. I meant no disrespect. Spoke without thinking."

"Not an attractive quality in someone with your aspirations, Bill."

"I simply meant that I thought you might have an idea."

"I might."

At that instant, Roscoe could have strangled Penrose, imagining his bald pate turning purple as he slowly choked the life out of the man. Instead, he smiled affably. "Will you share it?"

Penrose cut another hunk of steak and started chewing manfully again. "You know the name Harry Price?"

"Who doesn't?"

"Right. It's easy. You have Harry Price pay Miss Payne a visit, do what he does. Five hundred bucks, and the problem goes away forever. And have him search her house after he does the job. Simple. We get the letters, and we don't have her pecking away at us anymore. Miss Payne might not know jack shit about detective work, but she's gotten pretty good at rattling cages around the city. I've had it up to here with her."

Roscoe folded his napkin carefully and placed it next to his plate. "Wouldn't that raise some eyebrows?" he said. "Point back to us, even?"

"Not even a little," Penrose said. "She's yesterday's news. Not to mention that her employee, the lovelorn Mr. Murphy, has revealed a certain vindictive streak to the assistant district attorney himself that could easily have fatal consequences. Things like that can quickly spiral out of control."

Roscoe nodded.

"So—Murphy becomes the logical suspect if Miss Nebby winds up floating in the river. Right next to your fish," he added, gesturing toward Roscoe's abandoned lunch.

"Don't rub it in, Terry. I was hungry."

"Wouldn't hurt you to lose twenty pounds, Bill. You can't let the good life go to your middle. If you're DA one of these days, people won't respect you if you're fat. Fat people don't have any self-discipline. Literally do not know how to keep their mouths shut. Look at me," he said, flexing his biceps, "lean as rawhide. It's not easy to stay that way, but I do."

"I'll remember that," Roscoe said. "In the meantime, how can I find Price?"

"Talk to Baker, the fellow who took over collections from Pendle. Price goes along with him when he makes the monthly collection."

"I will. But there is one thing—that might be a problem."

Terry raised his eyebrows.

"She has a daughter," Roscoe said. "A little girl. If Price visits her some night—well . . ."

"I'm waiting to hear the problem."

"Um, the daughter. Little girl."

Terry wiped his mouth and tossed the napkin onto his plate, the crumpled white linen wicking up the puddle of blood. "I see," he said. "I understand. Let her have a nice Thanksgiving with her daughter. Then send Price over to see them."

"Before Christmas?"

"You going soft on me, Roscoe?"

Roscoe looked down at the pale, lifeless piece of fish he'd abandoned, and shook his head.

❦

THE ANNUAL MASKED BALL at the Buffalo Club was always memorable, although never spoken of afterward. Each year, the biggest men of the city turned out for a sprawling buffet, drinks, music, and—to cap it off—a costumed dancing girl revue. This year, the girls were from Pittsburgh—not terribly good-looking, but sturdy and willing. There were enough of them for the half of the men who wanted to continue the spectacle upstairs, in the club's lodgings. The other half were mostly superannuated, dried-up old coots, harmless to anyone but their equally desiccated wives.

Bert had been trying to talk with Terry Penrose all evening. The DA had been seated on a raised platform at the front of the banquet hall, and thus unapproachable by any but a very few select club men. After the dancing show had concluded, and cigars smoked down to nubs, the men had gotten up from their tables and were now milling around, a few preparing to leave, but most getting better acquainted with the dancing girls. Bert saw Terry chatting up one of the better-looking dancers who, Sadie Hawkins style, had sought out the DA at the dais. Penrose was now heading in Bert's direction, toward the elevators, through a throng that parted for him like the Red Sea for Moses.

"Mr. Penrose," Bert said, tugging on Penrose's elbow as the DA passed by with the obviously tipsy dancing girl on his other arm, "a moment?"

Penrose stopped and smiled wryly at Hartshorn. "Better be very quick, Bert. I told Miss"—he lowered his voice—"whatever her name is—I promised her a tour of the private rooms upstairs."

"Only a minute, I swear."

"Now, don't wander off, dear," Penrose said to the young lady. He raised his hand and snapped his fingers to summon a waiter. "Waiter, please get our guest another of whatever she's having."

Penrose then turned toward Bert, leaving the dancing girl wobbling. "This had better be good," he said. "If I don't get her upstairs in the next five minutes, she's going to be out cold. She's already three sheets to the wind."

"Yes, I understand. Look, here it is in a nutshell. Mrs. Miller's bequest from Arthur Pendle. She and I went to talk to John Pendle, as you suggested—"

"I didn't *suggest* it," Terry said. "I merely pointed out that his objections have to be answered before anything can happen."

"When we spoke with him, he said that if you were supportive, he would be."

"He's the man's brother and one of his heirs," Terry said. "I'm an executor. I'm following his direction."

"Can you influence him?"

"Anything is possible, but as executor I have to have a compelling reason. You know that, Bert. Now if you'll excuse me—" Terry turned back to his dancing girl, who had already downed her latest drink and was listing rather heavily onto the DA's shoulder.

"I'm sure we could find something that you would find compelling," Bert said. "If the rumors I hear are true, I understand you may be considering a run for governor."

Penrose forgot about the girl. "Now where did you hear that?"

"A little birdie told me."

"Maybe it would be worth a conversation," Penrose said. "Call my office and we'll get something set."

"I will do so. I very much appreciate it."

Penrose nodded and tugged his companion toward the elevators, slapping her gently on the cheek.

❦

"MAN LEFT SOMETHING FOR you," Jess's Chinese landlady said to him when he got home after a long, angry walk. She held out a small leather pouch, sewn shut at the top.

"Thanks," Jess mumbled, and took the stairs two at a time to his apartment, above the restaurant. He let himself in and looked around. No sign of Phil or George, thank goodness. Not yet, but they'll be back soon.

He took a small pocketknife from his vest and sawed carefully through the stitching. The knife was a cheap one, and dull, and it almost closed on his fingers three or four times. After a fair amount of diligent effort, he cut away the last of the stitches. He turned the bag upside down.

A cylindrical roll of paper fell out, which was secured by a piece of twine wrapped around its midriff. He cut the twine and unrolled the paper. Inside were ten crisp $10 notes, each with an engraved buffalo in the center, flanked by portraits of Lewis and Clark. He counted them out, twice. A hundred bucks? That's all that Sarah's deepest secret was worth to them?

He hurled the notes away as hard as he could throw them, but they didn't go anywhere, merely fluttered down around his feet as if the air itself refused them. He kicked the notes, stamped on them until they were torn, then grabbed a broom and swept the crumpled remains under the old wardrobe, where he couldn't see them anymore. Breathing hard, he stood in the middle of his apartment, wanting to smash something, anything.

He stormed out of the room, slamming the door, not bothering to lock it. I don't care if they find the money, I don't care if someone takes it. A hundred lousy bucks! I should throw myself in the goddamned canal. He raced down the stairs and past the astonished landlady toward the door.

30

AT GLEN CREEK FARM

Bert telephoned the DA's office on Monday afternoon, and the secretary said that she'd been expecting his call. A good sign. It meant that Penrose had given her his blessing for a conference. The DA's schedule meant that the meeting would have to wait until after Thanksgiving, so with nothing to do until then, Alicia and Bert escaped the city the next day for Hamburg, where the Hartshorns had a farm, Glen Creek.

He'd thought it would be a natural way to coax Allie from her near isolation, but even removed from familiar surroundings she remained unusually quiet. At first, Bert tried to draw her out, without much success. She would read quietly in the front room of the farmhouse, or he'd find her scribbling away in her diary. He wished he could read what she was thinking, but he knew better than to ask. The children loved the rural setting and occupied themselves making hideaways in the hayloft of the barn. To the delight of all, Mrs. Hall had taken the opportunity to visit some relatives near Rochester.

After two days of quiet, though, there was a shift in the wind. First it was a neighbor from the next farm over along Creek Road, and then another, more distant—who'd had to walk quite a distance in the brisk November air—to the Hartshorn farmhouse, ostensibly to pay their respects to the long-absent Bert and drop off a pie. Each time, he'd do as etiquette demanded: invite the neighbor in for thirty minutes of chitchat. And each time, however, they seemed to be curious mostly about Bert's other guests. Allie and the girls steered clear of these social calls, but it was obvious that word was getting around about the mysterious women holed up at the Hartshorn farm.

On the third day, Bert was smoking a cigar in his study when he heard a scream from the parlor. Pausing only to do a wild dance to stamp out the embers from the ejected stogie, he ran for the parlor, trailing smoke. He met Allie in the hallway, coming equally fast in his direction. "Whatever is the matter?" he said, catching her.

"I was reading, and felt someone's eyes on me. I looked up, and there was a face at the window—staring in!" she said. "One of your goddamned neighbors was spying!"

"For the love of God," Bert muttered and continued down the hallway. He wrenched open the front door and looked out. No one. In his shirt-sleeves, he stepped onto the front porch and then into the yard, looking this way and that. And then he saw the lady from next door hustling across the stubbly cornfield that separated their properties. He popped back into the house and collected his jacket, threw on a coat and hat, and went in hot pursuit.

He rapped on the neighbor's front door, and the woman duly answered, still red in the cheeks from her jog home. "Did we miss your call?" Bert said, none too warmly. "My guest said you stopped by, but didn't ring."

The lady brushed back her hair with a hand. "I meant to say hello," she said, "but as I passed by the window, I saw you had a guest already, so I didn't want to intrude."

"I see. My guest was rather startled by your appearance. You gave her quite a scare."

"I'm very sorry. Please give my apologies to Miss—"

Oh, to hell with it, Bert thought. "Mrs. Miller. I will."

The neighbor's mouth quivered, then made up its mind and landed on a smug smile. "You know, I thought that might be Mrs. Miller with you. And her daughters."

"Yes, she's my client. And it's the first time the family has left Buffalo since all the unpleasantness. Surely you can understand their desire for privacy."

"Of course. After all they've been through."

"Please know you're always welcome," Bert said, "but while the Millers are recovering, it would be best if you'd alert me before your next visit."

The woman looked a bit miffed, but nodded. "I shall certainly do that, Mr. Hartshorn."

He thanked her and hurried back to the farmhouse. There was no sign of Alicia, so he walked upstairs to her bedroom and rapped on the door. "Alicia? Are you in there?"

Alicia opened the door and blocked the doorway. She had changed out of her black mourning dress and was wearing a deep green cycling skirt—a skirt split all the way up, to allow straddling a bicycle—and a form-fitting cream-colored sweater with gigot sleeves. It became her, but without a bicycle at hand seemed a little out of place.

"It's all I had that wasn't black," she said. "I don't know why I brought it."

"Why did you change?" he said.

"I'm sick and tired of wearing mourning. I don't even know who I'm supposed to be mourning. And I'm sure your neighborhood spy, and all the rest of them, would prefer to see the harlot in mufti. Give the people what they want, they say."

"It was the lady from the next farm over," he said. "I walked over and talked with her."

"That was very noble of you."

"Not at all. She had no business peering through our windows, invading our privacy."

"I'm sure word is getting around that you have the Whore of Babylon and her imps bunking with you."

"Please stop that, Alicia. No one thinks that."

"Bert, I know it's only November, but I'm making an early New Year's resolution. Ready? Here it is: *I'm not taking any more bullshit. From anyone.*"

"Noted," he said. "Now why, really, are you in your cycling attire?"

"I was being honest. Wearing mourning has no purpose. I don't feel mournful, or at least not about what I'm supposed to. And this is all I have with me that's not deep black."

"So long as you are wearing what you like, and not what you think these yokels want from you."

Alicia stubbed a stockinged toe into the floorboards. "You're right. How would you feel if we returned to Buffalo a little early?"

"Doesn't matter to me. I thought it might do you and the girls some good to get away from the city for a while."

"And it has. But what's following me—it's everywhere," she said. "Here, Buffalo. Same."

"What's following you?"

"Why are you so interested in me, all of a sudden?"

"That's not very kind. I am interested in you."

"Do you want to come in? Has it been too long? Is that it?" She stepped aside.

"For God's sake, Alicia. I haven't been banging down your door for that since—that day with Pendle. I know you're suffering."

She scrutinized his face. "I won't be this way forever."

"However long it takes, it takes."

"Where are the girls?"

"Out in the barn, presumably. I've never seen three young ladies who have found such amusement in an old barn. But it's nice to see them laugh."

"It is," she said. "I wonder if I'll ever laugh again. You know, I used to. You know, people thought I was very witty, years ago. Why, when I was in high school, my nickname was 'Sweet Alicia.' But it's been a long time now."

"You will be happy again, my dear. You must believe that. What you've lived through these past, I don't know, half a dozen years would have killed most people. Not you. You're stronger than that."

She looked up at the ceiling, leaning against the doorframe. Then she fixed him with that look he knew.

"You *sure* you don't want to come in?" she said quietly. "Why should the girls have all the fun?"

He scuffed his foot. "You know I'd love that. But I don't think it's the best thing for you right now."

"Why not let me be the judge of that?"

"Because sometimes what we want isn't what we need."

She gave him a half-smile. "All right, then, Bert. That's actually very sweet. And when you decide that I'm ready," she said, "better make sure you are, too."

"Oh Lord," Bert said. "I've got to get out of here. Now why don't you take a little nap, and if by tonight you still want to go back to Buffalo, we can go in the morning."

"I will. And I'll ask the girls. If they're having such fun, they might want to stay."

Bert nodded and left Allie standing in her doorway, watching his back as he slowly walked back downstairs. Then she closed the door and sat down on the edge of the bed, feeling not merely alone but terribly lonely in her cycling attire. She closed her eyes and once more felt the wind in her hair, the playful bump of Arthur's bicycle wheel against hers—which always made her cry out in mock terror, and always to his great amusement—and smelled again the summer clover of Delaware Park, releasing its fragrance beneath their picnic blanket, heard their murmured endearments over the hum of bees, and one final time raising a toast to their future with warm lemonade, so conspicuous as to be hiding in plain sight.

Never again, she thought, but perhaps it never was, at that. Arthur had been Penrose's man then, too, more than he'd been hers. Penrose had created Arthur Pendle, like a golem, fashioned him into what he had needed for a time, and then—when Arthur had outlived his utility—had casually smashed him to bits. Whatever she'd had of Arthur, she'd borrowed from Terry Penrose, without knowing it. Arthur had lied, but he had been frailer than she'd known, and she could forgive him. But Terry Penrose . . . now that was a very different story.

MAKING CONVERSATION

JESS CAME INTO THE OFFICE LATE WEDNESDAY AFTERNOON, THE day before Thanksgiving, scowling.

"What's the matter with you now?" Annie said.

"Hat store stuff," he said. "Thanks to you, I'll soon be working there full-time again."

"Thanks to *me*? I didn't kiss my boss. You did."

"And I've been trying to make amends ever since. But it's as though I've been given the death penalty. For one stupid kiss."

"Stupid, I'll give you," Annie said.

"Why do you even talk to me? I wish you wouldn't."

"Making conversation. Miss Sarah says that as long as we're working together, we have to try to get along."

"Look on the bright side. You won't have me around much longer."

"Here comes the self-pity," Annie said under her breath.

"It's a fact. Not self-pity."

"What was the problem with the hat store today?" she persisted. "Why are you in such a bad mood?"

"If you really want to know, at Adair's we sell two dollar hats, three dollar hats, mostly," he said. "Hats for regular fellows, not rich swells. Straw hats in the spring and summer, felts in the fall and winter. No one buys felt hats in the summer, or straws in the winter. But even though our prices are cheap, we still get the smart alecks who come in and see if they can jew us down on last season's models. I almost got into a fistfight with one of them today. 'Look at all these hats sitting here,' he says. 'Why wouldn't you sell me one for a dollar instead of having it gather dust?'"

"What do you care? It's not your hat store," Annie said.

"It's the principle of it."

"It's a *hat*, not a principle."

"Well, I don't like that kind of thing. People always trying to put one over."

"Seems to me like you're always spoiling for a fight."

"Yeah, maybe. If you were a man, we would have already had it out," he said. "But you're a girl, so you're safe."

"Anytime, pal," Annie said. "Take your swing, girl or no girl. I'll knock your block off."

"You would like hell."

"Try it."

"Don't tempt me. Why don't you just shut up?"

"Why don't you just die," she muttered, bending over her desk.

"I heard that."

"Glad you did."

"You really are a nasty little—"

The front door opened and Sarah came in, carrying a steaming pot of coffee. Her smile was smothered by the tension in the office.

"Are you two squabbling again? Before Thanksgiving?"

"What does it matter?" Jess said. "I'll be gone soon. And Annie will have you all to herself, like she's wanted from the start."

"For God's sake," Annie said. "If you only knew how excited I was when I heard that Miss Sarah had hired a man."

"You hate men," Jess said flatly.

"Now—" Sarah began, setting the coffee down.

"I don't hate *all* men," Annie said.

Jess looked up at Sarah and pointed at Annie. "Do you see what I have to put up with?" he said. "And, you know, I think I know you well enough—*Miss Payne*—that if it were up to you, you would have forgiven me by now, and given me a second chance. But I'm sure this one"—he stabbed his finger toward Annie—"this man-hater, has poisoned you against me. Good and proper."

"I have done nothing of the sort," Annie shot back. "Miss Sarah can think for herself. In fact, she's never once asked me for my opinion about your employment here."

"If she had," he said, "I can guess what you'd say."

"I see. You're a mind reader, too, now. Maybe at the hat shop you can set up a little phrenology table and feel for lumps."

"Uh-huh, I'll give you a lump—"

"Both of you—stop it right now!" Sarah yelled, surprising even herself. "I can't stand this. Jess, if you want to be angry with someone, you ought to be angry with me."

"I could never be angry with you, Miss Payne," he said. "You're a good, honest, earnest soul. That's why you call this 'Avenging Angel.' It was only you, once."

Sarah looked dismayed. "I don't think I'm an angel. I thought that *justice* is like an angel, that looks out for the innocent and finds the guilty. It was never intended to be about me."

PART FOUR

REVELATIONS

ALLIE'S THANKSGIVING STORY

THE GIRLS PREVAILED UPON ALICIA NOT TO RETURN EARLY TO THE city but instead to stay at Glen Creek Farm through Thanksgiving. Alicia then wrote to her mother, asking her not to go back directly to Buffalo but rather to join them at the farm for a proper Thanksgiving meal.

On the great day, Bert, Allie, the girls, and Mrs. Hall had made a respectable showing of the feast and were sitting quietly in front of the ruined turkey, looking for excuses to leave the table.

"When I was growing up, Thanksgiving was an even bigger event than Christmas," Bert offered. "At our house, anyway. I looked forward to it all year."

"What made it so special, Bert?" Allie said, already bored.

"The food, of course. My mother was from down South, and she made the most delicious stuffing—out of sweet potatoes and molasses. I ate only enough turkey to make my pile of stuffing look modest." He laughed.

"That does sound delicious," Mrs. Hall said. "I always made chestnut stuffing—exactly like this. Allie learned the recipe from me. No one makes it the way I did."

"Cook made this," Allie said. "It's not your recipe."

"Well, it looks and tastes the same as mine."

"Maybe there are other people in the world who know how to make stuffing," Allie mumbled.

Bert cleared his throat. "Well, then, Mrs. Hall, do you remember any Thanksgiving in particular?"

"Oh yes, I most certainly do," she said, looking at Alicia.

"Mother, please, not this story again," Allie said.

"Bert's never heard it, dear."

"Nor does he need to. I don't like it, Mother. It's upsetting."

"You see, Mr. Hartshorn," Mrs. Hall said, "it's not every Thanksgiving your little girl runs away from home."

"Here we go," Allie said.

"You don't say," Bert said, dropping his napkin in his lap. "Now, Alicia, this does seem like quite a story."

"Mother, please don't tell that story again," Allie said.

Mrs. Hall primly settled back in her chair. "Mr. Hartshorn, Alicia scared the dickens out of us one Thanksgiving. Well, it was the day before Thanksgiving. She was old enough then to run errands on her own—"

"Not really, Mother," Alicia said. "Bert, you know the neighborhood I grew up in. No young girl had any business being out alone there."

"You grew up down near the canal, as I recall," Bert said.

"Yes, at the foot of Georgia Street. Bunch of criminals."

"It was not like that," Mrs. Hall said. "My late husband was in the harness trade, and naturally we needed to live near the canal. The boatmen were always in need of new tack for their teams. Repairs and so forth."

"That's still a pretty rough part of the city, even now," Bert said.

"Well, that's where we had to live, and we had to make the best of it," Mrs. Hall said sternly. "In any case, Allie grew up there and we knew everyone nearby. It was no more dangerous than this neighborhood. Look at the unspeakable things that have happened in Ashwood."

At this, little Millie started to cry, got up, and ran upstairs.

"For heaven's sake, Mother, sometimes," Allie said. "Mary Anne, please go tend to your sister. Besides, you don't need to hear this story again."

"May I go, too, Mama?" Caroline asked.

"Yes you may, dear," Allie said, and the two older girls ran upstairs to look after Millie.

"Are you happy now, Mother?" Allie said. "You've chased everyone away but your captive audience."

Mrs. Hall ignored her. "Mr. Hartshorn, as I was trying to say, our neighborhood wasn't nearly so bad as Alicia would make it out. When this one was still a girl—how old were you that year, Allie?"

Alicia scowled. "I was fourteen. No, that's not right. Thirteen."

"Thirteen, then. Plenty old enough to be helping me with errands, I think you'd agree, Mr. Hartshorn. But as I recall, Allie was going through some growing pains, and was quarrelling with both Mr. Hall and myself something terrible that year."

"Bert, please make a note. This was *all my fault*."

Mrs. Hall went on. "I asked Alicia if she would run down to the market and buy a few things that I needed for Thanksgiving dinner. She was more than happy to leave—angry about whatever she was angry about, you know—and off she went. This must have been around three in the afternoon."

"It was nearly four," Allie said. "To be precise."

"How you can remember something like that, I'll never know," Mrs. Hall said.

"Where was the market?" Bert asked.

"Down next to the canal," Allie said. "It was a market mainly used by canal boat families, but we went there because it was cheap."

"You make us sound like real lowlifes," Mrs. Hall said indignantly. "There is not a thing wrong about saving a penny when you can."

"So Alicia went to the market. What happened next?"

"Well, she didn't come back. The sun set, and no Allie. Poor, distraught Mr. Hall and I went up and down the streets with a lamp, looking for her, but it got too dark. We thought that she was playing at something, or perhaps decided to stay with a friend. To teach us a lesson, you know. Good and proper. Allie was like that. Willful."

"I was not *like* anything, Mother."

"And do you know, Mr. Hartshorn, she worried us sick for two full days! We told the police. We asked people to look for her. And neither hide nor hair of her, the whole time. Two full nights."

"That must have been terrifying for you and your husband," Bert said.

"It was! I can't tell you how we suffered. We thought she might have fallen into the canal and drowned. But then, the morning of the day after Thanksgiving, who do we find huddled on our doorstep but Alicia—her clothes all torn and muddy and a little string around her wrist that I think I put there to hold her little change purse."

"And what did she say? What did you say?" Bert asked.

"She told us, 'I ran away from home, but now I'm back.' Just like that, matter-of-fact, no expression. As though that sort of thing happens every day. We were terribly relieved, of course, but also quite furious. Why, Mr.

Hall gave her a real switching that evening, and there was no dinner for her, either."

"You certainly taught me a lesson, didn't you?" Alicia said with a bitter smile.

"You certainly didn't run away again," Mrs. Hall said.

"I'm glad it had a happy ending," Bert said, "but it sounds awfully trying for all of you."

Alicia was staring at her plate and at last looked up with a strange bland expression. "Are you happy now, Mother, that you've told Bert our little secret?"

"It oughtn't be a secret, dear. It happened."

Alicia pushed back from the table slightly. "Not the way you tell it, it didn't."

"What did I leave out, then? Tell me, what have I got wrong?" Mrs. Hall said.

"What's the point?" Allie said. "It's your favorite story. I'm not going to spoil it for you at this late date."

"Now you can't say something like that and not back it up," the old woman said.

"What is your version of events, Alicia?" Bert asked.

"My *version*, to use your word, is something that my mother knows nothing about. No one does. Except me. Well, one other person, too, but that's it."

"Forever throwing down the gauntlet," Mrs. Hall murmured.

"All right, then, I suppose it's time. It's only us three all-knowing, wise adults, and the children are upstairs, consoling one another."

"Let's hear it, then," Mrs. Hall said. "I've always wondered why it was you ran away. Maybe we'll learn something."

"Oh, I very much doubt you'll *learn* anything," Allie said. "But here it is. I walked down to the canal market. That part is true. I didn't have any money with me—there was no change purse, and no string. We bought everything on account and then my father would settle up each month."

"She is right about that," Mrs. Hall said. "I may have been mistaken about the change purse."

"The market was down alongside the canal, and there were a few canal boats tied up nearby. The canal was open late that year—either there were big shipments that had to be made or it was warm, I don't remember. But I do recall that normally there wouldn't be many boats left by Thanksgiving. Maybe one or two. That year there were a dozen or so, all moored up for the holiday. I expect that after the holiday they'd then go back home, and the canal would close for the winter."

Allie took a sip of water and continued. "I used to like walking past the boats, because of the mules. They'd be standing on the towpath and I sometimes could pet them, or watch them."

"You must have been a darling little girl," Bert said with a smile.

"Not so little. Thirteen's an odd age—neither girl nor woman. And I suppose my mother's right that I wasn't a girl anymore, but in some ways I was still. Anyway. On the way to the market, I took the towpath and I was passing one boat that was tied up away from all the others, and there was a boatman sitting on the deck, smoking.

"He waved to me, and I waved back. Then he called over and said that his dog had had a litter of puppies, and that his wife was either going to give them away or drown them before he had to head back east, and did I want one?"

"She was always after her father and me for a puppy," Mrs. Hall said. "But we could barely feed three mouths, let alone a dog."

"What did you say to the fellow?" Bert said.

"I don't recall, but I was very excited about the puppies, and he said I could come over and pick one out for myself. I was thinking about that, and quick as you please, he slid over the gangplank from the boat to the towpath, and I went on."

"Whatever were you thinking?" Mrs. Hall said.

Allie shrugged. "He seemed like a nice man, and I wanted a puppy. And I certainly didn't want his wife to drown them. Beyond that, I don't think I thought much about it at all."

"What happened then?" Bert said, looking a trifle worried.

"You know, canal boats have their little cabins below deck, where the boatmen and their families live. My fellow motioned me to follow him down the stairs. There was a lamp going down there and I remember it was tiny little space, one narrow bunk about a foot off the planking and not much else. A tiny cookstove for heat. I can still smell the way it smelled, like damp but also something else, a good smell, like bacon. I looked around, and didn't see a wife and certainly no puppies."

"You should have known better than to get on a canal boat," Mrs. Hall said.

"I suppose," Allie said. "But we do lots of stupid things in life, and we don't know they're stupid because they turn out all right."

"Did you turn and leave?" Bert said.

"When I saw there weren't any puppies, I got very frightened," Allie said. "I was going to leave, but he was blocking the little stairs. And now, Mother—here's where the string came from. He wrestled me down on the little bunk and tied my feet and hands to the little legs."

"Oh my God," Bert whispered.

"There was no God down there, Bert," Allie said. "So I was spread-eagle on the bunk, and I could smell how dirty the mattress was, sweat and ash and smoke. And my new friend told me to be quiet, or he'd kill me. He put a rag into my mouth and took his time about undressing me."

"You're not serious," Mrs. Hall said.

"I may have told a lie now and again in my time, Mother, but I'm not telling one now. Do you want to hear the rest of it?"

"Alicia, you don't have to say anything more," Bert said.

"But now it feels so good to tell it, Bert," Alicia said. "After all these years, to get this off my chest, makes me feel like I am capable of anything. So here you go, you two. As I was saying. He took his time about undressing me, and then he stood there admiring me, telling me how beautiful I was, while he took off his coveralls. I'd never seen a man naked before—you can only imagine the effect it had, seeing him standing out at attention like that, in the lamplight right over me. It was both terrifying and magical, the way his thing rose and got bigger and bigger—and then he climbed on top of me—"

"Enough of this hideous fable," Mrs. Hall said. "You ran away. Why do you have to make up such a horrible tall tale? To impress Mr. Hartshorn here? I'm sure it's not going to have the intended—"

"The first time," Allie went on, ignoring her mother entirely, "hurt. And I mean *hurt*. He was a rough son of a bitch, like all those canal types. At first, anyway. But after he was done, he sat there on the bunk next to me and smoothed my hair and covered me up with a scratchy wool blanket.

He was really very nice, then. And the next time he got on me—which couldn't have been more than an hour or two after and a couple shots of whiskey—he was almost tender.

"And here's where you get your wish, Mother. Whenever he'd be pumping away on me, I found I could pretend I was someplace else, and I always pretended I'd run away from home and that what was happening was only part of the story, not real, another something I had dreamed up. I got pretty good at not even being there. After the first day, you know what? Having his weight on me, smelling his sweat, became like a magic carpet, something out of *One Thousand and One Nights*. I knew I would be going somewhere wonderful, and all I had to do was let him do what he was so obviously enjoying. And I will admit it was flattering, in a way. Not at the time, but as I think back—I don't think a man could have had more fun than he did with me. It must have been eons since the last time the lonely fellow had any release."

"Oh for—" Bert breathed.

"Hang on, Bert, I'm almost finished. I honestly didn't have any idea of how much time went by. It was always dark down there, with only the lamp. He gave me some biscuits and water to keep me going, let me sleep, and then tap-tap-tap, he'd wake me up and start up again. After some time, though—I guess I know now it was two nights and Thanksgiving was done—he woke me up again and cut the cords that kept me down, and said that I could go. That's where that string came from, Mother."

Bert and Mrs. Hall were staring at her, stupefied.

"Now here's the most interesting part," Allie said. "I sat up and rubbed my wrists and ankles for a bit, with him watching me from his chair by the stove. And yes, I was very stiff and sore, but I didn't run away. I wasn't frightened anymore. Instead, I felt *sad*. Sad that I wasn't useful anymore, or something like that. He was done with me, after all we'd *shared*. So do you know what I did? No, of course you wouldn't know," she said, not waiting for a reply. "I lay back down, and I asked him to do it one more time."

"Sweet Jesus," Mrs. Hall said, crossing herself. "Sweet Jesus." Bert had gone pale.

"So there you have it," Allie said. "That's the whole story of my 'running away from home.' Partly true, in a way. But as is always the case, there was a lot more to that story than any single person knew. Until today. And that's why I told you that I'd run away from home—and you know what else? While Papa was whipping me, and you were starving me down, I ran away in my mind, again, exactly as I'd done for two days on a canal boat."

Allie folded her napkin neatly and placed it beside her plate. "Any questions?" she said brightly. "I'm an open book today, it seems, so now's the time."

"I think I'm going to be sick," Bert said. "If you would excuse me—" He got up quickly and trotted toward the front of the house. Allie and Mrs. Hall were left alone to survey the carnage of the Thanksgiving dinner.

Alicia stood too, as graceful and controlled as a thoroughbred. "I'll excuse myself, too, Mother," she said, smiling. "And please do know that should you choose to tell that story again, to anyone—the minister, the doctor, the neighbor—I'll tell my part of it, too. After all these years, I found it was much easier than I thought it would be."

33

HELEN WARREN'S RETURN

"Sarah, dear!" Helen exclaimed when Sarah opened the door. "Happy Day-After-Thanksgiving!"

The two embraced, and while Helen Warren was not a large woman, she favored voluminous, confectionary clothing and hats that seemed to dwarf any other woman in her vicinity.

"I'm awfully sorry it's taken me so long," Helen said.

Helen Warren had wasted no time reinserting herself forcibly into the social life of the Ashwood Set. Two years in Cleveland had left her starved for human connection, presumably. Her husband, Dr. Frederick Warren, had been a successful Buffalo surgeon, and he and Helen had been fixtures at the Ashwood Social Club. Then, two years ago, Helen had dropped off leave-taking cards at each of her friends' homes, tidily and appropriately engraved with P.P.C. in the corner, for *pour prendre congé*, to denote that she and Dr. Warren were leaving Buffalo.

This was a puzzlement to all the ladies of the Ashwood Set, and to most of the gentlemen as well. As the story went, the doctoring business in Cleveland was booming, and ambitious Dr. Warren wished to seize on the opportunity. The reason seemed thin, though, because if Cleveland was booming, Buffalo was booming bigger, and to have established a practice among the Ashwood Set was nothing short of a sinecure. There had been rumors, though, of trouble between Dr. and Mrs. Warren, horrendous quarrels that spilled out onto the street in front of their spacious home on Lexington, not far from the Pendles' place.

And there had been a kind of altercation, between Dr. Warren and none other than Edward Miller, in the clubhouse of the Red Jacket Golf Club, where both men were prominent members. It had started in the locker room, after a contentious nine holes. Edward had prevailed, by two strokes, but intimated to another club member, in a not too subtle aside, that he would have won by four strokes had not the esteemed Dr. Warren improved his lie on a critical hole with a little kick of a cleat. Overheard by one of the doctor's friends, the accusation spread like a grass fire from the locker room to the main clubroom, where Dr. Warren was enjoying a few cocktails and just tipsy enough to welcome a confrontation.

Edward had appeared in the clubroom after his shower and was, in short order, buttonholed by the angry surgeon, who informed him in no uncertain terms that he did not need to cheat to win at golf, and that Edward had best keep a civil tongue in his head, if he knew what was good for him. Dr. Warren, a large and bluff six-footer, failed to intimidate Ed, who on tiptoe managed five feet four, and the words flew and voices elevated until it seemed the two would come to fisticuffs. Ed was restrained by Howie Gaines, and the burly doctor by a couple of his allies, but before Warren had returned to the bar and his cocktail, he'd jabbed a finger at Ed and said, for all to hear, 'And if you make one more move toward my wife, I'll kill you.'

Ed Miller had been unperturbed, and had replied with equal venom, 'And I'll be ready for you when you do.' After that little exchange, the rumor mill went into overdrive. It was true that Ed Miller spent very little time with his own wife at Ashwood Social Club dances, but that was surely because Alicia was one of the best dancers in Buffalo, and Ed had two left feet. Still, it was true that he spent most of those long, boozy evenings chatting intently with either Sarah Payne or Helen Warren, and it was natural that—given the troubles in all three households—people came to believe that something had to be going on.

Then the Warrens abruptly pulled up stakes for Cleveland. Far from spreading oil on the simmering rumors, their mysterious removal from the scene had the effect of a bucket of gasoline poured on a bed of embers. Everyone wanted to know why, for the love of God, a man like Dr. Warren—and a handsome, forty-year-old woman like Mrs. Warren, still in her prime—would leave Ashwood, of all places, for *Cleveland*. No answer, other than the one of medical ambition, was ever forthcoming. And off the Warrens went, and stayed, for two long years. It didn't go unnoticed, however, that Ed's business travel—he had large contracts in Pittsburgh, Indianapolis, and Columbus—now frequently extended to Cleveland.

But then, just as suddenly, the Warrens were back, though in a much more modest house at 780 Bird Avenue, not far from Forest Lawn Cemetery and outside the northern boundary of the Ashwood section. Or, at least, Helen Warren had returned. Presumably the doctor was occupied in closing his nascent practice back in Cleveland, and would be along presently. Yet, why the somewhat scanty new quarters on a backstreet, instead of another grand mansion in the heart of Ashwood? Surely something had gone amiss and the Warrens' circumstances had been reduced while they'd been away.

Two months had passed since Helen Warren had reintroduced herself to Allie, soon after taking the house on Bird Avenue. Alicia had been the first woman she'd visited, officially, though no one could fathom why. She and Alicia had not been close, even in the headiest days of the Ashwood Set—the air having been taken from that balloon after the murder—and the contretemps between Dr. Warren and Ed Miller had forced the two women to choose sides. Yet Alicia had been the first on her round, while Helen was still waiting for her husband to return.

It took the full sixty days—the longest time acceptable in polite society—for a calling card to be dropped off with Ruth. Sarah must have been near the very bottom of Helen's list of Ashwood ladies. Such a long silence seemed odd, since Sarah and Helen had been rather good friends. Thus, when Sarah came home from the office one afternoon and found Helen's card waiting in the little silver tray by the front door, in truth she felt a little relieved. She'd begun to wonder if Alicia had turned her former friend against her.

But today, Helen seemed all smiles, and if there were any hard feelings, she wasn't wearing them on her sleeve.

"Not a word of it, Helen," Sarah said to her friend's apology. "I'm sure you've been very busy. Do come in. Ruth has some tea and cake for us."

"You'll understand perfectly why it's taken me all this time. I have been rather preoccupied these past weeks."

They settled in the parlor, and Sarah poured tea for her friend. "I trust you and Dr. Warren are well, though?" she said. "You've not been ailing, I hope."

"No, no, although what Frederick is doing, other than tormenting me, is a mystery."

Sarah put her piece of cake down on the plate and swallowed daintily. "I confess I am not following you," she said.

"My, you *have* been away from the neighborhood gossip! Freddie and I are getting a divorce. My only contact with him these days is through our attorneys, sparring over who gets this and that."

"I'm terribly sorry to hear it, Helen," Sarah said. "I didn't know."

"You've been too busy with your detective agency, I'm sure, to do much else."

"I suppose, but I'm ashamed that I didn't reach out to you. If I'd known—"

"Nothing of it, dear," Mrs. Warren said. "There's nothing you could have done. It's a legal matter, that's all. This has been coming on for a long, long time."

"I had no idea."

"That's because you've never been a gossip, like some of the others. We moved away to Cleveland because Frederick thought that I was coming under a spell here in Buffalo. He thought he could spirit me away and save me. Or save himself, I'm not sure which. I'm sure you heard the rumors."

Sarah straightened up in her chair. "One hears things from time to time, but it doesn't pay to give them any credence. Rumors are almost never nice."

Helen smiled. "Unfortunately, simply because they're not nice doesn't always mean they're not true. Freddie and I were at each other's throats for a full year before he dragged me off to Cleveland."

Sarah sipped her tea. "Would you mind if I asked why?"

"Not in the slightest," Helen said. "And I'd rather you hear about it from me anyway. What rumors did you hear about me? Or Frederick?"

"I heard about the dustup that almost happened at the golf club."

"Oh, *that*," she said. "That was merely the straw that broke the camel's back."

"How so?"

"The rumors about me and Ed Miller—you know—that we had some sort of affinity."

"Which I always knew was nonsense," Sarah said.

Helen sat back in her chair so hard that she almost spilled her teacup into her lap. "Oh, my, no—as I said, not *all* rumors are incorrect. Teddy found out about me and Ed, and that was the end of it."

"*You and Ed*?" Sarah said, feeling lightheaded. "I knew you were friends, but nothing more."

Helen set her cup down and leaned toward Sarah. "We're both adult women, and modern women at that," she said. "We were friends, yes. At first. But then it became much more, and Freddie got wind of it."

"How?" Sarah asked, not really wanting to know, but unable to rein in her curiosity.

"Well," Helen whispered, "Frederick and I were—sharing an intimate moment, and what did I do but blurt out, 'Oh, Eddie!' Eddie, Freddie—the names are too close to each other for their own good. Slip of the tongue, you know? And he, of course, got very angry, and asked me if I meant Eddie Miller, and I said, 'Of course not, I said, *Freddie*,' but he was suspicious after that.

"Then—as luck would have it—Eddie came through town a few weeks later, and I was careless and left—oh, this is horrible—one of Ed's cufflinks in my handbag. He'd lost it in my room, and I was terrified Frederick would find it. Then, of course, even though I found it—I put it in my handbag and didn't give it back before Frederick went in there looking for something. He found it and knew it immediately."

"How could he be sure it belonged to Eddie—Edward, I mean?"

"Ed had gold cufflinks engraved with his initials. ELM, like the tree. Who else's would they be? Frederick may be many things, but he's not stupid. I was cornered, and so I 'fessed up,' as the young people say. What was the point of denying it? He'd caught me red-handed."

Sarah didn't want any more cake, but she forced herself to take a tiny bite. "And that's why you went to Cleveland?"

"That's what lit the fuse for that argument they had, in the Red Jacket Golf Club. Ed wasn't about to back down. He loved me, he really did, and he had a lot of fight in him. Frederick laid down the law and told me we were moving away. That's where he underestimated Ed, though."

Sarah nodded. "He visited with you on his business trips."

"It was a lot less proper than *visiting*, but yes, he did. I think we had more fun on his visits than we did here in Buffalo. No one knew him, and by that point, I didn't care what Frederick thought. Last December,

I told him that I wanted a divorce, that I was coming back to Buffalo to be with Ed. Who was, as you remember, getting his divorce then, too."

"I remember it well," Sarah murmured. "But then—"

"Yes," Helen said. "I had already told Frederick and was packing up my things, when Ed was—when he died. It was the worst day of my life, Sarah. You can't begin to imagine how I felt."

If you only knew, Sarah thought. "It must have been horrible," she said.

"Oh, it was. And of course there was no prospect of reconciliation with Freddie by that point. But I came ahead to Buffalo, and soon I'll be a merry divorcée. Who knows, maybe I can turn the head of another doctor. Fortunately, I've secured a generous settlement and so won't be without attractions."

"Not you, Helen," Sarah said, "you don't need money to be attractive. You have something most women will never have."

"That's very kind of you to say," Helen said. "But what might that be?"

"Peace of mind, I think."

"That's a very curious thing to say, but so like you, Sarah. Very profound. You've always been that way. A thinker."

"That's kind," Sarah said. "Though I find out every day how little I know for certain."

"That's age, dear. But you're still young. Wait until you get to be my age. You'll have peace of mind by then, too. You'll have no choice!"

Sarah laughed, wondering how phony it must have sounded. But Helen Warren was on to the next topic, clothing and who were the best milliners these days in Buffalo, and could Sarah make an introduction . . .

She kept at it with Helen for the mandated ninety minutes, at which time precisely her guest excused herself politely and left Sarah with a parting hug. After the front door clicked shut, Sarah stood in the foyer, her hand resting lightly on the knob. She wanted to call after Helen, ask her to come back and beg her to say that it had all been a fable, a terrible waking dream, a sorry excuse for a practical joke. Yet as she removed her hand from the cold doorknob, she knew all too well that no amount of fiction can ever completely bury the truth.

.

REUNION & SEPARATION

December 1, 1902
Monday Morning

Sarah knew she should be in the office, after four days away, but the thought of it turned her stomach. The situation with Jess was bad enough on a personal level, but it was also compelling her to delay getting to work on the much-needed paying engagement with Charles Kendall until Jess was gone.

Nor did she want to be at home, watching the colors on the Christmas tree they had put up over Thanksgiving. The cheerful evergreen ought to have marked the beginning of a happy season, but this year she wished she could pass it all by without notice. And looking ahead to the New Year, no list of half-hearted resolutions about the future would make it easier to climb out of the ruins of the present. This was to have been *their* year, but Eddie hadn't made it out of the last. And even that memory, of love almost won and then utterly lost, was more bitter than bittersweet after what Helen Warren had said.

Sarah picked her way down the icy slope to the lakefront, hiking her fur collar high around her neck against the wind. The faltering, cold sun smoldered peach and coral, hovering just above a reef of low clouds, mirror images of the early ice floes in the mouth of Lake Erie, jostling for their chance to take their final, wild ride down the Niagara River. It was damp and frigid down here, along the grey shoreline.

She sat on a rotting bench near the water's edge and took out the little cabinet photo of Ed that she carried in her purse. She found herself peeking at it from time to time, to recall the curve of his lips or the way he combed his hair. In it, he looked so resolute, so firm, jaw set and eyes fixed on the horizon—a face of unwavering purpose. In life, he had been anything but the image he'd tried so hard to portray. The real Eddie had been confused, vainglorious, and had bounced like a shuttlecock between duty and desire, never settling for very long on either. He had made confounding and contradictory decisions, including the one that cost him his life.

Was that really him, this tiny sepia face? This likeness didn't capture his smile, or the way he would glance away when something pained him. Those details were now a jumble of loose memories, unmoored and drifting away. It disturbed her that—already!—she couldn't quite conjure the sound of his voice, or the smell of his cologne, or a hundred little details about him whose once sharp edges were softening, day by day. Did the memories predate the photo, or did the photo supply them? And which was more real?

But worse than his flickering image receding into her deeper mind was that she couldn't quite remember the woman she had been when he was alive. That person, too, was gone, or disfigured. She'd imagined that since December 1901 she'd been marking time, watching the world slip by like the little chunks of ice scudding past her rickety bench, when in fact she too had been moving inexorably along, like it or not. There was no place to rest from the relentless calendar round of days, months, and seasons. Treading water was impossible.

She picked at a finger of her glove and saw that the leather had torn, probably in getting down from the trolley. There would be holiday sales going on at all the big department stores downtown, a short walk from her bench. Might as well. Thinking isn't doing any good, and it'll be nice to be warm again. She took a last look at the lake and then turned away to begin the slow climb toward the Main Street shopping district.

❦

A half hour later, Sarah was rummaging around in a bin full of second-quality kid gloves at the H. A. Meldrum store on Main Street. Meldrum's didn't carry very nice things, but the prices were right and one could find everything under a single roof. And Maggie was excited by the new Green Stamps that Meldrum's gave out with every purchase, and eagerly pasted them into the little books that eventually—though it might take years—could be traded in for a credit on Sarah's account.

For all the apparent convenience of being able to buy a dress and have a tooth extracted in the same vast building, Sarah didn't care much for the new department stores. And she was fast losing what little patience she had left for the place as she dug through the heaps of gloves. There were never two gloves that matched correctly, and when she found two that did, they were different sizes. "Four thousand gloves and not a matching pair among them," she muttered under her breath.

She had almost reached the bottom of the bin, and the mountain of discarded gloves that she'd created in one corner was starting to collapse in on itself, an avalanche of rejects threatening to cascade down onto the few that still held promise. Nearing the bottom, she bent over the bin in a most unladylike position, head and shoulders deep in the void but as determined as ever to leave not a glove unturned. Then she heard a woman's voice behind her.

"Should I be throwing money?"

Sarah sprang up like a jack-in-the-box, her face flushed and a few wisps of stray hair drooping from under a hat that she had very nearly left behind in the glove bin. She brushed away the hair and turned to see a woman standing behind her, immaculately dressed in a deep purple day dress and wearing a hat even larger and more extravagant than her own.

Alicia Miller.

"Of all—" she said, smoothing her skirt and looking down at herself. "My, how dreadful."

"Not dreadful to see me, I hope," Alicia said with her thin smile. "It's been quite some time, you know."

"I meant—this spectacle I've been making of myself. And all for a pair of fifty-cent gloves." She noticed ruefully that in her one hand was clutched the single glove that had passed muster. She tossed it onto the mound, with all the other discards.

"Not at all," Alicia said.

"I wouldn't expect to see you in this place," Sarah said.

"Nor I you. But it's a good place for bargains."

They stood there, eyeing each other, for a long moment.

"As I said, it's been quite a while," Allie ventured. "You and Maggie are both well, I trust?"

"Yes, we're very well. And you?" she said, gritting her teeth.

"The same as ever. Life goes on. You know."

"That it does." Sarah shifted from one foot to the other, smoothed her skirt again.

"I was very sorry to hear about Seth's passing," Alicia said.

"He hadn't been well for some time."

"Still. I understand you have a detective agency now."

"Yes—yes I do. That's keeping me busy."

"I'd love to hear more about it. My own experience with detectives has been limited to being stalked by them." She chuckled, almost to herself.

Sarah wasn't sure what to say, and so gave Allie a half-smile. She brushed an errant wisp of hair out of her eyes.

"Why don't you come over to the house?" Alicia said. "Pay us a visit and see our Christmas tree."

Sarah wasn't sure what to do with this invitation.

"I'd love to," she heard herself say. "When would you like?"

"How about Wednesday? Around two o'clock?"

"All right, I can manage that."

"Good. We have a lot to catch up on. In the meantime, good luck with the gloves."

"Oh, I think I'll give up on that," Sarah said.

Alicia smiled. "You're not the giving-up type," she said. "See you tomorrow." And with that, she whirled around and left Sarah standing by the tangle of gloves, a thousand fingers all pointing in a thousand different directions.

❦

THE BRIEF SHOPPING TRIP, and the encounter with Alicia, hadn't made Sarah any more eager to go to work, but it was long past time to stop dithering and get on with it. The cutting wind seemed to be howling against her, regardless of which direction she walked, the whole way from Meldrum's to the Hudson Building. She took the stairs to the office, if only to get her blood pumping again.

"Did you have a good Thanksgiving?" Jess said brightly when she walked in.

"Uneventful," Sarah lied, walking past his desk and into her office. "You?"

"For it being three men eating Chinese food on the great day, I suppose," he said. "And then all weekend I had to sell hats."

"Sale season," Sarah said. "I was downtown just now."

"That's right. Saturday was the busiest I've seen it since I've been there. Made the time go by quickly, though."

"That's always good. I'd better get busy myself. Late start."

"Say, where's Annie?"

"She'll be along presently. She had a couple errands she wanted to run."

"Any more conversation with Mr. Kendall?" he said.

"He's accepted our proposal. His letter was in the mail yesterday." She sat down, put her reading glasses on, and ran a piece of paper through her typewriter.

"When do we start?" he called from the next room.

"Not until the New Year, Jess."

He stood up and walked over to Sarah's door. "You're going to need help on that case," he said. "It's a big one, if I understand it."

She looked up from her Underwood and quickly took off her glasses. "Let's not start, Jess."

He leaned his head against the doorframe. "I've been trying to make it up to you. You have to know how sorry I am."

She sat back in her chair. "I don't need a hundred apologies, Jess. We don't need to talk about this again and again. I've made up my mind, and I am sorry, but that's the way it's going to be. I know it's not pleasant hearing that, but it's not any fun for me to say, either."

"There must be a way I can make it up to you," he said quietly. "I'd do *anything*, if you'd only say to me 'Jess, I've changed my mind and I want you to stay.' I'd do anything."

"Jess—"

"I don't know what I'm going to do with myself," he said mournfully. "Everything I touch goes to ruin. I should just do away with myself."

"Please don't talk that way. You haven't ruined anything. You're going to be just fine. You're a talented person, a fine writer, and you have a sharp mind. Any number of firms would be delighted to hire you. And I'll give you a good reference, always. What happened with us does not reflect at all on your ability."

"Then why can't you let bygones be bygones? You can even keep me on day-to-day. If anything happens you don't like on any given day, then send me packing. But I feel as though I'm awaiting my execution, coming in here every day and—"

Sarah nodded. "I confess I didn't think of it that way. I thought I was being lenient, giving you so much time to adjust, and to get through the holidays. But I can understand how it would be difficult to come into an office, knowing—that it's not permanent."

"Yes, that's right," he said.

"Don't feel you have to come in. We'll pay you, same as always. Stay at home, look for another position, whatever you like. I'm not trying to make you suffer."

"Please don't make me stay away," he said. "I won't bring it up again, and you might change your mind when you see how good I can be."

"You're welcome to be here, Jess, but let's not talk about this again."

"All right," he mumbled, turning away and slouching back to his desk. "You can't blame a fellow for trying," he called out.

Sarah morosely put her glasses back on, not caring if Jess saw them, and straightened the paper in the Underwood. *Maybe I am being too hard*, she thought. *Everyone makes mistakes. I'll talk to Annie and see what she thinks.*

❧

WHEN ALICIA RETURNED FROM downtown late that afternoon, after taking in a rare Monday matinee, Bert hailed her from the parlor, where he was savoring a cocktail.

"I hope you've not been outdoors since you left," he said. "It's like the North Pole today."

"Oh, no," Allie said. "I went to Teck's Theater and saw *The Mikado*."

"Golly, I would have liked to see that."

"It'll be here through Christmas. You can still go."

"I thought we might go together, though."

"You never want to be seen with me."

"That's not true," he said. "I've wanted to be discreet, that's all."

"Bert, discretion and shame are twin sisters."

"Where did you hear that?"

"I made it up."

"All that aside," he said, "I have some news. My conference with Penrose is set. Tomorrow at ten."

"Finally," she said. "I thought he'd forgotten."

Allie finished hanging up her coat and hat and came into the parlor, lips vermilion and face flushed with the cold. She flopped down on the sofa.

"You look ravishing," Bert said. "The fresh air does you good."

"Please, Bert," she said, rolling her eyes, "I know you want up my skirt. Be patient, I'll let you have a peek when I thaw out."

"You know, I don't always have an ulterior motive for a compliment."

"That's a good practice. I need to adopt it. Penrose is on, then?"

"Yep," he said, raising his glass. "How about I pour you one?"

"Won't turn it down," she said. "Now what's your plan for the conference?"

"Same as we talked about. Offer him a contribution in exchange for getting Pendle to agree. He's going to run for governor, and that takes money. Lots and lots of money."

"And where do we get this money?"

"It would come out of your bequest."

"How much?"

"I think it could be as much as ten percent."

"Five thousand dollars?" Alicia said. "That's almost what this house cost."

"You'd keep forty-five thousand. And just about now you've got—zero."

"Then offer him ten percent, if that's what it takes. Not a penny more, though, unless we talk about it first. Don't make some Sam Patch leap on your own."

"I promise I will not."

"Then it's settled," she said. "If it doesn't go tomorrow, I don't know if it'll go at all."

"We mustn't give up. Arthur Pendle made that bequest of his own free will, and by right it's yours."

Alicia sniffed. "'By right.' You really are rather quaint sometimes, Bert, especially for a lawyer. Rights don't exist unless you win them."

"Then we will have to win, won't we?" he said.

"Yes, I suppose so. Now if we're done with that—I've got news, too."

"What's that?"

"You'll never guess who I bumped into at Meldrum's this morning."

"No, I probably wouldn't."

"Sarah Payne. Haven't seen her since the inquest, and after less than a week back in the city, what do you know."

"Interesting," Bert said cautiously. "How did you feel about that?"

"About what?"

"About seeing her."

"Other than wanting to claw her eyes out, you mean?"

Bert chuckled. "She's not that bad, Alicia."

"Bert, don't start on me about her. Brings back bad memories. The inquest, you know? When Ed was canonized and Silly Sarah was the sweetheart of all Buffalo. And I was Jezebel."

"It's not worth hating her for it," Bert said.

Allie whistled. "You have it so wrong. I don't hate her. I *envy* her."

"Envy her?"

"Of course. Not only for being lionized by Buffalo society. Mainly because she sashayed in and, in a matter of months, carved out the best part of Ed for herself—and left me with the part that for nineteen years had kept me in my place, made little of me and much of himself. Because he was a *businessman*, and I was only a mother. Did you know that my father was the one who set him up in business? You never would have heard it from him. Ed always was happy to take all the credit for himself.

"And in the meantime, I had to watch Silly Sarah lollygagging around with her 'Eddie,' having chocolate creams and batting her long eyelashes, and I was nothing more than the worn-out old hag who had to put up with his shitty little comments, year after year. And then when I had the nerve to find someone I loved, what then? He threw me out of the house. *His* house. He got to stay in *his* house after he'd found *his* one true love. And she would have moved in here with him, you can bet your bottom dollar. You think I'm going to forgive either of them for that? But I do envy them. Or her, since he's gone."

"That's all died down now. Life goes on."

"For you, maybe. I'm not quite ready for it to."

"Then I can only imagine what you said to Miss Payne. Did you give her a piece of your mind?"

"I invited her over for a visit. She'll be here the day after tomorrow."

Bert sat up straighter in his chair. "You're full of surprises," he said. "I thought you wanted to claw out her eyes?"

"I do," Allie said placidly. "But she doesn't need to know that. She may be useful."

"How so?"

"I don't know yet. But I don't have to like her to—make her an ally."

"Be careful," he said. "She doesn't like Penrose, and he doesn't like her."

"I'm sure I like him less than she does."

"You seem to get along with him rather well."

"You jealous, Bert? What am I supposed to do instead? All roads to my $50,000 go through Penrose. I'll do whatever it takes to get it. I'll suck the man's cock if I have to."

"I have no doubt."

Allie stood up. "You'd better mind your manners."

"It was a crude thing to say, that's all."

"Well then, how about this one? If Sarah Payne can get me my $50,000, without paying Penrose ten percent, I'll eat her pussy. And you can watch."

"Oh for God's sake, Alicia."

Alicia's mouth turned up at the corner. "Will you look at *you*, you naughty old boy," she said, pointing to his trouser front. "You *like* that idea, don't you?"

Bert shifted in his chair and dropped the newspaper in his lap. "I most certainly do not. Back to Penrose. I know he's a thorn in our side, but why hate the man so much?"

"I'm not sure I trust you enough yet to say."

"You don't trust me? I'm your attorney—"

"Among other things."

"Well, yes, fine, but as your attorney, every single syllable of anything you tell me is privileged. I couldn't reveal any of it without being disbarred. It's basic ethics."

"Hmm. You seem to pick and choose your ethical high ground as you go along."

"That's not fair. I've stood beside you since the inquest, and I still do."

Allie smoothed back her hair, pulled it into a little bun behind her head. She looks almost girlish when she does that, Bert thought. "Yes, you have, Bert," Allie said. "And you do. I sometimes wonder why."

"It's my job."

"Is that all it is?"

"That's enough, isn't it? You've said that to me more times than I can count."

"Yes, I have," she said. "But I've not always been fair with you, you know."

Bert looked at her, not sure whether she was setting him up. He felt like he might tear up, so he blinked and looked down at his lap.

"Bert?" she said.

He didn't look up, afraid he'd weep.

She knelt in front of him. "Look at me," she said in her husky voice. "Come on, Bert."

He looked up, biting his lip. "Yes, Alicia?"

"I *do* trust you," she said. "I'm sorry I said that. I do have more to tell you, and I will. It's that now's not the time. But I promise I will."

"That means a great deal to me, Alicia," he said, struggling. "And I am awfully sorry about that—horrible thing that happened to you when you were so young. It's been eating at me ever since Thanksgiving."

She reached out and smoothed down a cowlick in what little hair he had on the side of his head. He so carefully cultivated the little ring of hair, and always let it grow a little too long. "Enough of this," she said. "Everything will be all right. It always is. Bad things make us into better people."

"I'm not so sure," Bert said.

"I am. And," she said, laying her head on his lap, "let's not quarrel. What say we go upstairs for a while, instead?"

"That doesn't make everything right, Alicia. You're right, you know. Maybe I don't have any ethics."

"Now don't say that. You do."

"I have a lot of soul-searching to do, Alicia."

"And you will. We both will. But for now, let's forget all that." She paused. "You ought to know that I can only talk about cocks and pussies for so long before I have to do something about them."

"Oh for—"

She laughed, her deep, wicked, contagious laugh. "Come on, my boy. Don't be such a prude."

PART FIVE

TEMPEST

35

BERT'S MEETING
WITH PENROSE

"BERT! DO COME IN," TERRY PENROSE SAID AS HIS SECRETARY showed Bert into the DA's office. "Thank you for your patience with my schedule. I'm sorry it's taken so long."

"Thank you for accommodating me," Bert said. "I'm sure you don't have many idle moments."

Terry laughed. "Not too many. Some coffee?"

Bert and Terry sat at the long table in the corner of the office. A coffee service had been set out, and it was warming over a little alcohol burner. "I'd love some," Bert said.

"You ought to have stayed later at the masked ball," Terry said. "I could have arranged some companionship for you."

"That's very kind. There certainly were a lot of showgirls around."

Terry rolled his eyes. "And every one of them easily turned out by a man of a certain seasoning. That girl I had nearly crippled me."

Bert laughed. "Yet you live to tell the story."

"Thank heavens for that. Say, is it true that you and your wife are going your separate ways?"

"I'm afraid so," Bert replied. "Unpleasant business."

"Don't mean to pry, old man. I saw the filing."

"No, I didn't mean it that way. It's not a secret. I've been staying at Alicia Miller's house."

Terry raised his coffee cup in a mock toast. "You old dog," he said. "She's a fine-looking woman. Tough as they come, though."

"Right on both counts," Bert said. "And I am her legal counsel, too. Which is why I'd hoped we could meet."

"Yes, yes. What's on your mind?"

"Your run for governor—"

"Nothing's official, mind you," Terry said, raising a hand. "I'm exploring the possibility, so let's keep it under our hats."

"Naturally. If you do, though, I thought perhaps my client's interest and yours might intersect."

"Her bequest from Arthur Pendle."

"Indeed. You'll agree that for a widowed woman—one who likely has no prospect of ever finding another husband—that bequest represents a comfortable retirement from society. And it was clearly Mr. Pendle's intention that Mrs. Miller have it. Yet it seems we have Mr. Pendle's brother rather obstinately opposing it."

"Bad blood there," Penrose said. "He thinks that Mrs. Miller ruined his brother and brought about his death."

"That's a bit extreme, don't you think?"

"It doesn't matter what I think. John Pendle is of a mind that your client destroyed his brother's reputation, and either drove him to suicide—which I don't believe for a moment—or, at the very least, made him so distracted mentally that he was prone to an accident."

"I'm old-fashioned, I suppose," Bert said. "I tend to think that people are responsible for their own actions. It's easy to blame our misfortunes on someone else."

"True, true. Again, I'm not endorsing his view, merely stating it for convenience."

"Do you think it would be possible to change his mind? I mean, for you to change his mind?"

"Anything is possible."

"We'd be very grateful if you could," Bert said. "If my client could secure her $50,000, I can say confidently that she would have sufficient liquidity to contribute a full five percent to your campaign. Or, if you don't run, to whatever cause you select."

"I've always thought charities were the biggest sinkholes for money ever invented," Penrose said. "They're fine for people who haven't made a name for themselves, or who have a name they need to polish up a bit. I don't fall into either of those categories."

"No, you don't. That would be entirely at your discretion, of course. The donation would be made in whatever way you'd prefer."

"I'll tell you, Bert, it's going to take some doing to convince Pendle to stand aside. I'm thinking that a more typical finder's fee would be ten percent. After all, if I'm not successful, the amount becomes zero, so there's no risk to your client."

"It would take some doing on my part to convince Mrs. Miller to part with ten percent," Bert said. "But if I can manage it, would you make the attempt?"

The DA put his fingers together in a steeple and touched them to his lips. "Yes, Mr. Hartshorn, I would. I would do my best for you and Mrs. Miller."

"That's wonderful to hear," Bert said. "Mrs. Miller will be delighted—"

Terry's face grew hard. "There's one other condition," he said.

"And that is?"

"I trust you won't take this the wrong way. But I'm a little old-fashioned, too. Before we have a deal, I'll need to hear directly from Mrs. Miller that she agrees to our terms."

Bert frowned and drew some imaginary figure on the tabletop with his index finger. "Mr. Penrose, I assure you I speak for my client."

"And I'm sure you do. But in cases like this, I have to look in the other person's eyes."

"Very well, then. If that is your requirement, I feel sure that Mrs. Miller will agree to it. Perhaps we can invite you to the house for a little holiday cheer, and finish this matter then."

Terry smiled. "I'd like that," he said. "I've been to Mrs. Miller's home only once before, and that was under most unpleasant circumstances. It will be nice to get reacquainted with her under more auspicious ones."

"Agreed, then," Bert said, standing with Penrose. "How best should I follow up with you?"

"Why don't you give me a week or two?" Terry said. "Then call me, and if I've made progress, we can set a date for me to stop by. Until I speak with Pendle, I can't guarantee anything. He has to make up his own mind about this."

"I understand completely. Thank you, Mr. Penrose," Bert said.

"Oh," Penrose said, clapping Bert on the shoulder, "I do hope you'll call me Terry."

❦

Bert burst through the front door, bubbling over with his news. No sign of Alicia in the parlor.

"Alicia!" he called up the stairs. "Are you up there? I want to tell you about my conference with Penrose."

"I'm lying down," said Alicia's voice from above.

"Oh for heaven's sake," he muttered, taking the stairs two at a time. Her door was open, and he walked in.

"I'm just back from meeting with Penrose," he said.

"I know," she said, setting her book down. "I heard you bellowing from downstairs."

Bert looked up at the ceiling. "I thought you'd be eager to learn what Penrose had to say."

"I already know what he said."

"Oh, I see. Now you're clairvoyant."

"Smart aleck. It doesn't take a seer to know how this will go. Five thousand dollars is an awful lot of money, even to the likes of Terry Penrose. So doesn't it seem that he'd move heaven and earth to get at it?"

"Yes, it does, but I don't want to count on it."

"Wait and see," Alicia said. "And by the way. Even if Terry Penrose doesn't have any dirt on John Pendle—which I highly doubt—if Pendle doesn't agree to *get* out of the way, Penrose will *put* him out of the way."

Hartshorn tilted his head to one side. "He's the district attorney, Alicia," he said. "He doesn't have people killed."

She laughed so hard that she almost spit out her tea. "You dear man," she said. "If only you knew."

"Then enlighten me. You can't leave a comment like that floating around."

"Oh, but I can."

"If Penrose is as bad as you say, how does he keep it from becoming public?"

"Palm grease, of course. He makes sure everyone's in on the game. Then it's guaranteed that no one will ever talk. Bert, you're smarter than this." She brushed a few crumbs from her skirt. "Don't you realize that we'll be in precisely the same situation as everyone else he owns? We will have bribed a public official to obtain a payment. However legally that bequest was made, that will make it appear to be something shameful. Something we'll never be able to talk about. And John Pendle will know about it, too. All of us will be nothing more than conspirators."

"I don't think of it as a bribe," Bert said.

"And you may be my guest. But think about it this way: What if the newspapers ran a front-page story about how the infamous Mrs. Miller and her live-in attorney greased the palm of the Erie County district attorney to profit from the harlot's illicit love affair? You can bet we'll be the ones twisting in the wind and not Terry Penrose. He'll keep that Sword of Damocles hanging over our heads for as long as he needs it there."

"Why in the world did you go along with me, then, if you knew this?"

"You convinced me it was a risk worth taking. As you said, $45,000 is a lot of money. That will keep me, my mother, and the girls, until they get married, and then keep me and my mother for the rest of our lives. It's not riches, but it's security."

Bert looked out her front window to the snow swirling down Ashwood Street. "I feel we've done the wrong thing," he said. "I don't want this following me around the rest of my life."

"Funny how regrets always come too late, isn't it?" Allie said.

❦

THE FOLLOWING DAY, SARAH pushed the buzzer by the side of the Millers' front door. The last time she'd been to this spot was the night that Ed had been murdered. He'd greeted her at the door, sat down with her in the parlor, and she had talked and cajoled and pleaded with him to drop his divorce suit, that Arthur Pendle and who knew who else were dangerous people . . . And Eddie had agreed. He would call his attorney in the morning, and that afternoon he and Sarah would be on a westbound train.

But then again, she thought, perhaps he hadn't meant it at all. He may well have told Helen Warren the very same thing, keeping both plates spinning until he could devise a way to extricate himself. Ironic, she thought. Eddie mightn't have been so different from Arthur Pendle, running from pillar to post every day, borrowing time.

The two front windows of the den to the left of the front door stared out at her blankly, their shades drawn tight. She looked away, toward the other side of the porch, and at last heard the front door rattle.

"Help you, Miss?" a maid said, opening the door a crack.

"I'm Miss Payne. I'm to have tea with Mrs. Miller."

"Yes, of course. Right this way, Miss."

The maid took her coat, fur stole, and gloves, and showed her into the parlor across the hall from the den, the very parlor in which she'd met with Eddie. Sarah saw out of the corner of her eye that the den door was closed, and that was good enough. She dared not turn to face it directly, all the same.

"I'll let Mrs. Miller to know that you are here," the maid said.

Sarah stood in the parlor, looking around. The furniture, the slowly ticking ormolu clock on the mantel over the stone fireplace, even the smell of the oiled paneling—everything was exactly how and where it was that last night. She worked up the courage to look out toward the hallway, across to the den. Cheerless winter light was streaming down the staircase from the window at the top of the stairs, spreading a cold oblong on the floor in front of the den. A shadow crossed the bright spot, and Sarah half-expected to see Eddie round the corner and appear in the doorway, but instead it was Alicia who materialized, smiling her flat smile.

"Sarah," Alicia said, striding into the parlor and giving Sarah a little peck on the cheek. "Don't you look gorgeous today. It is good of you to come by."

"I appreciate the invitation," Sarah said. "You look lovely."

Alicia's dark brown hair was done up in a chignon that, Sarah thought, made her face look too large. She was wearing a crisp shirtwaist with a high lace collar atop a soft flannel skirt. Unlike the voluminous walking outfit she'd been wearing at Meldrum's, this one showed off her trim, petite figure.

"Do sit," Allie said. "Make yourself at home. Melissa will be along shortly with our tea."

Sarah sat, oddly in the same chair that Eddie had occupied that night, and Alicia in the one Sarah had sat in, pleading.

"How long has it been?" Alicia said. "Since you've been to the house?"

"Two years?" Sarah lied. "It's been quite a while."

"Let's hope you won't be a stranger around here anymore."

"Very kind of you to say. Tell me, have you been quite busy?"

"Oh yes, I have been," Allie said. "A bit of travel, to Mr. Hartshorn's farm in Hamburg. And the usual Ashwood-y things, you know."

"I haven't done much socializing myself," Sarah said.

"Why not? You were always so popular."

"I don't have a husband. I'm not sure I'd be welcome."

"I don't have one either," Allie said. "And I don't let it stop me."

"Well, then, I don't have any money."

"Now *that* could be a problem. You know how Ashwood is. But I'm sure that will be only temporary, as your new venture takes flight. A little joke there," Alicia said.

"Pardon?"

"A joke. Take flight. Take wing. Wings. Because your new agency is called Angel something."

"Oh," Sarah said, feigning a chuckle. "Yes, Avenging Angel Detective Agency."

"That's quite a heavenly-sounding title."

"You pay me quite a compliment, knowing the name of my agency. Or part of it."

Melissa arrived with the tea, and Allie watched the girl pour each cup and set out a little tray of crackers, cheese, and fruit tarts. Melissa seemed rather anxious under the scrutiny of the lady of the house, and quickly completed her tasks, curtsied, and scurried out to less nerve-wracking chores.

"She's not the best, but not the worst," Allie whispered. "Polite."

"She seems very pleasant."

"I entirely forgot to ask you—how is dear little Annie doing? I hear you took her on after she left our employ. And Ruth, too."

"They're both doing quite well," Sarah said.

"Please do tell them I said hello, wouldn't you?"

"They'll be delighted. I'll be happy to."

"Now do go on and tell me all about this agency of yours. Why did you name it 'Avenging Angel,' for instance?"

"It's a name I'd had in mind since I was a little girl. I'm not sure why, but that was always what I would name an agency, if I should have one."

"So you've wanted to be a detective for a long time, then. I had thought that perhaps you went into that line of work only because of—you know. The tragedy we all went through."

Allie's expression hadn't changed, even when bringing up the topic that Sarah had desperately hoped would not come up at all, but retained a bland, slightly abstracted air.

"No, it wasn't that," Sarah said quietly.

Allie blew on her tea, pursing her lips into a tiny red circle. "I should have sat where you are, dear," she said. "It was thoughtless of me, to have you looking at that door." She moved her head backward, to indicate the den behind her.

"It's not a problem," Sarah said quietly.

"Well, good. Now then. Are you working on your detective cases here in Buffalo? What have you got simmering away?"

"I'm only starting out. I may have one in Niagara Falls soon."

"Wonderful," Alicia said. She gestured to the tray of snacks. "Please, join me, won't you? All homemade."

"Why, thank you," Sarah said.

"Anyone special in your life, Sarah? A man? It's been some time since Seth passed. My condolences. Terrible shame."

"Thank you for saying so. No, no one special now."

Alicia studied her for a moment, and Sarah had a little glimpse of what was behind those deep, dark eyes.

"Aren't you going to offer your condolences to me, dear?" Allie said with a slight smile. "You know, I did lose my husband too."

Sarah felt the blood drain from her head. She slowly put down the little piece of tart she was holding. "It was a terrible loss," she said weakly. "My condolences."

Allie sat back. "It must feel awkward, talking about Ed with me."

"It does."

"I suppose there are no two ways around it. But we shouldn't play at it, Sarah. Games are such a waste of time."

"I'm not following you. Games?"

"Games. Playing pretend, as little girls do. Pretending that we both don't know all that went on. With me and Ed, and then with you and Ed. We experienced the same loss. In different ways, to be sure. But the same loss."

"It's a very difficult subject," Sarah said, her words catching in her throat.

"All the more reason we ought to clear the air. Anyway, what is any of this going to matter in a hundred years? All these petty concerns and cares? Eons passed before you and I opened our eyes, and eons more will pass after we've closed them. Our whole lives will be forgotten in short order. I think—if it's all going to be forgotten as soon as we're dead, why waste what little time we have alive thinking about it? Why not forget it now, while we can, and have the pleasure of a clean slate?"

"It's a fair point," Sarah said. "Yet I haven't been able to wipe the slate clean. I've tried."

"I'm sorry to say it, dear, but if you haven't done it, you haven't really tried. If you don't mind my saying, the reason that you aren't wiping it clean right now, *at this moment*, is that you have the luxury of time. You can afford to grieve, to spend a few years of your youth in melancholy. What will that cost you? A few wrinkles? That's all. I don't have that kind of time."

"Grief isn't a luxury only for the young," Sarah said.

"You're wrong about that. Grief is very much a luxury. An indulgence, the hobby of the leisured class. It's wasting precious time lamenting something you were used to having and don't have anymore, instead of going off and finding something new to replace it. Wasting time is only for the young. But if they waste enough of it, they repent it eventually."

"I don't think it's a waste of time to mourn for someone dear."

Allie's eyes creased in a little squint. "How old are you now, Sarah? If I may ask?"

"Twenty-eight."

"Twenty-eight," Allie sighed. "Can you believe I'm fifteen years older than you are? *Fifteen years*. One learns a lot about life in fifteen years. Things that you thought were true turn out to be false, and vice versa. You realize that everything is changing all the time, and there's nothing you can do to stop it."

"I can't disagree with that."

"I don't want to seem—I don't know—but would you be interested in a little advice? Middle-aged advice?"

"I've always been interested in what makes you tick."

"I'll take that as a compliment." Allie smiled and nibbled on a short-bread, then set it down on her dainty china plate. "You're still quite beautiful—really you are. Stunning. I do understand why Ed was so smitten with you."

Sarah didn't reply.

"But that won't last forever," Allie went on. "And if I'm not mistaken, when you smile, I *might* notice a couple little crow's feet."

"No doubt."

"It's inevitable, dear. It's the passage of time. It helps that I never had your advantages."

"What advantages, may I ask, would those be?"

"I was just about to tell you. Your beauty, certainly. But also your—I don't know a good word for it—let me think . . ."

"You may feel free, Allie."

"Then I would say your *glibness*. Yes, that's as close as I can come."

"Glibness?"

"Yes. It works for you too. You get away with it, because you're so beautiful. Beauty and glibness go hand in hand, and yet the great se-cret—hiding in plain sight—is that you had nothing to do with obtaining either of them. That said, beauty fades. And glib chatter—past a certain age—becomes grotesque. You're the perfect Gibson Girl, still. You can say silly things, and people will laugh, and they will say how darling you are. And they will want to do things for you."

"I see."

"You said you were willing to hear my advice," Alicia said.

"And I am."

"So then here it is: you need to find something more enduring."

Allie took a sip of her tea before continuing. "You see, when I say I never had your advantages, it's not a complaint, simply a statement of fact. I was never beautiful, nor was I particularly endowed with the gift of gab. I had a few other talents, on the dance floor and—if you don't mind my saying—in more private settings. So was it truly a disadvantage not to be born beautiful or with a silver tongue? Not at all, because I was compelled to find things that would last. That would *endure*. That's what I'm suggesting you do, dear."

"And will you tell me what things will endure?"

"Of course. You may be a detective now, but you'll be disappointed in me if you try to analyze me."

"Why?"

"Because you'll find that I am the least mysterious person you'll ever chance to meet. I'm an open book, though I well know that many people don't find me so. But in truth I am utterly obvious, even if others refuse to believe it."

"I haven't made up my mind about that," Sarah said.

"Get to know me better, and you'll see that it's a fact," Allie said. "Now to your question. What endures?"

"I'm sure I don't know."

"My advice is to look at what men have," Allie said. "Young men can be handsome, even beautiful. And they certainly can be glib. And many of them remain entirely insubstantial their whole lives. Yet a fifty-year-old, even a sixty-year-old, man can still be fascinating and—desirable—in a way most women of that age forgot they ever were. That's because men have located the Fountain of Youth, Sarah."

"Now is that a fact?"

"It is."

"And where is this Fountain of Youth?"

"Plainly it's not a *where*, it's a *what*. What men have discovered—the secret of eternal youth—is five things. Five little things, and only five, that you need to acquire. Ready?"

"As I'll ever be," Sarah said.

She counted them off on her fingers. "Wealth. Power. Influence. And I should add that with the first, you can buy the second and third. Fourth—secrets that you are willing and able to keep, until such time as they can be used to your advantage. And fifth"—she folded her thumb in to make a fist—"a conspicuous lack of introspection."

"Not children? That seems like an omission."

"Oh my, no. Children are competitors, dear. Even if you bring them up right—all the more so, in fact. They are lovable little leeches, but that's all. Waiting for their turn on the throne."

"I'm not surprised by the first four," Sarah said. "But lack of introspection?"

"That's as important as any. In fact, it may be the key to getting all the others. Women are constantly wondering: Am I pretty enough? Am I doing, saying, thinking, *being* the right thing? Am I a good enough mother? Shouldn't I have the vote? and on and on and on. Men? Do you think there's even a tiny space in their heads for that sort of lugubrious self-examination? That kind of self-doubt? No—not an atom's worth. They are bulls in their own china shops, dunderheads who take no thought to what they do, so long as it leads somewhere. To a woman's bed, to a bigger bank account, to whatever it is they desire next. They assume they deserve whatever it is they want, without the slightest doubt."

Sarah stared down at her plate. "I will say that is perhaps the most cynical thing I've ever heard."

"Faint praise, dear, but even if you are right, it doesn't make *me* wrong. And since you have been so gracious about all this, I don't mind offering up a sixth element that is another secret of mankind's success. A bonus!"

"I'm all ears."

"This is one that perhaps you and I can practice together," Allie said. "It's that men *don't hold grudges*. Women hold grudges. Men have short memories. A fellow might not receive any communication from another man for years, yet as soon as he does, the back-slapping resumes as if it had never left off. Most of the few grudges men do hold are because of women. A woman they lost to another fellow, or a grudge that one woman has against another and requires her husband to endorse and share." Alicia plopped her hands down in her lap. "And there you have it. Fifteen long years of experience that you haven't had yet, and all in five short minutes."

"I suppose thanks are in order."

"I should say so!"

Sarah set her teacup down carefully on the bone china saucer. "Now if you don't mind, Allie, I'd like to ask you a question."

"Anything."

"Why did you invite me here today? Surely not to offer up your wisdom. You and I have been at complete odds for years."

"Yes, we have," she said, nodding. "But the more I have thought about it, the more I think that it's time to bury the hatchet. Remember what I said about grudges."

Sarah looked startled.

"Oh, I'm sorry—that was a poor choice of words. I wasn't talking about our dear departed Ed," Allie said with a little smirk. "I mean to say that when I saw you fallen into that—tiger trap full of gloves, I will admit that I very nearly went on my way without saying a thing. Because, truth be told—I don't like you very well."

"I don't know what to say to that."

"You could say, 'And I don't like you very well either, Allie.' That would be honest."

"I'm not going to say that. But I will play along. Why didn't you pass on by and leave me with my gloves?"

"Simple. In the next heartbeat, I thought that there's no good reason I must *like* you to think of you as an ally, instead of an enemy. We're both rather spectacular women, if you don't mind my saying. Survivors. And again, men don't scruple about joining forces with people they don't particularly like. Or even ones they don't fully trust. They do, all the time, when it makes sense. Without a second thought."

"And why do you think that our being allies would make sense?"

"A feeling. A hunch, as you detectives might say."

"That doesn't seem very carefully thought out."

"Does it have to be? The worst decisions of my life have been the result of thinking too much. Remember what I said about introspection, dear. Waste of time."

"I'll have to think about it."

"Don't think too long," Allie said, sitting back. "Think of it as a clearance sale. Good for a limited time."

"Thank you for putting it into terms I can understand."

"I wonder. Do you? You may understand some things less well than you think."

"Like what?"

Alicia looked at the ceiling. "Oh, like my husband, for example."

"I'd rather not talk about him, thank you."

"And whyever not? I knew him far better than you did. Nineteen years of marriage—not all of them bad, either. Three children. There are many things I know that you could never possibly know."

"I knew him well enough."

"Well enough to run off with him, maybe," Allie said, smiling. "But you know something? Be happy you didn't. If you had, you would have ended up the same as I did. Under his thumb. You wouldn't have your detective agency, for one. He would never have allowed you to live the way you do now."

"We'll never know that for sure. What we do know is that someone didn't allow him to live at all."

"But you see, I *do* know. And that's perhaps why we could be allies. Because I have information you don't, and vice versa."

"What kind of information?" Sarah said.

"The other thing," Allie continued, as if she hadn't heard Sarah at all, "about Ed. Don't think for an instant that his interests were any more profound than any other man. He saw you as young and beautiful, and a chance to try being a husband again—after he'd failed so miserably with me."

"With the right woman, he may well have succeeded."

Allie laughed. "Oh, the 'right woman.' I gave you more credit, Sarah, than being the kind of someone who would believe that such a woman exists, outside of magazines."

"I simply can't be that misanthropic," Sarah said. "If that makes me naïve, so be it."

"You may still be too young to be a misanthrope," Allie said, "but you are most certainly too old to be naïve."

"Yet you decided that Eddie wasn't the right man for you," Sarah said. "Why was that?"

"That's such a personal question, dear," Allie said. "But I don't take any offense. We shared a man, in a way, and we have a special bond. I'll tell you. The 'right man' is the man who will let you become whoever you become, and not take credit for the outcome if he likes it or blame you if he doesn't. And that was not Ed."

"Anything else?"

"I can see why you'll make a topflight detective," Allie said. "You're so curious. And you're not afraid to ask pointed questions. Good for you. We're local girls, you and I, so I doubt you'll mind my being blunt."

"Not in the slightest."

"Well, then. Do you know what 'free love' is?"

"I know what I read in the newspapers."

"You'd think you'd have learned by now not to believe anything you read in the newspapers. But that is neither here nor there. Free love isn't nearly so scandalous as people like to make out. It simply means that the church and the state should have no interest in, or control over, who we love, how, or when. Marriage, divorce, public outrage—it's all phony, manufactured nonsense designed to keep people from achieving freedom where they deserve it most.

"Ed may not have told you, but I didn't want to divorce him, not even at the end. I'm not sure I ever wanted to divorce him. He was the one who brought the proceeding against me, had me banished from this house we are sitting in now, and separated me from my children and my mother. Wrote me out of his will, and left me almost completely disgraced. And why would he do such a thing?"

"Tell me."

Allie leaned forward. "Because I fell in love with another man, and that ate him alive. I liked being with Arthur more than I liked being with Ed. *That's* what Ed hated about me. He wanted to go out and find love, with you or with Helen—oh, I see you know about Helen—but when I found love, he had to have his vengeance, because I wasn't willing to eat his leftovers.

"And while Arthur was smarter, better looking, and richer than Ed, that wasn't why I loved him. I loved him because he was a man with the confidence to let me be myself. He knew that he or I might fall out of love one day, but he wasn't worrying about it. He was willing to seize the moment."

"If you fell in love with another man, that's called adultery. Eddie had every reason to divorce you."

"*Eddie,*" Allie said. "I like how you say his name. It's endearing, I'll give you that, but it keeps him from being a man—the *real* Edward Miller. 'Eddie' is a boy in short pants. But no matter—you really did love him. Oh, that's not a question." She looked in her teacup, saw that it was empty but for a few damp leaves.

"Where do I begin on this strange topic, 'adultery'? For one, when Ed fell in love with *you*, I didn't move to throw him out or disgrace him. It would have been fine with me for him to love you, or whatever passes for it. He and I could have stayed married forever, and he could go off and you'll pardon my French—fuck your beautiful brains out as much as he liked.

I wouldn't have blamed him a bit. In fact, it would have lifted from my shoulders the burden of having to be everything he wanted in a woman."

She waved her hand gaily and laughed. "And I would have been quite content doing the same with Arthur. If you only knew! I told Ed more than once—many times more than once—why don't you bring Sarah over here, and I'll get Arthur, and the four of us will have such fun that God himself will have to wake up and take notice."

"That's reprehensible," Sarah said. "It's obscene."

"Oh, my dear, one day you'll wake up and regret that you let that face and that body of yours go to waste. They won't last, so you might as well use them up while you can."

"It seems to me that this 'free love' of yours comes at a high price. One gives up things like loyalty and commitment and security. I can't trade that all away for—disdain."

Allie frowned. "Now, dear, don't be hypocritical. Without free love, you wouldn't have felt free to fall for my husband while he was still married to me, and you were still married to Seth. You were practicing one thing, and now you're preaching another."

"I never, *ever* was in an intimate way with Ed—Edward."

"So much more's the pity, because you can't truly know someone without that. And I don't mind saying that whether you were intimate with him physically or not, you did something far worse than letting him put one trivial little piece of himself inside of you." She tapped on her temple with a forefinger. "You were planning a life with him that would have taken him away from his children, from his business, and which would have painfully reduced my circumstances. And through no fault of any of us. Only because that's what *you* wanted. That's *theft*, Sarah. Plain and simple. You wanted something I had, and you took it. You didn't care, because the price was worth paying, so long as someone else was paying it. And all the while, I would have been perfectly accepting of an arrangement where Ed had as much of you as he wanted, or you wanted of him. Why did you have to be aggressive about it? So selfish! You made it *personal*. Did you think I was going to take that lying down?"

Sarah was losing what little control she had left. "You brought me here to lecture me, then?"

"Calm yourself down, little one," Allie said. "There's no need to fly off the handle."

"I knew it was a mistake to come here," Sarah said. "Imagine, the two of us being allies. I'd sooner die."

Allie looked a bit stunned. "Now that was certainly direct."

"I very much hope so. Now that we've said all that needs saying, I'd like to be on my way."

"You know, Sarah, if you don't want to be someone's ally—it's probably best not to tell them so."

"I'm not you, Allie." She was tempted to say, "Thank God," but swallowed the urge.

"You're more like me than you care to admit. We both loved men who loved themselves more than they loved us. Admit it to yourself, and you'll be healed."

Sarah stood. "I do thank you for your invitation today. And for the tea. Now I think it's best if I see myself out."

Alicia had barely time to stand when Sarah whisked by her. She was almost to the doorway when she ran smack into Bert Hartshorn, coming into the parlor.

"Is everything well?" he said. "I thought I heard a commotion."

"Sarah," Allie said with perfect composure, "surely you remember Mr. Hartshorn? He was Ed's attorney. Back when."

"I remember," she said, to neither of them.

"Pleasure to see you again, Mrs. Payne," Bert said. "I hope you have been—"

"Bert has been helping me sort out all the red tape from Ed's estate," Allie said. "He's more or less a permanent fixture around here these days."

Bert cleared his throat. "Yes, hoping to get all this unpleasantness behind us as quickly as we can," he said.

"Then Bert will make his escape," Allie said.

"That makes two of us," Sarah said, and squeezed by him and out into the foyer. Bert and Allie heard the front door close, and Sarah's quick steps down the hollow, wooden porch.

"Now what was that all about?" Bert said, motioning to the door. "I thought you were going to charm her."

"I tried. But having her here, looking at her—I couldn't stop myself."

"From baiting her."

"Even if I did, she deserves every bit of baiting she gets. Who pulled your chain, anyway?"

"You said you wanted her as an ally! I'm not making it up, Alicia."

"*I'm not making it up, Alicia*," she said, mimicking him. "Well, maybe an alliance isn't possible."

"Perhaps not, but we sure don't need another enemy."

"Don't lecture me, Bert. I don't appreciate it."

"Fine. Just try to contain yourself when Terry Penrose is here, all right? At least don't make an enemy of him."

"Five thousand dollars makes him a friend. That's all."

"It's part of it. But you also need to be charming. He's used to being fawned over."

"I'm not fawning over him, or anyone," Alicia said.

"You goddamned well better. I've worked too much on this—*case* of yours—for no money. I won't see you—"

"Listen to you! You *can* be a hard bastard, when you want to."

"You haven't seen the half of it, my dear," he said.

"What's it going to take to see the other half?"

"I'm not playing this game with you, Alicia. I'm going out for a walk."

"Bully for you," she said. "You could use the exercise."

"You know—don't wait up for me," he said angrily. "I'll stay at the club tonight, where I can have a moment's peace."

"You do that. Stay there forever, if you want. I don't care."

36

ALICIA'S ECHO

AFTER A LONG NIGHT FULL OF STRANGE DREAMS, SARAH HAD fallen into a deep sleep, all too soon interrupted by the sticky patter of freezing rain against the windows of her bedroom. Sarah sat up and looked around, not quite grasping where she was.

She turned up the lamp, which revealed only her humble room, with a slightly crooked dressing table across from the bed. She knelt on her bed and looked at herself in the mirror. Crow's feet? she thought, pulling at the skin next to her eyes. God, what would they look like a year from now?

The meeting with Alicia had left her more than a little rattled, disappointed with herself, and in a somber and reflective mood. She'd underestimated Mrs. Miller, again. She'd been easily outplayed, toyed with, and baited into losing her composure, and all she had done was give Alicia the satisfaction of the upper hand. And all while sitting in the very chair Eddie was sitting in only a couple of hours before his life—their life together—had been taken away. But had "Eddie" even been real, or an idol she'd created out of Edward Miller's flesh and blood?

She pulled on the crow's feet again, looking at herself in the mirror. Had she been wasting time? Letting her beauty fade? Maybe Allie was right—but then again, she had also said that women spend too much time thinking about such things, doubting themselves. What she'd said had made terrible sense when she was saying it, sitting in that awful parlor, but now it seemed jumbled, confused, circular.

On an impulse, she loosened the ribbon that secured her nightdress around her neck, and let it fall to the mattress. She examined her torso, ran her hands over the soft skin, the mounds of her breasts. It was true that she never knew what it might have felt like to feel Eddie's hands on her like this, to feel his skin against hers. And it had been so long since anyone had touched her. Seth had gone missing years ago. She slid her hand down, between her legs, something she'd vowed she'd never do, not this way. And at first it did feel wrong—sinful, even, and desperately lonely—but then she forgot about all that, and thought about nothing and no one, not even Eddie.

When she got out of bed and retied her nightdress, and smoothed it over her hips, one word that Allie had used kept running through her mind: *theft*. She'd never considered before that Eddie's attraction to her might well have been her doing. Had she lured the man away from a marriage that, however loveless it had become, was still something that wasn't hers, anyone's, to put asunder, as the liturgy said?

It was bothersome that Alicia had been right about so many things. No one else had called Edward Miller "Eddie," and he was sensitive, and could be astringent, about his size. He'd been a pipsqueak all his life, and diminutives of any kind awakened the memories of the taunts he'd endured as a boy. Sarah couldn't recall when she began calling him Eddie—along with a few other what she had considered terms of endearment. Her little envelope man, she used to say, and he would smile, and seemed charmed. But perhaps she had been wounding him, all along, and didn't realize it? Perhaps she'd been diminishing him, to build herself up? One thing she knew—thinking of him as Eddie now gave her a pang. That was done. He would have to be Edward.

❦

It was still early when Bert awoke. He sat up in bed as gingerly as he could, but his stirring awakened Alicia.

"What time did you come back?" she murmured. "I thought you were leaving for good, the way you stormed out of here."

"I don't know. After midnight sometime."

"I had no idea. You ought to have told me."

"You were sound asleep," he said.

"That's never stopped you before."

"I'm sorry I was a bear," he said. "I didn't tell you, but Mattie is filing for a divorce."

"Damned if I don't have the Midas touch," Allie muttered. "I'm terribly sorry, Bert. I know how that hurts."

"I must have written a hundred divorce complaints in my time, but reading one about myself was hard."

"No one knows how to hurt you like your spouse."

"All too true," he said. "But I guess I had it coming."

"Still. Seeing a document like that makes one want to retaliate somehow. Even the score."

"I did a lot of thinking about it at the club, and it gave me bad dreams."

"It must have been contagious," she said, to the ceiling. "I had one too."

"You did? Because of our quarrel?"

"No," she said slowly. "Christmastime always brings them on."

"Why?"

"I don't know. This dream was about something that happened a couple of years ago. Do you want to hear about it?"

"Your stories make me sad," he said.

"Don't be such a pansy, Bert. Life isn't a circus."

"Go ahead, then."

"Have I told you about the last time I cried? That's what I was dreaming about."

"I'm not sure I like the ring of this."

"Funny. That's actually what made me cry—a ring. The Christmas before last—the last Christmas we spent together—Ed gave me a diamond ring. Before he kicked me out. He was making lots of money, and he must have known that Arthur was spending a fortune on me. I suppose he wanted his balls back.

"He gave me a velvet box from Dickinson's, and on it was a card on which he'd written, 'To my little diamond in the rough.' I read the card and I said to him, 'What the hell is that supposed to mean? *Diamond in the rough*?'

"'I suppose this means you're perfect,' I said, 'and I'm the one who needs working on?'"

"What did he say?" Bert asked.

"I don't even remember. The point is that after I asked him that question—he looked at me with a horrid sneer, and what do you know? I started bawling, right then and there, and couldn't stop, even though I knew he was taking pleasure in hurting me. And as I'm crying my eyes out, it comes to me in a flash. He doesn't love me, and I don't love him, so what's left? Causing as much pain as we could. That's what it had come to.

"And I resolved that I wouldn't cry again after that. And I haven't. Not when Ed died, and—you can attest to this—not even when Arthur went. And I doubt I ever will again. That one little snippy card dried me up, Bert."

"I'm very sorry, Alicia," Bert said. "My marriage—you know—the way they end is always—"

"You'll have to respond," she said. "The question is—will you try to wound her back?"

"Unless I don't oppose it, I'll have to."

"Isn't that the strangest thing? You know you don't want to, but you haven't any choice. It's like being a gladiator—kill or be killed. I did the same with Ed. I started telling Arthur stories about Ed. What a bastard he was to me. And even told a few that weren't entirely true.

"They weren't false, either—they were more like parables, more about the way he made me feel than about things he'd actually done or said. And Arthur was something out of another age—chivalrous, if a little quaint about it—and he had antique ideas about 'honor' and how a lady should be treated. I knew the stories would enrage him. It didn't take much, either—especially after Ed stole all of Arthur's letters. Arthur decided that a divorce wasn't good enough anymore. He started to think that Ed would win. And Arthur was too competitive to let Ed win—at anything. Not at golf, not at tennis, not at making money—and certainly not at *me*.

"And this is when Arthur's legal mind got to turning. He reasoned that if Edward died before a final divorce, things would be different. Ed wouldn't be able to disinherit me, not entirely, and he'd pay for hurting me, for making me cry. One thing I'll say about Arthur—for a man in such a prim and proper profession, he didn't mind getting his hands dirty. He told me quite calmly that he would 'talk' with Ed—talk some sense into him. All he needed from me, since Edward had changed the locks on the house after throwing me out, was for me to ask Mother to leave the front door unlatched on New Year's Eve. Which we'd done for years, until Edward made enemies."

"It *was* you, then," Bert said softly. "Last night, at the club, that was part of my dream. That it was *you*."

"Was me what?"

"Who—gave the order."

"Gave what order?"

"To kill Ed. What else?"

"What the *fuck*?" She sat up, her nightdress falling off her shoulders. She didn't bother to pull it up. "That's what you've been thinking all these months?"

"Well—"

Allie looked up at the ceiling and gave a low moan. "I have to say—there's more to you than meets the eye. You've been in my house—in my bed—all this time, all the while believing that you were living with a *murderess*? What the hell does that say about *you*?"

"I don't know—I didn't want to believe—"

"But you thought, sure, she kills people, but I like fucking her. How the hell do you think that makes me feel, Bert?"

"Jesus, Alicia, I didn't see it that way. I didn't mean it that way. I concluded that you had ample reason, and now you said that about the front door—"

"Ample reason? To have a man *killed*? My children's father?"

"Well—I didn't—"

"Very sorry to disappoint you, Bert, after your profound musings by the fireplace in your precious club. But no, I had nothing to do with Ed's murder. I didn't love Ed. I came to hate him, certainly. But I wouldn't have ordered him killed. He had refused to meet with Arthur—my attorney. How else was the man going to get an audience with the great Ed Miller? Oh, if Arthur had roughed him up a little in the process, it would have been no more than he deserved. But that's the extent of it."

"But you said that you got Arthur—frenzied—"

"And I did. And for quite a while I worried that I'd pushed Arthur too far, and that he'd done away with Ed in a fit of passion. But what I didn't grasp, until that little tête-à-tête with John Pendle, was that Arthur would have done a lot of things for me, but he wouldn't kill. No."

"You don't think Arthur killed him, then?"

"Oh, Arthur killed Ed, without a doubt. But not out of passion for me, or because I told him to. He did it to save his own skin from the things he'd put in his stupid letters. And he did it at Terry Penrose's urging, I'm quite certain."

"You've got Terry Penrose on the brain," Bert said. "He's not a killer."

"Don't be so naïve, Bert," she said. "The man is willing to hold up a bequest until we give him a share. What he's doing to me is the tip of the iceberg. I know, because Arthur worked for the man. And what I know— which is also only the tip of another iceberg—included some nasty work."

"Nasty? Like what?"

"I know only my part of it," she went on. "There's a lot I don't know. Terry had been law partners with Arthur, and it wouldn't take much for Arthur to convince him that moving Ed along would benefit them both."

"Alicia—I don't think we should be discussing this."

"Didn't you say yourself that every word I say to you, every syllable, is *privileged*?"

"Yes, of course I did."

"Then who else can I discuss it with? I can't very well ask Terry Penrose."

"And if you did, he'd deny it."

"I know that all too well. He's like a greased pig. He committed the sin, and then happily let me live with the shame."

"I should never have taken on this matter," Bert said, almost to himself.

"Why not?"

He frowned. "I never thought—" he said, and stopped abruptly.

"You never thought *what*?"

"That it would be so *ugly*."

"I wonder if you know how nauseating your sanctimony is?" Alicia said. "You've made a very good living for decades in an ugly profession. The whole legal system is nothing but a confidence game."

"You may think that the law is nothing but a confidence game, but I still believe that laws should apply equally to everyone. There's not a different law for Terry Penrose."

"But there is. The man is revered, and I'm reviled. And yet he was the schemer who did away with Ed and left me with one-third of my own husband's estate. Then, to top it off, he told me personally not to see the man I loved because it might look suspicious for *me*. That I could be blamed simply for seeing the man he'd sent to do his dirty work! And I fell for it. When Arthur rang the bell for me, what did I do? I watched him drive on by. And I didn't go to him, Bert. Because of Penrose. Arthur then drove off to his death, and I never even—"

"Alicia, calm down now," Bert said. "You're getting hysterical."

"You haven't seen me hysterical. And you won't. But I have every right to be. Terry fucking Penrose took everything away from me. My husband, two-thirds of my inheritance, my reputation, and Arthur. And I'll be goddamned if I'm going to let him off the hook for any of it. Ever."

Bert held up his hands, trying to mollify her. "I agree with you, Alicia. I do. I mean only that we're working through all of that, a little at a time. Be patient. We'll get what you're due. But if what you say is true about Terry Penrose—that he was mixed up in a *murder*, of all things—he should be in jail, not in the Governor's Mansion," Bert said.

"Good luck with that."

"An eye for an eye," Bert said.

"That's the Old Testament, not the law, my friend."

"The law is founded on the Ten Commandments."

"This from a fellow who can hardly wait to break Number Seven every night of his life," she said. "Except last night, that is. I could have sat on your face and you would have still walked out on me."

"If you care to know, I don't feel too good about that, either. All of—everything."

"That doesn't seem to stop you from having your fun."

"I gave up everything—"

"For my pussy," she said. "Yes you did. And I'm flattered. I really, truly am."

"I thought—I hoped—for a long time that there could be more—between us—than *that*."

"What else does there need to be? It's a lot more than most people have. And you don't have to go out prowling like a tomcat looking for it."

"I'm not proud of myself, Alicia," Bert said. "I didn't think I'd feel this way. I am sorry. For so many things."

"Will you stop with the self-pity?"

Bert was silent for a moment, examining a curl of wallpaper next to the bed which needed pasting down. "Alicia, I can't do this anymore," he said.

"Can't do what?"

"Whatever it is that we are doing."

"Be serious."

"I am serious. And believe me, I have nothing to go back to. My wife's divorcing me, and my children have taken her side. They both hate me. Or worse, they no longer respect me. I've become a laughingstock among my peers—"

"Laughingstock? They ought to be slapping you on the back. What do they say?"

"They say I should have learned from poor Arthur Pendle."

"*Poor Arthur Pendle*?" She laughed. "Learned what?"

"That you've got a strange power over men."

"What a load of horseshit," she said, waving her hand. "I don't have any power over you. Not that you haven't given me willingly."

"And whatever I offered, then—you took. Willingly."

"Why don't you tell me what you want, Bert?"

"I don't know what I want. I know only that I feel awful most of the time."

She hissed through her teeth. "If you want to leave, leave. If you want to stay, stay. But either way—you're going to get my money paid out first, or I'll make a complaint about you to the Bar Association. That you seduced me with false promises about Arthur's bequest, and when you couldn't get the job done, you left me to fend for myself."

"You wouldn't do that," he said. "You'd leave me with nothing."

"Then don't leave *me* with nothing."

"Fine. I'll sort out your bequest, and then I'm going."

"Good. Go. I don't care one way or the other, so long as I get my money."

Bert leaned back against the pillows. "What a life," he muttered.

"You've got it good, mister," Allie said. "Spare me all the boo-hoo."

"What do you want from me, Alicia? Really?"

"I want you to stop treating me like I'm your problem. You moved in here of your own free will, and now you're sitting in my bed, moaning 'oh, what a life,' as if I—an actual, murdering bitch, by the way—am to blame for it?"

"I never said you were my problem."

"The truth is that you've had it easy most of your life," she said. "Farms left to you by your parents, your club, all your degrees and awards. And all that turned your head, made you think things should always come easy. Let's be honest—would you throw five thousand dollars of your own money—*five thousand dollars*—at Terry Penrose, to get something that's legally yours anyway? I rather doubt it. You'd spend the rest of your life scribbling out motions and countermotions. But since it's my money, you'll happily take a shortcut. To pay off a *real* murderer."

Bert was silent for a while. "That hurts," he said.

"I'm sure it does. But is it *wrong*?"

"No. It's not, I'm sorry to say."

"I didn't mean any of it to wound you," she said. "It is how I feel, though, and I might as well be honest."

"It's wrong to pay off Penrose," he said.

"We've been over this, Bert. Of course it's wrong. But it seems to be the only way."

"What if we could get him to do it without paying him?"

"If wishes were horses, the poor would ride," Allie said.

"I mean it. What if we could convince him he was getting a contribution—but wouldn't get one?"

"Idea or fantasy, Bert?"

"Idea."

"Well?"

"When he's here, you get him talking about what you are going to do for him, and what he's going to do for you. You confirm the terms of the deal. And you get him to talk about what he's already done for you. He incriminates himself, and as soon as you get your money, we go public with the dirt on him. You never have to pay him out—and his political career is over."

"Have you lost your mind?"

"I don't think so," Bert said.

"Even if he did say something incriminating, you yourself said that he would deny it all. Our word against his. No one taking notes. What's changed?"

Bert rubbed his palms together. "I haven't figured that part out yet. Though I know someone who might be able to."

"Who?"

"Sarah Payne."

"*Sarah Payne*? You really are insane."

"She's a detective, Alicia."

"Playing at being one, you mean."

"Maybe, but no one wants to bring down Terry Penrose more than she does. But since you shot yourself in the foot with her, our chance to ask for her help flew right out the window."

Allie pouted. "I can fix it," she said.

Bert rolled his eyes. "I've seen how you fix things, Alicia."

"No, you haven't. Because you know what I'm going to do?"

"No idea," he said.

"I'm going to apologize to Sarah Payne."

"You? Apologize?"

"You like watching me eat humble pie, don't you?" Alicia said. "Go ahead, stuff it down my throat all you want. I won't forget it, Bert."

"Fifty thousand dollars buys a lot of amnesia."

"Hmm. Well, you watch me. If you really think she can help us, I'll telephone little Miss Sarah this very day, and I will bow and scrape and grovel my way back into her good graces."

"If you can patch things up with her, then I'll talk with her about how to lay a trap for Penrose."

"You just want to see her wiggle her ass again."

"I'll let that go by. You do your part, and I'll do mine."

"Deal," Alicia said. "I'll charm the socks off Miss Payne today."

"And when Penrose is here, charm him."

"Sarah, I can handle," she said. "But Penrose? You think I'll be able to put one over on an old fox like him?"

"Oh, Alicia," he said, "about that, I have no doubt whatsoever."

"I'll take that as a compliment," she said. "But I'll tell you this—I'm not testifying against him. That'd be signing my own death warrant."

"None of us will testify against him. But I will have to see if Miss Payne can find anything up her sleeve, first."

"Up her skirt, you mean, you randy old bastard."

"You do have a way with words, Alicia," he said.

"You'd be pining away for me now, Bert, if you hadn't come back last night."

"You're probably right. But be that as it may, when this is done—with Penrose—and your money—"

"Yes?"

"After it's done, you let me go. We're square."

"Let you go? You're not a prisoner, Bert."

"It's a figure of speech. I don't want to do this anymore. I've got to salvage what little is left of my integrity."

He sighed and sat up in bed, swung his skinny legs over the edge. Allie tugged on his shoulder. He looked over at her, sitting there, her dark hair half-spilling over her breasts, her night dress crumpled up in the sheets.

"Bert," she said quietly, "I know you don't like me very much—"

"I never said—"

She put her finger on his lips. "No, it's fine. I can't blame you, really. I suppose I'm not the easiest person to like. I'm complicated. You can go, of course. But when you do, I want you to know that I will miss you, all the same."

"You will?"

"Yes, I will."

"What would you miss about me?" he said. "And please don't say—"

She gave a hoarse little laugh. "I will miss that, of course. But I'll miss other things too. Don't ask me to say it twice, but you're a very decent man. I sometimes feel as though you could make me into a better version of myself, if I let you."

He looked at her quizzically. "Are you being serious?"

Allie looked at him full in the face, examining him. "Yes," she said softly. "Yes, I think I am."

She sat back, propping the pillows up behind her, naked and unashamed. Bert looked at her and smiled. There are times when I'd like to put a bullet in my head, he thought, but then there are others—like this.

"Thank you, Alicia," he said.

"Don't mention it. Now you'd best run along. I know you have things to do. I think I'm going to go back to sleep for a little while, before I call Miss Sarah. I feel sad."

"Alicia—" he said tentatively.

"Yes?"

"Would it help to make love?"

"I thought you didn't want that anymore, Bert."

"I don't mean—the way it is sometimes. I mean—"

She smiled. "Ah, yes. I think I know what you mean. Yes, Bert, let's do that. Maybe this time you can show me how you'd like it to be. I can learn, you know."

And Bert slipped back under the covers, rejoining his complicated, beautiful, horrible creature, and thinking how if he could retrace his steps, he would have given away twice as much again for only this moment. It wasn't easy, but it had been worth it.

❦

"Annie, come and have a look," Ruth called over her shoulder. She was standing at the upstairs hallway window, looking out over Ashwood Street. "Isn't that the fellow you work with? Murphy?"

Annie trotted up to the front of the house from her bedroom. Ruth parted the curtains a little bit to allow her to peer out.

"That's him all right," Annie said.

"I don't know what compelled me to look out a little bit ago, but I saw him walking the other direction, on the other side of the street, and I thought I recognized him. He was looking over at the house, and walked up toward Utica. I lost sight of him. But then just a few minutes later, here he came again, on our side of the street, looking sidelong at the house."

"That's very strange." Annie pressed her face against the glass to see where Jess was going. "Looks like he's walking down toward Bryan. Let's see if he comes back this way."

Sure enough, within five minutes Jess was strolling north again, again on the opposite side of the street. Annie let the curtains drop closed. "I'm going out and confronting him," she said. "What does he think he's doing?"

"Do you think you ought to?" Ruth said.

"I'm not putting up with that. And besides, Miss Sarah could come back at any moment from her shopping. That's why he's out there. He knows she's out and about, and is trying to bump into her. No sirree."

Annie ran down the hall stairs and pulled on her coat. Ruth heard the front door slam and the thump of her sister's boots on the porch steps. She peered out the window again, saw Annie look up and down the street and then run across the lane to intercept Jess.

"Hey!" Annie shouted to Jess's back as he walked quickly toward Utica Street. "You heard me!" She trotted after him, calling his name, and after a few more attempts to ignore her, he turned and faced her on the sidewalk.

"What do you mean by walking up and down the street in front of our house?" she said.

"I happened to be in the neighborhood. So what?"

"You live in Chinatown, you said," Annie said. "That's a couple miles from here. And you happened to be passing by?"

"A two-mile walk is refreshing," Jess said. "Is there a law against taking a walk outside my own neighborhood?"

"Maybe not, but back and forth in front of our house? I think there is a law against being a Peeping Tom."

"You'd like it if I were peeping in at you," he said.

"Are you peeping at Miss Sarah, then?"

"If I were, it'd be the only way I'd ever see her. I'm not invited over here anymore, the way I used to be."

"You know very well why that is," Annie said, her voice raised.

"This man bothering you, Miss?" a deep voice asked. Patrolman McCormick, who walked the Ashwood beat, had sauntered up, swinging his stick. He was a big man to begin with, and in his woolen greatcoat and tall helmet, looked giant.

"I am no masher, Officer," Jess said. "I work with this young lady, and I happened to be taking a stroll when she came out of her house and accosted me."

"Is that so, now?" He looked at Annie.

"He's been walking up and down, up and down, past our house for some time. It was making me and my sister nervous."

"You live around here, pal? I don't know you," the patrolman said.

"I live near Michigan and Vine."

"You're quite a ways from home, aren't you now, to be taking a stroll?"

"As I've been trying to tell Miss Murray here, there's no law against walking in Ashwood, even if I don't live here."

"I'll be the judge of that," the big cop said. "I look out for Ashwood, and Ashwood people. Anybody else, I keep 'em moving along. So how about you walk on back down to Chinatown now? Word to the wise."

"I will, but under protest," Jess said. "I'll have you know—"

The cop had heard enough, and grabbed Jess by his coat collar and began tugging him down the street, toward Bryan. "How about I help you catch the next streetcar, how's about that?"

Annie stood on the sidewalk, angry but also thinking that she hadn't expected Jess to be hauled away by the police. The cop was saying something to Jess as he tugged him down the street away from her, and then she saw Jess wriggle free of the man's grip, point his finger at the man's badge, and bark a few words that she couldn't make out. The cop seemed to shift onto one leg, skeptically, and then Jess took from his vest pocket what looked like a calling card. He thrust it out toward the patrolman.

The patrolman studied the card for a few seconds, and then handed it back slowly, making a slight and obviously obsequious bow in Jess's direction. Jess smoothed off his shoulder where the cop's paw had wrinkled it, and snatched back the calling card. McCormick lifted his helmet to Jess, then quickly crossed the street and walked away. Jess looked down the sidewalk toward Annie and gave her a look that sent a shiver through her, a hard and unaccountable stare. Then Jess turned his back and walked off in the direction of Bryan Street, to the south—presumably back toward Chinatown.

More frightened than ever, Annie scuttled across the street, ran up the porch steps, and locked the door behind her.

❦

ANNIE MET SARAH AT the door when she returned from downtown, and told her in what might have been a single breath about her encounter with Jess Murphy.

"I'll ask him about it," Sarah said wearily. "His behavior isn't natural."

"Don't say anything to him! You didn't see the look he gave me. If he thinks I've told you about it, I don't know what he'll do."

"We can't have him spying on us in our own home."

"I have a better idea," Annie said. "We turn the tables on him."

"What do you mean?"

"I'll tail him to his lodgings. And I'm going to meet his roommates. Not under my own name, of course."

"Do you think that's wise? Perhaps it would be easier simply to let him go."

"Maybe. But if he's as crazy as I think he is, it'd be better if we know more about him before you give him the axe. I'll go tomorrow, when he's least likely to expect it."

❧

THE PHONE JANGLED IN the corridor. They'd finally had one connected, and now the damn thing never seemed to stop ringing. Sarah trotted downstairs and picked up the earpiece.

"Hello, yes?" she said, somewhat impatiently.

"Sarah?"

She knew the voice. "Mrs. Miller. I wasn't expecting to hear from you."

"This isn't encouraging," Alicia said. "I'm back to being Mrs. Miller again."

"Very well—Alicia. To what do I owe this pleasure?"

"I had to call you. I couldn't sleep a wink," Alicia said. "And I'm a good sleeper. Always have been."

"Clear conscience, they say."

"You can be quite droll, you know."

"May I help you with something?"

"I'm calling to apologize."

Sarah wasn't certain she'd heard correctly. "Apologize?"

"After you left yesterday, I thought perhaps I'd been too harsh. I was trying to be playful, but I went too far. I do that, sometimes. And I'm sorry."

Sarah looked quizzically at the earpiece. "That's very gracious, though not necessary. I oughtn't to have lost my temper. It's as much my fault as yours."

"I especially regret that we didn't have an opportunity to talk about something we do have in common. Something we both want."

"What would that be?"

"I'd rather not say on the telephone. If you don't mind, Bert will come by your office to tell you more. I predict you'll be interested."

"I'll keep an open mind," Sarah said.

"All I can ask. I'm glad you're giving me a second chance."

"Alicia, please. Let's not keep on like this."

"No, I merely wanted to thank you. I'll let you get back to your day. Bert will be in touch. Bye for now."

"Bye, Alicia," Sarah said, slowly replacing the earpiece on its cradle. She stood in the hallway for a long while, thinking.

DISGUISES

ANNIE WAITED IMPATIENTLY FOR A TROLLEY AS THE AFTERNOON sun balanced on the rooftops of Ashwood. Something was wrong on the line, and it took twenty minutes for one to rumble up to her stop.

She'd left work a little early, making some excuse that Jess would believe, and hustled back to the house. She ran upstairs and threw open the trunk that held most everything she owned in the world, dug around in it, and located the outfit she'd worn as the Millers' domestic.

She held it out at arm's length. After months of being folded in the bottom of a trunk, no amount of smoothing was going to take out the creases in the brown melton walking suit. There was no time to heat the iron, either. Even now, it would take luck to make it back to the office before Jess left for home.

She wriggled out of her office clothes, threw on the outfit from the trunk, and glanced at herself in the mirror. She ran her hands one final time over the fabric. The suit, high boots, and heavy woolen coat smelled faintly of cedar. The scent reminded her how delighted she'd been that first winter in service, when Mrs. Miller had purchased the clothing for her. And it had remained a source of considerable satisfaction for four long years. Upon being dismissed from the Miller household, she'd carefully stowed away the items, figuring that soon enough she'd be wearing them again at another fashionable Ashwood address. But Sarah had hired her instead, and the garments had gone to sleep, forgotten.

And a strange thing had happened in the darkness of her trunk—a transformation. When it emerged, the once-sleek walking suit looked hopelessly drab and shapeless, what had once seemed fine fabric was now coarse and common. She wondered for a fleeting moment, even, whether someone had pilfered *her* suit and left this one in its place. But no, there were her initials, sewn into the waistband of the skirt and behind the collar of the jacket: there could be no mistake. It was hers, yet almost unrecognizable. And she had changed, too, to such an extent that this suit, once her pride and joy, was now merely a prop, a disguise, an assumed identity intended to deceive.

Better get going, she thought. She wrapped a few spare items of clothing in brown paper, tied them with string, and trotted down the stairs and out the front door to catch the next trolley downtown.

❧

THE STREETCAR SEEMED TO make up some time on the way downtown, and by quarter after five, she was loitering across the street from the Hudson Building, watching the pedestal clock in front of the corner jewelry store. Jess was a punctual man, perhaps the result of working against deadlines in his former career, so she expected him to appear precisely at half-past five. She had wondered whether it might be better to wait near his lodgings, but she wasn't sure where on Michigan Street he lived, or on which side. It would be too easy to miss him on the busy sidewalk.

Five thirty passed her by, as she tapped her toe in time to the giant second hand of the jewelry store's clock. Five thirty five, then five forty ticked by, and she began to wonder whether he had left work early.

At quarter to six, the front door of the Avenging Angels' building banged open, hitting the brass doorstop mounted to the stone with a rap sharp enough to be audible over the passersby and end-of-day street traffic. Jess strode out of the building with his usual energy, turned down Delaware Avenue toward Niagara Square. So far, so good, she thought. He's walking in the general direction of Michigan and Vine. We'll know more when he rounds Niagara Square.

And Jess did turn briskly east at the great square in the center of the city, following Court Street. From there it would be a fifteen-minute walk to Michigan and Vine, but at Jess's pace, it might take only ten. Especially with an injured foot, Annie had a difficult time keeping up with her colleague's long legs, and he seemed to be walking unusually quickly too, dodging and weaving between pedestrians without so much as a "pardon me," almost as if angry at something.

He jogged to the right, onto Clinton, and covered the few blocks to Michigan Street so quickly that Annie lost him a couple of times. She spied him again just before he turned left on Michigan, toward Vine, a short half-block north. She darted around the corner, nearly plowing over a fat domestic lugging two enormous bundles of laundry under her arms, and didn't stop to excuse herself, despite the woman's torrent of abuse. She turned onto Vine Street just in time to see Jess disappear into the second building on her side of the street. She'd done it!

Annie planned to loaf on the corner for fifteen minutes, to allow Jess time to settle in, but then changed her mind. What was to say that he wouldn't make a quick change of clothing and head out again for an early supper? She tucked the twine-wrapped package of laundry under her arm and hustled to the front of his building, number 64. It might well have been number 164 or 264, too—there was a weathered, ghostly image of another bronze number that had either fallen off long before or been purloined by someone else in greater need of the digit.

Number 64 was a weather-beaten two-story frame building covered in wavy clapboard that hadn't seen a paintbrush in decades. The ground floor was occupied by Jum Lee's Chinese Market, which boasted two large and impossibly grimy plate-glass windows, flanking a central door. Above the market was a small second story and an attic tucked under a steeply pitched roof.

Three upper windows trimmed with elaborate gingerbread moulding faced the street, though strangely they weren't symmetrical, but instead the two on the left huddled cheek by jowl, with the one on the right nearly under the eave. The incongruous gingerbread trim also adorned the crest of the gable and the small attic dormer beneath, and unlike all the other wood, it seemed as if someone had risked life and limb to apply a fresh coat of brilliant white paint to each tiny detail.

Presumably, Jess lived above the market. Annie wasn't about to march past Jum Lee's patrons and look for the rear stairs, as Jess had plainly done. Instead, she eased down the narrow garbage-strewn side lot on the left of the building and to the rear, where there was a dark constricted alley barely wide enough to wheel out the ash cans stacked behind Jum Lee's store. There was a rear door there, near the corner of the building, unlocked. She stepped inside and let her eyes adjust.

Her eyes adjusted long before she could master the urge to gag. The smell in the place was overpowering, the stench of joss sticks and rancid cooking oil. The reek wasn't wafting from anywhere in particular, either—it seemed instead to have seeped into the pores of the structure itself. She gasped, wishing she had a handkerchief to put over her mouth, but in the next shallow breath decided that she was being craven and weak. Suppressing her squeamishness, she put her hand cautiously on the sticky handrail of a steep staircase leading up.

At the top of the stairs, the light was worse, and the smell close to intolerable. Whatever was bubbling downstairs in Jum Lee's market had percolated up through the floorboards. The narrow upper hallway connected what looked to be two separate rooms— there were two separate doors, between which was another small staircase opening, presumably leading down to the market below. One of these doors was Jess's, but which? Annie tiptoed down the corridor, heart pounding and breathlessly praying that the warped floorboards wouldn't give her away.

She had gone only a few steps, and was still ten feet from the first door, when she clearly heard Jess's voice, raised and urgent. She edged closer to his door and listened. He seemed to be having an argument with one of his roommates.

His voice was alternately rising and falling, growing louder and then fainter, crescendo and decrescendo, and it occurred to her that he must be pacing to and fro across the floor. How he could manage such a feat in so small a space, without bowling over his roommates, was a kind of marvel, but there was no other explanation for the odd rhythm of what sounded like a bitter tirade.

"That's a goddamned stupid question," he said. "Where do you come up with this junk?"

Annie was taken somewhat aback, surprised at the harsh talk directed at fellows Jess had always described as friends.

"Fine," she heard him say, sharply. The volume dropped to a bitter grumble as Jess moved away from her, and Annie leaned closer to the door. Nothing.

When the volume came up again, she heard something that sounded like "easy for you to say." Then Jess stopped very near the door, so near that she could hear him breathing hard, scaring her half witless that he was about to jerk the thing open and bowl her over before she could flee.

"Why don't you two shut up for a change?" he said, "I know very well what I've done. What choice did I have?" There was a pause, and Annie strained to hear.

Both of his roommates then, she thought, George and—what was the other's name? Philip. But the roommates must be on the far side of the room, because she couldn't make out a syllable of whatever they were saying to irritate Jess so.

"I said, *shut up*!" Jess shouted suddenly, so loud that he may as well have been in the hallway with Annie. "I've had enough of you. I'm going to get something to eat."

Sweet Jesus, Annie thought, breaking into a cold sweat. She thought she could hear his hand on the doorknob.

Heedless of the racket, she catapulted herself headlong down the corridor, back to the corner stairs. She hadn't time to step down them carefully, so on the second step she threw herself down flat, head toward the corridor, face an inch off the foul treads, trying to control her breathing. She could only hope that Jess didn't choose to come down this staircase, and instead take the central one.

She heard the door open and then bang closed, loud as a gunshot echoing down the hall. There were two dreaded footsteps in her direction, and then they stopped and turned. The door opened again and slammed shut. He must have left something behind in his room, she thought, and took the opportunity to clamber to her feet, gather up her bundle, and run down the staircase and out into the tiny alleyway. From there she ran full tilt back to Vine Street, where she huddled in the doorway of a laundry.

Annie peeked up the street toward Jess's lodgings, and only a few seconds had passed before she saw him emerge from the front door of the market and turn in her direction. She shrank back into the laundry doorway, and then realized that he might pass within a foot or two of her, so she reached behind her for the doorknob and turned it, backing hastily into the laundry just as Jess—walking even faster than usual—went by without so much as a sidelong glance. His face was flushed and contorted, and he was puffing hard on a cigarette. Didn't know he smoked, Annie thought.

"Laundry?" a middle-aged Chinese lady said to her, nodding toward the crushed bundle of clothing.

"Oh, no"—Annie patted the bundle—"this is clean."

The lady looked puzzled.

"I'm sorry," she said. "I have the wrong address."

Annie left the laundry, and on the street caught her breath. She'd evaded detection by her quarry, and felt a curious sense of exhilaration after her close shave, like a soldier who survives a pitched battle. Now that Jess was out of the way, for a little while at least, she thought it an acceptable risk to have another listen at the door, to see if she could pick up something from Phil and George.

She retraced her steps to the back alley and up the stairs. At Jess's door, she grew bold enough to put her ear an inch away from the wood, straining to hear anything. But there was only silence from inside. They probably left directly after he did, she thought, and since I don't know what they look like, I couldn't have known.

Annie walked back down the now-familiar side staircase, and in the vacant lot had what she thought was a quite brilliant idea. She was dressed for the part, and while the bundle was a bit mangled, that would hardly be a problem.

She stepped onto the Vine Street sidewalk, took four small steps, and went into the front door of Jum Lee's Market.

❦

IF THE SMELL IN the staircase and the upper corridor had been bad, the market itself set a new standard. Annie again fought the urge to retch. She walked briskly to the counter, where a very swarthy Chinese man with a long queue was eyeing her. Looks more like a lascar than a Chinaman, she thought.

Behind him was a twin gas burner, roaring away, atop which were two huge pots of something at a rolling boil, billowing steam. The source of the odor, presumably.

"Help you?" he said, not entirely helpfully.

"I have laundry to deliver, upstairs," she said, pointing at her bundle and then toward the ceiling.

The lascar called into the back of the market. In a moment, a woman parted a greasy curtain and came to the counter. She held out her hands.

"I have to deliver it," Annie said.

"I deliver." She motioned impatiently for Annie to give her the package.

"They're items of a personal nature, and I was told to deliver them myself. To Mr. Murphy."

"Mister Murphy not here."

"I know," Annie said. "I can put it in his room."

The Chinese woman scowled at her, then reached under the counter. Annie thought for an instant that she might be going for a gun. Instead, she pulled out a ring of keys. She jerked her head toward the back, came around the counter and made for the staircase in the back of the shop. Annie followed quietly.

At the top of the stairs, Annie thought she might try to ingratiate herself with the little woman, and learn a few things about Jess. As they shuffled down the corridor toward Jess's door, Annie cleared her throat. "You're Mrs. Lee?" she said.

The woman grunted.

"Thank you for your help, Mrs. Lee. Since he's not here I'm sure I can give this to his roommate."

Mrs. Lee looked at her strangely. Annie smiled back. "I understand they are very nice gentlemen, like Mr. Murphy," she offered. By this time, Mrs. Lee was working away at the lock, trying to find the correct key on the jailer's ring.

At last the door opened, and Mrs. Lee and Annie walked into Jess's lodging. As it turned out, it was only one large room, furnished with a very old wardrobe, a washstand, a single chair, and a small bed with a headboard that was missing the varnish in the places where years of pomade had dissolved it. Annie looked around. There was no one else there, though it smelled of recent cigarette smoke. On the washstand lay a collar and a set of soiled cuffs. There was no bedside table, so on the floor next to the sagging mattress was a small stack of books. No sign of the roommates—and how would, or did, three men share one small bed?

"You deliver or no deliver?" Mrs. Lee said.

"Oh—" Annie stammered, "I just noticed that I brought the wrong bundle. I'll come back. I'm terribly sorry."

Mrs. Lee emitted a hiss of disgust and gave Annie a shove toward the door.

In the hallway, Annie pointed to the other door farther down. She thought perhaps Jess's roommates might live there, and have a connecting door with Jess. "Another apartment?" she asked.

Mrs. Lee shook her head emphatically. "Water closet."

"I don't understand. Mr. Murphy has two roommates. Where are they?"

The shopwoman squinted at her. "He better not," she said. She held up one finger ominously. "Single man room. Like in newspaper."

Annie was soon back on Vine Street, clutching her tattered paper bundle under her arm, the twine trailing behind her like the tail of an errant kite. There was only one conclusion, one theory that explained what she'd seen and heard. Jess didn't have roommates. Whatever discussion, argument, or debate he had been having, had been only with himself.

38

TRICKING THE DA

"He *what*?" Sarah said, her violet eyes going wide.

"He was talking to himself," Annie said. "There are no roommates. They're figments of his imagination. I saw the room with my own eyes."

Sarah looked down at her desk and shook her head slowly. "I don't know what to make of this," she said, more to herself than to Annie. "I truly don't." She swiveled around to stare out the office window for a minute.

"How does a person confabulate an entire life?" Sarah said, looking around again. "Is he really from Newport? Is Jess even his name?"

"We're going to have to figure how to handle this," Annie said. "Someone living a delusion might well be a danger to himself. Or to us."

They both gave a start when the heard the front office door creak open. "Hello? Miss Payne?" a gentleman's voice said tentatively.

"I'll see who it is," Annie said, moving to the outer office.

"Good day," the man said, removing his derby. "I'm Bert Hartshorn, to see Miss Payne."

Sarah greeted him in her doorway. "Good to see you again, Mr. Hartshorn. Please, come in."

"Thank you for meeting with me," Bert said.

"I want to apologize for my demeanor at our last meeting," Sarah said. "I wasn't at my best. You probably saved Alicia and me from coming to blows."

"Don't mention it. Alicia can be challenging. But she has a higher opinion of you than you may suspect. She's not irredeemable."

"No one is," Sarah said. "Though I'm afraid that Allie and I seem to rub each other the wrong way, even when we aren't trying to. It was very gracious of her to call me and apologize, however. I don't think I could have been so magnanimous."

"Time may heal those wounds, Miss Payne. I hope that my coming here today may help."

"I will admit I'm curious about the interests that Allie said I may have in common. Please, make yourself comfortable."

Hartshorn pulled up the guest chair, which looked like it would be easy on his sore back. "I'll come right to the point, Miss Payne. I have it on good authority that the murder of Edward Miller was orchestrated, at least in part, by the Erie County district attorney, Terence Penrose."

"That's a bold statement, especially coming from a man in your position."

"I wouldn't make it if I didn't think it had a basis in fact."

"How did you obtain this information?"

"I can't say. It's privileged."

"Mrs. Miller, then, I assume."

"I'm sorry, but I can't say."

"It's of no consequence. I suppose, though, that this is secondhand information. I'm not a lawyer, but I know enough to be wary of hearsay and speculation."

"And that's precisely why I'm here. I—Mrs. Miller and I—thought perhaps your new detective agency can devise a way to collect the first-hand evidence that would put an end to Terry Penrose's political career."

"Alicia thought that?"

"Yes, she did. She knows I'm here and is fully in support."

Sarah shook her head slowly. "How interesting."

"Miss Payne?" Bert said, after a few long moments of quiet.

"I'm sorry, yes. Evidence, you said. Firsthand evidence."

"That's it. If we are to put Terry Penrose out of business, once and for all, he'll have to incriminate himself."

"Given the personality there, that seems like a long putt," Sarah said. "He's awfully cagey."

"He is that. But we have the better of him on that front." He smiled.

"How so?"

"Mrs. Miller," he said. "Penrose is going to join us for dinner soon. After a few cocktails and the application of Mrs. Miller's considerable charm, we think we can get him to say something incriminating."

Sarah frowned. "Mr. Hartshorn, if you don't mind my saying—and this may seem rather rude—"

"Yes?"

"I'm not sure that I can trust anyone who counts Terence Penrose among his social circle."

Bert held out his palms. "Oh no, it's not like that at all. I've asked him to discuss how he might arrange to have Mrs. Miller's bequest paid out at last. The bequest made in her favor by Mr. Pendle prior to his death."

"I see," Sarah said. "That will require some palm grease, I'm sure."

"Precisely," Bert said. "And we are going to make him ask Mrs. Miller for a bribe. That will be tantamount to an admission of corruption. After that, he's done."

"Your plan may well work," she said, "but I can't see how our agency can help. We can't very well hide behind your draperies, listen in, and take notes. And even that wouldn't do the trick."

"Exactly right," Bert said. "And that's precisely what we need—a *trick*. Some type of—I don't know what. Detectives are clever people, when it comes to coming up with such things."

"There are far more clever detective agencies than ours, I'm sure," Sarah said. "The Pinkertons, for example."

"I can't trust any of the established firms. There's no telling whether they are connected to Penrose."

"That's certainly a risk. Mr. Hartshorn, I must say that while I'm sincerely flattered that you and Allie would consider us for this matter, I don't think it's something we can help with. Short of having Terry Penrose sign a written confession, whatever admissions he makes to you or Mrs. Miller will be just another one of his many backroom conversations. Untraceable."

"Please, Miss Payne," Bert said. "Alicia—Mrs. Miller and I know that you can manage it. We don't know how, but we do know that you can. Will you at least give it some thought, before you decline? Wouldn't you, too, like to see Terry Penrose get his comeuppance?"

Sarah folded her hands on the desk in front of her and looked down at them. "Yes, of course I would like to see that. I'm sorry to say, though, that I've almost given up hope that I will."

"Sleep on it, at least," he said. "That's all I ask. If you then decide you can't help, I'll understand."

She nodded. "Very well, Mr. Hartshorn. I will do as you request."

"We will certainly pay you more than adequately."

Sarah hesitated. "That's not . . ."

"Is it the notion of working with Mrs. Miller? Is that what's troubling you?"

"You said you can't trust other agencies—and for good reason, too. Likewise, and to be very forthright with you, sir, it's very difficult for me to trust Mrs. Miller. I have good reason to believe, in fact, that it was Allie who put Terence Penrose up to sending his thugs to my house in the middle of the night."

"That was a long time ago, Miss Payne," he said. "Alicia was angry then. Very angry. And when she's angry, she can—"

"No need to say more," Sarah said. "It's not going to help. You've already sold me, Mr. Hartshorn, on giving this my full consideration. Don't sell it back now."

Bert laughed. "There's great wisdom in that old saying 'Quit while you are ahead'!"

She smiled. "Yes, that's a much nicer way of saying it."

Sarah stood and extended her hand. "Thank you for your confidence in us," she said. "I give you my word that we will give this careful attention. Whatever my personal misgivings."

"If you can't yet trust Mrs. Miller—then perhaps you can trust *me*, Miss Payne. Ed Miller did, for many years. He was my client, yes, but he was also one of my best friends. I know a little about what you meant to him, and he to you. Please know I would not deceive you, for his sake."

"That's a compelling argument. Edward always spoke highly of you."

Bert shook her outstretched hand. "Thank you for saying it, Miss Payne."

Sarah walked him to the outer door. "Oh—one other thing," she said, as he was about to leave. "When is Mr. Penrose coming to your home?"

"Next Thursday evening."

"That doesn't leave us much time. I'll telephone you no later than tomorrow evening and tell you if we think we can help."

"That is all I can ask, Miss Payne. And I thank you."

"You're more than welcome," she said, and closed the door behind him.

After Hartshorn left, Sarah exhaled, went back to her desk, and looked around at the little collection of office equipment she'd mastered, piece by piece, in secretarial school. It wasn't much, yet, this Avenging Angel Detective Agency, but it was beginning to feel like something that might just work, after all.

Sarah called out to Annie. "Annie, can you spare a minute?"

Annie walked in and sat down opposite Sarah. "Yes, boss?" she said.

"I may have a challenge for you."

"Music to my ears. What is it?"

Sarah related her conversation with Hartshorn. Annie looked at Sarah for a few minutes, then around the room, and then squeezed her eyes tightly shut, as she did when she was thinking. She stretched her legs out under the partner's desk, kicking Sarah solidly in the shin.

"Beg your pardon," she said, opening her eyes.

"It's quite all right. Fortunately, I have two legs. Where did you go just now?"

"I was trying to picture something in my mind."

"Any luck?"

Annie smiled and said, "I don't think we're going to need any. Luck, that is. I have an idea. Tell Hartshorn we can do this. I need two days."

"Are you joking?"

"I am not. But I need to get started right away."

"How can I help?"

"The most important thing I need is this office to myself. Without any distractions or prying eyes. And that means *no Jess*. So, I don't know, we tell him there's been a water leak or something, so I can be by myself."

"That won't be a problem. He's been staying away a lot anyway. He may have given up trying to stay. Anything else you need?"

"I'll need a few tools from the shed in our backyard."

"Help yourself," Sarah said.

❦

TWO DAYS LATER, WITH the office still shut up due to the fictitious water leak, Hartshorn arrived precisely on schedule. Sarah and Annie were waiting in the outer office, chatting. On Jess's vacant desk was a thick cotton duck cloth draped over something that might have been a large table lamp, to judge by its size and shape.

"Ought we to be encouraged, Miss Payne?" Hartshorn said. "I wish you'd given me a hint on the telephone yesterday—I wasn't able to sleep at all last night."

"I couldn't have if I'd wanted to," Sarah said with a laugh. "This is all Annie's work, and as usual, she's playing her cards close to the chest. What solution she has devised will be as new to me today as it is to you."

"I'm sure we're both eager to hear her thoughts, then."

Annie stood. "Mr. Hartshorn, I understand the problem facing us is one of gathering direct evidence against a particular person of interest. Otherwise, what we have is hearsay or at second hand, and no one who will dare testify against him."

"That's it exactly," Bert said. "Only direct evidence will suffice, in this case."

"I believe this will do the trick," Annie said, and stepped over to Jess's desk. "Ready?"

"We are," Sarah said.

"Voila!" Annie said, pulling off the cloth.

No one said a word as they stared at the object on the desk. It was a beautifully lacquered box, about eighteen inches on a side and a foot tall, made of what might have been rosewood. There was a crank handle protruding from one side of the box. On the top was a black cylinder with a metal stylus resting on it, and suspended from a wire frame was a large black funnel, the small end positioned just above the stylus and the large end facing out, looking very much like a lightweight version of a tuba's bell.

"A phonograph?" Hartshorn said.

"That looks awfully like *my* phonograph," Sarah said.

"You said I could borrow some things," Annie said.

"I'm perplexed," Hartshorn said, rubbing his temple.

Annie held out her hand. "Patience."

She moved behind the machine. "First, I wind it up, as I would any phonograph." She gave the protruding crank a half-dozen turns. "Now I move this lever, here, to start it playing." She flicked a little lever, and the cylinder began to rotate. The opening bars of a Scott Joplin rag tune came blaring out of the sound horn.

"So it *is* a phonograph," Hartshorn said.

"Playing my Scott Joplin cylinder," said Sarah.

Annie made a wry face. "You're both correct. But what makes this phonograph different," she said over the ragtime cornet, "is a second little lever, on the back. It used to be a thing that allowed you to change the drive belt. But I turned it into a lever that changes what this thing *does*. Watch what happens when I push the rear lever to its opposite position."

She moved her hand behind the rosewood box, and the music abruptly stopped. The cylinder stopped rotating, but from inside the box the motor and clockworks could still be heard whirring away. Annie stepped back from the device.

Hartshorn leaned forward. "Doesn't seem like anything's happening," he said.

"You'll see," Annie said.

She reached behind the machine again and flipped the second lever, and Joplin came blaring back. She then stopped the machine altogether, and with a small screwdriver opened a panel in the side of the rosewood box.

"This panel normally gives the user access to the motor and gears," she said. "For lubrication and repair."

She reached into the opening behind the panel and withdrew a second black cylinder. She removed the Joplin cylinder from under the stylus and replaced it with the one from inside the machine. She closed the panel again and, with a grand gesture, slid the starter lever on the top of the box.

Nothing.

The cylinder turned on its long axis as had the Joplin cylinder, and the stylus rode over the its smooth surface obediently, but from the sound bell came only a static scratch.

"What—" Hartshorn began, but Annie put her finger to her lips to stop him.

Then, from the sound bell, the static scratching was replaced by the clear sound of Hartshorn's voice. *"Doesn't seem like anything's happening."*

"You'll see," Annie's ghostly voice replied.

Annie stopped the cylinder and looked at her audience with a little smile. Sarah and Bert stared at the machine, then at Annie.

"What in the devil?" Bert stammered.

"When Miss Payne told me about our little problem, we were sitting in her office. And I was looking around while she was explaining what was needed—"

"And you saw my Dictaphone," Sarah said.

"You guessed it. Now, we all know that a Dictaphone records a man's voice so that a secretary can transcribe it later. Miss Payne has had one since her school days, in her office on the side table. Lovely little machine, too.

"So when Miss Payne said she had a challenge for me, I said, 'That's music to my ears.' And then, as I was listening to her, I saw that Dictaphone sitting on the table in its little box, and I thought: music to my ears, Dictaphone . . . you know.

"You see, a Dictaphone is nothing more than a phonograph in reverse. It uses the same kind of cylinder to *record* sound that a phonograph uses to *make* sound. And it uses the same kind of little spring motor. I reasoned that if I could combine the two—fit the Dictaphone into the body of the phonograph, and make it possible to switch from *playing* sound to *recording* it—we'd have everything we need. And it worked like a charm."

"That's simply brilliant," Sarah said.

Bert was grinning broadly. "Miss Murray, you could be a second Thomas Edison!"

"I hardly think so," Annie said, "but it will serve our purpose. On Thursday, you organize a little concert for our friend the district attorney, and let Mrs. Miller—"

"Work her magic," Bert said.

"That about sums it up," Annie said. "And when she does, we'll have the DA's confession—in his own voice."

"Miss Payne, Miss Murray, you do underestimate yourselves," Hartshorn said. "I can't think of another agency that could have contrived such an elegant solution."

"I'm so proud of you, Annie," Sarah said. "This is genius."

Annie smiled. "Thank you both. I love tinkering with things—I learned it all from Mr. Miller, too, so it will feel good to put some of that knowledge to catch his killer."

Hartshorn nodded. "That will be especially gratifying. Now, show me how to work this thing, and then I'll carry it downstairs and hail a carriage back to the house."

Sarah shook her head. "I think it's better to have the phonograph delivered directly, in case someone is spying," she said. "It's bad enough that you're here—I ought to have suggested we meet elsewhere. But if you should be spotted, at least you won't be in possession of our novel little device."

STRANGE BEDFELLOWS

ALONG WITH A FEW STUBBORN LEAVES AND DITHERING BIRDS IN the December trees, the days seemed to hang on, too, while waiting for the district attorney's visit.

Ashwood was unusually quiet, anticipating the rush of Christmas dances and dinners. This year's annual display of prosperity among the Ashwood Set was shaping up to be one for the record books. Women were anxiously goading their dressmakers, milliners were griping over a shortage of paradise plumes—egrets, herons, and ospreys were getting terribly scarce—and jewelers were spreading out their remaining stock to make their cases look less empty.

Alicia had hoped to sit this year's social season out entirely. Last year, she'd been banished, but that time seemed a long way off—not-quite-real and not-quite-dream. This year, everything was all too real, hard-edged, and she had no appetite for any of it. She would put on a good show for Penrose, and that would be a whole Christmas season's worth of phony distilled into a single evening.

As the sun dived behind the houses across the street, Allie grew tired of staring at the tree, and went to her room with a cup of tea, propped up some pillows behind her, and put some soft music on the phonograph near her dressing table. From her window, the clouds were thick and dark to the west, over the lake. That meant snow was coming, and a lot of it.

She was in a sort of trance when Bert rapped on her door and stuck his head in. "Penny for your thoughts," he said.

"They're not worth that much," she said.

"May I keep you company?"

"If you like."

Bert came in and sat on the edge of the bed.

"Are you ready for tonight?"

"Ready as I'll ever be, I guess. But they're calling for a blizzard. This whole thing might not happen."

"Maybe," Bert said. "But Penrose seemed pretty excited about tonight when I saw him at the club yesterday. I'm not sure that a blizzard would keep him away from seeing you by candlelight, my dear."

"To see the color of my money, you mean, not my sparkling eyes," Alicia said.

"Don't sell yourself short," he said, patting her leg. "Do we need a plan? Specifics, who does what?"

"You know how to use the magic phonograph well enough?"

"Yes, Miss Payne and Miss Murray made me practice it until I was proficient. It's simple. Now it'll be up to you, dear."

"I'll try to steer him around to saying something incriminating. God knows there are plenty of possibilities, but he's wily. It may not be easy."

"We can record a little more than three minutes' worth of chat," Bert said. "It doesn't sound like much, but if I turn it on and off a few times, three minutes will be plenty."

"I must say I didn't see Sarah Payne pulling this rabbit out of her hat."

"You doubted me. I told you that her agency could help."

"I did doubt you. But you were right."

"She's confident you can charm Penrose, too."

"Let's not count our chickens, Bert. You must have done some serious charming yourself, to induce her to do something that would help me."

"She respects you more than you know," he said. "But even if not, as they say, 'The enemy of my enemy is my friend.' She wants Penrose taken down a peg as much as you do."

Alicia nodded. "Misery has made us strange bedfellows."

"Well said."

"Speaking of which, I'd love to know what Penrose had to offer John Pendle to get him to sign away his objections."

"If I had to guess, there were a couple smaller policies that were held up by the insurance companies. For reasons that had nothing to do with you—suicide clauses and such. He probably funneled those to Pendle. Now of course Pendle had to swallow a bitter pill, because your getting his brother's bequest does give you quite a bit of legitimacy."

"Money beats sentiment, every time," Allie said.

"Not always, dear. Let's stay optimistic, if we can. Now why don't you rest up a little before your big performance."

THE TROJAN PHONOGRAPH

December 11, 1902
Thursday

THE SNOW WAS COMING DOWN AT A CLIP WHEN MELISSA SHOWED the district attorney into the parlor, where Alicia and Bert were waiting.

"Good to see you, Terry," Bert said. They shook hands.

"Mrs. Miller," Penrose said. "You are simply radiant."

"It's the candlelight, I'm sure," she said. Alicia was wearing a black velvet gown with a plunging neckline, her torc blazing gold, in full view against her skin.

Alicia extended her hand, and Terry shook it gently. "It's very kind of you to invite me to your home."

"You are always welcome here, Mr. Penrose. Make yourself comfortable. We've already poured the cocktails."

"Don't mind if I do," Terry said, sitting. "What an unusual necklace, if you don't mind my saying. An ouroboros."

Alicia ran her fingers down her neck, gently caressing the golden snake. "Bravo, sir. Not many people know what this is."

"You may not detect an accent now, but I was born in England and lived there until I was fifteen," he said. "I have seen that device many a time on ancient Celtic monuments. Yours seems particularly well done."

"Please," she said, leaning toward him and letting her gown gape open. "Take a closer look."

Penrose bent forward and studied the torc, stealing a glance into the shadows below. "Magnificent," he said.

"I'm happy you like it. Now, please, let us pour you a cocktail."

Melissa, who had been standing in the doorway with a pitcher and glasses, poured generous drinks for them, and then left, leaving the tray behind.

"Now we're officially under way," Alicia said. "Mr. Penrose, look at what Bert bought me for Christmas." She gestured to the phonograph. "Do you enjoy dancing? Or is that something district attorneys don't do?"

"I do like to dance, though my sources tell me that you're the best dancer in the city. I'd look like I had two left feet compared to you."

"Crank the phonograph, Bert," she said. "Let's see what our guest is made of."

Hartshorn wound up the phonograph, and when the first notes of Debussy's *Valse Romantique* began pouring out of the sound horn, Terry Penrose stood and held out his hand.

"May I have the honor of this dance, Mrs. Miller?"

"Your wish is my command," Alicia said, rising and fitting herself into his hold.

"Now tell me, how do you find Buffalo, Mr. Penrose?" she said, as they waltzed.

"I like it, though I never considered living here. You know it was Arthur Pendle who brought me here. When we graduated, he convinced me that Buffalo would be a gold mine for up-and-coming lawyers."

"I know all about that," Alicia said. She leaned close to his ear as they waltzed. "Now that all the drama is behind us . . . surely you knew— even if you didn't let on—about me and Arthur? Beyond the lawyering part, that is."

"I didn't want to presume."

"You needn't worry about that," she said. "In any case, I'm glad Arthur convinced you to make Buffalo your home."

"As am I. Did you know that when Arthur and I closed our law practice together—in 1898—he was planning to go off to the Klondike?"

"That I didn't know."

"Yes, he was keen to seek his fortune in the gold fields."

"He never mentioned it. I wonder why he didn't?"

"I'll claim credit. I asked him to help me with a few of my cases, and he stayed."

The waltz stopped abruptly, replaced by a scratching sound from the bell of the phonograph.

"Is something wrong with the player, Bert?" Allie said as she and Terry stood awkwardly, holding each other.

"Sorry, I must have jostled it," Bert said. "I'll get it going again in a second."

"Just like Bert," she whispered in Terry's ear. "The machinery works only half the time, and even then you have to crank it hard to get anything out of it."

Penrose laughed. "Oh, I'm sure it's not as bad as all that, Mrs. Miller."

Alicia and Penrose gave up on the music and sat down on the sofa, rather close to each other. Terry was plainly taken with Alicia's décolletage, the creamy swells of white skin outlined by the scalloped velvet of her dress, which pushed her up and out, a few freckles drawing his eye down into the depths. He extended his arm along the back of the sofa and glanced over whenever she looked away for a moment.

The two of them sipped their refreshments. Terry held his glass up to the light. "You make a good stiff one, Mrs. Miller," he said, looking approvingly at his cocktail.

Allie leaned toward him again, letting her cleavage fall directly into his line of sight. "You must know that's a terribly wicked thing to say. Though I won't disagree with you."

He cleared his throat. "Disagree that I'm wicked?"

"I don't know you well enough yet to render a verdict, Mr. District Attorney," she cooed. "Now tell me—where did you learn to dance so well?"

"My mother was a stage actress. She taught me to dance when I was just a lad."

"An actress? How interesting."

"Yes, in England. My father moved the family here when I was quite young. Well, not to Buffalo—to Philadelphia. My mother never forgave him for that."

"Philadelphia is unforgiveable," Allie said. "But imagine, it might have been Cleveland."

"You have a good sense of humor, Mrs. Miller," the DA said. "But yes, moving to Cleveland would have been sufficient grounds for divorce. Even in Ohio."

"Bert, any progress on the music?" Alicia said.

Hartshorn smiled over at the two of them, sitting too close on the sofa, drinks in their hands. The phonograph suddenly squawked back to life.

"See?" he said, "I told you it was only a matter of time before I got it working again."

"Better late than never. Now let's have some more fun," Allie said. "Another dance?" she said to Penrose, and he nodded eagerly.

They danced and then sat down again to their drinks. Penrose's throat was dry after the dance in the steam-heated parlor, and he finished off his tumbler of strong whiskey punch in two loud swallows. He dribbled a little on his chin, and dried it with a swipe of his sleeve. Alicia refilled his glass.

"Bert, will you put on another tune?" Alicia said. "How about something a little faster."

"Yes, Allie," Bert said from his chair next to the phonograph.

Bert dug around in the box of Edison cylinders, put one on, and the machine squawked to life. Meanwhile, Terry sidled closer to Alicia, starting to feel the effects of his cocktail. She turned and looked at him full in the face, challenging.

"You're more handsome than I remembered," she said. "Though I suppose in politics good looks are a requirement."

Penrose's pate flushed pink. "I find it fascinating," he said, a little shakily, "that a woman like yourself would take an interest in politics."

"A woman like myself? What kind of woman is that?"

"One of considerable refinement, taste—and beauty."

"I think you are trying to turn my head, Mr. Penrose."

"Let me know if I succeed," he laughed.

"You are doing pretty well," she purred, playfully tracing a line with her fingernail on the back of his hand. He knew he should pull it away, but didn't. "Now then. Why would I not take an interest in politics?"

"It's too grubby a business for a lady," he said. "But perhaps you are a suffragist?"

She sniffed. "Oh no, I don't care a fig for the vote. Let men pretend they make the decisions. I am happy behind the scenes."

"Very wise, Mrs. Miller. Very wise."

"Perhaps I'm more interested in the exploits of a certain politician than in politics generally."

THE TROJAN PHONOGRAPH

The music stopped with a screech. "What's wrong?" Alicia said to Bert.

"Not sure. I'll get it going," he said.

Alicia looked back at Terry and rolled her eyes. "Well then, while we're waiting. I understand Bert told you about my contribution to your campaign fund."

"He did—and it's most generous, madam."

"He said you wanted to hear the terms from me directly."

"Oh, I trust you, but so that we have a common understanding, it's always beneficial to talk face-to-face."

"My understanding of our agreement is that you will pull whatever strings a man like you pulls," she said, "and get John Pendle and the insurance companies to step aside and pay my bequest. In exchange, you get ten percent of my proceeds. That means five thousand dollars for your campaign fund."

Terry smiled. "That's exactly my understanding as well. Then this is for you." He pulled a thin envelope out of his breast pocket with a flourish and handed it to her.

"What's this?"

"An affidavit, signed by John Pendle as Trustee, and by myself as Executor, withdrawing all opposition to your bequest."

"You're an absolute prince! How can I thank you enough?"

"I'm sure we'll think of something, madam," Penrose said.

"I've got it working!" Bert exclaimed as the music started up again. It was a soft, slow piece, almost a dirge.

"Let's sit this one out," Alicia said. "However did Bert choose this one? You'd think we were at a funeral."

Terry chuckled and finished his second cocktail. Alicia poured him another.

"Now that our financial business is concluded, let's talk politics," he said to Allie, raising his glass.

She touched his glass with hers. "Very well, where do we begin?"

"I've been thinking," he said, brushing his foot against hers, "that it could be useful to have a woman working closely with me—as you say, behind the scenes. These days, a woman of substance, well-connected here in Buffalo, could influence women who will then influence their men to vote the right way."

Allie gave him a slow blink, studying his face. "Yes, I would agree. A woman like that could be very useful."

"Is it something you might consider yourself?"

"I don't know," Allie said. "I have a few other things weighing on my mind at present."

"And what are those? Perhaps I could be helpful."

"Bert tells me you've already done a great deal on my behalf."

Terry sipped his drink, which didn't seem as strong as the first two. "He couldn't possibly know," he said in a stage whisper.

Alicia turned to face him. "You'll tell me, though, won't you?"

The melancholy tune playing on the gramophone turned into static.

"God *damn*, Bert," Allie said. "Tomorrow that thing goes back to the store. Did you get it on sale?"

"I said I'll figure it out," Bert shot back. "It's acting up."

"I'm terribly sorry," Alicia said to Terry. "You were saying?"

"You might say I've been your guardian angel for quite some time," Terry said. "Even if you didn't know it."

The room seemed heavy with quiet, with only the rhythmic *scritch-scritch* coming from the malfunctioning phonograph, the sound of a cricket trapped inside the wooden cabinet.

"I must be a very lucky woman," she said.

"Nothing to do with luck," he said, flinging back the rest of his cocktail and smacking his lips. "I don't mean to be indelicate, but you do realize that if your late husband had lived, and Arthur too, you'd be in—shall we say, a very different situation from this one?" He opened his arms wide, gesturing around the paneled parlor, gleaming in the gaslight.

"That's either deliberately unkind or impossibly provocative," she said. "Bert? Have you given up over there?"

"I know what's wrong," Terry said over his shoulder to Bert. "I've had similar problems with mine. It sounds like the little clutch inside is slipping."

"It's fine, Terry," Bert said. "I'll figure it out."

"Listen. You can hear the mechanism inside going along fine," the DA said, standing and walking over to where Bert was kneeling by the phonograph. "But the cylinder's not turning." He pointed to the side of the wooden case. "Behind this little door is all the clockwork. Do you have a screwdriver handy? I'll have it going in a jiffy."

Bert was about to stammer out some excuse, but Allie came to his rescue.

"Bert Hartshorn! We are not putting the future governor of New York State to work as a repairman. Mr. Penrose, please. Come and sit with me." She patted the sofa with one hand.

"Oh, all right," Terry said. "I don't mind, though. I like mechanical things." He gave up and sat back down next to Alicia. No sooner had he taken his seat than the music started up again.

"God, he's such an idiot," Allie said to Penrose. "Bert," Alicia said over her shoulder, "now that you've got that fool thing going again, go ask Melissa to fix some more cocktails." Bert hustled out of the room.

Alicia slide quickly over next to Terry, shoving him against the end of the couch, forcing him to look down her décolletage.

"Quick, while he's gone," she whispered, "give me a kiss. A *real* one, too."

"Mrs. Miller—"

"*Alicia*. Come on," she moaned, "I want to thank you. Are you going to make me beg for it? I will if I have to."

"I—" he began, and she shut him up by planting her lips squarely on his, slipping her tongue quickly between his teeth. She could feel him inhale sharply. Then she slid back to the middle of the sofa, as if nothing had happened.

Alicia looked down at the DA's trouser front and smiled at him. He smiled back, breathing hard. She nodded. "Now then," she said, "that's one more secret you and I share. And I like secrets, Mr. District Attorney. Don't you?"

"They're my stock-in-trade, Alicia," Terry whispered, trying to catch his breath.

Bert returned and announced that Melissa would be bringing the cocktails right away. "I'll change the cylinder, too," he said, "while we're waiting."

"Now then, where were we?" Allie said. "Mr. Penrose, my guardian angel. You said that had my husband lived, I'd be divorced and on the street by now. And I think you're saying that had Arthur lived, I wouldn't have my bequest."

"Yes, that's right."

"But I'm confused. Those unfortunate events had nothing to do with you."

Penrose's eyes narrowed. "My dear, I have something to do with *everything* that happens in this city."

"Tell me the secret, then," she said. "I want to learn. How did you manage it? With Ed—and Arthur? I know you did."

Terry swirled the ice around in his empty glass. "Your husband and Arthur had only themselves to blame. They did some very imprudent things, left some very loose ends. I couldn't have that. They created the leaning tower. I merely pushed it over."

The cocktails arrived, and Alicia waved Melissa away and refilled Terry's glass. He seemed warm, and took a swig as the phonograph clicked and scratched.

"Don't let it run down without a cylinder on it," Terry said.

"Got it," Bert said, cranking the machine.

"He'll never understand," Alicia said wearily. "Now then, would I be wrong if I said that it was your strategy to have Arthur take care of my husband? Put him out of the way?"

"Of course. But not only Arthur," he said with a wave of his hand. "I had someone else ready, if that didn't work out. Ed Miller wasn't going to see the New Year, one way or the other."

"And I am grateful for that, of course," she said. "Ed got exactly what he had coming."

"You really did hate him, then," Terry said.

"I am a woman of strong passions, Mr. Penrose. But I am curious. What was it that brought you into my little marital dispute?"

"You recall the trouble with your correspondence?"

She sipped her drink. "It was hardly *trouble*," she said. "It was outright theft."

"They still escaped, though, didn't they? Flew away." He fluttered his hand like a couple of birds.

"Nothing ever came of them," she said.

"But that's where you're not giving me enough credit," Terry said. "Their public release in a divorce trial would have been ruinous. For Arthur, and for me."

She smiled at him, her eyes sparkling. "Surely not for you, too?"

Terry fidgeted, jiggling his one knee impatiently. "May I be frank?"

She looked directly into his eyes. "Forthrightness is the thing I value most."

"I've learned where the letters are," he said. "And as we speak, a man is—taking care of the problem. Permanently."

"I thought Arthur found those letters in Edward's den and burned them?"

"He was supposed to, but they weren't there. He took care of your husband, as I'd instructed him, but no letters. Poor Arthur. His luck was doubly bad that night. He committed a murder for nothing."

Allie gave him a thin smile.

"And to make matters worse"—Penrose looked at the ceiling and sighed—"he lost his composure entirely. He left behind the murder weapon. A damned big wrench. It was there the next day. If I hadn't had my men pick it up and dispose of it, it would have pointed right to Arthur."

"Arthur must have been very grateful," she said.

"I didn't tell him the part about disposing of it."

"You didn't tell him?"

"No. I told him we'd found it, and that it would soon be evidence. Arthur wasn't stupid. He wasn't going to prison for murder. He wasn't going to lose all that life insurance, not being able to pay the premiums behind bars. He knew he had one choice, and one only."

"To kill himself."

"I'm afraid so."

"That is play worthy of a grandmaster," Alicia said.

"You said you were interested in politics. And that is how it works. I simply wanted to explain that I've done far more for you than arrange a bequest to be paid out in exchange for a little piece of the pie. And I can—and will—do much more for you as governor. And Bill Roscoe, who's worked hand in glove with me on everything, will still be here in Buffalo to assist with local matters."

The music started up again, and Alicia glanced over at Bert.

"Well, at long last, Bert comes through," she said. "I wouldn't have bet you a nickel he'd get it working again."

Bert smiled over at the two of them. "See?" he said, "I told you it was only a matter of time."

"Better late than never. Now we can stop talking and start dancing again, before it's time for dinner?" Allie said. "Another spin around the floor, Mr. Penrose?"

He smiled and took her hand.

"Mr. Penrose, you have a real sense of rhythm," she said, as they danced. "Or perhaps I should call you Mr. District Attorney? Or Mr. Governor?"

"I'd like it if you'd call me Terry," he said. "Now that we know each other a little better, we can be closer."

She looked up at his face and pressed her hips against him, hard. "I don't want any distance between us," she said.

He took her uplifted hand, drew her in as the music swelled, and her body curved to fit his as closely as though they'd been one creature once, and then divided. He'd poked merciless fun at Arthur for falling so hard for this middle-aged, middle-class woman, but now he understood how she could coil herself around a man's will.

Bert turned his back and let the dancing continue, smiling to himself.

HARRY PRICE

December 11, 1902
Later That Same Evening

THE BLIZZARD HAD STILLED THE STREETCARS AN HOUR EARLIER. Delaware Avenue was silent, save for the muffled wheels of the occasional carriage, hauling home drunk young men who ought to know better than to be out slumming in a squall. Alone in her darkened office, five floors above the snow-swept boulevard and the amber haloes of the streetlamps, Sarah was as unreachable as a lookout in a crow's nest.

The wind rattling the sash wasn't making it easy to get anything done, but she knew that was an excuse. She'd known when the snow started to fly she'd have a devil of a time getting home, unless she got a move on. Instead, she'd idly watched the eddies of snow scour the cobblestones, far below her frosted windowpane. For the first time in her life, being alone had begun to suit her.

The tower clock of St. Paul's chimed ten, its booming echo smothered in snow. I suppose I *could* still hire a carriage, she thought. No, that would cost me a small fortune, which I don't have. It'll have to be the couch. I'll telephone and tell them I'll be home in the morning. Poor Maggie. She'll go to bed—again—without seeing me. Ruth takes good care of her, but it's not right.

One by one, she removed the clips and pins that kept her elaborate Gibson Girl hairdo in place and set them on the desk. She ran her fingers through her lush hair, fluffed it out, letting the strawberry blonde waves fall in a thick cascade over one shoulder.

Then from the outer office, Sarah thought she heard the front door open quietly. The thought jolted her out of her trance, and she lifted her little desk lamp, playing shadows over the far wall of the outer office. Dim light from the corridor seeped in through the reeded glass of the front door.

She rubbed her eyes and squinted. There seemed to be a patch of shadow crouching near the door that looked deeper than the rest, a well of darkness. Sarah was about to get up and investigate, and then thought better of it. She reached into her drawer and took out her revolver, its bright nickel plating glinting in the lamplight. She tucked her hand behind her typewriter, and tried to slow her breathing.

The shadow shifted and then moved quickly toward her. Three feet from her doorway, a hollow face bloomed out of the darkness, pale and yellow in the lamplight, appearing like a drowned body bobbing up from dark water. A half-second later, the face was joined by a heavy woolen overcoat, a crust of snow melting from the shoulders.

The intruder removed his hat, slicked his hair back with a forearm, and leaned against the doorframe. He kept his right hand jammed deep into his overcoat. She recognized the face—deeply pitted from an old case of smallpox—the indolent slouch, the dark, dead eyes.

"Mr. Price," she said. She moved her hand from behind the typewriter and pointed the gun. The man didn't so much as flinch, looking almost bored. "You're here to kill me, I imagine."

"Miss Payne," he said. "I am truly sorry."

"Don't bother with the apology," Sarah said, keeping the gun trained. "But I'll warn you—I have a little girl at home waiting for me. I'm not about to let you leave her an orphan."

He shook his head. "I'm not here to hurt you."

Sarah tried to keep the revolver steady, aimed at Price's belly. He watched it placidly. The snow sliding off his coat and hat plopped audibly onto the wooden floor.

"But that's what you do, isn't it?"

Despite his bland manner and modest physical presence, Harry Price had a fearsome reputation. He was often heard of, but rarely seen, and most people who met him in the flesh didn't survive the encounter. Price was combustible, merciless, and in demand—to settle scores that called for the focused application of violence. How he'd come to his line of work wasn't known. What was known was that on a long-ago payday bender, he had contracted syphilis from a tainted hired girl. One cell at a time, the disease had eaten away the limits that most men have, and left him with a hair trigger.

"Not tonight I don't."

"Then why are you here?"

"To tell you that there's a contract on your head."

"On me?"

"Why else do you think I'm here? A social call? A fellow gave me five hundred dollars to do the job."

She jabbed the gun at him. "Very funny. Are you going to keep me in suspense, or do I shoot you where you stand?"

He exhaled loudly. "You'd be doing me a service. But you're safer with me around."

"Should I thank you for sneaking into my office?"

He shook his head. "Look, the guy asked me to visit you at home, you know? I wasn't about to do that. I saw your light from the street, so I came up."

"You could have called. A man with your reputation, showing up in my office—"

"You've got a reputation, too," he said sharply.

"Is that so?"

"Yeah, it's so. For being a little green at this game. Sitting around alone, at night, in an unlocked office? You don't understand the people you're dealing with. You whack a hornet's nest, you'd better run like hell."

"You seem to have become quite the Good Samaritan."

Price shifted his weight, keeping his hand deep in his pocket. "I know, it's out of character. But it's the truth."

"The *truth*? This from the man who spent how many years doing Arthur Pendle's dirty work."

Price looked toward the ceiling and blinked, more a kind of spasm of the eyes than a blink. "Mr. Pendle wasn't a bad sort. He had balls—I mean—"

"I know what that means."

"He never asked me to do anything he wouldn't have done himself. I feel bad for him. He got played."

"I'll take your word for it. And now that you've gone to the trouble to warn me, will you tell me who wants me dead?"

"Bill Roscoe," he said. "In the DA's office."

"How do I know you're not lying to me?"

"I've no reason to."

Sarah wasn't sure how to respond.

"Would you answer a question, then? Honestly?"

"If I can," he said.

"Did you kill my Edward?"

"Edward Miller?"

She nodded.

"No," Price said. "Not my doing."

"Do you know who did?"

Price gave what he might have intended as a smile, but was instead an odd puckering of his large, flat lips. "Not for certain. But everyone knew he'd made enemies. Except him, I guess."

"He had too much faith in people."

"He hadn't met enough of 'em, then."

Sarah was about to respond when Harry abruptly stood up straight and began to pull something from the depths of the coat. She jabbed the gun in his direction.

"Careful," she said, trying to keep her voice level.

"Easy," he said. "I'll take my hand out slow. If there's anything in it you don't like, shoot." She nodded.

He drew his hand out of his pocket. In it was a wad of bills. He gingerly leaned forward and put the money on Sarah's desk. He tapped it with two fingers.

"That's the five hundred," he said. "It's yours."

"That's not necessary."

"Well, I don't want it."

"Then I'll put it toward getting justice for people like Edward Miller."

He looked down and scuffed his foot, spread around the little pool of water that had collected under his coat hem. "Justice," he mumbled, "is a funny thing. Most times you got to dole it out yourself. And you're not going to do that."

"What's that supposed to mean?"

"You're not the killing kind."

"How would you know?"

"If you were, you'd have shot me already."

"I'm not going to shoot a man in cold blood," Sarah said. "If you had attacked me—"

"Cold blood is the *only* way to shoot a man," Price interrupted. "Once he makes his play, you're too late. If I wanted to come over that desk at you, you could put two in me"—he nodded in the direction of her little revolver—"and I'd still have time to slit your throat and toss you out that window."

This time he smiled confidently, a horrible smile showing a mouthful of bad teeth.

Sarah's hand was trembling and seemed numb as she tried to tighten her grip on the revolver.

"I hope it won't come to that."

"I'm not trying to frighten you. But you need to keep a weather eye out. Get yourself some muscle. You may need it."

"As if I would know where to get 'muscle,' Mr. Price."

"Then do what I'm doing. Get out of the city. Once Roscoe and his gang get wind that I've skipped on them, they'll send someone else. These people don't give up." He popped his hat back on his head. "Anyhow, I am sorry I startled you."

Sarah set the gun down on her desk and flexed her frozen fingers.

"I suppose I owe you thanks for doing the right thing by me, Mr. Price. And my little girl."

"Wouldn't have laid a hand on you."

He turned on his heel, and was melting into the shadows of the outer office when he turned back. Sarah eased her hand over the revolver again.

"There was one other thing Roscoe asked me to do," Harry Price said. "Might be worth knowing."

"What was that?"

"Toss your place. Search it. He said you have some letters that they want, bad. I got the feeling he cared more about them than he did about putting you out of the way."

"What letters?"

"A boxful. From Mr. Pendle."

OUT OF DARKNESS

"I see."

"That's it, then," Price said. "Look after yourself. These people won't stop unless you stop 'em first." Then his eyes went black and dead, and he seemed to be looking past her, over her shoulder. "And they know you have a little girl."

She nodded dumbly, her heart in her stomach. "Yes, I understand," she murmured.

"Good that you do. 'Night, Miss Payne." He nodded and then melted silently back into the dark outer office.

When Sarah heard the door click closed behind him, she sagged forward, her head in her hands. She wanted to scream, or pound the desk, or run. Instead, she got up unsteadily and locked the outer door, and then locked herself in her office, tilting the back of a chair under the knob, wondering if she could ever feel safe again. Then she sat down in her creaky desk chair and picked up the telephone with a shaking hand, as the gusts outside rattled the sash, trying to pry their way in.

❦

JESS SHOWED UP AT work the next morning. When he did, Sarah came out of her office and sat down with him and Annie. "I have something I need to tell you both," she said. "Last evening, here, I had visit from a man named Harry Price."

The two looked at her blankly.

"There's no reason you'd know the name. I knew about him only from those letters I showed you."

"What did he want?" Jess said.

"Mr. Price is a hired killer. An assassin."

"Oh my God!" Annie said. "I should never have let you stay here alone!" Jess suddenly looked deathly white.

"I'm glad you weren't here," Sarah said. "If Mr. Price had been serious, I don't like to think of what would have happened. Fortunately for me, he came to warn me that someone wants me dead. And gave him five hundred dollars to do the deed."

"Who would want you dead?" Jess said. "Who in the world would think such a thing?"

"William Roscoe, the man whose initials you identified in that document I have."

Jess looked even more ashen, and had to put his head between his knees.

"Penrose must see me as a problem that needs to be taken care of before his run for governor. I don't think he's interested in anyone but me, but I had to tell you both so that you can keep a sharp eye out."

"Miss," Annie said, "what can we do?"

"The most important thing is that you must be very careful. I don't think any of us should be alone without someone else around."

"I have to run a quick errand this morning," Jess said.

"Someone should go with you," Sarah said.

"I don't need an escort," he said.

"You've got your roommates," Annie said. "I'm sure they would go with you."

"I'll be fine on my own," Jess said, blushing. "I'm very sorry about what happened to you, Sarah. Miss Payne, I mean."

"Just be careful," she said.

After Jess had gone, Annie asked Sarah if she had heard from Hartshorn.

"Not yet," Sarah said, "but their dinner was only last night."

"I hope the machine worked as advertised."

"I'm sure your invention worked flawlessly—the question is whether Mrs. Miller could get Penrose to admit anything."

"Miss, this Harry Price fellow—I wonder if we're doing the right thing by trying to trap Mr. Penrose."

"I don't think I have a choice, if I ever want to feel safe again. But it might be a good idea for you to step away until—"

"You stop that right now!" Annie said, to Sarah's surprise. "Please don't say that to me. We're in this together."

"I never wanted to expose you to danger," Sarah said.

"It's the nature of the business. He doesn't scare me, either. We'll get him."

"You're one in a million, Annie."

"We're a good team, that's all. You knew we would be."

"That I did. And—about this Harry Price. There was something I couldn't say about his visit. In front of Jess."

"Yes?"

"He knew about the Pendle letters. That I have them."

"He did?"

"Yes, and he said that was the reason Roscoe—and Penrose, I'm sure—wanted me put out of the way. Roscoe paid him to take care of me and Maggie, and search the house for the letters."

"It's simply awful," Annie said, shuddering. "Which raises the obvious question—how did Roscoe know you have the letters? Unless I'm mistaken, the only people who know you have them are you, me—"

"And Jess."

JESS WANTS OUT

JESS LEFT THE AVENGING ANGEL OFFICE AND WALKED AT DOUBLE time to city hall, and sprinted up the stairs to the DA's office, pounding his feet hard on the marble treads.

The secretary opened Roscoe's door a crack and stuck her head in. "It's that Jesse Murphy again, Mr. Roscoe. He wants to see you. And he's not taking no for an answer."

"Oh, fine then," Roscoe said, covering up his case piles with other papers. "Send him in."

The door swung open. Jess walked in and stood opposite Roscoe's desk.

"Mr. Murphy, I wasn't expecting you. You have news?"

"I wasn't expecting a lot of things I wasn't expecting. I came here in good faith, to do my duty, and what did you do? You sent a—an assassin to take care of Miss Payne."

"Please keep your voice down, Mr. Murphy. And we don't send assassins anywhere here, except to the electric chair. Have you heard of Leon Czolgosz?"

"You know what you did. I know it was you because I told you about those letters. I never thought you'd do that. And I want no part of it. I want out."

Roscoe sat back, removed his glasses, and tossed them onto a stack of paper. "You want out? Of what, exactly?"

"Yes. I want out. It's one thing to keep an eye on someone, but then—this," he spluttered. "That was not our agreement."

Roscoe stared at him. "I don't recall our having an agreement. I tend to remember things like that. I do recall you telling me some things that the district attorney and I should take in hand, and that's all. And I recall that you were paid. Weren't you?"

"A hundred dollars. For someone's life? My—my *Sarah's* life?"

"You were paid for *information*. What we *do* with that information is not your concern. And how would you know what we've done or haven't done? Do I report to you? I don't believe I do."

"I assumed that you would—"

"Mr. Murphy," Roscoe interjected, "for the second time now, you've barged in here, throwing about some very serious allegations—even though I'm not sure quite what they are. And I don't need to know. What I would like to know, though, is what can I do for you today so that I can go back to work?"

"You can forget I ever came here, ever. Forget what I told you about Sarah Payne. Forget you ever heard her name. Leave her alone."

"Is this remorse, Mr. Murphy? Catholic guilt?"

"Call it whatever you like. I'm through."

"You know the story of the thirty pieces of silver?" Roscoe asked. "From the Bible?"

"Of course I know the story."

"Well, then, you know the way it goes is that *Judas*"—he drew the name out to its full length—"repented of having betrayed his Lord. And full of remorse, he went back to the high priests and tried to give them back their money. And what did they say? The head Jew told him, I'm terribly sorry to hear it and all, but it's nonreturnable. Same goes for you, Mr. Jesse Murphy. You took the money and that—as they say in your reporter trade—is *the end of the story*."

Jess was silent.

"You do understand the parable, don't you?"

"Parable or no parable, there's nothing about this woman that merits your further attention," Jess said.

"You know that's not true," Roscoe said. "You said yourself that she's getting too close to certain things. But what of it? I would assume that this so-called assassin of yours didn't give full value for his wage, either, or you'd be really upset."

"Lucky for you he didn't," Jess said.

"You're a very interesting fellow," Roscoe said, pursing his lips. "Last time you were in this office, you told me that as much as you loved Miss Payne, you loved duty more. And now you seem to have completely reversed yourself. To the point of offering up a veiled threat to the assistant district attorney."

"I've told you too much already. And I believe our business can be concluded, Mr. Roscoe."

Roscoe put his fingers together in a little steeple, kissed the apex gently.

"If I understand, then—you're telling me that you want to do the *honorable* thing."

"Yes. That's right."

"A noble goal," Roscoe said. "Then am I to take it that you wouldn't mind if Miss Payne knew that you've been spying on her? Informing on her? And if your allegations about an assassin are true—and I don't concede that they are—that your spying almost got her and her daughter killed? Because that's the only way you get out of this honorably. To come clean."

Jess fumed for a moment. "I wonder how that would make you look, Mr. Roscoe?"

"Of course, there's no telling whether she'd believe you. And if she did, what of it? Your credibility would be shot to hell. Besides, this office conducts surveillance on persons of interest every single day, and I wouldn't confirm nor deny any such arrangement. But now if a confidential informant—such as yourself—were to talk openly about such surveillance, I suppose you know that would be called 'obstruction of justice.' You'd go to prison."

"It would be worth it. Do you think I care about prison?"

"If you don't care, it's because you've never been in one, my friend," Roscoe said. "And as I understand it, the only reason you're not already in one is because of the generosity and kindness of this very office to your distraught father."

"Don't bring him into this," Jess said.

"Instead of getting all worked up, why don't we think about what new arrangement might benefit us both? Then we can conclude our business, and part as friends."

"Just tell me how I can be done with you."

"You know that's impolite, Mr. Murphy, but I understand you are upset. I'll let it pass by. We'll conclude our business soon enough."

"I'm not an indentured servant. I don't plan to work for you for the rest of my life."

"Life can be short or long," Roscoe said with a shrug.

Jess rose shakily to his feet, clutching the brim of his derby, unsure of whether to strangle Roscoe or run for his life.

"Say—come to think of it," Roscoe said, tapping his forehead with his index finger, "there may be one way to make a graceful exit, if you're interested. Without leaving any trace with Miss Payne."

Jess knit his eyebrows together in a question. "And?"

"You get those letters for us yourself. Or someone else will come to her house. There's always someone who can do a job if you can't."

"They're not in her house," Jess said.

"Did you give me a bum steer, then?"

"No, I was mistaken. I underestimated her. Sarah's too cautious to keep something like that in her home, where her child is, for God's sake."

Roscoe shifted in his chair. "And do you know where they can be located?"

Jess had already dreamed up an answer.

"If I tell you, will our business be concluded?"

"If you tell me *and* you retrieve them," Roscoe said, "yes, that would do the trick. But I'm not going to be led on another wild goose chase, from one false lead to the next. If you know where they are—bring them to me. Then we'll be square."

"I can live with that," Jess said.

"But you do have to tell me where they are. I'll give you the first opportunity to retrieve them before—someone else does. If you fail, though, then I'll take matters into my own hands. And you won't like that very much."

"Fine. I was talking with her recently about them, and she said that Ed Miller was laughing about having those letters. How they were going to be the ruin of Arthur Pendle."

"Go on."

"She said that what amused Mr. Miller most was that he was keeping the letters right under the nose of the man who wrote them. 'Inches away,' he said."

"Intriguing," Roscoe said, tapping his pen on the blotter, too hard, and splattering drops of ink on his shirtsleeve.

"Yes," Jess said, warming up. "Miss Payne said he knew those letters were dangerous."

"He was right about that," Roscoe murmured. "But let's think about that statement for a minute. If he meant it literally, what would be only inches away from Arthur Pendle? A hiding place, I suppose. Maybe in the Pendle residence."

"Not a chance," Jess said. "That place was gone over thoroughly in the search for the estate papers. And how would Ed Miller be able to hide something there, given his estrangement from his former friend?"

"I suppose you're right."

"But I *do* know a place that fits that description—'inches away'—and which wasn't searched then, nor has been, up to now."

Roscoe tapped his front teeth with an inky finger. "Where?"

"What did Miller and Penrose love most?"

"I don't know. Money? Women?"

"No," Jess said. "Golf. They were both fanatics about the sport."

"I recall that."

"And Miller and Pendle were both charter members of the Red Jacket Golf Club—near Delaware Park. I'm sure you know it."

"Indeed. A fine course. Where is this leading?"

"Edward Miller was president of that club. Arthur Pendle was the club's best golfer. And if they both had to change clothing from street dress into golf togs—"

"The locker room!" Roscoe said, starting up from his chair.

"Exactly. Inches away. They had adjacent lockers."

Roscoe resumed his bland expression. "You may be onto something," he said. "I'm quite sure no one searched the Red Jacket Golf Club after either death. Whatever was in their lockers before that would still be there."

"My point exactly. It all fits. The letters have been hiding in plain sight, all this time."

Bill Roscoe stared directly into Jess's eyes. "Then, as I said, go get them. Bring them to me, and when you do, we'll be done. In fact, I don't mind negotiating against myself by saying that not only will we be done but I'll owe you a favor."

"I don't have any way into the clubhouse."

"What do you want from me, a passkey? The place is shut up for the winter. No one's there except probably some caretaker a couple days a week. Go over on a Sunday evening and find a way in. It's not a bank. It can't be too hard."

"And what if I can't find Miller's locker? Or Pendle's?"

"Do you want me to send someone more competent, Mr. Murphy? I thought you wanted a chance here."

"What I'm saying is that there may be a great number of lockers."

Roscoe sat back in his chair, exasperated. "You really are a tyro. Open all of them, one by one, if you have to. If you can't, dynamite the place. Burn it down, if you have to. I don't care what you do. Find them or destroy them, either way. You figure it out."

"Will you leave my Sarah alone?"

"I'm not admitting I haven't left her alone, but I will give you a week before she might not be left so alone. If I don't have them by then, all bets are off."

"Two weeks," Jess said. "I'll go next Sunday. And in the meantime, Sarah is off-limits."

"Until next Sunday, then."

"You'll hear from me by that Monday," Jess said.

"Good. Now will you let me get back to my work? It's Friday, and I have my standing lunch with the DA in less than an hour. And if you think Miss Payne's mystery visitor was frightening, you don't know Terry Penrose very well."

❦

"YOU GAVE HIM ANOTHER chance?" Penrose said at their usual table at The Dainty.

"He's scared shitless," Roscoe said. "She might be his fantasy lover, but he doesn't want anything to happen to her."

"And Price has run off to the hills of Pennsylvania with our money, without getting the job done?"

"No one could have predicted that. He's touched in the head. We knew he'd snap eventually. Anyway, it's only five hundred bucks, and he's not the type to name names."

"Um hmm," Terry said. "You don't think he spilled anything to Sarah Payne about who gave him the money?"

"Not a chance. He's nuttier than a fruitcake, but he's not a rat. That fellow lives by rules of his own."

"Fair point," Terry said, slurping down his champagne and waving for a refill. "So now what?"

"I gave Murphy until next Sunday to get the letters."

"Good. Last night I sealed the deal with Alicia Miller. I gave her the affidavit I got from Pendle, and that'll mean a nice round five thousand dollars to us from the grateful lady. And, by the way, I'm hoping she'll show her gratitude in other ways too."

Roscoe laughed.

"I have to tell you," Terry said, "I had a raging hard-on the whole night. Bad case of blue balls by the time I got home, I don't mind saying. My poor wife didn't know what hit her."

"Mrs. Miller's definitely got something," Roscoe said. "Even when I was questioning her at the inquest, I couldn't stop thinking—well, forget it. She's all yours. What the hell does she see in that old clod Hartshorn, anyway?"

"She's not stupid. She's got a full-time attorney bolted to her side, and he is a good one. So? She holds her nose and gives him a taste every once and a while, so long as he's useful. I'm sure once she gets her payout, he'll be pounding the pavement. Instead of her. Ha ha."

Roscoe shook his head. "Nice work, I have to say. Five thousand is a real war chest."

"It is. As soon as the payments are made—a week or two—I can declare my candidacy."

"It's all working out perfectly."

"Perfection only in the next life, Bill," Penrose said. "Many's the slip twixt cup and lip."

CUTTING BOTH WAYS

THE WEEKEND PASSED QUIETLY, WITHOUT ANY NEWS FROM Hartshorn. Sarah and Annie stayed close to home, mindful of Harry Price's admonition that once word got out that he'd left the city, another one of his kind would take his place.

By Monday, though, they were both getting slightly stir-crazy. Reasoning that they'd be safe enough during business hours in bustling downtown, they took the trolley together to the office. Sarah had her little revolver in her bag, in case. At the office, Sarah placed a call to the Miller residence.

Melissa answered, and told them that Mr. Hartshorn had gone out, but would be back in the afternoon or evening. Sarah asked the girl to have Hartshorn call her that evening, after four o'clock. She and Annie planned to get home before dark and lock themselves in for the night.

They arrived home well before sundown, and were unbuttoning their overshoes when a flustered-looking Ruth met them in the foyer.

"Thank heavens you're back safe and sound," she said, looking a little spooked.

"Is something wrong?" Sarah asked.

"Well, I don't know," Ruth said. "A strange-looking man passed by the house several times this afternoon."

"Did you recognize him?" Annie said.

"No, he was a horrible-looking creature. At last I walked out and confronted him."

"You oughtn't to have done that, Ruth," Sarah said.

"I told him to shoo."

"Well, don't do that again, please. Did you speak to him? Did he identify himself?"

"I did speak with him, and asked him what he meant by lurking around our house. He said he knew you, but I wasn't sure about that. I asked him his name, and he wouldn't tell me—he said I wouldn't recognize it. I told him you weren't home, and he left. I haven't seen him in an hour or so. Oh, he was even worse-looking up close. Dreadful."

"I'm glad you're all right, Ruth," Sarah said, feeling almost like throwing up.

"He said he'd come back—"

At that moment the doorbell rang, and Ruth, Annie, and Sarah jumped as though a firecracker had gone off.

"Run upstairs," Annie said to Sarah. "Ruth and I can handle this."

"Not a chance," Sarah said. "You two have already done enough."

"Maybe we oughtn't to open it at all," Ruth said.

"I refuse to be a prisoner in my own home," Sarah said. "You two—git!"

"We're not 'gitting' anywhere," Annie said. "Better there are three of us, anyway."

"Hand me my bag then, if you're going to be that way," Sarah said. She fished the gun out and turned to the door, opening it a crack. Standing on the step, ankle-deep in snow, was Harry Price, hands in his coat pockets.

"Miss Payne," he said.

"Mr. Price," Sarah said. "I didn't expect to see you again so soon." She held the gun behind her back and readied herself to slam the door if he moved a muscle.

"I came by earlier," he said. "Your girl sent me away. I like her. She's spunky."

"You haven't—changed your mind about things?"

He shook his head. "Everything's fine. I only wanted to talk for a minute."

"I was afraid you might be the someone else you said they might send after me. Won't you come in?" Sarah said, opening the door halfway.

"Sarah!" Annie blurted. "Don't let him in!"

"Slam the door on him!" Ruth yelled.

Too late. Harry had already sidestepped in and leaned against the door to close it. He removed his hat, tipping it to the three ladies.

"You may have overheard," he said to Ruth. "I really like you."

Annie stepped in front of Ruth and Sarah and put her hands on her hips.

"I wish I could say the same," Ruth said, frowning at him from behind Annie. "The nerve you have. Coming around here and scaring us half to death."

"It'd be a nice change of pace not to frighten people all the time," he said. "But it's too late for that, I suppose. Miss Payne, after I left you on Thursday night—"

"*This* is the man you told us about?" Annie blurted. "You get out of here, before I call the police!"

"It's fine, Annie," Sarah said. "Mr. Price is on our side."

"Oh for heaven's sake," Ruth muttered. "You're going to get yourself killed one of these days, Miss, and then whatever will your little one do without—"

"And that's why I'm here," Harry Price said. "After I left you, Miss Payne, I walked all the way to the station, had my ticket to Pittsburgh in hand, you know—and then I thought, this ain't right. Leaving you and your kid here to deal with these people. I couldn't have lived with myself. So I didn't go."

"I don't know what to say," Sarah said. "I never would have expected you to take such a personal interest in us."

"Going soft in my old age, maybe. But I thought you could use a watchful eye."

"And where have you been since then?" Sarah said.

He scratched the back of his neck and then hooked his thumb toward the back of the house. "In your toolshed, out back. I tailed you and Miss Annie home Friday evening, when you left the office."

Ruth's face went beet red. "You mean to tell us that you have been living in a *shed*, in our *back yard*? Without our knowledge? What in the world!"

Price held out his hands, large and dark, the strong hands of a man used to hard labor. "I did it because I was afraid someone might come here," he said. "If someone had, I'd have the drop on him. And if you'd known I was out there, you woulda called the cops on me."

"You'd better believe we would have," Ruth said. "And I think we ought to call them right now, if you ask me."

Sarah smiled. "Mr. Price, Ruth and Annie are my two best friends—and allies," she said. "Annie's my business partner, and Ruth looks after our household."

"Like I said, I like her," he said, nodding toward Ruth, who scowled ferociously back. "She's the kind you want to have around. And so am I. That's what I wanted to talk over with you."

"May I offer you a seat in our parlor? Some tea? Or—maybe you'd prefer a glass of something stronger?"

"Oh no, Miss," he said. "Let's just talk here. I wouldn't feel right sitting in such a nice place. This won't take but a minute. What I wanted to say was that I think it might be a good idea if I stayed around here for a while. If anyone makes a move on you, they'll get quite a surprise. I'll stay out in the shed, and keep an eye on things."

"Like a junkyard dog?" Ruth said. "You must be out of your mind."

"Not quite, not yet," Harry said. "Ask Miss Payne. I can be useful to you. You won't even see me. You haven't, for more than two days, and I've been fifteen yards away the whole time."

"Mr. Price, I truly do appreciate your offer. I can't tell you how much easier I will feel about things with someone like yourself nearby. But I can't very well have you staying in a freezing toolshed," Sarah said. "You may use one of the spare rooms here." Ruth gasped audibly.

"No need," Harry said. "I've slept rougher than your shed, I'll tell you. It's really very comfortable. I'm not a man accustomed to more. A couple blankets would be nice."

"Of course. And we will bring you your meals, at least."

He bowed. "Thank you, Miss. And don't worry," he said, looking at Ruth, "I won't stay forever. When things are on an even keel, I'll go. You don't have a thing to worry about."

"Says you," Ruth mumbled.

"Mr. Price, I'll admit I don't quite know what to make of you," Sarah said. "'Thank you' doesn't seem very grand, but I am grateful. You have been very kind."

"There's a first time for everything," Harry said with his odd, flat smile.

"Ruth, would you mind preparing something for Mr. Price to eat? Something hot. When it's ready, I'll bring it out to you, and we can talk more, if you wish."

"Thank you kindly," he said, bowing again. "Miss Annie. Miss Ruth. Pleasure to meet you, and if you need me—you know where to find me." He settled his hat on his head, and eased himself back out the front door.

"Oh, Miss Ruth," he said, turning on the doorstep. "If you ever want a part-time job, you let me know. You've got the killer instinct." He laughed, showing his mouthful of snaggly teeth.

"Shoo, you horrible thing!" Ruth said, and Price laughed again. He then walked noiselessly down the porch steps and disappeared into the snowy shrubbery.

"Do you really think this is a good idea?" Annie asked, once the door was closed. "I must agree with Ruth. He looks like a dangerous—vagrant."

"Thank you, sister," Ruth said. "I think we ought to call the police right away."

Sarah gave a little stamp of her foot. "You two. You're going to have to trust me on this. I wouldn't put either of you, or Maggie, in the slightest danger, if I thought Mr. Price were anything but sincere. But having him around until things get sorted out—and it won't be long now, I expect, if the news from Mr. Hartshorn is good—well, you'll understand how good it is to have him watching over us. Now then, before I shuck these glad rags, if you can give me something hearty to feed the man, I'll be right back and we'll lock up for the night."

❦

SARAH'S BOOTS WERE TOO short to keep the snow out of the tops, and by the time she rapped on the door of the toolshed, her stockings were soaked through and her feet already cold.

The door opened, and Harry was standing there in his vest and shirt-sleeves. He was carefully folding a straight razor, which he tucked into his trouser pocket. "Can't be too careful," he said. He opened the door wide and she stepped in, and then he shut it halfway.

She was carrying a large lunch pail that Ruth had supplied. "Here's something to warm you up," she said, setting it onto the old workbench in the shed. "Some of Ruth's stew. It's excellent."

"Thank you much, Miss," he said. "Much obliged. And I'm sorry I rattled your friends."

"They've already gotten over it. I'm sorry to say it, Mr. Price, but you do know how to give someone a scare."

"Hell of a talent to have," he said. "Pardon me, I mean, yes."

"I'll let you eat your supper," she said, "but if you don't mind, if I may—are there any other precautions we should take? Should we tell you when we're at home or going out, for example?"

"You don't need to. I'll know."

"And if we should need to talk with you about anything?"

"If you're at home, I'll be here. Anytime you like."

"What's next, then?"

"Keep your wits about you, that's all. They'll hire someone else, now that they know I skipped on them. I'll keep my ear to the ground, and when I hear anything, I'll hang a kerchief on the doorknob, and you'll know I have news."

"Why won't you come to the front door?"

"Best not to be spotted by your neighbors. Once is the limit. If anyone asks, say it was a tramp who wandered off the main drag, looking for a handout. If someone sees me hanging around, they'll sic the cops on me. That won't do us any good."

Sarah looked around the toolshed. "Are you sure you're going to be all right out here? Wouldn't you rather sleep inside?"

"No, Miss, I can keep an eye on things better out here, and get the jump on anyone if I need to. Thank you, though."

"There's nothing else we need to do?"

"That little gun of yours," he said. "I'd leave it at home. It's useless."

"It's for my protection."

"*I'm* for your protection. And I don't carry a gun. Why should you?"

"I'm surprised," she said.

He shook his head. "Guns attract attention—everyone within a half-mile knows when one goes off. They run out of ammunition. You can go to prison for concealing one, if you don't have a license. But my trusty blade"—he patted his trouser pocket—"is quiet, cuts in two directions at once, and there's no law against keeping shaving gear on your person."

"I never thought about it that way," Sarah said.

"Guns also give people a sense of—what is it?—false security, which is dangerous. We talked about that the other night. In the time it takes someone to pull out their gun, aim, and decide to fire—which isn't easy, if you're not used to it—"

"I remember all too well."

He rubbed his chin, which had been shaved but was so pocked that the whiskers filled up the craters in his skin. "Sorry," he said. "Didn't mean to go into all that."

"Not at all. I'm eager to learn."

"That's good. In your new line of work," he said, "it's *not* knowing things that will get you hurt. I've seen lots of people learn too late. Or thought they knew already and didn't need to learn. Anything you want to know, say the word."

"I will. For one thing, I'd like to make some contacts in the underworld."

Harry smiled, the strange grimace he had when something struck him as funny. "The *underworld*, you say?"

"Yes, the underworld. Don't you think that it'd be useful for me to have sources placed here and there?"

"Cops have sources, but they have something to trade for information. Usually a free pass. You have to have something to offer for information. Money."

"That I don't have, other than the five hundred dollars you gave me."

"Then I think it's best if you stay away from the underworld. It ain't all it's cracked up to be, anyhow. Let me be your go-between. I know the right people."

"That's very generous, and forgive me for saying, but I can't have you doing anything—anything that isn't legal."

Price's eyes narrowed. "And if you don't mind my saying—legal, illegal . . . who decides? The cops and the guys in city hall? One of the highest muckety-mucks of all gave me five hundred bones to do you and your kid in. Does that make it legal?"

"Are you telling me I oughtn't to care?"

"What I'm saying is to follow your own rules."

"May I ask, then, what rules you follow, Mr. Price?"

"I may be a bad example."

"But would you tell me?"

"I don't work for cowards. I don't hurt innocent women or children. I decide how far I'm willing to go beforehand, and then I don't think about it again. I guess that's about it. Oh, I forgot. I hit the other guy first, with everything I've got."

"And what you do—it doesn't bother you, afterward?"

"The people I deal with have it coming to them, every last one of them. And a lot of them hide behind the law, whatever that is. They're hard people to like."

"I'm sure that's true. Thank you. That's very helpful. I would like to think about it a bit. In the meantime, I will trust you to do what you think is right, since I'm obviously a little quaint in my notions of law and order."

"Understood."

"Now before your food goes completely cold, I want to let you eat it. I'll look for your signal in case you need anything. And thank you again."

Harry inclined his head. "Thank you, Miss. Believe me, it's my pleasure. I learned a long time ago not to go around with a chip on my shoulder, but this time I'm half hoping that someone tries something. Because I want to see the look on his face when he realizes what's coming. Best part of my job."

❦

BERT HARTSHORN LEFT THE Miller residence before sunup on Wednesday and caught the first trolley that rumbled down Ashwood Street. He needed time to think before he met with Bill Roscoe. A shave and a good breakfast would do it.

He stepped down from the streetcar at the Iroquois Hotel, at Main and Eagle. The hot towels perked him up after the ride in the drafty trolley. After his shave, he walked a few minutes south to The Dainty, at 44 West Swan, where he knew Roscoe and Penrose ate, so it would be away from prying eyes.

Bert asked to sit in the back of the place, away from the plate-glass front windows, so that he wouldn't be spotted by anyone he might know. On his third cup of coffee, and after his second trip to the bathroom, he had his strategy set.

Roscoe lived in a three-story brick walk-up at the corner of Swan and Oak. Fortunately, it was only a five-minute walk from The Dainty. The recent blizzard had brought with it clear and penetrating cold, and Bert had left his warmest winter clothes behind when his wife had kicked him out. Now she was plainly taking some pleasure in thinking of Bert shivering in nothing more than a raincoat.

Roscoe's building, The Criterion, had a bustling restaurant at street level, with a second street entrance to a small tiled lobby serving the residents on the floors above. Hartshorn opened the door and was nearly blown backwards by an escaping blast of hot, humid air, as though he'd opened a bake oven. He forged past it and, in the tiny lobby, spied the cause—a leaking radiator, hissing and steaming, turning the whole space into a Turkish bath. Rivulets of cold condensation were tracing sooty veins down the tiled walls, puddling in low spots on the floor. He tried to hold his breath, but that was futile, and so he stepped over to the address board. The board was locked up in a brass frame, whose glass was so thickly beaded with dew that Bert had to use the forearm of his coat to clear it away. W. R. Roscoe was in 3F, which probably meant front since there was someone in 3R.

Bert was almost grateful to climb the three steep flights up a chilly staircase, if only to get away from the sauna in the lobby. At the top of the stairs, he turned to face the street and found the door to Number 3 about a third of the way down the hallway. He knocked and waited. There was no response, so he knocked again, harder. He was winding up for a third try when the door opened, and there was Bill Roscoe in his trousers and shirtsleeves, his belly straining against the front seam of his shirt.

"Very sorry, Mr. Roscoe," Bert said. "I may be a touch early. I can come back after you've finished dressing."

"Not at all, Mr. Hartshorn," he said, stepping aside. "You're right on time. Do come in, if you don't mind seeing me without my waistcoat."

"Not a problem," he said, taking off his hat and stepping into Roscoe's flat.

The apartment did, in fact, face Swan Street, and was brilliantly lit by a half-dozen large windows lined up along the facing wall. The bright, large space—apparently one entire side of the top floor of the building—could have been made more cheerful with a woman's touch. Instead, it was furnished with dark, heavy furniture and rugs, which sucked up the light pouring in from outside, and in a quick glance, Bert could see that there was nothing hung on the plaster save for a calendar from a Main

Street business. There was a distinct smell of cooking wafting up from the restaurant on the ground floor, enticing but slightly dispiriting, as though the lone resident of the flat would always be reminded of people sharing meals two floors beneath his little dining table under the right-most window.

"Please, make yourself comfortable," Roscoe said, gesturing to an overstuffed chair. Bert folded his coat over the back of the chair and sat, keeping his leather case next to him.

"Thank you for seeing me on such short notice, Mr. Roscoe," he said as Roscoe sat on the couch opposite.

"Of course. Your reputation commands serious attention from any gentleman in Buffalo," Roscoe said. "The Merrill case, a few years ago. Penrose and I nearly killed ourselves trying to get that one done. But you prevailed, fair and square. Damn good lawyering, as difficult as it is to admit."

"You made for a tough opponent. I felt like Gentleman Jim must have against John Sullivan."

Roscoe laughed. "Perfect! And like Corbett, you won with your brains. Hats off to you, sir."

"Very gracious of you to say."

"Credit where credit is due. Now then, I confess I am a little curious about what you have in mind for me. You were emphatic about meeting away from my office—"

"It's a matter that requires some delicacy. And privacy."

"I assumed so. But your interest in whether I have a gramophone struck me as rather queer. I can't imagine you came here to enjoy musical entertainment."

"No," Bert said, reaching into his bag and removing an Edison cylinder. "Though I would like you to listen to something, if you wouldn't mind."

"Happy to," Roscoe said, getting up and holding out his hand. Hartshorn was momentarily uncertain whether the assistant DA wanted to help him up from his chair, but then understood. He handed him the cylinder, trying with only partial success to keep his hand steady. He followed Roscoe over to the far corner, where a phonograph stood on an oak table. Roscoe placed the cylinder and wound the clockworks. He was about to drop the stylus when he looked over his shoulder at Bert.

"No overture?" Roscoe said. "Nothing I ought to know before I start?"

"I think you'll find it requires no introduction."

Roscoe started the cylinder revolving, and set the needle down.

The two stared stolidly at the phonograph horn while the cylinder played for its three brutal minutes, neither daring to look over at the other. After it was done, Roscoe lifted the stylus and quietly stopped the cylinder. He stood there, still looking at the phonograph, his chin in one hand, elbow resting on his other arm. At last he turned toward Bert.

"What do you expect me to say?" he said.

"I don't have a particular expectation," Bert replied.

"Well, it's very clever, I'll give you that. *Very* clever. Though if I'm being honest, a bit beneath you, Hartshorn. Not terribly gentlemanly. Underhanded, in fact."

"It was not done lightly, nor without some debate within myself. Given the stakes involved, however, it seemed like the only way to bring this business to a close."

"What business do you have in mind?"

"Mr. Roscoe, as you have heard, you make a guest appearance in this recording—a rather important one—but you are not the star of the show."

"Go on."

"Terry Penrose is a cancer growing in this city. I'm willing to believe that he's inveigled you into things that you would have rather not done. Our interest is in seeing him removed from office."

"You're not looking to prosecute?"

"Not if he vacates his office, and his campaign for governor, voluntarily and unequivocally."

"Very wise, Mr. Hartshorn. You wouldn't obtain a conviction. You would merely succeed in sullying the reputation of a man who has put innumerable criminals behind bars. Including McKinley's assassin, at that."

"I don't share the view that the end always justifies the means, Mr. Roscoe, but I am cognizant of the district attorney's contributions to justice during his terms in office."

"And what about me?" Roscoe asked.

"You still get to be district attorney."

Roscoe smiled. "Bert Hartshorn, kingmaker."

"I have no interest in being a kingmaker, or any role in city politics. For me, you're the lesser of two evils."

"I suppose that's a compliment."

"If you like."

"What do I have to do to avail myself of your generosity?"

"Call off whatever you have going, now and forever, involving Sarah Payne, her child, or her associates."

"Done," Roscoe said.

"Ensure that my client, Mrs. Miller, receives her $50,000 bequest from Arthur Pendle, within the next two weeks. With no deduction for campaign funding."

"That's already in the works. Two weeks though—that's not up to me. That's the insurance company's business."

"Two weeks, Mr. Roscoe."

"If I have to pay it myself, it'll get paid. Within two weeks."

"Good."

"Anything else?"

"You'll give this cylinder to Terry Penrose personally, and conduct all conversations with him. You'll ensure that he complies. We wish to avoid any contact with the man."

"Of course you do," Roscoe said. "It's so much easier to be furtive, isn't it?"

"Now, Mr. Roscoe, let's not start down that road. You may mock me, but I am being generous, and I needn't have been."

"Fine. Let us conclude, then. Is there anything else you want?"

"A pledge from you not to interfere with any of us any further, in any way."

"Gladly and freely given," Roscoe said, extending his hand. "Do we have a deal, then?"

"How long will you require to discuss this matter with Mr. Penrose?"

"I'll speak with him on Friday. We have a standing lunch then. I assume you'll leave me with the cylinder."

"Then it's agreed," Hartshorn said, shaking Roscoe's hand. He nodded toward the phonograph. "It hardly need be said that the cylinder is a copy. The original is quite safe, and should any harm befall any of us, copies will be sent to several newspapers, to the mayor, and to the governor."

"Just what do you think we are, Mr. Hartshorn?"

Bert smiled. "I would suppose you can gather that without my help. Now I bid you good day, Mr. Roscoe. You may reach me at any hour at the Miller residence."

"You'll hear from me by Monday, I'd expect."

Bert was tempted to apologize, to fall back on his decades of always rising above the fray. He tamped down the urge.

"Good. If I don't—whatever the outcome—I will consider our deal null and void."

For the first time, Roscoe looked slightly nervous. "I'm at the mercy of Terry Penrose's timing, as you surely understand."

"I'm sure you've grown accustomed to being at his mercy," Bert said. "Look on the bright side. In a few days, you'll be your own master."

With that, Bert left and hustled down the stairs, through the Turkish bath, and out into the cold. He turned west on Swan Street and jogged one long block away from The Criterion. He darted into a narrow alley near Washington Street, where he bent double, panting, and in the dirty snow threw up everything he'd eaten for breakfast.

IN THE RED JACKET
GOLF CLUB

THERE WAS A RING AROUND THE MOON THAT SUNDAY NIGHT, which was bright enough to spill bluish light down the serpentine path that led from Parkside Avenue to the Red Jacket clubhouse. A brisk northerly wind brought with it the scent of snow. By tomorrow morning, there would probably be a foot of the stuff atop the hipped roof, and the fresh fall would fill Jess's tracks and erase any trace of his errand.

The walkway snaked up the contours of a low hill to the imposing stone clubhouse's wide veranda. Behind the porch were narrow leaded windows that extended from the porch planking almost to the brow of the overhanging roof. In fine weather, these windows could be swiveled open on gimbals, letting the cool lake breeze waft over the veranda and into the large front room.

In the moonlight, walking directly up the path to the front of the building would make him too conspicuous, so Jess pulled his muffler tight around his throat and walked past the club without so much as a sidelong glance, then veered off onto Florence Avenue. Like any other pedestrian headed home after Sunday night Mass, he shuffled along purposefully, mostly looking down at his feet.

When he reached the northwest corner of the clubhouse, he darted across the wide lawn to the back of the building, where the groundskeeper's equipment was stored and the sprawling nine-hole course undulated away into the night. In the lee of the clubhouse, he would be entirely hidden from view. He would enter there, get his business done, and get out.

Along the back side of the structure was a man-sized door and two carriage doors that opened wide enough to allow the groundskeeping equipment to come and go from the storage room inside. The man-sized door was a heavy oaken thing that looked like a portal into a castle keep. It would be impossible to force with only the small pry bar he had in his coat pocket.

Not so the carriage doors, however. They were secured by a large hasp and lock, but five years of wet Buffalo weather, and constant opening and closing by the grounds crew, had worked loose the screws that affixed the iron hasp to the wood of the carriage doors. It was a simple matter for Jess to slip his pry bar under the strap and pull it free of the decaying wood, screws and all. He swung one of the doors open enough to slip inside, and closed it carefully again.

He was in the groundskeeper's equipment area, a large addition fused to the back of the structure. There was enough moonlight creeping in through a skylight that Jess could navigate around the club's horse-drawn lawnmowers, which occupied one half of the space, and a small steamroller—a traction engine fitted with heavy rollers, to keep the greens perfectly even—which took up most of the other half. There was a gasoline tractor in a vacant corner, near the carriage doors. Various tools, rakes, and shovels hung neatly on pegs along the walls, and a heavy workbench extended along the left side wall. Under the bench were cans and carboys of fuel and oil for the machines.

He squeezed between the hulking pieces of equipment and, at the front of the storage room, stood before the door into the clubhouse proper. Here, he was deep enough into the building that he could squat, take a match from his pocket match safe, and light the small skater's lantern he had clipped to his belt, under his coat. Once he had the little flame going, he turned the doorknob. The door was unlocked, and so he stepped over the threshold and into the clubhouse.

Jess now found himself in the kitchen and pantry area, where the club's cooks prepared meals for the golfers and their guests. He arced the lantern toward the front of the room and located a swinging door, which, as he expected, opened into the small dining hall. Chairs were turned upside down on the tables, waiting for spring and the return of—Jess thought with a smirk—familiar asses.

One more door, and Jess had come all the way through the Red Jacket clubhouse, emerging into the main front room, just behind the veranda. He took a quick look around, playing his beam over the massive stone fireplace that occupied the entire back wall, and the long wood-topped bar nearby. Canvas was draped over the furniture. He took care not to direct his lantern toward the veranda, however, lest it be spied down the hill on Parkside, flashing away like a lighthouse.

There were doors on either side of the giant fireplace. To the left, the door read Women's Apartments. That would be the ladies' parlor and locker room, so he retraced his steps to the right side of the hearth. There, an identical door read Men's Apartments. He went in and passed through a small lounge area, and was at last in the men's locker room.

His lantern revealed neat ranks of identical oak-fronted lockers, each taller than a man to allow space for clothing and golf clubs. Oak benches were bolted to the floor in front of the lockers. The lockers themselves were numbered, but not named, and each was guarded by a silver-dollar-sized thumbwheel with letters around the perimeter, very much like a post office box lock. He thought for a moment whether it might look better to pry open a few, but then reconsidered. It would be a waste of time—no one would know if any had been opened anyway, once the whole place was rubble.

Burn it down, if you have to, Roscoe had said—doubtless half-jokingly, but Jess had known better. The letters weren't there, never had been, so the only believable story he could peddle to Roscoe afterward was that he hadn't had time to find and open the right lockers, and had had to resort to extreme measures.

Jess felt a brief ripple of sorrow, but let it pass by. It was a beautiful building, to be sure, but at the same time only another private enclave where the plutocrats of Buffalo—people like his father—could slap one another's backs. They didn't deserve to keep it all to themselves, any more than Kendall deserved Sarah for himself, and only because he had money. And who was here, on a wintry Sunday night in December, putting himself at risk—again—for Sarah's benefit? Who was doing whatever it took to ensure her safety? It certainly wasn't the great, self-made Mr. Kendall!

Jess blew out the skater's lantern, waited for the burner to cool, and then unscrewed it from the font. He lit a match and found the corner of the room, where two banks of wooden lockers came together. He upended the little lantern, pouring out the remainder of its kerosene under the lockers, and touched the match to the small oily pool. It fizzled out with a hiss.

He tried again, but the floor was cold, and without a wick in it, the kerosene wouldn't catch. He pulled the wick out of the skater's lamp and set it on edge in the little patch of liquid. This he was able to light, but the pitiful little flame refused to ignite anything, not even the spilled fuel oil. He moved the wick around, hoping to heat the kerosene enough to get it going, but then accidentally tipped it over. It, too, fizzled out, smothered in its own fuel.

Jess felt in his match safe for another match. He'd never expected this much difficulty, so he had brought only what matches were in the little container. Now the container held but one remaining match, and he couldn't risk it on another failed attempt. He would need something else to get a bigger, hotter fire going.

He stood in the dark locker room, which now smelled of brimstone and kerosene, frustrated and wondering what to do. After a moment the obvious solution appeared: the bottles of fuel back in the groundskeeper's area. Full of purpose now, and with a sense of the layout of the clubhouse, he returned to the storage area. The tractor in the far corner suggested that there would be bottles of gasoline around—still a novel fuel, more volatile than kerosene, and one he knew would burn fast and hot.

Feeling around under the workbench, he found a demijohn about three-quarters full of about two gallons of clear liquid. He gave it a little nudge. It was difficult to tell for sure, but the fluid looked to be thinner than kerosene, so it was probably what was left of the season's gasoline. He eased the container out from under the bench. Cradling it in his arms, he walked back to the locker room, feeling at home in the place now, even without light.

In the dark locker room, he set the gasoline down on one of the benches. He stood in the darkness, letting his eyes adjust and rehearsing. He tried to open the demijohn, but the cap was wired to the neck of the damn thing and his fumbling, cold fingers couldn't work it loose. No matter, he thought. He would smash the demijohn in the corner of the lockers and back away, open his match safe, take out a match, toss it into the pool of gasoline, and get out. He knew the way by now and could retrace his steps easily. Once out the carriage doors in the rear, he'd hustle across the lawn to Florence Avenue again, turn right, and in five minutes he'd be on Main Street, not far from the trolley stop. Easy.

He'd been fiddling around in the clubhouse for a good ten minutes now, and so there wasn't any more time to waste. There could be no guarantee that his light had not been spotted, or that some pesky beat cop might not rattle the hasp on the back of the Red Jacket Golf Club as a matter of routine. He picked up the bottle of gasoline, held it over his head, and threw it as hard as he could against the lockers.

The bottle landed with a dull thud and clattered around on the tile floor, but the thick, heavy glass did not break. Jess cursed softly and crouched to retrieve the bottle for another try. The impact may have failed to smash the demijohn, but it had succeeded in loosening the wired cap, and there was now a steady stream of liquid dribbling onto the floor and saturating his hands and coat sleeves. He knocked the neck of the bottle against the bench and jarred the cap the rest of the way off. Now he didn't need to smash anything. He splashed some of the fuel on the floor, on the bench, and on the fronts of the lockers.

He backed away, ruefully shaking his soaked and stinking arms and trouser cuffs. They would dry by the time he got to the trolley. Must be old gasoline, he thought, thinner and without any tangy petroleum scent. Even in the cold locker room the volatile fuel quickly filled the space with vapor, and in the tight confines, the thick fumes made him suddenly dizzy. Jess hastily retrieved the match safe from his coat pocket and flipped it open, feeling for his last match. The reek was almost intolerable now, cloyingly sweet, fogging up his head. He found the rough patch on the bottom of the match safe and put the matchhead against it.

His hand was already moving when the thought occurred that this wasn't old gasoline—it wasn't gasoline at all. It smelled like something he'd smelled before, like sour cotton candy. Then he remembered. *The darkroom.* Sarah's tiny vial of ether, whose flammable fumes had frightened her so. The groundskeeper must have kept this bottle on hand, knowing that only a few drops of the highly volatile liquid ignited in the cylinders of a cold tractor engine would provide enough explosive power to get it turning over. But now the room—and Jess—was soaked with more than a gallon of the stuff, and his final match was flaring into life.

His sleeve caught first, not that it would have made any difference. The atmosphere was so heavy with the ether fumes that the air itself ignited, starting low, near the floor. The roiling flames rose so quickly, though, that his next breath was superheated air. He tried to scream, but his scorched lungs managed only a thick gurgle. He dropped to his knees, waving his arms wildly, like a man who has disturbed a hornet's nest. Flames were everywhere, and the half-empty demijohn, red-hot, began pinwheeling around the floor like a firework. The whirling jug spewed flames from its neck, until it smashed itself to pieces against the iron support of the burning bench.

Jess was fully engulfed now, encircled by a nimbus of flame. His trousers and coat were ablaze, and the skin on his calves and hands was starting to bubble and peel. Even if he had known the way out, he couldn't have made it to Parkside alive. But Jess Murphy would never leave the Red Jacket Golf Club. As he fell forward, facedown into the spreading pool of burning ether, he thought it odd that there was no pain. He could recognize that he'd made a terrible mistake, but there was no disappointment in it. In the deepest whorls of his brain, far from the fire, his final thought was that he had done what he had come to do, and that Sarah was safe.

❦

"The Red Jacket Golf Club clubhouse burned to the ground last evening," Annie read the next morning over their breakfast. "A faulty gas connection is blamed for the loss, it says here."

Sarah put down her section of the paper and shook her head slowly. "That was Ed's club, you know," she said. "Seth's, too, and Arthur's. In the good old days, all of us would go golfing there. We had some very nice times, before all the trouble. Now nothing's left."

"It seems that everyone and everything in the whole Ashwood circle is doomed," Annie said.

"For heaven's sake, don't say that out loud!" Sarah said.

"I didn't mean it that way, it's—"

"No, you're right, Annie. I sometimes shiver when I think that whatever sins we committed will catch up to us eventually. Clearly we have displeased"—she pointed to the ceiling and whispered—"*someone*."

❦

When Annie and Sarah arrived at the office, they walked slowly down the corridor, thawing out after the bitter walk from the trolley stop.

At their door, Annie put her hand on the knob, took a deep breath, and looked over at Sarah. Every Monday it was the same, dreading seeing Jess after two days without that anxiety. She exhaled and turned the knob, but the door was still locked. He hadn't arrived.

Sarah unlocked the door and they breezed in with as much sangfroid as they could muster up, just in case he was there. But there was no sign of Jess. The office was warm and cozy, the honey oak furniture solid and comforting. The telephones stood at attention, waiting for the day to begin.

"Let's hope he's sick today," Annie said.

"Now, Annie, be nice," Sarah said with mock sternness.

Sarah sat down behind her desk and scanned the few trinkets she had arrayed in front of her. A Pan-American Exposition letter opener and paperweight. A little clay animal that Maggie had made—a quadruped, it must have been, but with a downturned tail long enough to make it look as though it was some queer, newly discovered five-legged species. She shuffled through the few pieces of mail, picked up the letter opener, and then put it down again, starting off into space.

She sat there for a good quarter of an hour when the telephone jangled and made her jump. Maybe it was Hartshorn. She took a deep breath and picked up the earpiece.

❦

"'MORNING, ROSCOE," PENROSE SAID from behind his desk as the assistant DA tried to pass by and get to his office unnoticed.

"Good morning," Roscoe said, not turning his head to look at his boss. He walked into his office and sat down unsteadily. He'd been so queasy that morning he hadn't had his favorite breakfast—a bacon sandwich and fried potatoes—at the city hall commissary. Without anything in his stomach, he felt even more nauseated and was having an uncomfortable attack of flatulence.

He'd been sitting for a few minutes when Terry Penrose appeared in his doorway. "A minute, Bill?" he said, walking in without waiting for a response. He sat down in the chair across from Roscoe, leaned back, and pushed the office door closed.

"Good night, it stinks in here," Penrose said, pinching his nose. "What have you been eating?"

"I'm sorry. My stomach's upset."

"As it would be, as it would be. Yes. Well, then, speaking of shit—I listened to that piece of music you gave me," Penrose said. "A couple times."

Roscoe tugged on his collar. "Yes. And?"

Terry looked around the office, craning his neck. "There isn't any magic phonograph going in here, is there, Bill?"

Roscoe shook his head.

"I suppose I have a couple questions for you," Terry said. "I thought of them over the weekend. At first, I thought I'd storm in here and cry out, 'Et tu, Brute?' at the top of my lungs, but then what good would that do? The classics are almost forgotten these days. You might not even understand the reference."

"I know the reference," Roscoe said.

"Bad example, then. My first thought, though, was: Who is the Brutus in this story? Was it Bill Roscoe, betraying me in such a novel and cunning way? And I decided that it couldn't have been your idea. You're neither creative nor especially cunning.

"Let's set the *who* aside for a moment. The *why*, the motive, was at first a mystery. But if I've learned anything in this office, it's that men do things only for a few main reasons." He ticked them off his fingers. "Ambition. Greed, which is ambition in another form. Hatred. Sex. And, last but certainly not least, fear. Let's look at each one.

"First, ambition. You were almost certain to become the next DA. Stabbing me in the back wasn't necessary, and it would turn me into an enemy, instead of an ally. So it couldn't be simple ambition. And knowing that you weren't motivated by ambition eliminated one thing I might have offered you to call this charade off—namely, to be my lieutenant governor. An ambitious man would have wanted something like that, and would have made a play for it. You didn't."

Roscoe was silent.

"Are you following along, Bill? All right. Let's look at greed. Not a chance. One always makes more money working in the bank than robbing it.

"Hatred? No, not that either. Not strong enough in your case. You don't like me, and never have. And in truth I've never liked you. But in politics who does, really? No one.

"Which brings us to sex. Cherchez la femme! Or, in this case, *femmes*, with an 's'. Because I figure that not one but two women were behind this trick of yours. And yes, I know very well who they are, so don't bother denying it. But, on the other hand, I also know very well that neither Mrs. Miller nor Miss Payne would fuck you, Bill. Not even if you were marooned with them on a desert island, without any hope of rescue. So sex is out as a motive."

Roscoe was about to say something, but Penrose held up a hand. "Be a little patient with me, Bill, will you? You do owe me that, at least, after all we have shared. And I'm almost to the end, having ruled out everything but *fear*. Fear comes in more flavors than Lang's ice cream, Bill. And a man like you, well, *is* a man like you because of fear. You're the man *behind* the throne, an *éminence grise*, because you're not brave enough to be the man *on* the throne.

"You're a parasite, Bill. Yes, yes, I know that's harsh, but it really is the only word for you. A parasite, living off the substance of creatures stronger than you. You attach yourself to a man like me, who is in the arena every day, fighting, winning, and yes, sometimes losing, but always fighting, while you stand safely by in the wings and decide whether to put your thumb up or down.

"And so, after all this, I have decided that it was fear that made you do it. Hearing your name mentioned on that cylinder"—he waved his hand vigorously in front of his nose—"scared you shitless, if you'll pardon the expression. Am I right, Bill?"

"You heard it. There's good reason to be scared."

"They have one little cylinder. Big deal. In time, we can figure out how to get our hands on that. Look at those stupid letters—how long did it take to eliminate those? But we did. It took our mad friend Mr. Murphy—who seems to have managed to incinerate himself over the weekend—to destroy them, but what of it? Same goes for the original cylinder. In time, we find out where it is, and we have it destroyed. Bill, we're in a better position now, with one troublesome cylinder to worry about, than we were twenty-four hours ago, with hundreds of letters in the wind."

Roscoe looked confused, as though he'd never considered this. Penrose looked at him and then chuckled, shaking his head.

"What are you sniggering about?"

"I'm sorry, Bill. I'm chuckling because you're not that smart, and you're a pussy. Fact is, they played you, and you fell for it. You could have stalled, could have come to me with the cylinder, and we could have worked something out together. But you got scared, and panicked. And in the process, fucked things up for me—and also for yourself. It's probably a good thing you won't be DA, after all."

"What's that mean? I'll step into your position."

"And what fun you'll have, my friend. When you do, I'll be back in private practice, with everyone who owes me a favor lined up. And I'll see to it that you don't sit in my office for more than a day. Come to think of it, I may let you do it for a week or two, simply for the pleasure of seeing you removed."

"I suppose we'll have to see about that."

"Oh, we will, Bill. We most certainly will."

Roscoe looked at Penrose, and then looked quickly away.

Penrose rapped his knuckles on Roscoe's desk so sharply that Roscoe jumped.

"But you know, Bill," he said, "even after all this, I'm still of two minds about what to do next."

"What does that mean?"

"I can be a very forgiving man, you know," Terry said, "with only the slightest encouragement. And I can also be—well, I'm not proud to say it—*vindictive*. So I think it's only fair if I offer you a choice of which Terry Penrose you'd rather see in your near future."

"I'm listening," Roscoe said quietly.

"Good. Option one reflects the less magnanimous side of my nature," Terry said. "You go ahead as you planned, and tell Bert Hartshorn and his womenfolk that I'll quit as DA, drop out of the governor's race, and return to private practice. And you get to be DA—if temporarily. And while I'm finding ways to make your two weeks on the job miserable, guess what else?" He paused and leaned forward expectantly.

"What?" Roscoe said, without thinking.

"You don't sleep a wink that whole time without one eye open. You don't live another hour of your life without looking over your shoulder.

Because you've chosen the wrong man to fuck with, and you ought to have known that."

Roscoe stared into his lap.

"Now for the second option. As previously, I still step down for some bullshit made-up reason. My family, or an illness, or some other thing. We'll figure that part out. You get to sit in my chair, still temporarily, but you use this office to help me get my hands on that goddamned cylinder and destroy it. Once we do, I step back into my position, and you go back to yours."

"It doesn't sound that different to me," Roscoe said, "from the first case."

"Bill, if you please—it's worlds' different!" Terry said with a broad smile. "In this second case, I don't hound you out of office. I don't order someone to peel your skin off with pliers, then cut all your tendons and toss your body into the Buffalo River. Most of all, I let bygones be bygones—because that's what gentlemen do. And I'll run for governor, as planned. With you as my successor here."

"You would do that?"

"Which part?"

"Let bygones be bygones."

Terry clapped his hand down hard on the arm of his chair. "Bill, it's like I said. I don't like you. Never have. And I like you less now than ever. But I'm not going to shoot myself in the foot for the sake of a childish grudge. With you in this office, my chances of getting my hands on that cylinder increase dramatically. I don't have to like you to know that's the better course for me. And I think it's the far better course for you, too."

"Then I'll choose the second option," Roscoe said.

"Wise choice," Penrose said, standing up. "You're smarter than you come across sometimes, Bill. Now, how about you and I go out for lunch today and think through our strategy."

❦

SARAH HUNG UP THE telephone and wandered slowly out into the outer office. She sat down deliberately in the guest chair next to Annie's desk.

"What's wrong, Miss?" Annie said. "You look like you've seen a ghost."

"In a manner of speaking," Sarah mumbled. "I just now hung up the phone with the morgue."

"The morgue? At the newspaper?"

"No. The *morgue* morgue. Where they do the autopsies. It was Dr. Gerlach who called."

"Why would he be calling us?"

"It's Jess," she said. "He's—dead."

"*Dead?*"

"Yes, dead. He said the police think Jess was the one who set the Red Jacket Golf clubhouse on fire last night, and was trapped in it. They found our agency card in what was left of his wallet. Dr. Gerlach didn't know who else to call. Didn't even know his name. I had to tell him."

The two sat silently, trying not to look at Jess's desk.

"I don't know what to say," Annie said. "I just don't."

"Neither do I. Dr. Gerlach wants me to come down to identify the body."

"I can do that, if you're not up to it."

"No, no, it's my responsibility."

"Why would he do such a thing?" Annie said, after another long silence.

"I have no earthly idea."

"We have to get word to his family," Annie murmured.

"He said he was from Newport. Maybe we can locate his parents."

"I'll track them down. The library should have a telephone directory for Newport."

"There may be quite a few Murphys."

"I'll tackle them one by one then. We'd better get going."

The two locked up the Avenging Angel office and walked slowly down the stairs, not wanting to see anyone in the elevator. They stopped on the front steps of the Hudson Building, looking up and down the street at God knows what. Then Annie turned to Sarah and threw her arms around her, burrowing her face into her coat. Sarah hugged her back, hard.

"Oh, Sarah," Annie's muffled voice said. "I'm sorry I hated him so. I told him I wished he'd die. I feel like I killed him."

Sarah held her out at arm's length and wiped Annie's face with her glove. "No, Annie," she said, shaking her head. "You dear thing. Don't think that. You never hated him—you were afraid for me. And you're not responsible for his death. Whatever notion he took to burn the golf club down, we'll never know. But it wasn't a sane one. He was not a well young man, and that's sad."

Annie sniffed. "I'll find his parents, and I'll say good things about him when I tell them."

"I know you will. You have the best heart of anyone I know. Wherever Jess is now, he's free of all the . . . torment he must have felt in life. We can try to remember the good things about him."

Annie gave a weak smile and nodded. Sarah hugged her again, and then the two went in different directions, Annie toward the public library and Sarah toward the morgue at the foot of West Eagle Street.

At the morgue, she asked for Dr. Gerlach and, after a few moments, was greeted by an impossibly handsome young doctor. "I'm looking for Dr. Gerlach," she said.

"I'm Dr. Gerlach."

She had expected some pale, shriveled ghoul, not a tall, strapping college man. "Oh, well, then, doctor—I'm Sarah Payne. You called me about Jess Murphy. Jesse James Murphy is his full name, actually."

"Thank you," the doctor said. "My condolences. Right this way. We'll get this over as quickly as we can."

The morgue building was damp, and smelled of chemicals and bleach. Dr. Gerlach escorted Sarah down a long hallway, to a tiled room with a low ceiling. This room had a cloying smell of charcoal and sulfur, a nauseating combination of persistent and penetrating odors so strong that Sarah could taste them more than smell them. She clutched her handkerchief to her mouth.

"Sorry about the smell," Gerlach said. "I do need to prepare you. He's very badly burned, and it's not a pretty sight. If you can either identify him as Mr. Murphy or not, that's all you must do. Less than a minute. Can you bear up?"

"Yes, I can," she said.

The doctor walked her over to a long exam table draped with a sheet. "Are you ready? May I steady you, Miss?"

"I'm ready. I'll be fine, thank you."

"All right," he said, and drew back the sheet.

She had entirely underestimated the sight. On the table was a black figure that looked to be carved out of charcoal, arms curled in a boxer's pose, legs drawn up tight to the midsection, the way she and the other children had jumped from a rope swing into a pond when she was a girl. The body—such as it was—was naked, hairless, and, in places, without skin at all, only charred bone.

The palms—the fingers were mostly blackened nubs—covered the face in what must have been a futile protective reflex. Dr. Gerlach gently moved the hands down, the frozen arms making a horrible crackling sound. The face underneath was—

"It's him," she said, trying not to vomit.

"You're sure?"

"Entirely, yes."

"Thank you," Dr. Gerlach said, and pulled the sheet over the remains. "I'm sorry you had to see that."

"It's well that I did, doctor," Sarah said. "We can't live in a dreamworld, no matter how we might like to, can we?"

❦

BERT HARTSHORN CALLED SARAH that same evening. It had been such a terrible day—the news, the morgue, Annie spending hours dialing every Murphy in Newport, until finding the right one and then having to tell them about the death of their son—that Sarah almost didn't care about Hartshorn, or Penrose, or Roscoe. She covered the mouthpiece of the phone with one hand and signaled to Annie.

"It's Hartshorn," she said. "He wants to come over and tell us about Penrose and the phonograph. Are we up to it?"

"Not really, but let's brace up and do it anyway," she said.

After Sarah hung up, she took Annie by the hand. "I've said it before, but I don't know what I'd do without you."

"And I've said it before—you won't have to. When is he coming over?"

"He said a half hour. I figured that would give us time to freshen up."

"I know I look hideous," Annie said, "but I'm almost happy to say, for the first time, you don't look so good yourself."

They laughed and trudged up the stairs to try to repair some of the day's damage before Mr. Hartshorn showed up.

🦃

THE DOORBELL AT NORWOOD Street rang precisely thirty minutes after Hartshorn's call, and Ruth answered the door. Standing on the icy front porch were Bert Hartshorn and Alicia Miller. Bert was holding a small box, wrapped with Christmas paper and tied in a satin bow.

"We're here to see Miss Payne," Bert said.

"Yes, they're in the parlor already," Ruth said. "Let me take your wraps."

Allie and Bert walked into the parlor, where a fire was blazing cheerfully in the hearth and a graceful spruce tree was glittering with tinsel and glass in the corner of the room. The flickering gaslights made the paneling glow amber and yellow.

"How cozy!" Alicia exclaimed, walking in and holding out her arms to embrace Sarah. "Sarah, you look lovely as always. And Annie," she said, holding out her hand, "your new wardrobe certainly becomes you."

Annie shook the proffered hand. "Why thank you, Mrs. Miller. You're looking very well, too."

"Can you believe that all of this—hell—is nearly behind us?" Alicia said as the four of them took a seat. "There have been entire months when I thought I'd never see the day."

"That's encouraging," Sarah said. "I hope Mr. Hartshorn has some good news for us about Annie's invention."

"That was *your* invention?" Allie said to Annie. "Clever girl."

"I've always liked tinkering with things."

"Me too," Allie said. "Right, Bert?" She laughed.

"For heaven's sake, Alicia," he said. He cleared his throat. "We wanted to see you personally to tell you that Miss Annie's invention worked famously. And I must compliment Mrs. Miller, too, on a bravura performance worthy of Mrs. Bernhardt. She had Penrose admitting to things no sane man would repeat, even in the confessional. Oh, and this is for you." He handed the little Christmas present to Sarah.

"You didn't have to do that," Sarah said.

"Open it," Alicia said. "Go on."

Sarah slid the ribbon off and tore the paper. Inside was a little wooden box with Japanese characters on the top.

"How lovely," Sarah said. "Why, thank you."

"It's not the box," Allie said. "I got that at the Pan-American. You can keep it, though, if you like. It's what's *in* the box that matters. Open it."

Sarah lifted the hinged top of the little box. Inside, sitting on a bed of snowy cotton, was a phonograph cylinder.

"A copy of the original," Bert said. "It's all on there. The end of Terry Penrose's criminal career. I gave a copy to William Roscoe, and he shared it with Penrose."

"And?" Annie said. "What did he say?"

"Roscoe wants to meet with me tomorrow to make it official, but it would seem that we have prevailed."

"That's wonderful news, Mr. Hartshorn," Sarah said. "What terms did Penrose agree to?"

"Penrose will vacate his office on December 31. Roscoe becomes DA, and he pledges to leave all of us alone, for good."

Sarah stared into her lap for a few seconds.

"Is something wrong, dear?" Alicia asked.

"It seems to me that they're getting off scot-free," Sarah said. "Compared to all the evil that they've done."

"I hardly think that's so, Miss Payne," Bert said. "A man like Penrose, stepping down from high office when on the cusp of becoming the next governor of New York—that's quite a fall."

"Maybe, but he'll be raking it in in his private practice," Sarah said. "And without any public disgrace, everyone will still be willing to dance to his tune. And Roscoe as DA? Why, on the night this cylinder was being recorded, those two sent a man to execute me and my daughter."

"Whatever do you mean?" Bert said.

Sarah told him about Harry Price's visit.

"Penrose and Roscoe would happily have my blood—and my little girl's—on his hands today, if they'd had their way."

Alicia whistled. "She's got a point, Bert. We may have been played."

"Well, I didn't know about any of that," he said. "I hardly can be expected to know about something . . . I didn't know anything about."

"Bert has such a way with words, wouldn't you agree?" Allie said to the other two ladies.

"They ought both to be in prison," Annie said.

"*Terry Penrose* isn't going to prison," Hartshorn said sharply, shaking his head. "It's simply not possible. But this way, he won't be governor, or be further rewarded for his crimes."

"And you're both happy with this?" Sarah asked.

"I'm happy," Bert said.

"I'm content," Alicia said.

"I'd imagine $50,000 buys a lot of contentment," Sarah said.

"What the hell is that supposed to mean?" Allie said.

"You know what it means. I know very well that you got Penrose to unjam your $50,000 bequest."

"However did you know about that?"

"I didn't. You just told me."

Alicia laughed. "My God! Sarah, you are a force to be reckoned with. Well played!"

"If I may say, Miss Payne," Bert said, "you're not being very fair to Mrs. Miller. That money belongs to her, and Penrose was holding it up. Illegally. If there had been no money at stake for her, the deal would have been the same."

"*Fair* is one thing, and *just* is another, Mr. Hartshorn. I took this case up for the sake of *justice*. And justice is *not* done by letting these two off the hook, even if you"—she pointed her finger at Alicia—"got all that money. These men are *murderers*. They had Edward killed. They forced Arthur Pendle to take his own life, and his wife's. And for all of that, Penrose gets rewarded with a fat private practice, and Roscoe gets a promotion?"

There was a thick silence in the parlor, broken only by the settling of the coal in the grate and the ticking of the mantel clock.

Bert was getting red in the face. "I can't very well go back to Roscoe and tell him the deal's off," he said. "The deal is *done*. He's agreed to the terms I presented. What's changed?"

"What's *changed*?" Annie said. "Other than those two having sent someone to murder Sarah and her child? And, by the way, what is to prevent them from ordering *all* our deaths? Their word of honor?"

"And we know what that's worth," Sarah added. "These men will just keep coming, unless we can put a stop to them permanently."

"Why wouldn't we simply give the cylinder to the newspapers?" Annie asked.

"Oh, no you don't," Alicia said. "My voice is on that cylinder too, and I don't need any more publicity. Bluffing is one thing, but as I told Bert, testifying against Terry Penrose is quite another. And *that* I am *not* doing—not in court, and not in the press."

"Then this was all for a *bluff*?" Annie said. "That's all the cylinder means? You never intended to use it as evidence against them?"

Alicia folded her arms and glared at Annie. "It bought us time, didn't it?" she said.

"That cylinder isn't our *only* evidence against Terry Penrose," Sarah said at last. "Nor what frightens him the most—and the reason he wants me dead."

Bert and Annie looked puzzled.

A slow smile spread across Alicia's face—a horrible, cold smile. "I know what you mean," she said, leaning toward Sarah. "I can read your mind, little lady."

"What *do* I mean, then?" Sarah asked.

"My letters," Alicia said. "Arthur's letters. *You* have them. You've had them all this time."

"I give you credit," Sarah said. "You *can* read minds."

"I wish you could read mine, right now," Allie said.

"I'll pass."

"And I'd bet you every last cent of my fifty thousand you've read them all, too. I hope you enjoyed them."

"Truthfully, I'm not proud of anything relating to your letters, Alicia," Sarah said. "You may not believe me, but they've been a source of considerable pain—and risk of bodily harm—since the day Edward gave them to me. But now, for the first time, I'm happy I kept them. Because we can use them to have our revenge—*permanent* revenge—on Terry Penrose."

"We're not doing anything of the sort," Alicia said. "Those letters are my private property. And Arthur's name has already been dragged through enough mud. His letters to me are not *evidence*. They are all I have left of him. And I want them back, tonight."

"Allie," Sarah said, "I never wanted the letters. Edward wanted me to safeguard them, that's all. And I wanted to do right by him. I am sorry that you were hurt by that."

"You're too kind," Alicia said. "And I'll try to overlook that the reason he wanted them safeguarded, as you put it, was to use them against me. And that you wanted to have him to yourself."

Sarah bristled. "I did—"

"Ladies," Bert said, "this will get us nowhere. I realize that we don't have any guarantee that Penrose and Roscoe will go away quietly. Perhaps if we let some time pass, though—"

"Terry Penrose doesn't have a short memory, Bert," Allie said.

The four sat quietly, watching the fire.

"How much danger are we in?" Annie mused out loud.

"My house is the most-watched house in Buffalo, and has been for quite a while," Alicia said. "I'm more concerned about the four of you here."

"I'm sure that's very kind of you, but you needn't worry about us," Sarah said. "We're safer than Fort Knox."

"How's that?" Alicia said.

"The Avenging Angels have a new bodyguard."

"I've been thinking that might be a good investment myself," Bert said to Alicia. "What agency did you engage, if I may ask?"

"No agency," Sarah replied. "It's an individual. The man that Roscoe sent to murder me, actually."

Alicia laughed. "I swear, Sarah, it must be those eyes of yours. You charmed the socks off a hired killer."

"It had nothing to do with me. He's got a conscience."

"Who is this captivating devil?" Allie said.

"His name is Harry Price."

Alicia's face creased into her flat smile. "Oh, I know very well who Harry Price is," she said. "Arthur used to mention him. However did you manage to tame that one? You must have strong juju."

"When Mr. Price came to visit me, we got to talking, and he decided on his own that he wanted to look out for us. He's been living in the toolshed behind my house since then."

Alicia laughed again. "I dare say, you are chock-full of surprises tonight. But even the fearsome Harry Price has to sleep. And Penrose has enough lackeys to run three shifts, if he had to."

"Then it seems to me," Bert said, "that unless you change your mind about releasing that cylinder, the best we can do is to keep a low profile."

"I won't be changing my mind," Allie said.

"To think I was so happy just a little while ago," Annie said. "But now I feel more unsettled than ever."

"Welcome to Planet Earth, missy. Bert, we'd best be going," Alicia said. "I need a drink."

Alicia and Bert stood to go, and Sarah and Annie walked them to the front door. In the foyer, Alicia turned and confronted Sarah.

"Aren't you forgetting something?" she said.

"I don't think so."

"Think harder, dear."

"Oh," Sarah said. "Your letters."

"I *knew* you'd remember," Allie said. "I'll thank you for, er, *safeguarding* them, but now I want them back."

Sarah nodded and ran up the staircase. She returned with the box of letters held out in front of her. "Here you go, and I can't say I'm sorry that they're leaving," she said.

Alicia took the box from Sarah's hands and hefted it. "Who'd have thought?" she murmured, almost to herself. "Thank you, Sarah." She turned to go, and then turned back.

"Do you want to know something, Sarah?" she said. "Something I wish?"

"I can't begin to imagine."

"I wish you could believe that I really do admire you. There it is, and I won't say it twice."

Sarah stared at her. "I—"

Alicia waved her hand in the air. "It's fine. Now, Bert, let's get going. After all this, I need two drinks now. At least."

❦

AT SUNDOWN THE FOLLOWING day, Bert returned to 101 Ashwood Street after his meeting with Roscoe. The girls and Mrs. Hall were playing a board game in the kitchen, so after he'd said a quick hello, he trotted up the stairs to find Alicia sitting naked in her bedroom, having a glass of whiskey.

"How'd it go?" she said when he sat down at her dressing table.

"He swore they'll abide by our terms."

"But?" she said.

"But there was something in his manner that I didn't like."

"Other than the obvious? That he's a fat, sweaty, duplicitous little shit?"

"Besides that. He didn't seem so frightened as before, when I played the cylinder for him. And Bill Roscoe is not a brave man. I think he and Penrose are planning a double cross."

"People don't change, Bert," she said.

"He may be bluffing, of course."

Alicia swirled her bourbon, making the ice clink, and took a sip. "Oh, I don't think for a second that he's bluffing," she said to Bert. "He's already had one member of this household murdered, you know. What are a few more?"

"Alicia, we have to release that cylinder, or we'll never be safe again in our own home."

"I'm *not* releasing that cylinder, under any circumstance, so you can stop going on about it. But don't you worry, Bertie boy. I'll think of something. I always do."

"Well, you'd better do it fast. I'm concerned."

"I can see that. You're also a sentimental old fool."

"Whyever would you say that? Because I'm worried about you?"

"No. Because you said you were worried that we won't be safe in our own home. *Our* home." She put one leg up on Bert's lap.

"It must have slipped out," he said. "I wasn't trying to assert any ownership rights—"

"You really couldn't find your ass with both hands sometimes, Hartshorn," she said, and finished her whiskey.

PEARLS BEFORE SWINE

January 1, 1903
New Year's Day

SARAH SWEPT THE SNOW FROM A LIKELY BENCH AND SAT, COLD BUT happy to see the clear blue sky, the few high clouds. The ice in the lake was thick now, jostling and bumping along in front of her, beginning its trip down the Niagara River.

New Year's Day. She'd lost Edward a full year ago. She hadn't wanted to let him go, then or ever, but it had never been up to her. The choice had been made long before that final night in his den, without her permission or approval. There had never been a thing she could do about it. Yes, tracking down the culprits had been satisfying, but it hadn't given her anything back that had already been irrevocably taken away.

Nor—contrary to her understanding of the term—had any real *justice* been done. Terry Penrose had stepped down, but he wouldn't stay down, that was certain. Besides, no one knew the real reason why he had withdrawn. There was only his tepid public statement about needing to attend to some unspecified family matter. So as far as everyone outside of a pitifully small circle was concerned, every laurel he'd won while DA still sat snugly on his head. But now he was angry, and vengeful, and would be looking to settle the score.

And the dead were still dead. Their shades most probably hadn't the barest inkling that someone had followed their trail to its terminus. If those spirits were indeed looking down on humankind, as so many asserted, there was at least a fair chance that they were having a good laugh, counting their earthly lives paltry stuff, comparatively, from their births to their brief and violent deaths. Even those, too, might have been a mercy. Who knows if they mightn't have lingered in pain for months or years, their bodies and their dignity murdered in slow-motion by age or disease or senility?

Perhaps it had been only her curiosity that had been satisfied. Was it enough? Did it matter? It would have to suffice. Sarah understood at last what it meant when people said that "life goes on." She'd always thought that comment callous and unfeeling, an insensitive cliché—yet in the natural brutality of the notion, there was contained a great truth that could be denied but never refuted. Life always went on, and always would. Ed, Arthur, Jess, Penrose, herself—every one of them was only along for the ride, bumping along like so many hunks of ice headed for the Falls.

Allie is the only one who ever *understood* that, Sarah thought. She never gave anything of herself away without careful consideration of the potential risks and rewards. Sarah had accorded that to selfishness, but now it seemed different. Allie had simply grasped that something so precious as her dreams and desires could never mean to another as much as they did to her. *Pearls before swine*, she would probably say.

"I thought I might find you down here," said a voice behind her. Sarah whirled around to see Alicia walking down the stone steps to her bench.

"Speak of the devil," Sarah said. "I was just thinking about you."

"You still think me the Devil, then." She didn't wait for an answer to continue. "Mind if I join you?"

"Be my guest," Sarah said, and Allie sat down next to her. "And no, I don't think you're the Devil."

"That's a nice change," Alicia said. "And guess what?"

"What?"

"I don't want to claw your eyes out anymore."

Sarah laughed and looked over at Allie, her violet eyes as blue as the winter sky. "You're funny," she said.

"I can be."

"What are you doing down here," Sarah asked, "on a cold New Year's Day?"

"I spent New Year's Eve by myself, at my parents' old house. I did the same two years ago, thinking that it might bring me luck. And it brought me Arthur." She laughed softly. "Perhaps I should be more careful about what I wish for."

"You can say that again," Sarah said.

Allie looked out over the lake, watching the ice. "You said you were thinking about me just now. What about, if I may ask?"

"I was thinking how I used to think you were the most selfish, horrible person on Earth, but now I think you may have been right all along. I gave myself away too easily. I didn't keep anything back."

"Don't be so hard on yourself. Not a one of us knows what the hell we're doing as we go along. We live, and if we're lucky, we learn. But usually the hard way."

"Can't disagree with that," Sarah said, watching the ice scudding by. "So, Allie—what's next? For you, your family? Bert?"

Alicia sighed. "Ah, Bert. Seems like I've been rather smitten by the old fart," she said. "Can you imagine? Just yesterday, I asked him if he'd stay, and he said he would. My mother is my mother. And as for the children—it's been a difficult year for them, but they'll recover."

"Children are resilient. Maggie's been through hell this year, too, but she's as sweet as ever."

"That's good. And what's next for you? And the Avenging Angels?"

"I'm sorry to say it, but right about now Buffalo is haunted by too many memories," Sarah said. "There's someone in Niagara Falls who—wants me to work for him. I won't go far, but it'll be good for me to go."

"Ah," Alicia said. "You'll move the agency to the Falls?"

"No. Annie's going to run the Buffalo office. I'll be in Niagara Falls. For a while. How long, I don't know. I'll have to see."

"I never thought I'd say it, but I'll miss bumping into you at the glove bin," Alicia said.

"I promise to come back for the sales. Maybe I'll see you in Niagara Falls sometime."

"Where are you going to be?"

"I'm going to be at Kendall House, north of the city."

"Kendall? As in *Charles* Kendall?"

"You know Charles Kendall?"

Allie gave her flat smile. "I know *of* him. Lucky you."

"He's only a client. And I don't know if I can ever love anyone again after—" She blinked. "Oh, I'm sorry. That slipped out."

Alicia looked her full in the face, her dark eyes taking the measure of the younger woman. "It's fine. If there's anything I've learned, it's that we don't really choose whom or how we love."

"That's very kind of you to say."

"Aren't you simply full of goodwill for me today?" Allie said. "I ought to leave now, while I'm ahead."

"Are you getting cold?"

"No, dear," Alicia said, suddenly slipping her arm around Sarah's shoulder and pulling her in. "I'm a Buffalo girl, born and raised. I was wondering, though, if you'd care to have a hot chocolate in town? Perhaps you can tell me more about your upcoming work for the mysterious Charles Kendall."

Sarah squeezed Allie's hand where it dangled next to her face. "Does this mean we are to be allies, after all?" she said.

"At least. Who knows? Maybe even friends."

Allie stood, and offered Sarah her hand. Sarah joined her, and the two women started up the long hill toward Buffalo, arm in arm.

"It is a shame, though, isn't it," Sarah said, "that after all this, even our cylinder won't stop Terry Penrose for good. I suppose no matter how dirty you are, so long as you have power, you're safe."

Alicia looked over and gave her a strange smile. "Oh, I'm not at all sure about that," she said.

"You're not?"

"No, I'm not." They walked on a couple of steps, and then Alicia stopped, catching Sarah by the arm. "Since we're allies now, Sarah," Alicia said, "and maybe even friends, I have a little confession to make."

"Do I want to hear it?"

Alicia considered this. "Yes, I think you'll want to," she said. "You see, I didn't tell you, but I walked over to your house yesterday."

"You didn't leave a card."

"No, I didn't need to. I came over to borrow something from your toolshed."

Sarah laughed. "Whatever could you want in my toolshed?"

"It wasn't a *whatever*, it was a *whoever*," Allie said. "I had a little talk with Harry Price. About Terry Penrose."

Sarah stopped and looked at her, full in the face, and then they both burst out laughing. "You're serious, aren't you?" she said.

"Do I strike you as the lying kind?" Alicia said.

"No, I have to say that you do not."

"Then let's toast the New Year with our hot chocolate. I have a hunch that 1903 is going to be our year."

The End

ROBERT BRIGHTON'S
AVENGING ANGEL DETECTIVE
AGENCY™ MYSTERIES

THE UNSEALING

THE FIRST NOVEL
OF THE SERIES AND
WHERE IT ALL BEGAN

A MURDER IN ASHWOOD

THE SECOND NOVEL

CURRENT OF DARKNESS

THE THIRD NOVEL
COMING SOON!

STAY TUNED FOR MORE!

ASHWOOD PRESS

ACKNOWLEDGMENTS

I'D LIKE TO THANK my eighth-grade teacher, Mr. Paul Houser, whose influence on me—in kindling a lifelong love of language and learning—cannot be adequately described or repaid.

Thanks to Mark Summers, one of the world's greatest illustrators, for helping bring this book to life. Mark, you're a pleasure to work with, and your talent never fails to astonish me.

My publisher and representative, Ashwood Press, is small but mighty, and I am delighted to be associated with them.

I am deeply grateful to Mark, Olivia, and Chaney at Bizango, LLC (bizango.com), who do such an amazing job with my website and all things graphic design. Such fun people, too.

Extra-special thanks and wild acclaim are due my editor, Kimberly Laurel (thetrustybookmark.com), who is the first and only person I've ever met who gives my manuscripts the amount of care and diligence that I give to them myself. Thank you, Kimberly, for your dedication and erudition.

My deepest gratitude goes to my wife, Laura, for her constant support and encouragement. There is no one else like her.

And I remain ever in debt to Alicia, Sarah, Arthur, Edward, Bert, Annie, Harry, Ruth, and all the rest of you who inspired this tale. A large part of who I am exists solely because of who you are, and I hope I will always do you justice. I love you all.

Robert Brighton
May 2023

ABOUT THE AUTHOR

AWARD-WINNING NOVELIST, ROBERT BRIGHTON is an authority on the Gilded Age, and a believer that the Victorian era was anything but stuffy.

When he is not sniffing out unsolved mysteries, Brighton is a wanderer. He has traveled in more than fifty countries around the world, personally throwing himself into every situation his characters will face—from underground ruins to opium dens—and (so far) living to tell about it.

A graduate of the Sorbonne, Paris, Brighton is an avid student of early twentieth century history and literature, an ardent and relentless investigator, and an admirer of Emily Dickinson and Jim Morrison. He lives in Virginia with his wife and their two cats.

For more information visit:
RobertBrightonAuthor.com

Sign up for my newsletter to get
VIP updates and special offers!